FIVE-STAR

J. SANTIAGO

Other Novels by J. Santiago

Lex and Lu

Bliss

SUPERSTAR DUET
Five-Star
Superstar

Published by Angela St. James, LLC

Visit my website at https://jsantiagoauthor.com
Cover designer: Elizabeth Mackey, www.elizabethmackeygraphics.com
Cover images: Shutterstock and Adobe Stock.
Editor and Interior Designer: Jovana Shirley, Unforeseen Editing, www.unforeseenediting.com

Print ISBN: 978-0-9969558-3-6

To Brandi and Ochuko—
Thank you for my best professional memories.

To my PSL boys and those who know—
Here's to family nights, Ninja, and Left, Right, Center.

To Tauara, Xander, Nico, and Lucas.

PROLOGUE

SIGNING DAY

Athletic Director Sammy Day stood back to survey the scene. They set it up in the back of the media center. The black pipe and drape hung against the back wall. A skirted table, flanked by two artificial trees, took center stage underneath the fiery mane of their mascot, the Lion.

Sammy wasn't one to invite attention, but the celebrated football season and the national attention on his students had forced Middleton High, buried under the three 6A schools in his county, into the limelight. Since this was a first for his small school, he wanted to make sure that the people watching would be impressed with what they saw.

Turning to the football coach, Don Hayes, he asked, "Should we move it to the gym? It's a much newer facility. Might look better on TV."

Don patted Sammy on the shoulder. "No one is going to see anything but Tank and the banner. And maybe his mama. You know how this works."

"I've watched, but I've never been a part of it." He pointed to his tie. "You ever see me wear one of these on a Wednesday morning?"

Don smiled. "You look great, Sammy."

"I've got all the hats. Just waiting for the table to be set up." Sammy looked over at Don. "Seems a little silly to be doing all of this. Everyone knows where Tank's gonna go."

Don laughed, somewhat humorlessly. "Yeah. He would have committed a long time ago if it weren't for his dad. Tank's not one for all this attention."

Don thought back over the last two years since Tank Howard had been discovered by the college football coaches of America. He imagined that Tank had probably received over two thousand pieces of mail in his junior year alone. He'd changed his cell phone number three times. Don chalked that up to Tank also avoiding his father as much as overzealous recruiters.

It wasn't only Tank who had been receiving attention. Don, his coaching staff, and even Sammy had been caught up in the media hype of having a five-star recruit in their midst. During the contact periods, it'd seemed like college coaches were roaming their halls on a daily basis. He could see how some high school coaches got caught up in the merciless tide of recruiting with phone calls pounding like waves in a constant stream. Yes, Don was ready for this day to be over. Unfortunately, Tank's father had arranged for Tank to be the final signee of the day. That meant, it wasn't over yet.

Chantel Jones woke up, knowing. She had that feeling in the pit of her stomach—the one that told you something wasn't right with the day, the one that made you want to crawl back into bed and start all over. But this was Tank's big day. There was no starting over. It had taken too long to get here. So, she got out of bed and headed for the shower.

She'd had her hair re-twisted yesterday. She'd bought a neutral-colored outfit to protect Tank's choice.

Her boy.

She couldn't believe it had already come to this. Her son was to the point where he was making decisions about his life. He was maneuvering people and events. Somewhere along the way, her precocious, charming boy had grown up, despite being denied, then ignored, and then embraced by That Man.

She couldn't think about That Man without getting heated. And not a good heated. This was a gut-wrenching, pissed-off, wanting-to-throw-something heated. That wasn't normally her style, and it made her all that much madder. Catching a glimpse of herself in the mirror, she stopped her mad. It was that quick. She'd definitely wasted enough mad on That Man in her lifetime. And today wasn't about the insignificant fact that his sperm had fertilized her egg. It was about the amazing result. Antony Howard, aka Tank.

Chantel finished getting dressed and checked the time. It was six forty-five a.m. She had to get Tank up.

Leaving her room, she began their daily ritual. "Tank, time's up. You need to get out of bed."

She walked toward his room, expecting their normal morning struggle. Tank had always been a night owl. But she opened his door and found him sitting on the edge of his bed, fully dressed, elbows braced on his knees, his beaten-down hat in his hands.

She stopped abruptly. "Hey, baby!" she exclaimed in an overly loud voice.

But she knew then and there that the quivering feeling in her stomach was right on. Because she'd never seen Tank up before his alarm. And she mentally braced herself because she knew today wasn't going to go as planned.

At six thirty a.m., the activity in the offensive war room at State rivaled the trading floor on the New York Stock Exchange. Ten coaches, one player personal director, one director of football operations, and several minions filled the conference room. The television was set to ESPN, but for now, it was muted.

Surrounding them was the recruiting board. They'd played this board for months, moving pieces based on their evaluations, rearranging by commitment and position needs, dreaming of bringing in specific players. All of their work came down to twenty-five seventeen- and eighteen-year-old boys. That was one of the ironies of all of this. Yeah, coaches made a shitload of money, but in the end, their fate was in the hands of children.

In the midst of the chaos, head coach Mickey Whitehurst leaned back in his chair and crossed his arms behind his head. A success story in the making, he surveyed his domain. He had assembled this group with care.

"Well," he said—instantly, silence ensued—"it all comes down to this. We can either have a top twenty-five recruiting class or a number one recruiting class. We've worked our asses off. We've got nineteen commitments and six wild cards. We get five of those six wild cards, and we'll be in the top ten. We get Tank Howard, and hands down, we'll be number one."

"You heard from him, Whitey?"

Tank Howard had a recruiting coach, but he was special enough that the head coach was heavily involved.

"Yeah, he called last night."

The faces around the table looked at him expectantly. He shifted positions and moved toward the table. Dropping his elbows on the edge, he leaned forward and picked up his Sharpie, doodling on the list in front of him.

Whitey had been in the game for a long time, and he was quite certain he hadn't met any kid like this one. Tank was smart—football smart, people smart, classroom smart. Talking to Tank, one would never know that they were conversing with an eighteen-year-old. Whitey wanted this kid more than he wanted a recruit in his illustrious career.

He and Tank had spoken for a while last night. In his methodical way, Tank had asked Whitey the plans for the team and how he'd fit into those plans. Whitey wasn't sure if the questions were Tank's or if his mother, Coach Hayes, or his father but the kid knew what to ask and how to ask it.

It was no secret that Tank had grown up as a State fan. It was also no secret that he had wanted to commit a long time ago, but his father had wanted him to keep his options open and had convinced his mother that it was the smart thing to do. And he was probably right. Whitey would advise his own son to do the same.

He looked back up at the faces around the table. "Everything tells me that we should get Tank. That when ESPN points their cameras toward him, he's gonna pick up our hat and say he's coming here." His announcement was greeted with smiles.

"But"—he paused—"it ain't over till the fat lady sings. And until it's four thirty-two when the announcements have been made and I see our damn hat on his head with a freshly signed National Letter of Intent, you just never know."

Coach Mike Franco surveyed his new offensive coaches' meeting room with both trepidation and elation. Finally a head coach at a Division I institution, he couldn't stop the small grin that stole across his face. He'd had one month to recruit for his alma mater—one crucial short month to attempt to put together a recruiting class that the top seventy-five hadn't seen, one month to shift gears from recruiting coach at a major program, a Division I perennial power, to a coach of a blip on the radar of college football.

Franco didn't mind being the number two. In fact, he'd sort of relished being the sounding board but not the buck-stops-here person. Yet, when the president of the university had called, he'd surprised himself with his quick answer. He had been poised at State to sign the most impressive recruiting class to ever be assembled, set to coach the most promising high school prospect in history. But Franco had called his agent and negotiated his contract in record time. Then, he'd hit the recruiting trail in different colors.

The first stop he'd made was to the hometown of Tank Howard. He knew Tank would never, could never sign with his school. But he'd been recruiting the kid for three years. They had a relationship. Franco wanted, if nothing else, to explain. He'd also wanted to assure Tank that he'd still have a place at State, still get a top-notch coach, still be part of a national championship program. He didn't have to do that, but he had worked hard to put State on top. And even if he couldn't be there to reap the rewards, he still thought they deserved it most. And maybe he'd squeezed in an offer for an official visit to Kensington State and the promise of a scholarship if Tank wanted another option. But, even as he'd made it, he had known it was like trying to substitute Goodwill for Neiman Marcus.

They'd gotten all of their National Letter of Intents back. It wasn't a rock-star recruiting class that the college football analysts would be salivating over, but it was solid. And Franco had been smart enough to demand time to put his team together.

Glancing at the newly installed TV, something else he'd negotiated, Franco sat back and waited for Tank to appear. He almost called Whitey but figured he'd wait until he could officially congratulate the State coach on the addition of Tank Howard to his team.

Tank sat—well, hid really—in his coach's office. He'd been calm all day, but now, thirty minutes before airtime, he could no longer contain his excitement. His face was split wide by a white-toothed smile, and his eyes sparkled. He couldn't wait to make it official.

They would be the number one class, potentially one of the best ever brought together. Most of them had met at seven-on-seven camps they'd traveled to throughout the southeast. They'd kept up their tentative friendships via Facebook and text-messaging. They'd offered each other congratulations when their respective teams had won big games. They'd taken official visits together. And he'd turned a few of them. Not sure where they were going to go, he had exerted gentle pressure as the unofficial president of the recruiting class.

Tank hadn't liked waiting. He really didn't need this big announcement. He didn't want to be on TV. He'd wanted to commit two years ago when Coach Whitey had been named the head coach. It seemed stupid to wait, as it was surely the worst kept secret in college football. He wasn't sure how his father had convinced his mother that this was a good idea. They hadn't had a civil conversation since he'd shown up in their lives after years of denial. So, why she'd listened and forced Tank to keep his options open was beyond him. Since he wasn't going to go against his mother, he had gone on his five official visits and honestly listened to what all the coaches were trying to sell him. But he wasn't stupid. He didn't believe most of what they'd said.

On his only visit to a non-BCS conference school, Tank had been hosted by a Tilly Lace. Tilly was a freshman lineman, who had been honest with Tank. He'd told Tank not to believe what he heard on his visits.

"Tank," he'd said, "I'm gonna be real with ya. When I got here, I asked my coach about something he'd told me. He said, 'Did I say that during recruiting?' I said, 'Yeah.' He said, 'Till, if I said it during recruiting, don't believe it.'"

Tank had listened. And he'd listened to the coaches and the people he met with. He knew what was real and what wasn't. But he was glad that he'd gone into the rest of his visits with Tilly's advice filtering what he'd heard. He was also glad that he'd already known where he wanted to go. It made the whole process a lot easier.

"Tank, you ready?" Coach Hayes asked, bringing him out of his memories.

Tank stood and accepted his mentor's hand. Coach pulled him into a quick one-armed man hug and released him.

"Let's do this!" he said, clapping his hands once for emphasis.

Tank followed him out of the room and into his future.

Long before today, the administration of Middleton High had delivered the message to the school that only the senior football players and the faculty and staff could be at Tank's signing. So, while many people weren't there, the size of the library made it seem like thousands were in the audience.

In front of where Tank would sit, the microphone and five hats had been arranged. Tank entered the library with his mother and his coach. Already miked up, he made his way to the small stage and escorted his mother to her chair.

Tank surveyed the hats. They'd briefly discussed how to arrange them. He was pretty sure Mr. Day had watched YouTube to see how the signees from last year had set up their hats. Tank wasn't sure what had been decided, but he studied the hats and their alignment, so he knew where his was.

"All right, Tank. Ready?" asked the producer.

"Yes, sir," Tank replied.

"We're about to go live. We're going to show you sitting with your mother, and then we'll go to a commercial break. You'll have about two minutes. Then, it will be your show." He smiled at Tank and said, "Good luck."

Tank leaned back in his chair and turned to Chantel. "Well, Mama, here we go."

She reached out and laid her hand on his cheek. "I'm so proud of you, baby."

"All right, Tank, we're on you."

Tank wasn't sure what people were seeing, so he kept his arm around his mother and smiled at the camera.

"We'll be right back with our last, most-anticipated announcement of the day."

"We're off."

"You ready?" Chantel asked. "You know what you're going to say?"

"Yes, ma'am. I'm so ready for this."

"I know. And I know this isn't the way you wanted to do this, but I'm glad that you went on all of your visits and that you took some time to consider what would be best…even though you wanted to be grown and pick a long time ago." She finished with a smile.

"Mama," he whispered, "I think the TV people can hear you." He laughed.

"We're ready in five, four, three, two, one."

"Tank, you are the last signee of the day. People have been waiting to hear this announcement for a long time. Are you ready?"

"Yes, sir."

"Where will you be going to school in the fall?"

Tank paused. "I'd like to say thank you for all the support I've gotten over the last couple of years. It has meant a lot to me to have so many people cheering for me."

He waited as cheering and clapping broke out in the crowd. During the pause, the library door opened.

"I'd also like to thank all of the schools that recruited me. There are a lot of great programs and that made my decision tough."

Tank paused. In the back of the room a small commotion began. Tank heard the word *father*. He turned quickly to look at his mother, and the expression on her face filled him with dread.

Richard Howard made his way through the parted crowd. He was a big man, which made him hard to miss. He pinned Tank with his eyes, but all Tank could see was the State billboard the sperm donor was wearing from head to toe. Towering over all, Richard muscled his way up onto the stage, casting his large shadow over the skirted table and eclipsing the spotlight reserved for Tank. Even with his faded good looks and his dubious past, Richard still knew how to command a room. He faced the masses, wearing State's hat. The stunned crowd didn't know what to do. Someone clapped, and everyone else joined in.

Tank surveyed the mess. He knew he was on live TV, and he couldn't imagine what the audience was seeing and thinking. Pissed off and frustrated, Tank looked at the hats in front of him. He thought of the places he'd been, the coaches he'd met, the programs that wanted him. He thought of Whitey, the man he'd wanted to be his coach, and Franco, the recruiter he'd liked the best. He thought of Tilly Lace. Then, he looked at his father one last time, draped in what would have been his future team's colors.

Filled with a calm but determined rage, he reached over and plucked the Bears hat off the table.

He turned to the room, placed the hat on his head, and said, "I'm going to Kensington State. I'm going to be a Bear!"

ONE

Tank Howard, a third-year starter, entered the team locker room for the start of the football season. A sucker for tradition and Karma, Tank reached out for the Touch of the green Bear painted on the wall. In some mild hazing incident, he'd been tricked as a freshman. All the players were supposed to pat the Bear twice on their way into and out of the locker room, he'd been told. It wasn't until the fifth or sixth game of that season when he'd noticed that he was the only one doing it. After the game, he'd walked up to Haze, one of the seniors, and asked about it.

"Yeah, bro," he'd said, a shit-eating grin on his face, "we were totally fucking with you. Got bets on how long it'd take your stupid ass to notice."

As if to accentuate his point, three of the guys standing around reached into their lockboxes, pulled out twenty-dollar bills, and handed them to Marsh, the center.

Taken aback, Tank turned to Marsh and said, "You bet against me?"

"Nah, I bet for you," he said as he grabbed Tank's shoulders. "Everyone else picked next season!"

"Fucking jokesters," Tank said to the locker room at large before turning to Marsh and saying, "What's my cut of your take?" He appreciated a good practical joke.

But it had become a part of his ritual, and because it was already the fifth game of the season, it was too late. He couldn't stop it.

Marsh watched him now and smiled, remembering the origin of the Touch. "You were a stupid fucking freshman," he commented as he followed Tank into the locker room.

With a smile, Tank reminded him, "You still owe me my cut."

"You haven't collected yet," he responded with a shrug. "I think my money's safe."

Tank finished donning his practice gear—just shorts and a jersey for the first practice. Excited about the start of the season and the team his coaches had assembled, he was ready to go. "You know the good thing about this year, Marsh?" He looked over at his center. At Marsh's nod, he continued, "We are in the conversation." With a smile, he headed toward the door, wanting to catch up with Coach before practice started.

As he made his way out of the locker room, Tank did a quick assessment of the last two years. Since joining the Bears, their rise had been *meteoric*—not his word, but it worked. They were undefeated in the regular season, losing only their bowl game last year, when Tank had been sidelined with a concussion. Two years ago, if you hadn't lived in Georgia, you wouldn't have even known Kensington State existed. Now, this year, during preseason, they were being talked about—and not just because of his signing day shocker, but because they were good. They were breaking barriers for non-BCS schools, and Tank could barely contain his excitement.

Heisman talk abounded, too, but Tank didn't get caught up in that. More than the coveted Heisman, Tank wanted the opportunity for his team to play for the national championship. While the practical side of him knew they wouldn't get the chance, he was going to make sure that there was some debate. He wouldn't call himself a crusader for Cinderella rights, but while he was doing what he knew how to do, he didn't mind advocating at the same time. He'd leave it up to the reporters to tell the story. That was what they were there for anyway.

His phone vibrated with a text message. Pulling it out, he smiled at the name on his screen.

Lamarcus Steele.

Check Instagram.

Quickly following the instructions, Tank laughed at the picture of Lamarcus in the locker room at State, surrounded by most of the guys who should have been Tank's recruiting class, all of them flipping off the camera.

Tank responded.

Didn't your sports info peeps school you about doing stupid shit on the Internet?

Lamarcus texted back.

Yep.

Tank laughed again.

Fool. Whitey will be pissed when that ends up on the ticker.

Only till we start whooping people's asses. Then, he won't care about nothing.

Lol. True.

Tank pocketed his phone but entered the football offices with the residual evidence of a smile occupying his face. After his monumental impulse decision on signing day two and a half years ago, Tank had figured he would be persona non grata by the carefully constructed all-time best recruiting class at State. He'd handed his phone to his mother and become the hardest-to-reach eighteen-year-old on the planet. In the forty-eight-hour phone ban, he'd received over one thousand text messages. Rather than go back and read them, he'd gone to the Sprint store and changed phones and numbers. Coming off of that self-imposed silence, Tank had reentered the world of Facebook and Twitter with the aplomb of someone who lived in his skin quite comfortably. No one would have ever guessed that Tank Howard had ever wanted anything other than to be a Kensington State Bear. It was this sense of innate confidence that made Tank so valuable.

Tank entered Coach Mike Franco's office, fired up.

This man waiting for him was the reason that the Kensington State hat had even been on the signing day buffet. Franco had recruited him hard for Coach Whitey, making him the cornerstone of the class early on. It was a smart move that Tank had just recently begun to realize had been calculated long before anyone else in college football had caught on to his importance. Franco had continued to recruit like that, which was why they had been able to dominate their conference and were poised to be a national contender. Tank's respect for his coach had only grown over the last few years. And from his vast social network, he knew that continuing to respect your coach wasn't always a guarantee.

After grabbing on to the shoulder of Cy Greenburg while reaching out for his hand, Tank took the only remaining seat directly in front of Coach. "Cy, how's it going?"

Cy, like everyone else who worked closely with Tank, smiled fondly back, his genuine pleasure at seeing Tank evident on his face.

"How are you, Tank? Ready to go?" Cy asked even though he knew the answer.

"Always ready, sir."

That was the thing about Tank. His mother hadn't raised no fool, as she liked to point out whenever they talked. Respect was paramount for everyone Tank came into contact with.

Clapping his hands together twice as he took his seat, Tank looked expectantly up at Franco. "What's up, Coach? Have to be on the field in fifteen."

Franco chuckled as he leaned back in his seat. "Yeah, I'm pretty aware of when *we* need to be on the field."

At Tank's big smile, Franco laughed again.

Theirs was an easy relationship. Fate had tied them together when Tank was only fifteen. Tank had known then that he wanted to play for Whitey and Franco. Then, a month before his dream could materialize, Franco had gotten the call to become the head coach at Kensington. Tank had known there had never been any intention for Franco to bring Tank with him. Why would the number one prospect in the country, a true five-star talent, with scholarship offers from everywhere, want to go to a school that could never be in the running for a national title? And Franco would never have even suggested it. In fact, he'd specifically continued to recruit Tank for Whitey, even after Franco had left. Little had either of them known how it would all turn out. Tank had liked Franco when he recruited him. Now, he respected Franco—not only as his coach, but also as a man.

Tank looked at his coach, curious about this conversation. They talked often but not normally with Cy lurking, so whatever they would be discussing didn't seem to be Xs and Os.

"This will be quick."

"Whatcha got, Coach?"

"It's about tonight."

Of all the things they could be discussing, Coach was concerned about what was going to happen off the field. It was a bit charming. Tank could make this really easy for his coach, but he was in one of those practical joking moods.

"What about tonight?" Tank asked, a look of feigned innocence on his face.

"Don't give me that shit, Tank. I was a part of the team that started the tradition. Don't act like you don't know that I know."

Tank couldn't help it. He laughed and made it just a little bit harder on Franco. "Tradition?"

"The bar. Tonight. The first night of preseason. The breaking in of the freshmen." He stopped there.

Cy picked up the mantle. "We're in the spotlight now. Our team can't all go out and party on the first night of preseason without drawing some attention. I know this is a time-honored tradition, but you all need to be careful."

Tank wanted to make them both suffer some more, but his desire to be on the field was greater.

"Don't worry, Coach. We'll take it easy." He looked over at Cy. "We won't tweet, Facebook, or post anything on Instagram. We do this every year, and we've never gotten out of hand."

Right up until that moment, Tank hadn't even considered their preseason bash. Coach and Cy were right. It was just something they did every year, no exceptions. But, now, they could be big time, and they needed to take it easy. He appreciated the reminder.

Tank stood up and backed out of the room. "I got you, Coach."

TWO

Amber rolled over, found the clock with her bleary gaze, and bolted out of bed. Almost late for her second shift at the bar, she hopped into the shower, threw on her sorry excuse for a uniform, and pulled her hair into a haphazard ponytail.

Because of the hours her dad worked, they hadn't seen each other before she left for work last night. Hoping that his workaholic ways would save her again, she strolled out of her room and made a beeline for the kitchen. She didn't have time to eat, but she could at least grab a snack on her way out. It was unfortunate that her dad was waiting for her.

She saw him glance at her outfit and watched him literally bite his tongue. Things with them had been rough since she moved back in, and he tried to pick his battles, which she definitely appreciated.

"Hey, Pops!" she enthused, attempting to disarm him. Making a show of glancing at her watch, she looked up at him again. "Not working late tonight?"

"I wanted to try and catch you before your shift," he said warily, as if that small showing of parental concern might be taken the wrong way.

"Well, you did, but I'm running late." Moving toward the pantry, Amber exaggerated her need to rush by, slipping past him. "Something up?" she said with as little interest as possible while she loudly scoured the shelves, shuffling boxes of all the things she didn't want, huffing as she came up empty. "Want to leave me some money tomorrow, so I can buy some real food?" Catching the brattiness of her tone, she winced, glad her father couldn't see her.

"Sure. I'm sorry. I'm not used to buying for anyone but me."

The sincerity of his statement washed over her as she continued to hide in the pantry. Feeling petty and bitchy, she hung her head, giving herself a quick shake. Conceding that this was difficult for both of them, she made a quick promise to try to stop being such a brat. Her being here right now was not her father's fault. Gathering up her courage, she barreled out of the pantry and planted her ass on the counter, ready to give her father the five remaining minutes she had.

"I know. But I can do the shopping." Lifting her shoulders in a snarky shrug, she grinned at him and said, "I know what I like."

When she was playful like that, she was hard to resist, and he returned her smile, forgiving her for her attitude, she thought.

"How was rehab today? You don't seem too stiff."

Remembering her promise to herself not even thirty seconds ago, she tried not to sigh in exasperation as she answered him, "Pretty good. I like the physical therapist they set me up with. Thanks for that, by the way." At his nod of acknowledgment, she continued, "I don't think I'm going to lose any ground by transferring to this center."

"Good. That's really good." He looked like he was about to reach out to her, but then he thought better of it and ran his hand through his hair before grabbing the back of his neck. She knew then that he wasn't as relaxed as he seemed. "So, bartending last night was okay?"

They'd fought this battle before she moved back home, and she knew that she'd won. Her arguments were better than his. But because of the major skirmish, she wouldn't ever give him the satisfaction of knowing that he was right. It was taxing on her leg to stand for that long, and at least on the first night, on her brain. She hadn't had to make conversation with strangers in a while, and she was as exhausted mentally as she was physically. But he'd never get to hear that.

"It was good. Fun. Nice to be back."

"Good. That's good." He moved away from her then and leaned back against the opposite counter. "Things are going to be pretty busy for me from here on out. I kind of hoped you weren't working tonight."

"Dad, you don't have to explain about your schedule. I know what it's like. I know how much you work."

"I know, but you just got back, and you're just getting settled. I feel like I need to be available at least."

She pushed off the counter and stood in front of him. Shrugging, she said, "I know where to find you if I need you."

Even when she was standing on her tiptoes, he had to lean down so that she could plant a kiss on his cheek.

"I'll see you when I see you," she said.

He grabbed her arm before she could get too far away. "You know what tonight is. Be careful, okay?"

"Always," she responded.

But neither of them could look the other in the eyes because, if she were always careful, they wouldn't be standing together, having this conversation.

The Bear's Den had been around for longer than Amber had. On the eve of the dawning of the sports bar genre, they had closed for a month, during which they had completely gutted and renovated the place. When they'd reopened, it was amid a blaze of televisions, pool tables, dartboards, and Bear paraphernalia. Like most of the places in town, the Bears reigned supreme. Everything was green and silver, and while they'd serve you if you weren't in fact a Bears fan, they tended not to like you as much.

Amber had grown up in the Bear's Den on Bear's fare, dressed in Bears' colors. Her best friend, Keira's, parents had owned and operated the place since it opened its doors forever ago. In this bar, Keira's sister, Kaycee, had shown her how to use a tampon. She'd left for her sophomore sock hop and junior/senior prom from the restaurant. Her prom pictures boasted the green and silver in the background. The first drink she'd pilfered was from the bar back by the pool tables. And this was where she'd brought her college acceptance letter and opened it up among Keira's family. Naturally, when she'd been a little broken, she'd come here to heal. It was why she'd won that battle. As hard as it might have been for her father, this had been her home when he was gone.

"Just because you're family doesn't mean you can be late," Mark bellowed.

Amber stuffed her things under the bar, thinking she'd flown in under the radar. Glancing at her watch, she was quick to point out, "It's eight fifty-five. My shift doesn't start until nine." She sashayed over to Mark. "I'm not late yet."

He merely smirked at her as he moved out from behind the bar.

Keira laughed. "You know she thinks she can get away with anything. You were too easy on her, growing up. I told you that you should have spread the torturing around."

Amber gave Keira a mock-angry look. "Help a sister out, will ya?"

"I thought that maybe your dad had put his foot down and wouldn't let you work tonight," she quipped.

Amber knew she was fishing. "He issued a warning, but that was it. No dramatics."

"Good. I was worried when I didn't hear from you all day."

"Sorry, sister," Amber said, genuinely meaning it. "I was beat from last night. Then, I had rehab. And then I crashed and woke up about forty-five minutes ago."

"I'm just glad you're good." Keira reached out and squeezed Amber's hand. Nodding slightly, she asked, "You wearing your hair like that?"

Reaching up, Amber remembered that it was still in a ponytail. Suddenly, it clicked, and she remembered her father reaching out to her before quickly withdrawing. She hadn't even thought about the fact that her hair was up, and he was probably seeing the angry red scar for the first time. "Uh, definitely not."

Sliding under the door of the bar, she turned back to Keira before she ran to the back. "Anything else need to be prepped while I'm in the back?"

"We'll need another bar kit. Lemons and limes, for sure."

"Okay, I'll grab them." She turned to run to the back but stopped to look at her friend. "Is it as bad as you thought?"

She could tell Keira didn't want to answer her question by her slight hesitation. Keira wasn't one to consider her words. She looked away from Amber's eyes and let herself look down at the right side of her mouth, chin, and neck.

She didn't wince and didn't waver to look Amber in the eyes when she replied, "It's pretty bad, champ."

Amber shrugged. "Yeah."

"But you're still beautiful." Her words were so heartfelt and so devoid of pity that Amber felt tears threaten. "Now, pull yourself together. We have a very long night ahead of us."

"I'm going, I'm going," she bitched, trying to follow Keira's lead and lighten the mood. "Where's Mark? I think I'm going to need his hat."

"Probably getting a keg from downstairs."

"I'm on it."

Amber made her way through the kitchen to find Mark, pulling her ponytail down as she went. She didn't have much time and could only think of one way to hide her face.

"Need your hat, dude," she called down to Mark in the beer cellar.

He didn't answer, but his hat came flying up and almost smacked her in the face. Grabbing it, she ran to the restroom. Pulling her platinum-blonde hair over to her right side, she braided it so that it came over her shoulder and fell just above the swell of her breast. She pulled on the hat, which provided the shadow she needed. Looking at herself in the mirror, she could barely see anything, and with the dark of the bar, she figured she'd be all right.

She ran back through the kitchen and picked up a premade garnish kit and a couple of sliced lemons and limes. Feeling pressed for time, she hustled back through the kitchen and out to the bar. Placing everything on the sleek surface, she slid underneath the gate and moved around the square until she stood in front of Keira.

"Better?" she asked.

"Yep. You ready?"

"Always," she repeated for the second time tonight.

Only, this time, there were no recriminations because she might not always be careful but as Keira could attest, Amber was always ready.

THREE

The legend went something like this. Way back in 1993, the Kensington State football team, lamenting over their first full day of practice, had decided that what they needed was a night out. None of them had mentioned that it was only their first day of practice or had they bothered to state the obvious that it was merely the beginning of a very long season. Even back then, it was never clear who had come up with the brilliant idea. Whoever was responsible might well live in infamy in their small college town, but the secret had seemed to be well protected. Regardless, the team's trip to the Bear's Den had marked the beginning of a tradition that thrived now, almost twenty years later.

"So, we aren't really going to make any money tonight, are we?" Amber asked as the bar started to fill with the team. "I mean, they're mostly broke college students."

Keira looked over at her as she filled a mug from the tap. "You would think that, right? But word's gotten out over the years." Shrugging her shoulders as she leaned across the bar to exchange the beer for money, she said, "It's the other people who come to mingle with them that tip us well. I made bank last year—and the year before, come to think of it. It's the Tank Howard Effect."

At Amber's questioning look, Keira continued, "He's a walking economic incentive for this town. After the whole signing day spectacle, I feel like the whole town showed up two years ago. And aside from all the controversy surrounding him, he's worth coming out to see."

"Why's that?" Amber asked as she headed to take an order from a customer.

"Have you been living under a rock?" She quickly apologized. "Sorry. I wasn't thinking, but seriously, Amber, the man is hot."

Shaking her head, she replied, "Aren't they all?"

"You'll see. He's smoking hot—and nice, as far as I can tell."

After that, there wasn't much time to chat. The crowd at the bar was three deep. Amber would fill an order, collect the cash, and move on to the next. The noises from the bar and the pounding of the music made conversation difficult. Even taking an order required either great lip-reading skills or a provocative lean across the bar.

Briefly, Amber wondered how many more people Mark could admit without a citation for a fire hazard. But the rhythm of the bar didn't allow her much time to think. Much like the seven-minute lull in a conversation, an unexpected break would hit when they could catch their breaths and look out with wonder on the scene.

It was pushing up against midnight when Mark made the call to shut it down. They went one for one—one person out, one person in. Finally, with that move, things became manageable again, and they were able to take much-needed breaks.

As Amber made her way to kitchen, where she could take a breather, she decided she appreciated being behind the bar because trying to get through this crowd was like a mouse trying to weave through a herd of elephants. The football players' big bodies took up more space than the average person and blocked the small opportunities for light that bars made available. And the girls. Draped on virtually every player, a scantily clad girl fussed and fawned. Amber saw more skin on the way to the kitchen than she had at the beach.

Her leg was sore, and her head was pounding. She'd worked up a sweat, moving through the crowd. She could see the light at the end of the tunnel.

Putting her hand on the small of an enormous human's back, she stood up as far as she could and yelled, "Excuse me," so she could slip past him and through the double doors to safety. It was the wrong thing to do.

The female on the other side of him must not have heard what she'd said. Before Amber could even react, a large woman, dressed in tights that obviously hadn't come with a warning label, wrenched Amber's hand off the back of the guy in front of her. The sudden jerking was too much for Amber's tired right leg. It crumpled and even though she fought to regain her balance, she hit the floor.

Tank stood in the midst of the crowd, chilling with Marsh and Tilly. He'd been available for a while, mingling with everyone at the bar. Not that it was a chore. He loved the fans, loved their enthusiasm and their gratitude. Not one to analyze his feelings, he imagined that, if he spent sometime thinking about it, he'd admit that he liked being in the spotlight. He enjoyed being the go-to person, and for this town, he was it. And that meant he had to mingle.

Cy would make him do all sorts of stupid bullshit that he supposed most people wouldn't enjoy. But Tank liked meeting the donors and the bigwigs, liked chitchatting with the president of the university. Franco would give him a hard time, but Tank wouldn't take it too seriously because he knew that Franco was the master of mingling. Most of the time, the bullshit he had to attend, his coach would have to attend, too.

But tonight was about the team and tradition. Tank had done his part and now, he was tucked away from the crowd with the insulation his teammates provided. It was nice, having friends who weighed over three hundred pounds. Tended to keep one safe.

There were some token cleat-chasers hanging around, but it wouldn't be a party without them. Tank had learned how to keep himself insulated from that, too. He indulged, like the rest of them, but he tended to think that he was smarter than everyone else about keeping himself in line. Most of his teammates didn't have Chantel Jones to mother them, so he chalked it up to her.

The team knew most of the girls who hung around, who were sometimes like flies you wanted to swat. So, the girl with the platinum-blonde hair who came charging through like she was on a mission caught him off guard. When he saw her reach her hand out to Marsh, visions of his conversation with Franco and Cy about tonight flashed through his head. Cynthia, Marsh's girlfriend took no shit from no one and wouldn't take kindly to the spindly Gwen Stefani–looking girl touching her man.

Briefly, he wondered if they would get in trouble for a girl fight.

Could they post that on Instagram if they weren't in the picture?

He stepped forward, hoping to thwart Cynthia, when the blonde went down—hard.

"What the fuck, Cyn? Are you crazy?" Marsh asked, showing that he had a pair of balls.

But Tank knew better. Marsh would be sucking up to Cynthia for the next couple of days after talking to her like that. Trying not to smirk, Tank glanced at Tilly and rolled his eyes before dropping to his knee and scooping up the sprite.

Tilly's gold teeth flashed as he caught Tank's expression.

Shrugging his shoulders as he lifted her, Tank nodded to the kitchen doors behind them, and Tilly pushed them open for the three of them to go through.

"Think she's okay?" Tilly asked, still smiling over Marsh's peril.

"She's out cold." Tank didn't want to lay her on the ground. Spying the clean stainless steel countertops, he moved toward the wall and laid her down.

Looking her over, he took note of her almost skinny frame. Her head fell to the side, and he was struck still by the angry red scar that pulled down the corner of her mouth spanning out like a web on the bottom part of her chin along her jawline and down her neck.

"Shit," he muttered.

Tilly followed his gaze.

"Looks like a glass shattered around her head," Tilly observed.

"Wearing a Bear's Den shirt. Wanna go get Mark?"

Tilly nodded and left the kitchen. Tank continued his perusal down her neck to her ample chest, small waist, and very long legs. She'd looked tiny on the floor, but she appeared taller than he'd first thought. She was hot, even with the scar. His gaze worked its way back up her body to her scar. As he stared at it, he wondered not about how it had gotten there, but about what color her eyes were.

He didn't have to wonder. He looked up, right into a pair of dark chocolate eyes.

Smiling, he said, "Good. You're awake."

Scowling, she replied, "Did you get a good enough look, perv?"

Still smiling, Tank nodded. "Great, hostility. I'll chalk that up to getting knocked on your ass and hitting your head. Do you feel okay?"

Seriously? That was her first thought. Her second was, *I have the luck of the damned.*

Without needing an introduction, Amber knew she was staring into the light-green eyes of one Tank Howard. Although she wasn't sure how her body would react, her dignity and pride demanded that she sit up and break out of the damsel-in-distress role. Swinging her legs over the side of the counter at the same time as she sat up, Amber pulled her braid over her neck in an attempt to cover the scar. Bracing herself for the dizziness she knew would hit her, she secured her hands on the side of the counter and held on.

"I don't think you are supposed to move that fast after you lost consciousness," Tank observed.

His damn smile drew her attention to his mouth and the dimples in his cheeks.

"I'm fine," she replied while fighting the dizziness that threatened to win. Inhaling sharply, she slowly looked up and met his eyes. "A friend of yours out there?" she asked with a glint in her eye.

"Yeah," he said.

"Nice girl." She noticed that he stayed close, and she knew he was waiting for her to topple over. *Over my dead body*, she thought. "Does she know those pants come with a weight limit?"

"Wow!" he exclaimed. He threw his head back and laughed. "Should we ask her? Or how about you ask her, and I watch? I'm supposed to keep the guys out of trouble tonight. Think my coach would be okay if we just witnessed a catfight? I thought about it right before your head hit the ground. Then, I got distracted."

"Yeah, into necrophilia much?" She paused. "Need a dictionary?"

"Ah, dumb-jock jokes. Very original. So, you have anyone who can claim you, so I can get you off my hands?"

As if on cue, Keira and Mark burst through the kitchen doors with Tilly in tow. Keira rushed over to Amber while Mark stopped to clasp Tank's hand.

"Thanks, man," he said.

Keira spoke softly to Amber, "You okay?"

"Yeah. I just need to get out of here. I'm fine." To prove she was okay, Amber jumped down off the counter without flinching.

"Keira, it's starting to die down out there. Why don't you take Amber home?"

"All right," Keira agreed.

"It's okay, Mark. I can drive."

Keira, Tank, and Mark all said, "No!" at the same time.

Conceding defeat, Amber shrugged her shoulders. "Fine. My stuff's at the bar."

Still leaning on the counter, Amber watched as Mark left with Keira to retrieve their bags. Left alone with Tank and Tilly, Amber knew she needed to thank them.

Amber looked up into those amazing green eyes. "Thanks for the white-knight routine."

Rolling his eyes, Tank moved toward her. "Take care of yourself."

"I will. Thanks."

He reached out to shake her hand. Like a politician, he was too smooth and shiny to be trusted. Meeting him halfway, her hand slid into his. His large hand engulfed her small one. All at once, the slimy feeling melted away as a shocking warmth stole through her. Her eyes widened as they clung to his. But, just as quickly, she slid the shutters closed, the electricity doused before the spark could ignite. And they were once again just two people who had happened to meet.

Tank released her hand, and with an irritated sigh, he walked away.

"See ya around," Tilly said as he followed Tank back out through the swinging kitchen doors.

FOUR

Molly Magee listened to the message on her voice mail with some trepidation. There wasn't a Compliance Director in the country who enjoyed getting a message from the NCAA, but when it involved a Heisman Trophy candidate, dread couldn't begin to explain it. When it was over, she listened to it again. And, just to be sure, she listened to it a third time. Unfortunately, it was short on details.

Heaving a long sigh, she leaned back in her chair and closed her eyes.

She knew she had to call them back, if for nothing else to satisfy her curiosity and assuage some of her anxiety. It could merely be a courtesy call. She still had friends in Indianapolis. But she didn't immediately pick up the phone because, once she made that call, things would become chaotic. No matter what they did, there would be no way to keep the situation from spiraling out of control.

She decided to savor her ignorance, and thus tranquility, for just a little bit longer. Rather than reaching for the phone again, she pushed out of her chair, deciding to head out to practice. Without saying anything to the her tiny staff, she made her way out of the office, out of the building, and over to the football field.

Waving to the security guards who gave her free access, she strolled over to the sideline and took up her usual spot.

Molly had been here for almost three years, the same three years in which the football program had begun its meteoric rise. From consistently being in the top five of their conference over the last three years, the Bears had become a BCS spoiler. They still hadn't captured the elusive national recognition and credibility, but after an undefeated finish last year, they could taste it.

They'd come in together—she and Mike Franco. The way she figured it, when the decision had been made to hire Franco, someone had realized that they probably needed a compliance person who knew their way around the NCAA manual—not that anyone thought Franco would cheat, but he'd want to do more than the previous coach. He'd want to push the envelope. They needed someone who could tell him no. Better yet, they needed someone who knew whether or not to tell him no. The previous compliance director didn't know the difference between a head count and equivalency sport. She'd have never been able to figure out if they could direct message on Facebook or send a notecard with a picture of a player on it.

And if Molly were really honest, she'd admit that Franco was smarter than most compliance people. If she cited a bylaw that told him no, he'd ask her to check the interps. What frickin' coach even knew about the NCAA interpretations? He'd make her find loopholes to some of the most formidable rules. And the shit part of it was, he was right more than he was wrong, which only fed his enormous ego. At this point, Molly was fairly certain that Franco challenged everything she said because he liked sparring with her. Or maybe that was her ego talking.

Looking in Franco's direction, she saw him throw his hands up, not liking something he'd seen. Pulling Tank away from the line, he directed the player to do something. She couldn't tell what he was saying, but he looked frustrated. Tank nodded and then sort of hung his head in acquiescence. She saw a look of confusion skirt across Franco's face before he bent over, focused Tank on him, said something, and then rapped him on the side of the helmet. Stepping up to the line, they ran the play. Tank delivered the perfect pass to his new freshman receiver, and then he looked back at Franco, who merely nodded his approval. And they ran it again.

When Molly had arrived on campus, she hadn't figured that she'd spend a lot of time at practices. Some of her peers had suggested she show up every once in a while—not to spy really, but just to be aware of what was going on. Once the coaches got over their wariness of having the Compliance Cop on their sideline, they'd pretty much embraced her presence. Of course, she'd had to earn their respect and trust along that way, but she'd had to do that to be good at her job. Three years in, they trusted her.

A basketball girl herself, she'd thought that was where she'd spend a lot of her time. She liked football okay—you didn't work at a Division I college if you didn't like the sport—but it wasn't what she loved. She hadn't known the difference between the spread offense and the I formation. She did now, of course. When one had Tank Howard to watch, one learned to love the game—although, it wasn't Tank she loved to watch as much as his coach.

There wasn't a woman, age twenty-eight to sixty-five, who could resist the appeal of Mike Franco—okay, and the looks. Franco was hot. Putting Franco and Tank together had been brilliant. It was a Hollywood version of college athletics right here on her campus. Add that to an almost undefeated record for two years, and you had something. She certainly had something. A big-ass crush. It didn't stop her from saying no, and it certainly didn't stop her from challenging him at every turn, but it lurked within her. Sometimes, she thought he felt it, too—this low-level sexual tension. But then she'd see him smile at the next girl, and she remembered his charm. She was sure Franco got as much play as Tank.

Molly watched Tank get the snap, survey the field, and deliver another perfect spiral into the hands of Iman. He was amazing. He hadn't stopped stunning the college sports world since he'd chosen their little school over all the major BCS teams. It was a story that was retold every year, both on signing days and on the opening days of the season. But even hearing the story over and over again, no one really knew why Tank had ended up here. His motivations and reasons had never really been divulged.

Knowing she had procrastinated long enough, she headed back to the office to make her phone call.

When she hung up with the NCAA staff, she laid her head on her desk with a sense of relief. She'd enjoyed an hour of stress for nothing. They'd only reported something that she'd already known. They were monitoring Tank's Facebook, watching out for agents and runners. *Duh!* She was surprised it had taken them two years to add them to their watch list. She would have put him on there after his freshman season. She needed to let Franco know even though it seemed to be common sense. He'd have some opinion about it.

Picking up the phone, she called Miss Beverly, Coach's administrative assistant.

"Miss Beverly, it's Molly."

"Hi, Molly," she answered. She'd been the football secretary for as long as Molly had been alive.

"Can you have Coach call me as soon as he can?"

"Okay. He won't come off the field for a while yet, and then they'll do film and meet as a coaching staff. It might be late."

"Miss Beverly, have him call me tonight—no matter what time, the first available time. I need to talk to him."

That was the other thing about Franco. He hated not knowing if something was going on with his players, Tank or not. And she got that.

"Absolutely. I'll make sure he knows."

"Thanks, Miss Beverly." Dropping the phone back into its cradle, Molly leaned back in her chair.

She glanced at her watch. It was five thirty. The football staff probably wouldn't be done until nine thirty or ten.

She pushed out of her chair, grabbed her bag, and headed out the door. She'd go home for a bit and then come back to talk to Franco. She wanted to deliver her news in person.

She tried not to think about the reason.

Franco pushed his chair back and propped his feet on the table. He quickly noted the time and called Molly. Thinking she wouldn't answer and he could enjoy a reprieve until tomorrow, he started when she picked up.

"What's up, Molly?" he asked without preamble as he rubbed the back of his neck, weary from the day.

"You still in the building, or have you left?"

Coming up in the chair, putting his feet on the ground, he laid his head on the table, wishing he could bang it a couple of times. "I'm here. You?"

"Yeah, I'll be right up," she said before she hung up.

Franco sighed heavily. He wasn't up for a compliance debate tonight. Molly, he was up for anytime, but their conversations would often become antagonistic, as they'd each defend their positions. Sometimes, he would say the sky was red just to get a rise out her. She was fun to bait, and her arguments never disappointed. She was also fun to look at. Her shoulder-length curly blonde hair and deep blue eyes contributed to her all-American persona. She hailed from some Midwestern town and had the twang to prove it. Her height intrigued him because he didn't feel like he dwarfed her, which he kind of liked. If he didn't work with her, if she were just some woman he'd met socially, he'd have had her a long time ago. But, alas, they did work together. And that was all they did—unfortunately, for him.

Disturbed that she'd stayed late to talk to him, Franco braced himself for bad news. All his freshmen had been cleared to practice and were deemed qualifiers, so he could scratch that off the list. Summer grades had posted, and as far as he knew, everyone was eligible. *Check.* He knew they had a waiver on file with the NCAA, but having that particular kid on the field wouldn't make or break his year. Tank Howard would.

Fuck, he thought, *don't let this be about Tank.*

As if sensing his rising panic, Molly opened the door, came in, and sat down at the table with him.

Picking his head up, he asked, "How bad is this? Do I need to get the bottle of Jack I have stowed under my desk?"

She smiled. "No. But it's good to know that you have some Jack in the building. You might want to keep tabs on that bottle."

Right away, she put him at ease. Her easy manner dispelled his panic. Yet another thing he liked about her.

Molly leaned forward and rested both elbows on the table. Franco followed suit. Sitting up, he rolled his chair closer and then leaned back again, hoping his relaxed stance would reveal a confidence lacking at that particular moment. He looked at her expectantly.

"I really didn't mean to alarm you, but I also didn't want to leave this until tomorrow, which could turn into three days from now with your schedule."

He acknowledged the statement with a nod, knowing the truth in it.

"I mean, don't you have the *Sports Illustrated* cover to shoot?" she teased.

"Ha. That was a couple of months ago." He waved off her teasing, wanting her to get to the point.

"The NCAA called. They wanted to inform me that Tank Howard was now on their watch list. Frankly, I am a bit surprised he wasn't on there sooner, ever since signing day. But, I suppose, with him being eligible for the draft after this year, they want to monitor him for agent activity."

More alert now but not alarmed, Franco nodded slowly. "So, what does that mean exactly?"

"They'll monitor his social network accounts, specifically looking for particular names. Agents are using runners now to get close to the players. The NCAA wants to make sure Tank's not communicating with agents before it's time—and, of course, that he doesn't show up to school in a brand-new car."

Relieved, Franco stood and made his way to the door. "I'm not worried about Tank and agents. The NCAA is wasting their time. He and I have discussed the timeline. He has a plan. Trust me, Molly, this is not an issue."

Knowing she was being dismissed, Molly stood. "I agree to some extent. But Tank needs to be careful. A runner could be anyone—girls on campus, people in his class. I don't know if you've had that discussion with him, but it needs to be had. You can send him to me, and I can explain it to him."

Franco stopped and turned around to her. "Tank doesn't need to be tutored on this, Molly. He gets it. He knows. He's careful. I need for him to be focused on the season—not agents, not runners, not the goddamn Heisman. He's already more distracted than I've seen him. I appreciate the heads-up, Molly," he added to soften his outburst, "but this is not an issue."

Trying to disguise her hurt, Molly moved quickly through the door that Franco still held, his exit interrupted by his anger.

"Just thought you'd want to know," she murmured.

"No one needs to watch Tank. The person they should all be watching is that piece-of-shit sperm donor of his. If anyone is going to fuck this up for Tank, it's going to be Richard Howard."

He watched Molly continue to walk swiftly down the hall, looking for her brief nod of acknowledgment. But she didn't turn or nod, just kept walking.

Cursing himself for his attitude and his secret fears, Franco slammed the offensive room door a little harder than necessary.

As he headed to his car, Franco lamented over his irrational fears of conjuring Richard Howard just by murmuring his name.

Great, he thought. *Fucking Harry Potter references.*

FIVE

A few days before the first game of the season, the physical therapist Amber worked with cleared her for limited activity. Anxious to get back into working out, she found herself strolling through the athletic department, looking for the sports medicine area at zero dark thirty. The woman her father had hooked her up with worked with the athletic department on a contract basis. But, with the fall season underway, the time slots were slim.

She'd met with the trainer, Glenna Davis, the day before to map out her rehab. This morning, she would walk on the treadmill in the pool. Although she wasn't sure how long she'd be able to last because it'd been so long since she'd been mobile. It used to be that she could move for hours. Now, she felt beaten and battered after her shifts at the bar. If nothing else, her goal was to be able to make it through her shift without needing twenty-four hours to recover.

Glenna got her in the water and hooked up to the treadmill.

"Thanks for doing this for me," Amber told her.

Glenna adjusted the speed on the treadmill. "Of course. Remember, we are taking it easy today. Let's just get a baseline."

"Okay." Amber began to walk, surprised at the resistance provided by the water. "It sounded so easy, but it doesn't feel easy," she commented as her breathing began to labor.

"You've been down for how long?" Glenna asked.

"It's been a year and a half since the accident."

"So, the key word is going to be *patience*."

"Not persistence," Amber quipped.

Glenna shook her head and smiled. "I think you've got the persistence thing down."

Amber smiled back at her, liking her immensely.

"I've got some stuff I need to do, so I am going to leave you for a few minutes." Glancing at her watch, Glenna said, "We have treatments starting at eight, so I'll try to let you off the hook around seven forty."

At Amber's nod, Glenna left. While she had appreciated the company, Amber would rather suffer alone. Talking would make her concentrate on doing two things at once. The walking taxed her enough without having to engage in conversation. But, after a few minutes of being alone, she remembered why the solitude wasn't all that good either. It allowed her time to think.

Over the last few weeks, she'd settled in. Between rehab and working at the Bear's Den, she'd come up with a routine that worked for her and allowed her to avoid her father on most days. When they did see each other, there wasn't time for in-depth conversations. They existed in this odd purgatory where they circled around each other and what had happened. She thought that if he looked at her with something other than pity, she'd be able to talk to him. But the moment their eyes met, mirror images of each other, sorrow for her would flood his eyes, and she'd find herself looking away.

Her dad was really young when the girl he had been seeing had gotten pregnant. The ins and outs of what had happened had long ago stopped mattering to Amber. The woman who had given birth to her had given her up to her father and his parents. Essentially, her grandparents had raised her. Perhaps her mother had looked at his family and known that Amber would always be loved, or perhaps she hadn't cared. Amber had never really felt the loss of her mother because she'd never lacked for love. With her father being the oldest of eight, she'd grown up alongside her aunts and uncles and never experienced a lonely day in her life. Up until his career had taken him away from her, her dad had been involved in everything. And even after he'd left, his every free moment was spent with her.

This new chasm that existed between them hurt, but sort of like the new skin forming on her jaw and neck, numbness reigned.

She kept waiting for the feeling to rush back—in her face and in her mind. But there wasn't much that penetrated. Her therapist, whom she still had a hard time admitting to, had said that it was probably her mind's defense against the accident. But Amber didn't know if she bought that. She waited...waited to feel something—guilt, sorrow, fear, anger.

Shouldn't I be angry when I look in the mirror and see the mess that's my face? Or sad because of the situation I left behind? Or guilty because I couldn't even look my father in the face without hating the pity I see there?

Unfortunately, Tank Howard had made her feel something, which was just fucking typical for her. During the banter with him and while her hand had been in his, she'd felt all sorts of things. But the Tank Howards of the world were the reason that her face was all jacked up.

Couldn't I just once bypass the big man on campus? Nope, not me.

Because she was *that* girl—the one who was with the guy everyone else wanted.

In high school, it was Jake Michaels, star football player, who'd gone on to play at Syracuse. At Ole Miss, it was Rowdy Daniels, the Tank Howard of Ole Miss. He wasn't on anyone's Heisman list, but he was a good football player with NFL prospects. In retrospect, her attraction to a football player shouldn't have been surprising, but she'd thought that Rowdy would have cured her of that proclivity. It was the least he could have done.

She glanced down at the monitor. *Only sixty more seconds*, she thought with relief.

As the treadmill ground to a halt, Amber stopped walking. She looked around for Glenna and found herself staring directly at the beautiful Tank Howard, smirking at her.

Yep, luck of the damned.

"Hey there, Sunshine. How are you?" he asked solicitously.

Tank sat on the edge of the pool with his feet dangling. She was fairly certain that anyone else would have been shooed away but not him. Her hand automatically reached up and pulled her hair over her right side in an attempt to hide her scar. She saw him notice, his mouth tightening before he relaxed. She wanted to be able to get away from him, to exit with some dignity, but she was still hooked up to the machine and had no idea how to extricate herself from it.

Noticing her dilemma, he smiled at her again. "I'd help you out, but Glenna would kick my ass."

"I'm sure you'd just talk yourself out of any trouble," she responded sweetly, sharing a fake smile. "I mean, you are Tank Howard. Who stays mad at you for long?"

"Apparently, you," he quipped, getting the better of her.

Frustrated with being effectively trapped and pissed because he'd won that small word skirmish, Amber looked around, desperate for an escape. He must have noted her rising panic because he stood up from the side of the pool and walked into the main training room. There was nothing to do but watch him strut. He had to be six-four, two hundred and thirty pounds. His shirt pulled across his back as he moved. His muscles rippled under his taut cocoa-brown skin. She knew, without seeing it, that his stomach was ripped and sculpted. If his body wasn't enough to tempt a girl, his light-green eyes, in contrast to his caramel skin, could just about push you over the edge. She felt her body temperature rise as she observed him move gracefully toward the offices at the front of the training room.

And she prayed silently for distance from him.

Tank came back with Glenna in tow and then stayed to watch the release. Avoiding his eyes at all costs, Amber tried to make conversation with Glenna.

"So, same time tomorrow?" Amber asked.

"With the game on Saturday, it might be difficult. We'll probably have to wait until Monday," Glenna responded.

She was all business now, and Amber couldn't think of any other way to prolong her presence. As soon as Amber was free, Glenna gave her a quick good-job pat on the shoulder and left Amber and Tank alone.

As she climbed out of the pool, she noticed that Tank was holding out a towel for her. Grabbing it, she made for the bench on the back wall because her legs felt like jelly. Tank stayed where he was, on the edge of the pool, giving her space.

"I haven't seen you on campus before. I actually haven't seen you before the Bear's Den. How'd you score Glenna's services?"

Amber shrugged. "I know people."

"Do you go to school here?"

Deliberately rolling her eyes, she responded, "I've been on a school hiatus. But I transferred and should graduate at the end of fall."

"What's your major?" he continued.

"Is this Twenty Questions?"

Throwing up his hands, he said, "Fine. Don't answer that super personal question. You going to the game on Saturday?"

"What's a girl have to do to get rid of you?"

"Answer my questions," he said.

He presented her with a self-deprecating grin that showcased his dimples and sent her hormones into overdrive.

"Ugh! Broadcast journalism, which I'm pretty sure is out now. And I haven't decided about the game. I have to work that night. Driving to Athens for the game would make it a long day. Now, I've answered your questions. There's the door," she said, gesturing with her hand.

"See you Saturday, Sunshine," he said. He turned and started for the door.

"I didn't say I was going, and I don't think Sunshine is an appropriate nickname."

He kept walking. "See you Saturday, and I didn't think it'd be nice to call you *bitch*, which is about the only appropriate nickname for you."

"Tank?" she called out sweetly.

He kept walking but turned to look back at her.

"Fuck you!" she said with an innocent smile back on her face.

"Right back at you, Sunshine."

What is it about this girl? Tank thought as he went in search of Glenna.

He'd thought about Amber more than once since she'd literally fallen at Marsh's feet. He'd searched for her without even knowing he was doing it. He hadn't gone as far as asking about her, but he was about to cross over that line as soon as he found Glenna. If he could find out Amber's last name, he could at least cyberstalk her and probably garner a whole lot about who she was. It would probably cure him.

Although she intrigued him, he knew it was because she was a bit of a mystery. And, in this town, that was something of a novelty. Sure, when the new freshmen came in every year, the thrill of the chase would be back on. But five weeks into practice and two weeks into school, he'd gotten bored with the selection. He was fairly certain he wouldn't be bored with her.

Not that he needed this right now. What he needed to be doing right now was thinking about the game and focusing. Focus had never been one of Tank's issues, but recently, Franco had been all over him about getting his head in the game. Franco was normally spot-on, and Tank had to agree that he was this time, too. Tank would never have thought that he'd succumb to pressure. He'd sailed through high school and even the first two years of college. Maybe, he admitted to himself, it was because there hadn't ever been any expectations.

After the mess on signing day, most people had been ready to write him off. They'd thought he'd disappear into the oblivion of a small school in one of the many programs that didn't play before a sold-out crowd of tens of thousands, dallying on the sidelines of the national stage whose colleges and universities struggled to operate their programs in the black.

But here they were, three days away from playing the University of Georgia in what had become a highly anticipated matchup. So, yeah, KSU was in it for the guaranteed money it would bring them. But he was in it to win.

So, why was he spending anytime thinking about this very hostile girl?

He finally spotted Glenna, walking out of her office headed to where Iman sat on one of the tables. Harriman Perry was going to be a star. Tank loved the kid. He was raw, but God had graced him with talent. Tank had originally made his way to the training room earlier to check up on the kid.

Sitting himself on the rehab table opposite Iman, Tank reached out and clasped the hand that Iman held out.

"Wassup?" Iman asked as Glenna hooked him up.

"Just came to see how you were. You feeling good?" Tank asked him.

"Oh, yeah. I'll be ready."

Tank nodded. He really wasn't concerned about the kid being ready, but he was a freshman, and his first collegiate game would be against a ranked team with a rich history.

Iman nodded to the door of the pool area. "Who is *that*?" he asked Tank and Glenna.

Tank did a quick prayer of thanks that Iman was leading him exactly where he wanted to go without making him walk in that direction.

"Not sure. Who is she, Glenna?"

Glenna took note of him and Tank hated that she was such an observant woman who knew him too well not to understand his interest.

Shaking her head, she said, "Sorry, boys. Doctor-patient privilege and all that."

Again, Iman took up the mantle. "Shit, you ain't no doctor," he stated. "We ain't asking for her medical information. Just her name. Right, Tank?"

He nodded toward Tank, and Tank promised himself he'd hook Iman up later.

Again, he saw Glenna eye him. "Her name's Amber Johnson."

"She an athlete?" Iman continued.

"Not here," she responded as she continued to watch Tank.

Tank felt the question looming on his face and wished Glenna couldn't read him so well.

"Why is she here then?" Tank asked.

"She knows people," Glenna responded. Then, she flicked on the switch and moved on to the next person, effectively cutting off the conversation.

Satisfied that he at least had Amber's last name, Tank stood and looked down at Iman. "I owe you one."

Iman laughed. "All right."

Reaching over, Tank lightly tapped his shoulder.

Iman flinched. "Careful. I just got a new tat." Lifting the sleeve on his shirt, he showed Tank the intricate design. Against his dark skin, it was a bit difficult to make out.

Rolling his eyes a little, Tank asked, "How much did that run you?"

"Not too much," Iman answered proudly.

"Try not to spend all your money right away."

"I got Pell, too," Iman said with a gleam in his eye. "There's some new Jordans I want."

Tank remembered the feeling of having all that money in his account his freshman year. Staring at a couple thousand dollars when you'd never had your own money was pretty cool. But Tank had learned the hard way.

"Look, man, I'm just saying. It might seem like a lot of money. But if you go spending it all, when it comes to paying rent in January, you're gonna wish you'd saved some." On that note, Tank headed out.

He'd do his treatment later. He had a girl he wanted to check on.

SIX

"I'm telling you, it's like this girl doesn't exist. What twenty-something person doesn't have a Facebook or Instagram account?" Tank sat in the cold tub, across from Tilly, explaining his fruitless search to him. "So, say you're over Facebook, but no Instagram or Twitter? It's not natural."

Tilly merely watched him. "Maybe she's got some religious thing," he said, trying to mess with Tank.

"Trust me, this girl isn't Amish. Not with the mouth on her. She told me to fuck off this morning. If she were religious, I think she would have held back."

Tilly laughed. "You mean some girl you haven't even slept with yet is already telling you to fuck off?"

"Ha-ha. Real funny." Tank was too annoyed to find it amusing.

"Why not ask Mark? Looked like he knew her that night," Tilly suggested.

"Nah. You should have seen Glenna watching me like a hawk this morning when Iman was asking questions about her. I don't need Mark giving me shit. You and Steele give me enough as it is."

"You talked to Steele about this?"

Tank's sheepish shrug told Tilly all he needed to know.

"What'd he have to say?"

Tank smiled. "Something like, 'Hit it or someone else, and you'll snap out of it.'"

Tilly roared with laughter, sending rippling waves through the cold tub, which sent the water higher up his chest. "Sounds like good advice," he said between laughs.

Getting out of the tub, Tank smiled back. "Exactly what I need. But I have to actually be in the same vicinity as her to get that done."

Tilly followed him out. "We know where she works."

"Yeah."

"The Bear's Den sounds good to me," Tilly said.

Tank watched him, weighing the suggestion. He'd pretty much avoided the place since he'd met her. Maybe not consciously, but now that he thought about it, he hadn't been there since that night, which was unusual. Tank didn't chase. But…

"What is it about this girl?" Tilly asked him, all traces of joking gone.

"I have no freaking idea."

"Well, let's see if you can work her out of your system."

"So, I ran into Tank Howard today," Amber mentioned as casually as possible as she continued to wipe down the bar.

Thursdays were busy, so she'd come in a bit early to help Keira set up. Keira was behind her, so Amber couldn't see her face, and Keira couldn't see Amber's, which provided the anonymity of a phone conversation with just tone of voice to give her away.

At the silence that followed this pronouncement, Amber turned around to look at Keira.

Leaning against the bar, Amber waited for a response. Cocking her head to the side, she prompted, "You got nothing?"

Keira stood, frozen, the beers she was stocking in the fridge dangling from her fingers. "You need to stay away from Tank Howard, Amber."

Not that she'd been expecting a different response, but Amber was still taken aback by the vehemence in Keira's tone and the fierce look on her face. "Wow!" she said as she reared back a little to emphasize her surprise at Keira's attitude.

"Haven't you learned anything?"

Now hurt, Amber's formidable defenses kicked in. "Apparently not," she responded sarcastically. Pissed and wounded was a bad combination for her.

Amber turned back around and continued her chore of prepping for the night. When she felt Keira's hand on her shoulder, Amber pulled away and moved to the opposite side of the bar.

Keira followed. "Look, I just think you are still healing. The last thing you need is to get involved with any guy."

Amber shook her off. "That's not what you meant."

"You can't even talk about what happened. And those months before the accident, no one knows what was going on with you because you disappeared. Do you really think you are ready to be with anyone, let alone Tank? Your father would freak."

"I don't give a shit about what my father thinks."

Of Keira's litany, the part about her father was the easiest to handle.

"And who says I want to be with Tank? Maybe I just want to screw him." Snarky was something Amber could always do.

Keira let out a maniacal-sounding laugh. "Yeah, right! You've never been that girl."

Amber looked her in the eyes. "Let's be honest, Keira. You have no idea what kind of girl I am."

Amber had secretly been hoping for a denial, a good old-fashioned proclamation of sisterhood, and when none was forthcoming, she felt something within her wither. So, maybe she wasn't as numb as she'd thought.

Turning away from her friend, Amber scooted under the bar, needing a minute. Practically running to the restroom, Amber pushed open the door, looking for refuge.

She found it in the handicap stall, the one with its own mirror and sink. Slinking toward the back, she leaned against the wall with the silver bar used for leverage wedging into her back. Avoiding the mirror, she dropped her head back, allowing the cool tile to ease her sudden headache. Reaching up, she ran her fingers across the scar by her mouth and down the spiderweb on her jaw to the lacerations running down her neck. She couldn't feel her fingers, sensing only a pleasant numbness, but the coolness against the scars eased the burn. Phantom pain, someone had told her. Phantom or not, the cold helped. And, once again, her world came into focus.

Walking to the sink, she ran the water over her wrists, patted her cheeks with her wet hands. She pulled some paper towels from the dispenser and wiped away the water. Fortified against Keira's betrayal, she made her way back to the bar.

As she slipped underneath the opening, she noticed Keira on the backside. Walking to the front of the bar, the most distance she could maintain, Amber straightened the already clean bar just to do something. As she leaned down to get a new bottle of tequila from the cabinet behind the bar, she heard the scrape of chairs. Thankful for a distraction, she grabbed the bottle, turned around, and found herself staring at Tank, Tilly, and a kid she'd never met.

"Hey, Sunshine. We meet again," Tank said amicably, as if her last words to him hadn't been to fuck off.

"Gentlemen," she responded, taking in all three of them with her greeting. "What can I get for you?"

"Couple of menus," Tilly responded.

"Sure," she said as she reached behind her and pulled out a menu for each of them. "Can I get you something to drink while you look?" She could be sunshine when she wanted.

They all asked for water at the same time. As she got their drinks, she remained careful not to look at Tank.

Setting their drinks down, she said, "You all ready for the big game on Saturday?"

As Tilly and the kid responded to her, she saw Tank sit back in his chair with his arms folded across his chest and an expression of, *Who the hell are you?*, on his face. Trying to concentrate on talking to the guys and not to make any eye contact with Tank, she rolled out her most charming self. She took their orders and moved down to the computer to input them. She knew Tank continued to watch her, but she refused to get into any verbal warfare with him.

Since she didn't have any other customers and Keira was busy on the other side of the bar, Amber took up residence in between Tilly and the kid. She didn't exclude Tank, but she also didn't include him. His gaze warmed her. She liked knowing he was there, staring at her. It infused her with this sense of female power that did wonders to stroke her ego after her falling-out with Keira. She could feel the tension between them. So, to distract herself, she struck up a conversation with his boys.

"I know these two jokers. Who are you?" she asked the baby-faced guy.

"Harriman Perry. But everyone calls me Iman."

"Ah, the receiver," she said before she could stop herself.

All three of them looked a little taken aback.

Tilly, without the gold teeth today, said, "You know who he is?" with an inflection of incredulity in his voice.

"Of course she does," Mark said, coming out of nowhere and inserting himself in the middle of the conversation. "Amber probably knows more about football than the three of you put together."

She almost groaned her consternation at Mark for putting her shit on the table, but it was hard for her to ever really get mad at him.

"Really?" Tilly said at the same time as Iman's, "Seriously?"

Tank, she noticed out of the corner of her eye, continued to sit there, observing.

"Oh, yeah. Stats, plays. It's pretty amazing."

"Interesting," Tilly said, shooting a look over at Tank.

Amber, desperate to get rid of Mark, said, "I think Keira said the Miller Lite keg is low."

Mark quickly took his leave to check on it.

Looking up at Tilly, she quickly explained, "Mark exaggerates. Everyone who has grown up in this town knows something about football."

To close down the conversation, she went to check on their food.

Between Keira and Tank, she felt overwhelmed. *Where is the numb when I need it?*

Peering around the corner, she saw that the guys were watching *SportsCenter*, and their drinks were full. She had a minute to escape. Trudging down the hall, she flew out the back door and leaned against the brick wall. Just as she closed her eyes for some solace, the door opened, and Tank appeared.

Tank wasn't quite sure which Amber he liked better—the bitter, sarcastic, caustic girl from the morning or the charming, solicitous girl who was waiting on them. This girl now wouldn't meet his eyes, so he'd probably choose the one from this morning. Regardless, his intrigue just ratcheted up a notch.

As he had seen her flee from behind the bar, he had known he was going to follow her even before Tilly had looked over and nodded his head in the direction of the back exit.

"Sunshine," Tank said.

Her head rolled in his direction, and their eyes met for the first time. The tether of their connection hit him hard and quick. Before he knew what he meant to do, he moved toward her, caged her in with his arms on both sides of her head, lowered his mouth, and ran it along the scar on her chin and mouth. He didn't touch her. He stayed just far enough away that she could duck out if she wanted to or lean into him. She did neither, instead closing her eyes. But he watched the pulse point in her neck jump and heard her stuttered breath. He was daring her to lean into him, but she wouldn't.

"You know where this is going, don't you?" he murmured, still a hairbreadth away from her scar, inching his lower body in closer but still giving her a choice.

"Nowhere," she said on an exhale that skidded and bumped out of her throat.

"Yes, it is," he continued, still moving along her jaw and mouth, hoping she would reach out for him.

She opened her eyes, and he drew away from her, so he could look into them. They were drugged with the lust that swirled around them.

"This can't—won't go anywhere. I'm bad news, Tank. I don't want to take you down, too."

A look of confusion passed over his face, "Too?"

"Just walk away," she muttered. "Please."

She ducked underneath him, taking the escape route he'd provided, and disappeared into the restaurant. Tank turned and leaned against the wall, grabbing her spot, absorbing the heat she'd left behind. Banging his head on the wall, Tank pushed away, moving toward the door.

The last thing he needed right now was a complicated girl. He wanted a national championship. He could win the Heisman. He couldn't have his focus split. Resolving to stay away from Amber, he entered the bar, threw some cash down where he'd been sitting, and left.

SEVEN

Over the next three weeks, the Bears made a statement. Game one of the regular season had had them playing the University of Georgia. In their only game that could propel them into the national ranks, the victory in Athens, even though it was the first game of the season, had had the analysts salivating. Tank had gone seventeen for twenty-five for three hundred thirty yards, rushed for seventy-nine yards, and had two touchdowns, earning him comparisons to Cam Newton. That week alone, he'd received hundreds of random friend requests and texts that he didn't answer. His numbers for the second game had been even more impressive, but because they'd played a conference school, it was merely a footnote on *SportsCenter*. By their third game, Tank had put up legendary numbers, and it didn't matter to anybody that he'd been playing Toledo.

In a scheduling fluke, their first three games had been on the road. So, when the team came home the third week in September, it was to a hero's welcome. Home football Saturdays had always held their own special charm. The town decked itself in green and silver. Most activities were suspended as everyone came out to cheer on their team. The sense of anticipation and excitement that permeated the town became palpable as they eagerly welcomed the the team home. In a town that embraced its football team, no matter how they were performing, when you sprinkled a dash of national attention and a cupful of Tank Howard, you had the recipe for a worshipful, adoring fan base.

Where their team had always enjoyed a modified celebrity status in town, now, they were recognized and fawned over everywhere they went. Even the walk-ons, the scout team members, got into the action. While everyone enjoyed their newfound recognition, Tank was the star. Screw the big man on campus image. Tank Howard was king of the world. Everyone was deferential. Professors, administrative assistants, coaches from other sports—they all wanted wanted to talk to him, shake his hand, be part of the dream.

In the Tank-is-god atmosphere, it was difficult to keep his head. On the football field, he didn't have a problem—partly because Franco had a way of keeping him grounded and partly because he had a healthy enough respect for the talents of other players that he knew he had to keep his head in it. But off the field, in Tank Is King of the World Land, he was invincible. For the first time in his life, he became indiscriminate with women. If they were offering, he would take. At first, he'd attempted to keep it to the night after a game. Now, the only night he was alone was the night before a game. If he seemed to have a preference, no one could figure it out. Willing seemed to be the only requirement.

Part of him, the part that was grounded on the football field, kept waiting for someone to rein him in or say no or ask for more. And another part of him marveled at the power a twenty-one-year-old football player could wield. Why was this so important to everyone? What made them think he was anything special? Because he could throw a football? Because he had amazing receivers who could catch anything he threw at them? Because his coach was amazing and scripted his play just enough to give him the ability to make decisions when the opportunity arose? *Why did his skill with a football really matter in the whole scheme of things?*

But then he'd step out of the locker room and move back into the world, and his questions would dissolve in a haze of reporters and fawning fans. It wasn't such a bad way to live.

The stadium maxed out at about 23,000 people, but for the Bears opening game, it was beyond capacity.

People were watching. And Tank didn't disappoint. He went twelve for fifteen, throwing for one hundred sixty-five yards. He also rushed twenty-three times for two hundred seventy-five yards. It wasn't the stats that Franco wanted, but a win was a win. And as they continued to garnish national attention, the last thing they wanted to do was stumble.

After the post-game interviews, Tank made his way to Franco's office because his presence had been requested. He already knew that Franco wasn't happy about his performance. His coaches didn't want him running the ball as much as he had been. He understood because he knew the game plan, but he didn't think that Franco could really argue with a victory. Again, he felt that pull of invincibility.

Let Franco bitch, he thought. *He can't win without me.*

And if Tank believed it was odd that he'd suddenly become the most important factor in the game in his mind, he brushed it off. He certainly didn't notice that, for the first time in his life, he was walking into a coach's office with a chip on his shoulder.

But Franco did.

Franco nodded briefly as Tank threw himself into the chair across from him. He didn't say anything for a moment—not necessarily to make Tank stew, but just to watch his level of frustration at being kept waiting. Looking down at something on his desk but watching Tank from below his lashes, he shuffled some papers. Tank shifted, rapping his fingers against the arm of the chair. Still, Franco waited.

Finally, Tank couldn't hold it back. "What the fuck, Coach?"

Franco looked up, a bit surprised at the hostility in Tank's tone. When he met Tank's eyes, he knew that Tank was shocked, too. But bravado being what it was, Franco watched him bow up some more.

"You want to try that again, Antony?" Franco asked, the hardness in his tone a distant but foggy reminder to Tank that he was in charge.

Franco saw the struggle in Tank—his ego doing battle with his innate sense of respect for other people.

He didn't apologize—the celebrity in him wouldn't allow him to—but his tone changed. "What's up, Coach?"

Franco leaned back in his chair, warily watching his star. "We'll talk about your performance on Monday during film. Right now, I want to discuss what you are doing off the field."

If Tank was surprised or pissed, he disguised it. Still drumming his fingers, he nodded his assent to the conversation. Franco didn't need that, but it helped.

"You've been on a tear. And I'm not going to stop you from having your fun. I've never been that guy, but I know what it's like to have offers, and I know how hard it can be to resist. So, I'm all right with that. But you need to be careful."

Franco saw the look steal across his face, as if to say, *Who are you? My mother?*

And, almost on cue, the door opened to one Chantel Jones. It couldn't have been better scripted in Hollywood. The shock on Tank's face was absolutely priceless after the attitude earlier. Franco stood to greet Chantel. He'd been around for a while, and Chantel trusted him. Leaning down to kiss her, Franco walked her to the chair next to a belligerent Tank. But, this time, the innate sense of respect won out, and Tank immediately stood to greet his mother.

"Hey, Mama," he said as he grabbed her for a long embrace. "Did you like the game?"

Chantel took her seat. "You ran the ball too much. But I'm pretty sure you know that, right?"

"Yes, ma'am."

Franco could see the struggle in Tank, could tell he wanted to know where this was all going. But he kept quiet and waited impatiently for them to tell him why they were meeting like this.

"Tank, you know that Franco and I have your best interests at heart."

This one was easy for Tank. "Yes, ma'am."

He could be all bravado, but Franco knew that Tank trusted him with his career.

"Well, Franco and I want you to be careful. Now's the time when people will come out of the woodwork." She didn't say it, but they all knew she was talking about Richard Howard. "You've been very free with yourself over the last few weeks."

Tank squirmed.

Franco watched as Tank experienced some horror that his mother knew what he'd been doing. If Tank took the time to ask his coach, he'd find out that Chantel had requested this meeting. She'd been watching his Facebook and Instagram accounts. She'd seen too many faces over the last couple of weeks, and she was concerned. But Tank wouldn't ask. He made some assumptions. At this moment, Franco knew what he hadn't foreseen. Tank was going to punish him for this somehow.

"Look, Mama, I'm just having some fun."

"Fun can get you in trouble. I shouldn't be having this conversation with you. You know better. Everyone's going to want a piece of you. All it takes is one girl. One screw-up. You can't afford that right now."

"I've got it!" Tank said with some emphasis that his mother didn't seem to like.

"Excuse me?" she said, standing up and walking over to him. "I don't care who all these people think you are. You are still my son, and you'd better talk to me the way I taught you to talk. Do you understand me?"

Franco wished he weren't here. He didn't need to see Tank dressed down by his diminutive mother. But Chantel had wanted him present, and he would do just about anything for her.

Tank rose, dwarfing his mom. "Yes, ma'am," he replied with the proper amount of deference. "I'll see you tomorrow at breakfast?" he asked as he bent to kiss her cheek.

"Yes. Eight o'clock sharp. I have to get back for work. You be careful tonight."

Tank nodded as he made his way to the door. He gently turned that knob. Then, he turned and blasted Franco with a look of contempt. Franco merely nodded and watched his star storm out.

Chantel sat heavily in the chair. Looking at Franco, she said, "I misplayed that, didn't I?"

Not one to rub salt in the wound, Franco merely said, "He'll be okay. He just hasn't gotten called out on anything for a while. And, right now, he's feeling a bit invincible. But it'll be okay."

Franco just wished he believed that.

EIGHT

Amber and Keira had reached a tentative truce over the last few weeks. During the incident with Tank outside the restaurant, Amber had grudgingly accepted that Keira was right. It was why she'd warned him, why she had been able to walk away when everything was telling her to stay, to take a chance. But she had stopped trusting herself after Rowdy, and she understood, right now, Keira knew what her best interests were better than she did. Not that she cared to admit that to Keira. She just forgave her friend for her brutal honesty.

Keira and Amber worked during the game that Saturday, the first home game of the season. Even though there had been a record crowd in attendance at the game, the Bear's Den had been packed with Bears fans. It had been a busy day.

Exhausted but amped up from the adrenaline of watching a good football game, Keira suggested they go out. About to refuse, Amber decided that she and Keira needed a good time out together. She hadn't really been social since the accident, and she really wanted to do something other than work, rehab, sleep, and evade her father.

They headed to Keira's apartment to get ready. There was some big party tonight, and although they both preferred a dance floor to a kegger in a field, Keira convinced Amber that this party would be worth it. She should have guessed that Keira wanted to go there for a reason, but she was too excited to be going out to worry over what was motivating her friend. Embracing their north Georgia heritage, which they both normally downplayed, they donned jean skirts, T-shirts, and their cowboy boots.

As they drove through town, Amber's curiosity finally won out. "What's up with wanting to go to this party?" she asked.

"Nothing," Keira said. "Just thought it would be fun. I'm pretty sure everyone nineteen to twenty-five who lives in the town is going to be there."

"*Oh-kay*," Amber replied, not really satisfied with that answer. "But is there someone in particular you are interested in seeing?"

Keira tucked her hair behind her ear and quickly glanced in Amber's direction. Then, she shrugged, which was a dead giveaway.

"Who, may I ask, are you interested in?" Amber teased.

It was so rare to see Keira shy and slightly uncomfortable that Amber laughed with the novelty of it.

"I don't want to tell you."

Taken aback, Amber's brows drew together in confusion. "Why not?" She tried to keep the hurt out of her voice, but really, who was she to force something out of her friend? How could she push her friend for information now without being a complete hypocrite?

As Keira hesitated, Amber swooped in to alleviate the tension. "Look, if you don't want to tell me, you don't have to."

Again, Keira looked over at her, briefly taking her eyes off the road. She drew in a deep sigh and said, "I don't want to tell you because I feel a bit like a hypocrite."

Amber choked out a laugh at the irony of Keira making that statement right at that moment. Shaking her head, she exonerated her friend. "Really, Keira, you don't have to tell me anything you don't want to."

"Don't pull that shit, Amber. If I had to do it all over again, I would still hound you for information. And maybe, if I'd kept at it, things would have been different. If you'd had someone you felt was actually there for you, no matter what, maybe things wouldn't be like they are."

Amber reached out for Keira's hand. "There is no way that anything you would have done could have changed the outcome. Please do not place any of the blame for what happened in my life on our friendship. My relationship with you is one of the only reasons I am sitting here, alive and somewhat healthy. You have to believe that."

Keira kept her eyes on the road.

Amber, needing her to acknowledge what she'd said, squeezed her hand again. "Really, Keira, that's the honest truth."

"I want to see Tilly," Keira said in a rush, as if saying it as fast as she could would take away the complete shock of her words.

Amber leaned back in her seat, her face a knot of confusion. "Tilly Lace? The hulking, big black man with the sometimes gold grill in his mouth, on the football team?"

Keira merely nodded. Then, Amber couldn't help it; she laughed her ass off.

Keira looked annoyed. Amber tried to say something, but she couldn't stop laughing long enough to formulate a response.

"I knew you'd be pissed because I told you to stay away from Tank. But the last couple of times Tilly's been into the bar, I've talked to him. He's a really cool guy. And, the last time they were there, he was really concerned about you when you disappeared outside with Tank. I don't know. I like him."

They arrived at the field, and as Keira turned off the car, Amber got ahold of her laughter.

"He does seem to be really nice," Amber conceded. "Just take your own advice and be careful. Right now, those boys are getting girls left and right. That's what happens when you're really good and the whole country is talking about you. Trust me on this! You need to be cautious, okay?"

Keira merely nodded. Amber caught the look in her eyes and almost groaned. She recognized the look because it would stare back at her in the mirror whenever she thought about Tank Howard.

Amber and Keira brought their own drinks. They weren't all that interested in drinking beer, and they didn't trust any of the guys there to watch out for them. This way, they could control what went into their bodies. There was a DJ set up not far from them, providing some decent music. But, no matter how many amenities the organizer had attempted to provide, they were still in the middle of a field.

They picked out an old picnic table where they sat watching the crowd. After they had been there for an hour and hadn't seen anyone of interest, one Tilly Lace specifically, they decided to pack it in. Just as they made that decision, a big bear of a man and his lanky sidekick moved on to the dance floor. Amber noticed them at the same time Tilly noticed Keira. Walking through the crowd, he was quickly in front of them.

"How are my two favorite bartenders?" he asked, his gold grill flashing in the hazy light.

Keira, who hadn't noticed his arrival, smiled broadly. "We're good," she answered for both of them.

Since Tilly had recently seen Amber at two of her weakest moments, he waited for her answer.

Amber smiled and nodded. "We are."

"How come you're not working?" he asked.

"We worked during the game, so we got the night off," Keira responded.

Iman, who still reminded Amber of a twelve-year-old boy, puffed up as he asked, "You mean, you didn't get to watch us stomp on Akron?"

"Oh, we watched," Amber replied, "enough to know that you should have caught that third and long ball that Tank practically gifted into your hands."

Tilly laughed as he popped Iman in the back of his head. "Told ya," he said, as if they'd just discussed that play.

"Where is your third wheel?" Keira inquired.

If she were asking for Amber, Amber could have told her friend not to do her any favors. But when she looked over at Keira, she saw that Keira was just making conversation.

Tilly glanced briefly at Amber, perhaps to gauge her level of interest. "Not really sure."

Iman just laughed. "Probably off with some girl. It's not only his stats on the field that are making headlines."

Again, Tilly popped him in the head, "Freshmen," he muttered.

Snickering, Iman gestured to the makeshift dance floor. "Wanna dance?"

The four of them got up to dance. It was dimmer over there, but someone had gotten some kind of strobe light that flashed intermittently, taking away some of the dark but not enough to make out faces.

They were quickly swallowed in the dancing crowd. Tilly and Iman stayed close, not letting anyone really get near them. But it was hard for them to keep the other girls at bay, and soon, Keira and Amber were jostling for position, trying to stay with the two guys.

Tilly kept Keira close, Amber noted, but Iman enjoyed soaking up the attention that was being lavished on him. Finding herself on the outskirts of the Iman circle, Amber flinched when someone grabbed her arm and pulled her backward into his chest. She started to protest and moved to stomp on his instep when she caught a whiff of his scent. Without even needing to see him, Amber knew that Tank was behind her. And against all her honorable intentions and trappings of self-preservation, she leaned back into him, allowing his hands to steal around her waist and his leg to creep between hers, before he pulled her ass back against him.

"I really hope," he breathed into her ear, "that you know it's me and have just agreed to stop trying to stay away from me."

In response, she moved her hands behind her and settled them on the backs of his thighs, molding herself to him by getting as close as possible without being absorbed by him. Somehow, her body had made the decision for her.

NINE

When Tank had left Franco's office, he'd been pissed—pissed at Franco and pissed at his mom. The fact that they'd teamed up on him messed with his invincibility, and that made him mad, too. How they could treat him like some eighteen-year-old freshman who needed to be told how he could act bordered on demeaning.

He hadn't known what to do with his mad, so he'd stayed away from the bash. On a night with the high of the game and the useless rage against the two people he respected most pumping through him, he had known he'd get himself in trouble. He'd hit the weight room and taken out his anger on the dumbbells. When he felt in control, he'd headed to the party.

His first sight of Amber had come the moment he stepped out of the car. That platinum hair had called to him like a beacon. He'd moved toward her with purpose. He hadn't stopped to talk. He'd just plowed his way through the dance crush, needing to get to her. He had seen her on the outside of the circle around Iman. Cursing the freshman for letting her slide from his view, Tank had grabbed her and hauled her to him. As she'd acquiesced, he'd felt the tension of the night drain from his body.

"Thank God," he breathed into her ear.

Then, he moved his mouth down, kissing the unmarred side of her throat. They stayed like that, molded to one another, as one song ran into the next. He couldn't stop touching her and got bolder and bolder as the dance wore on. He moved his hand under her T-shirt, inching up toward her amazing breasts. Before he knew it, his hand was under her bra, weighing her breast, rolling the nipple between his fingers. He felt rather than heard her moan. Her ass jerked against his pelvis, sending him into a tailspin. For a brief moment, he wanted to look at her, see her eyes, and make sure she was okay with this, with him. Then, that invincibility kicked in.

"I need you," he said, holding her close to him, toying with her breast, rubbing against her. "I need more."

Amber nodded her head. Removing his hand from under her shirt, he grabbed her hand in his and pulled her away from the crowd. He looked back at her as they moved through the field, a quick sweep that took in the boots and the skirt and her hair pulled to the side, covering her neck. Her body seemed to pulse with need. He could feel it mirroring his. Turning back, he moved toward the barn, the source of the power for the party. Pulling her forward, he turned the corner, and they disappeared around the side of the barn, away from the partygoers.

Gently pushing her up against the barn, Tank grabbed her hands and intertwined his fingers with hers while leaning in and pinning her with his body. Looking into her fathomless brown eyes, he was struck by his general sense of ease with her.

"Hi," he said, grinning down at her.

"Hey," she responded. She pulled her bottom lip between her teeth, putting her nervousness on display for him.

Dropping a quick kiss, he gently drew her lower lip into his mouth, mimicking her movements from a moment before. At her sharp intake of breath, he kissed her hard, possessing her mouth, hoping to swallow all of her warnings before she could make them. He pulled back, trying to slow himself down, recognizing his desire to possess her absolutely.

"Did you watch the game?" he said as he rested his forehead against hers.

"Yes," she responded. "You ran the ball too much," she added confidently.

Groaning, he released one of her hands and rolled away from her, leaning back on the barn. Squeezing her other hand, he said, "So I've been told."

She'd distracted him for a moment. He let the game scroll through his head.

"Third quarter, third and seven, on the forty-seven-yard line. Iman was wide open on the left side, but you didn't even look. Your first option was covered, but you had plenty of time. That was the most obvious one," she responded clinically, like she was dissecting the game for him.

Franco had wanted to review film, but this girl had made a spot-on assessment with only one viewing. Although he was annoyed with everyone else who had told him he ran too much, the analysis coming from her mouth made his lust blaze even hotter. Rolling his head to the side so that he could see her, he watched her pulse jump in her neck.

Then, he gave in to it.

He moved quickly. Releasing her hand, he spun back to face her, pinning her against the barn, taking possession of her mouth, grabbing her thighs and placing them around his waist. He pressed into her, and the contact of his erection with her pulsing center made them both moan loudly and move in a frenzied motion to get closer. Her boots hooking around his back allowed his hands the freedom to roam her body. As he pulled her shirt up, his mouth found her nipple through her bra, and she cried out as he gently bit down, feasting on her. He couldn't get close enough.

"I need to be inside you, Amber," he said raggedly in her ear as they continued to rub against each other. "Please tell me it's okay."

Amber was caught in a maelstrom, tossed about the sea, with no control over her body as the ocean shifted her about from place to place. Sometimes, she felt like she couldn't breathe, like the current was too much and she needed air. But her body knew the rhythm, knew how to swim with the current, knew the way to go without her mind being in it at all. That Tank Howard was the maelstrom didn't matter. He ruled her, like she was a tiny rowboat in the middle of a magnificent storm.

She wanted him. But she didn't know why she wanted him, and that scared the shit out of her.

Was just this her? A glorified cleat-chaser who just wanted to be with the next big thing? Or even scarier, did she just want this man in front of her, regardless of who he was or what he could do?

She didn't know.

As he toyed with her body and all but forced the decision from her with his clever hands, amazing mouth, and hot body, she tried to gather her senses. *Would having sex with him extricate her from this unbelievable desire?* She couldn't make a rational decision with her legs wrapped around him and his mouth on her breast. As time between his plea and her nonanswer marched on, he pulled his mouth away from her and started to slowly put distance between them.

He put his hand around the back of her neck and stroked up her scar with his thumb. Her legs were still around his waist, but he was no longer flush against her.

"It's okay," he said, his light eyes boring into her.

Without even knowing she'd made a decision, she brought her hand up to his, her palm pressing into the back of his hand. Turning her mouth to place a kiss there, she conceded to him.

So, she was surprised when he gently tugged his hand from beneath hers, and he unhooked her legs from around him. As her feet dropped to the ground, he held on to her waist, as if he knew he needed to steady her. Her startled gaze met his. She searched for some explanation in his shockingly green orbs. But he merely smirked before dropping his forehead to hers, effectively breaking eye contact. They stayed like that, their panting breaths calming, their wits returning.

He leaned away from her and then down, pressing kisses along the corner of her mouth, over the deep scar that pulled her mouth a touch lower, over the webbing on her jaw and neck. He settled there, learning her scars, peeling away layers of her hardened resistance. It was headier than any sex she'd ever had. Her head swam from the tenderness, and her body pulsed from the feeling of his warm, wet mouth on the mostly numb, puckered skin on her face and neck. Her heart rate kicked up, the pulse point in her neck thumping to some Tank-inspired rhythm.

He stepped away, dropping back to lean against the barn, leaving space between their shoulders, terminating their contact. It took a moment for the churning inside her to halt, for awareness to return.

She took in the scene around her. Shadows of reds and blues bounced around in the periphery of her vision. The sound of police sirens filtered in from the distance.

"Guess the party's over," she said flippantly, beating him to the punch. She felt the sting of his rejection.

Tank eyed her suspiciously. But the shutters were back in place, and she continued to straighten her clothes.

Straightening her skirt, she looked up to meet his eyes. "I have to go find Keira. And you need to slink out of here."

She started to walk away, but he grabbed her hand, staying her.

"Wait," he said. "Tilly won't let anything happen to Keira. We'll walk back together."

He started to move toward her, but she put her hand out on his chest to stop him.

"Tank, I'll find Keira on my own." She looked away from him, his green eyes too much to take in at the moment. She hated that she was hurt. She shouldn't have gone down this road. "Look," she said, "nothing good can come of this. Let's just leave it as it is."

She turned and started walking away. But he had to go in the same direction, so walking together was inevitable. They didn't touch, and there was enough space, physically and emotionally, that no one would put them together. As soon as they got near other people, it was easy for Amber to get lost in the crowd. So, she did.

TEN

At dinner the next night, Amber leaned against her grandmother's counter, pretending to be available if she needed help. But they both knew it was a front. Nona was the only person Amber allowed to mother her. Amber accepted Nona's coddling, fawning, desire to feed, and unconditional love.

"Why were you late?" Nona asked her.

Amber wove her hair around her finger, trying to concentrate on being in her grandmother's kitchen and not on her evening of almost debauchery with Tank Howard. "I was waiting for Dad. When he didn't come home by four, I figured he'd just end up meeting me here."

"Did you talk to him? It's almost five now, and he's still not here."

"Nah, I haven't talked to him."

Nona sighed. "When was the last time you spoke to him?"

Trying to exonerate both herself and her father, she explained, "We work opposite hours, and he's obviously been super busy."

Nona rolled her eyes, making Amber laugh. "I know you think I am naive and don't know the way things work. But you living with him now is not the right thing. You should be here with me and Papa. We'd be able to take care of you."

"We've been over this. I need to be on my own now, Nona. I truly appreciate your generosity and love, but it's time for me to confront my issues. I'm twenty-three. I don't need to be taken care of." She tried to disguise her irritation because she loved her grandparents so much, but she didn't want to have this same conversation yet again.

"You were in a very serious car accident recently. When I think that we could have lost you…" Nona stopped talking, her eyes filling with tears, the way they did whenever the accident was mentioned. Her grandmother turned away and grabbed a tissue to pat her eyes.

As she did every time this happened, Amber laughed it off. "You're being dramatic. And I'm fine. Look at me." But that was the wrong thing to say.

There weren't many people who could look at her and not flinch at the scars. *Except for Tank*, she remembered. Almost as if she were up against the barn, she felt his kisses along her scars and her body's reaction to the gesture.

Feeling her face get warm, embarrassed to be thinking about her desire in her grandmother's kitchen, she moved to hug out her guilt with a quick embrace. "It's all good. I promise."

"Well, I'm worried about your father. I'm going to call him to see what's taking him so long."

The only hours during the week when Amber could not evade her father were from four to seven o'clock every Sunday when the whole family was expected for Sunday dinner. He always dropped whatever he was doing to pick her up at a quarter to four to head to her grandparents' house. Normally, it would be a quiet ride once they got past the meaningless questions about rehab, work, and her disposition. Beyond that, they shared nothing, each wrapped up in their own thoughts on the way to dinner. On the way home, they'd typically have one family scandal, issue, or problem they could discuss to fill the gap. He would drop her off at home and head back to work. She could then avoid him for the rest of the week until Sunday rolled around again.

After the accident, the family had all expected her to come home and live with her grandparents. But she'd known from day one that she would go to her father's house instead. His house offered the solitude she wanted without the probing but gentle presence of her Nona. It had been a battle. No one was fooled, especially not her father. They'd created a crevasse in their relationship that neither seemed willing or able to traverse. He accepted that she needed a place to heal how she saw fit, and he'd offered it to her because, quite frankly, he wouldn't deny her anything she ever wanted.

"He's got too much going on at work. He's not going to make it tonight," Nona informed her.

Amber breathed a sigh of relief at the news that she wouldn't have to deal with his guilt-ridden presence tonight. She had enough craziness going on inside.

It never dawned on her that her father rarely missed a meal at her grandparents'. Nor did she contemplate the enormity of whatever the problem could be that kept him away that night.

When Amber pulled into the driveway of her dad's house, it was close to nine. After dinner, she'd stayed to help clean up since her father wasn't hustling off to get back to work. She saw her dad's car but rejoiced over the dark house, figuring he was asleep. Almost skipping with glee at the way her Sunday was turning out, she opened the door, dropped her keys on the table, and headed toward her room. As she made her way through the living room, she noticed a shadow and almost jumped out of her skin.

"What the hell? Shit, you scared me to death!" she exclaimed as she saw him sitting on the couch in the corner with a drink in his hand. "Why is it so damn dark in here?"

"That's three cuss words in three sentences. I hope you didn't expose your grandparents to that mouth," he said somewhat drolly, like he felt the need to mention it but didn't care one way or the other.

Amber moved toward the wall and hit the switch for the light. Her father drew back, closing his eyes, as if the light blinded him. She heard the ice move in his glass and saw a tumbler in his hand filled with a rich golden liquid.

"Rough day at the office?" she quipped. She wasn't sticking around to find out why he looked like shit. She began to head toward her room.

"Don't take another fucking step," he said.

Shocked, Amber stopped walking and turned around to face her father. She didn't even know what to say or how to act or what to think about his statement. She merely stood there, in the middle of the room, looking at him.

"I'm not sure if you know this, but Cy, our sports information guy, monitors all the guys' social media accounts and any app that have their names in them. Facebook, websites, Instagram. It's his worst nightmare. Apparently, fans open up accounts in athletes' names, so watching all of that is a full-time job for an intern."

He didn't say anything else, but she felt her stomach plummet, and the food she'd inhaled at her grandmother's started to churn. She wasn't sure if she was supposed to acknowledge his statement or chalk it up to general information.

Unable to take the silence, she said, "Uh, I didn't know they had to do that, but I guess it's not surprising."

"You don't have social media."

Again, it was a statement that she wasn't sure what to do with. *Should she respond or not?*

"No. I don't have any of that stuff anymore."

"Hmm," was all she got.

Silence reigned supreme. She took him in, something she hadn't done in a while. Her dad was a good-looking dude. Their hair was the same color when she didn't dye hers—a blue-black. Their eyes were mirror images—chocolate brown. When she was little, she'd wanted blue eyes, but she'd gotten over that a long time ago. He was a big man with wide shoulders and a flat stomach. She knew he did well with the women although she supposed that had to stop now that she was living with him. That was one sacrifice she hadn't thought about when she made her plan.

Since he hadn't said anything in what seemed like an hour, Amber turned again to head to her room.

"We're not done."

"Done with what?" she snapped. "You haven't said a damn thing. You're just making stupid statements and looking at your drink."

He suddenly yet gracefully got up and set his drink down. He pulled his phone from his back pocket as he walked toward her, tapping keys as he went. "You want to explain to me what you were doing with Tank Howard?" he said as he shoved his phone into her line of vision.

The picture on the screen was erotic. It was when they were dancing. Their bodies were totally entwined, but neither one of them could see the other's face as Tank was behind her with his arms all over her body. Her face was a mask of ecstasy, her eyes drugged, her smile sexy. His mirrored hers. It was a picture of two lovers who were completely engrossed with each other. To her horror, she had to admit that it was soft porn. Someone could look at that picture and get hot quickly. She couldn't believe her father had seen this picture of his daughter. No wonder he was drinking.

"We were dancing," she answered, knowing it was insufficient but not knowing what else she could say.

"Looks to me like more than dancing, but what do I know?" He paused.

She could feel his anger vibrating through him. And she really couldn't blame him.

"I've heard that Tank has been with a different girl every night since the Georgia win. Is that what you are? A groupie whore? I just want to make sure I know if I've raised a girl who spreads her legs for the best athlete on campus."

A rage like no other jolted through her body. Before she knew what she was doing, she slapped him across the face. It didn't matter that she hadn't screwed Tank last night—she knew she would have if he hadn't stopped—but her father had already made up his mind.

He didn't even flinch. "Should I take that to mean that the truth hurts? When Rowdy's parents were hurling all those accusations, should I not have defended you? Is this who you are?" he said calmly, as if he were asking her if she wanted milk in her cereal.

"Fuck you!" she said, her voice devoid of inflection, as tears pooled in her eyes and began to run, unchecked, down her face.

"I was really proud when this picture was shoved in my face this morning. Really proud, Amber."

"I hate you. Don't sit there and disguise your parental concern. This has nothing to do with me. This has everything to do with your precious Tank Howard, your star fucking player, whose coattails you've been riding since signing day three years ago. Wouldn't want Tank to get any bad press, would you, Coach? What would people think about Tank if they knew he was with the girl who had brought down Rowdy Daniels? His fucking silver image would be tainted. Isn't that what you're worried about? Coach Franco's whore of a daughter shacking up with his protégé? They might even think you whored me out. Come to State, and I'll let you fuck my daughter. Well, let me tell you something, Coach.

When Tank was fucking me up against the wall last night, you, your fucking national championship, and the goddamn Heisman were the furthest things from his mind."

She saw it, the moment when she'd pushed too far. He raised his hand, and she waited for the slap that would send her flying across the room. God knew she deserved it. But the anger seeped out of him, and he stepped away from her.

"What the hell happened to you, Amber?" he said as he backed out of the room. He grabbed his keys and left the house.

"I don't know," she whispered as she crumpled slowly to the floor.

ELEVEN

Franco replayed it all as he walked as calmly as possible to his car. He got in, started it up, and placed it in gear. Each movement was exaggerated, tightly controlled.

Many people didn't know Franco had a twenty-three-year-old daughter. It was never because Franco was ashamed of her or even ashamed that he'd let his parents do most of her childrearing.

He was sixteen years old when she was born. His youngest sibling was three. It'd just made sense for her to grow up in his parents' house with her aunts and uncles as brothers and sisters. He'd been the one to get up with her at night. He'd fed her breakfast before leaving for school and dinner when he'd gotten home from whatever practice was in season. When he'd begun to receive scholarship offers, he'd chosen Kensington State because he didn't want to leave his daughter. It had worked out for him. He had been drafted to the Baltimore Ravens when she was seven. That was the first time he'd left her. Granted, they'd never lived in the same house again until two months ago, but they'd been close.

Cy Greenburg, Franco's sports information director, was one of a few people who knew about Amber's existence—and mostly because he needed to know as he managed the media for Franco. When Cy had come to see him this morning, Franco had thought nothing of it. This had become a daily ritual, even more important now after Chantel had shared her concerns about Tank's behavior off the field.

"You need to see this, Franco," Cy had said.

Maybe in retrospect, Franco should have seen the anxiety lurking behind Cy's eyes, but Cy was a nervous kind of guy. He'd have been much happier being the sports information director twenty years ago when social media didn't exist. Cy saw it all as a plot to destroy his sanity.

So, Franco had reached for Cy's phone, careful to conceal the sigh of resignation that automatically kicked in when Cy had something for him to see.

Franco's first thought had been that the picture was completely erotic. He hadn't even noticed the girl during his quick glance. He'd zeroed in on Tank's face and thought, *So, this is the distraction.*

He handed it back to Cy, saying, "How many does that make since Georgia?"

Cy hesitated.

When he didn't immediately answer, Franco looked up from his notes. "Cy?"

"Uh, sixteen."

At Cy's answer, Franco returned to his notes.

"Do you have any idea who keeps taking the pictures? We need to try to shut this down."

"Uh, Coach? Did you see the girl in the photo?"

Franco looked up again. "No."

Cy reached out with his phone again. Franco looked at him quizzically. Taking the phone from Cy, Franco looked at the picture again and froze. The air got stuck in his lungs, and he couldn't move. There she was, with the platinum-blonde hair that he couldn't quite get used to, in the sexiest picture he'd ever seen.

He quickly handed the phone back to Cy. Taking a deep breath, he said, "Chantel and I double-teamed Tank last night. Maybe he'll slow down."

He didn't mention that the picture had probably been taken after he'd spoken to Tank. Nor did he mention that his corneas were now seared with the image of his daughter virtually having sex with a kid who'd probably had sex with fifteen other girls in the last few weeks. He also didn't mention that this seemed to be his daughter's MO. He hadn't mention any of that, but in his mind, all he could think of was, *Which one of them should I save?*

As he drove through town, he was assailed by images of his daughter, sweet images to erase the photo of her that he'd stared at for far too long today. He could pinpoint the exact moment he'd lost her. It was twenty-three months ago, a couple of months before the accident. They'd been Skype junkies. They'd had conversations without the visual, but it just wasn't as much fun. Then, suddenly, the face-to-face phone conversations had stopped. Then, her daily text messages had become weekly.

So, the day after signing day, he'd jumped in his car and driven to Oxford.

He'd shown up, unannounced, at her apartment, which he'd done before. But, this time, she hadn't liked it. She'd been bitchy and short with him, telling him she had a couple of big tests that week. She'd told him that she was dating someone, but she hadn't said who the person was. They'd had a quick dinner, and he'd gotten back on the road.

Later, he would remember that and think that she'd held that back because the world of college athletics was small. Everyone knew everyone, and for some reason, she hadn't wanted him to know about Rowdy. When he'd called her the next day to let her know he'd made it home safely, the bottom had dropped out. She'd berated him for coming to see her, and he'd given it back for her rudeness.

That was it. That one conversation had sent them into an abyss.

As the details of her life before the accident had seeped out, he knew he'd failed her. Watching her fight for her life for all those weeks was the hardest thing he'd ever done. That, and watching her brave the storm of the fallout from it.

She'd been through hell, but seeing her with Tank made him think that she hadn't learned a damn thing.

He didn't know what was worse—the image of her in the picture or his memory of what she'd screamed at him.

"Well, let me tell you something, Coach. When Tank was fucking me up against the wall last night, you, your fucking national championship, and the goddamn Heisman were the furthest things from his mind."

It was on repeat in his head.

He hoped she'd been going for shock value. The father in him wanted to hunt down Tank Howard and beat the living shit out of him. The coach in him wanted to again counsel Tank about being distracted by groupies. After his confrontation with his daughter, he wasn't sure which part of him would win out. *And what kind of man did that make him?*

The thing about being emotionally stymied was that you did things you wouldn't normally do. Franco certainly wasn't aware of that though as he parked his car in Molly's driveway. This was not the place to come tonight, but his need for perspective, peace, refuge, and some sound girl advice had driven him here. Even though he knew it was a bad idea, he found himself knocking.

Molly's stunned expression when she opened the door almost had him retreating. But he'd already put himself out there, so to speak, so he soldiered on.

"Hey. I know it's late," he said, sounding lame.

Molly regained her composure and stepped back so that he could enter her home.

"You look like shit. What's going on?" she asked as he walked over the threshold.

He stood in the foyer, trying to figure out if he should move forward or cut bait.

But then she took the decision away from him by saying, "You're already in my house. Plus, I've got the game on. I'd offer you a beer, but I think a bourbon will suit you better." She gestured toward the family room. "Sit down. I'll be right back."

And, in the moment, he thought she was the most amazing woman he'd met. She knew he shouldn't be there, but he was, and she made him feel as if it were the most natural thing in the world.

"Sure," he said as he walked to where she'd invited him and moved to sit on the couch.

She came back into the room, handed him a tumbler, and sat on the recliner across from him. They watched the game in silence for a while. It wasn't particularly uncomfortable, but he felt odd about being there. As he finished his drink, he stood up to go.

"Uh, thanks. I needed the drink."

Molly looked questioningly at him. She hadn't pushed him to say anything since he'd gotten there.

"Okay," she said as she stood, too. "But you don't look like you're okay, Coach."

She didn't ever call him anything other than Coach, but just now, in this moment, it was a reminder that they worked together.

"Yeah. Thanks for letting me sit." He paused, not knowing what else to say but wanting to say something. He moved toward the door. As he reached for the doorknob, he felt her grab his arm.

"Franco"—she paused, keeping her hand on his forearm—"if you need to talk or…you need anything…I'm here for you." She looked away and then rephrased, subtracting the presumption, "I can be here for you."

Maybe it was her use of his name or perhaps her feather-like touch on his arm or the way she'd said *anything*, but something suddenly felt different between them. Not the uncomfortable silence of a few minutes ago or the uncertainty when he'd first walked in, but something electric, a charged feeling. He didn't really think much about what he was doing.

He moved his hand up and lightly caressed her cheek. "Anything?" he asked.

Molly moved her hand and placed it gently on top of his. She'd imagined him kissing her a number of different ways, times, and places but never in her foyer. With his sudden appearance at her house, Molly knew something big was going on. Something had chased him out into the night, and he'd sought refuge with her. Knowing that made her want him more.

"Molly?" His questioning tone and the look in his eyes told her that this was her decision. If anything happened between them, it would be her call.

She'd be lying to herself if she didn't admit that her career flashed before her eyes. Her integrity, her reputation—it could all spiral out of control. Men could get away with it. After all, college athletics was still really just a good ole boys' network. The token Senior Woman Administrator at every school was merely the world's way of trying to keep women in the game. So, crossing this line meant something. She didn't want to be the girl on the back of the coach's motorcycle.

But Franco was single and seemed to do things the right way. She respected him, she liked him, and she was attracted to him.

But even as she started to nod her head, she felt like she was moving in the wrong direction.

"Why here? Why did you come here tonight?" she said instead.

He took a deep breath and leaned against the wall of her foyer. She could see him weighing his decision in his head.

"I lost someone very special to me today. Actually, I've been losing her for a while but today…" He paused, closing his eyes, gathering his thoughts. "Today, I realized it. I started driving and ended up here." He opened his eyes and looked at her.

"I'm glad you did," Molly said softly.

He pushed away from the wall. "I should go."

He put his hand around the back of her neck and pulled her into his chest. He was tall enough that he could rest his chin on her head. She put her arms around him and hugged him back, hating the way her body wanted to betray her big-girl decision.

"Thanks again," he murmured before releasing her, opening the door, and heading out into the night.

TWELVE

Amber woke suddenly, disoriented and uncomfortable, huddled in the middle of the family room floor. Her eyes were swollen, and she ached all over. Getting her bearings, she sat up, cross-legged, and looked around. As if answering her unasked question, the grandfather clock belted out eleven bongs before retreating into silence. She could tell that her father hadn't returned.

Pulling her phone from her pocket, she texted Keira.

I need a place to crash.

As she waited for a response, she gingerly stood up. Even simple things like that now took more effort than any twenty-three-year-old should need to make. Sighing, she moved toward her room and started to pack a bag. Dropping her phone on the bed, she moved toward the bathroom, grabbing her toiletries.

When she returned, Keira had hit her back.

Of course.

She breathed a sigh of relief. She hadn't thought Keira would turn her down, but still, she felt better knowing it was okay. Swinging her bag on her shoulder, she left the house as quickly as she could. She should have been mature and left her father a note or dropped him a text, but she wasn't going to.

Let the motherfucker worry, she thought.

Keira's wasn't far away, so it didn't take Amber long to get there. Jumping out of the car, she climbed the steps to the third-story apartment. She tried really hard not to feel sorry for herself as every other step seemed to take a toll on her body.

As she opened the door to Keira's apartment, she stopped short. Sitting at Keira's kitchen table, playing what appeared to be a competitive game of spades, were Tilly, Iman, and Tank.

Luck of the fucking damned!

A startled, "Hey!" came out of her mouth.

Keira looked up, the smile on her face dying as she took in Amber's appearance.

"I didn't realize you had company."

Keira immediately got up from the table and came to her, her eyes wide with confusion and concern. "You okay?" she asked.

Looking only at Keira, she said as low as she could, "I'm out."

Turning, she walked right back out the door she'd just entered. She ran down the steps as fast as her stupid bum leg would allow. She heard Keira calling her back, but she couldn't face those guys right now—especially not Tank.

She made it to the second landing when a hand flew out, grabbed her around the upper arm, and pulled her back against the wall. As her body rebounded softly, she leaned her head back and looked directly into Tank's amazing eyes.

"You really are the last person I wanted to see tonight," she said in greeting.

Tank smirked as he took her in. "Ah, Sunshine's back. I was just thinking that I hadn't had my dose of smart-ass, bitchy women yet today."

"You just get that from me? What about all of the girls you've screwed since the Georgia game? None of them give you shit? They just lie down for you and fawn all over you when you're done?"

Tank reared back. "Wow! Extra Sunshine today." He studied her, taking in the swollen eyes, her super-pale coloring, her wild hair. His hand moved up to the back of her neck, and he rubbed his thumb along her jaw. "What happened?" he said.

He watched her eye him warily.

"Nothing happened," she answered, not a hint of shit in her tone.

He loved it when she just spoke without the bite of her attitude nipping at him.

He started at the top of her head and slowly perused her body, making sure that she observed him inspect every part of her, his thumb still caressing her. "You look like something happened, Sunshine," he said huskily, paying for his very thorough perusal.

He felt her pulse pick up, her breath quicken. She was like dynamite for his libido.

She stepped away from him so that his hand had to drop back to his side. "I'm good. I just need a place to crash."

"Okay," he said, letting her keep her secrets. "Come back upstairs. I swear, we'll leave you alone." He could see the resignation in her eyes.

He grabbed the bag off her shoulder and followed her upstairs. When they entered the apartment, Keira pointed to a door. Tank followed Amber to the door, pulled it open, and dumped her bag. After gently pushing her inside, he closed the door behind her and returned to the card game.

"She all right, man?" Tilly asked when Tank sat back down.

"I didn't get anything out of her." He looked at Keira. "Do you know what's going on?"

"No. But until she's ready to talk about it, we won't get to know," she answered. "Amber only gives out small bits and pieces of herself now." Keira looked up, directly at Tank.

"Now?" he asked.

"Since," she answered cryptically.

"Since?" he asked.

But Keira, recognizing that perhaps she had said too much, shook her head and returned her attention to the game.

His concentration broken, and the game—which, ten minutes ago, had been an enjoyable way to pass the time—had lost its luster. He played, but his head was no longer in it. He couldn't stop thinking about Amber all day, which confused him. A lot about her confused him. She seemed all wrapped up in anger and resistance, shit and vinegar. She was rarely nice, but something about her pulled at him.

"This fool," Tilly said, pulling Tank from his thoughts. "The end of September and broke like a bum."

Tank smiled. "I told him those tats and shoes were going to bring him down."

Tilly laughed again. "How many you got now, bro?"

Iman smiled big. "Shoes or tats?"

They all laughed.

"Fool!" Tilly repeated.

"At least I'm not named after women's clothing," Iman said.

"But your name is Harriman. It sounds like a seventy-year-old white guy's name."

"Your name is Chantilly Lace. How can you even hold your head up?" Iman shot back.

"Every day, I thank God for my genetics. Imagine if I'd been a scrawny-ass boy like you?" he said.

"Well then, you'd have been able to outrun 'em, bro."

Tank sat back and listened. After a bit, he decided he'd go check on Amber. He nodded briefly to Keira as he stood up. He saw her nod back. Taking that as consent, he strode to the bedroom door, and after knocking lightly, he stepped inside.

It was dark, but Amber lay with her hands behind her head, staring at the ceiling. She briefly glanced at him and then returned her eyes to the white space above her head.

Tank took that as an invitation to stay since she hadn't spewed any venom in his direction. Moving forward, he sat on the side of the bed with one knee up so that he faced her. She turned toward him but remained silent.

"Want to tell me what's going on?" he asked.

She merely gazed at him for a minute, studying him. He couldn't tell what she was hoping to discover with her intense stare.

"Want to tell me what happened on signing day?" she countered.

He sighed. "Sunshine, why do you have to make everything so complicated?" he asked.

"What's complicated? You go; I go."

"That's not the way it works."

"Well," she said, "I'm a one-for-one kind of girl. You give me something; I give you something. That's the only way it works."

She frustrated him. There were so many other places he could be right now, getting whatever he wanted for free, none of this exchanging shit.

Running his hand over his sheared head, he sighed heavily. "You're a shit-ton of work," he said.

She laughed. "That's where you're wrong, Tank. You don't have to work for me." She suddenly pulled off the sheets and got to her knees.

He watched uneasily as she pulled her shirt over her head, putting her breasts on display for him.

Moving toward him, she whispered, "You don't have to work at all for this, Tank." She picked up his hand from his lap and placed it on her breast. Grabbing his thumb and forefinger, she showed him what she wanted him to do.

He watched her as her breath caught, and her head lolled back.

"You get all this," she whispered. "All you have to do is make me forget."

He couldn't believe he was hesitating. His hand dropped, and she quickly glared at him. He didn't mind trying to make her forget; his body certainly didn't mind the request. He couldn't blame his delicate sensibilities or strict moral code because that hadn't reared its head in an amazingly long time. But—and here was where he stumbled—he didn't want to be just that to her. He wanted to know what he was making her forget. He wanted to see past all those dark shadows in her eyes and under the scars that told stories. He sighed at the inevitability of it all.

He watched her angrily grab her shirt, pull it over her head, and throw herself back on the bed, but this time, she put her back to him.

From out of nowhere, he laughed as he observed her temper tantrum. "Let me take a guess here. No one ever said no to you when you were a little girl. Because you definitely have the tantrum down to a science."

"Don't let the door hit you where the good Lord split you."

Again, he laughed. He couldn't help it. She was absolutely adorable in her huff.

Lying down on the bed but careful not to touch her, Tank pissed her off even more by saying, "I'm not going anywhere."

"Look, I don't want you here."

"You can't always get what you want," he murmured.

"Don't pull that Rolling Stones shit on me," she countered.

That made him laugh again. And, just to annoy her, he started singing the song. He made it through the first verse before stopping to flash her a dimpled smile.

"You've got to be fucking kidding me," she said, her tone a mix of wonder and annoyance.

"What?" he asked.

"God graced you with a voice, too? How unfair is that?"

Then, she genuinely smiled at him. It was a first. He felt the breath leave his lungs, like he'd just sustained a hit from a defensive lineman and lost fifteen yards. He tried to gather his wits, to gain some footing, but it felt like a useless struggle. Before he could even think about what he was doing, he rolled over her, trapping her beneath him, shoving his body between her legs. He grabbed her arms and lightly pinned them above her head. They stared at each other, both suddenly breathless.

"Remember this," he murmured.

He captured her mouth in a searing kiss, one he wanted her to take with her to shield her from some of the pain. It went on for what seemed like hours, this one kiss. It was a make-out session like he hadn't had since he was fifteen. When he ended it, he rested his forehead against hers and worked to slow his breathing. He wanted inside her now, too, just like the night before, but he wanted her to be begging for *him*, not for oblivion.

"Tank," she panted, "please."

He lifted his head and looked down into her brown eyes, which were liquid and dazed. "It can't be about forgetting," he said.

She pulled her hands from his, reached up, and put them on either side of his face. "I got that."

He slowly shook his head and rolled over, disengaging from her touch. "You don't yet," he murmured.

He rested on the pillow next to her before reaching over and pulling her onto his chest, settling her against him. She squirmed before she relaxed.

"But you will," he said.

THIRTEEN

Amber found Keira at the table, drinking a cup of coffee. Heading to the cabinet, she grabbed a cup and sat down heavily in the chair across from her.

"What did I miss Saturday night?" Keira said.

Amber looked up from her coffee and met her friend's questioning gaze. "Sorry?" she said, confused.

"Tank Howard seemed awfully concerned about you last night. Did you fuck him at that party?" Keira asked bluntly.

"What? No!" Amber sheepishly looked away. "Not that I wouldn't have, but he stopped."

"Seriously?"

"For real."

"So, what's going on with you two?"

"I have no idea."

"Interesting," Keira remarked.

Amber didn't even know where to start, so she said nothing. Keira toyed with her coffee cup, and Amber braced herself for what was coming.

"I feel like I waved a red flag in front of a raging bull," her friend said.

Amber took a deep breath. "You mean, when you told me to stay away from Tank?"

"Yeah, that's what I mean. Look, you know I love you deeply. But you have a whole bunch of shit going on. And he's about to be a star. This is not about anything other than you getting yourself together before you entangle yourself in a relationship that…is going to end."

She saw Keira tense for a fight, but Amber just didn't have it in her. "I know."

"Huh?"

"I know. I get it. I don't disagree. I don't want to be in this place with him. Because he seems to be one of the good guys. And I'm not."

"What happened last night?"

Amber owed it to Keira to tell her, but she was so used to hiding everything that she hesitated. If she laid it out there, what would happen?

"Forget it," Keira said, frustrated.

"No! I just need a second." She sat back in her chair. Then, she shifted forward. Then, she stood, trying to find a comfortable position for her body since her brain was all out of sorts. Something clicked, and she turned to head toward the bedroom.

Keira, the saint that she could be every once in a while, stayed, waiting patiently at the table.

Amber handed her phone to Keira. "Google *Tank Howard and girls.*"

Keira smirked. "Really?"

Amber nodded her head, smirking back. "Seriously."

Keira messed with the phone, and Amber knew the exact minute she saw the picture.

"Holy hell!" Keira murmured.

"Yeah. So, Franco and me had it out last night. It was ugly. He was angry, rightfully so. Imagine seeing that picture of your daughter with a kid you love like a son. I can't even begin to know what must be going through his mind. But then take that and add it to my past, and I'm my father's worst nightmare."

Keira continued to scroll through the pictures. "Have you seen the other pictures of Tank?"

"With all the others?" she asked.

"How many are there?"

"I'm not sure. My dad made some reference to Tank having sex with a different girl every night since the Georgia game."

She saw the look of horror on Keira's face.

"Uh, do you want to see?"

"I don't think so," Amber answered.

"Doesn't that bother you?"

Rolling her eyes, she sat at the table. "Because he's had sex? No. I'm sure all of his practice will pay off," she said, deadpan.

Keira merely rolled her eyes, knowing Amber liked to shock her.

"Seriously, Amber, what are you doing?"

Amber shrugged. "I'm not trying to do anything. I've been attracted to him since he swept me up off the floor that night, but I've truly tried to stay away from him. I mean, do I really need a repeat?"

"Well, I don't think Tank and Rowdy are in the same stratosphere. Tank's always impressed me as a good dude. And he was genuinely concerned about you last night. So, I'm not sure *repeat* is the correct term."

"Maybe not. But you get it, right? If I get entangled with Tank Howard, and for some reason it comes out, it would be bad."

"Yes, I get that. That's why I told you to stay away from him," Keira said, trying not to infuse the statement with the I-told-you-so tone.

"Yeah, yeah," Amber said, waving her off, "the red flag. The thing is, this conversation could be a complete waste of time. For all we know, Tank's done with me. He certainly doesn't have the reputation for being a girlfriend kinda guy."

"Point taken. Then, go back and tell me what happened with Franco," Keira said like she were asking about the weather.

Amber knew this was a big moment for their friendship. It was her second chance. Keira had tried really hard to be there for her with Rowdy, but Amber had frozen her out, much like everyone else. Amber hadn't wanted to let Franco back in because it was too much. But maybe, with Keira, she could take the first step.

Taking a deep breath, Amber laid it all out there, even the last part—the part where she'd falsely told her father that she had sex with Tank against a wall, outside, at a party.

Keira sat, listening, but when Amber dropped that on her, she couldn't help but react. "Oh, Amber, what were you thinking?" Keira asked, shaking her head.

"I wasn't. All the accusations he threw at me were things I'd been thinking, ya know? Am I a glorified cleat-chaser? How much fun have I made of those simpering girls my whole life? God, Keira, what if that's true?" For all of Amber's bravado, laying her insecurities on the table in front of her oldest friend was one of the hardest things she'd ever done. "And then, even more horrifying, what if this thing with Tank is just to fuck with Franco?"

"Amber, one of the worst things that came out of your disaster in Oxford is your belief that you aren't a good person. You have blamed yourself for everything that happened. And I know you don't want to listen to me letting you off the hook. But I don't think your relationships have anything to do with you being a cleat-chaser. I never have. Look, you and Jake, you were high school sweethearts, long before he became good at football. So, he doesn't even count in the equation. I don't know enough about your relationship with Rowdy, but I know you."

When Amber started to interject, Keira held up her hand.

"I do know you. You are not a horrible person who wants to be with a superstar just because of what it could get you. I don't know what happened leading up to the accident, but even knowing only bits and pieces, I know that you were the victim there. Not Rowdy Daniels. My objection to Tank wasn't really about who he was or his status. My objection has everything to do with you. You're all banged up and battered. I just don't know that you can give yourself over to a new relationship without forgiving yourself for what happened with Rowdy."

Not ready to travel down the road Keira wanted her to, Amber stood abruptly. Making a show of glancing at her watch, she gave herself an out. "I have rehab at ten."

But Keira knew her too well to buy the sudden departure. "This is exactly what I'm talking about, Amber," she said, shaking her head. "Should I expect you back here tonight?"

"Yeah, if that's okay," she said as she moved toward the room, needing the distance.

"Sure. I've got plenty of sand."

Amber stopped and looked at her questioningly.

"Ya know, for you to bury your head in."

"Clever," Amber replied as she turned away, hiding her smile. "Really fucking clever."

Between class, weights, practice, tutoring, and a trip to the training room, Tank spent the majority of his day moving from one activity to the next without much room for deviation. Although he'd been distracted by thoughts of Amber throughout the day, the moment he stepped onto the field, his focus sharpened. That invincibility returned with a vengeance, and he could see it permeating the team. Every player was on point.

He left the field, pumped up, the adrenaline freely flowing through his body.

As he came out of the locker room, freshly showered, he was surprised to find Cy waiting for him.

"Hey, Tank. Great practice."

"Thanks, Cy. What's up?"

"You have a couple of minutes? I'd like to show you something."

"Yes, sir."

"Coach is waiting for us."

Tank wasn't surprised by this statement. He'd wanted to stop by and talk to Franco today, but he hadn't had the time. This gave him the opportunity to do that.

He and Cy made their way to Franco's office.

"You're moving up the Heisman watch list. After last weekend, people are noticing."

Tank merely shrugged. They quickly found themselves in Franco's office.

"Hey, Coach. The team looked good today," Tank observed, still amped from their practice.

"Yeah, it was a good day."

Where Franco's excitement would usually match his, Tank noticed that he seemed off.

"Good? Were you watching what I was watching?"

Again, Franco played it off, not giving Tank the endorsement he was looking for. It took Tank a moment to remember the last time he'd talked to Franco and the little shit attitude he'd given his coach. So much had happened in the forty-eight hours since that he'd forgotten his anger over the ambush and moved on. Apparently, Franco hadn't. He'd fix that as soon as Cy had his say.

There was a brief knock before the door opened, and Miss Magee walked in. Tank was a little confused as to why the compliance lady was present. He looked over at Franco and noticed his eyes widened before he quickly masked his surprise.

"Sorry," Miss Magee said. "Cy asked me to come."

Franco seemed to take exception to that. "What the fuck's going on, Cy?"

Tank, Miss Magee, and Cy all looked at Franco with shock. Franco could throw it down on the field, but he had a thing about being respectful. He would cuss every once in a while, but for the most part, you could tell when he was pissed by the tone of his voice and the fierce look on his face. He normally wouldn't have to cuss to make a point. The fact that he'd just dropped the F-bomb—in front of a woman, no less—made Tank a little leery.

"Uh, Tank," Cy said, recovering first, "you know we've been monitoring any social media sites that have your name in them and one keeps posting pictures of you"—he paused to look at Tank—"with various women."

Tank was surprised. "What do you mean?" was all he could think to say.

"Someone's been taking pictures of you. I thought they were coming from one of your real accounts, but I think someone actually set one up in your name."

Tank felt like someone had taken a pin and popped his balloon of invincibility.

"Coach, can I pull it up on your computer?" Cy asked.

Tank wasn't sure he wanted to see what was out there. He did a quick inventory of what his life had been like over the last couple of weeks and actually broke into a sweat. Most of what he'd done was in private, he thought, except for Saturday night…with Amber. He felt his body slink lower in the chair as he waited for Cy to pull up the site and motion for them to come look. Getting up, Tank walked slowly around the desk and looked over Cy's shoulder.

The site that greeted him wasn't as bad as he'd thought. It was all images of him with different girls. But the pictures weren't horribly telling. He could tell that he was either getting or about to get some action with every girl pictured, but there were no naked or embarrassing photos. He knew it didn't bode well for his character, but it could have been a lot worse. He could hear their chatter around him, but he hadn't focused in on anything they'd been saying.

"If not for that last picture, it's not that horrible, Cy," Miss Magee said matter-of-factly.

Tank heard her words and looked for the picture she was concerned about. His whole body tensed when he saw it. He and Amber were all wrapped around each other, and from the looks on their faces, it seemed like they were having sex. He knew they weren't, but the picture was certainly incriminating. He heard Franco take a deep breath and watched him walk to the other side of his office.

"Yeah"—Tank winced—"that picture doesn't look very…wholesome."

"Wholesome!" Franco roared. "It looks like you are fucking that girl."

Tank didn't know what to do. He understood Franco's anger, but he'd never, ever seen his coach so worked up. "Coach, we weren't having sex."

"How many times have I told you that it's about perception? It only takes one girl to ruin your career. What the hell do you think you're doing?"

Tank's confusion rocketed up a notch. Cy and Miss Magee appeared to want to crawl under Franco's desk, and Tank might have joined them if they tried to make a run for it.

"Look, Coach, it's over. I'm done." He needed to explain to Franco that he wasn't going to be with any other girls right now, that he had this one girl he intended to—had to figure out. He wanted Franco to know that he'd met someone, but the forum wasn't appropriate, and he didn't want to lay his soul out for everyone. Just his coach.

"What's over?" Franco barked.

Tank looked at Franco, tried to meet his eyes and signal that he didn't want to talk about this with an audience. But Franco was relentless.

"How do you think those girls feel? What about their parents? You think they want to see their daughters plastered all over the Internet?"

Tank couldn't help it. Franco was starting to piss him off. "I didn't pursue those girls. Those propositions and test messages were sent to me. Those girls followed me around, telling me all the things they wanted me to do with them.. I didn't just go out and look for them. You of all people should know what it's like. And maybe their parents should have raised them not to be whores."

Tank knew he'd gone too far with his last line, but he was angry. He waited for Franco to fire back at him, but Franco's face went chalk white. Tank could see he was shaking with rage, but he also saw Franco get control. He turned away from Tank and stood, looking out the window of his office.

"I can't talk to you right now." His voice was deadly calm. "I need for you to leave."

"Coach," Tank began, his explanation and apology begging for an audience.

"Tank, I'm serious. Get the fuck out of my office."

Tank looked over at Cy and Miss Magee, all sorts of questions heavy in the air between them. Then, he turned and left the office. As he walked away, he felt a prickle of consciousness. Those girls hadn't meant anything to him. But Amber did.

FOURTEEN

Even after Tank's exit, the tension in the office radiated from Franco. Molly felt the same anger and confusion in him that she had the night before. He didn't seem like himself, but he wouldn't let her in. Neither she nor Cy had moved, and judging from the deep breath Cy drew, she thought that he might not have breathed during the confrontation between Tank and Franco. She wanted to leave, but professionalism demanded she stay.

She hadn't thought she would see Franco today. It was easy to avoid him during the season when the recruiting questions were at a minimum and everyone was involved with the business of winning football games. Last night had baffled her. He'd shown up on her doorstep for something—comfort, sex, conversation. She still wasn't sure what. She hadn't questioned her decision or actions from the night before. But, seeing him now, obviously not himself, she wondered what he'd been escaping from. She had to admit to herself that this frustrated, angry man staring out the window was more imposing than she'd known.

"What options do we have?" Franco's sudden question startled Molly and Cy out of their paralysis.

Both of them moved at the same time, Cy toward the computer and Molly out from around the desk to the chair. But neither of them answered his question.

He turned then and repeated himself. "Cy, Molly? What can we do?"

"There's not much we can do. It's the Internet," Cy responded with a scoff before walking around to join Molly in the seats across from Franco's desk.

Despite the intensity of the last moments, Cy's response elicited a wry smile from Franco. Suddenly, the tension seemed to dissipate from the room.

"Cy," Franco responded as he walked away from the window and took up his usual spot behind the desk, "the Internet was not invented to spite you personally."

He'd said it in a way that made Molly think that they'd had this conversation before.

"Might as well have been," Cy muttered under his breath, making Franco chuckle.

"So, there's nothing we can do about a website dedicated to the"—he paused and looked at the computer screen to his right—"Many Women of Tank Howard?" Rubbing the back of his neck, he mumbled, "Don't people have anything better to do with their time?"

"The good news is, the site is not Tank's, so we might be able to seek some type of cease and desist. It doesn't hold much weight. There's no legal recourse, but sometimes, proprietors don't want to mess with the NCAA. It's worth a shot."

"How can you do that to a website?" Franco asked.

"We can use the contact information on the site, if there is any." Cy returned to the computer and Franco rolled his chair back, out of the way. Messing with the mouse and clicking through the site, Cy said, "There's a place to upload photos of Tank."

"That'll work. I'll send it tonight," Molly said.

Franco leaned back in his chair, looking weary. Cy came around from behind Franco's desk again and returned to the chair.

"You went a little hard on him," Cy observed.

"Yeah," was his only response.

No one said anything for a bit.

"I thought I had my anger under control, but when I saw him, it took everything in me not to take it out on him. And I can't even really blame him, which makes it even worse. It's not like he knew and did it deliberately."

Molly had no idea what they were talking about, but she felt like an interloper. She needed to know what was happening. She'd already started to connect some pieces. Fairly certain that this was what had driven Franco to her house the night before, she really desired an explanation. But, for all her job responsibilities to ask questions and look under rocks, she was curiously struck silent.

Why was she losing her objectivity with this man? She couldn't do her job if she couldn't challenge him.

"Franco," she said quietly, as if Cy were not in the room, "what am I missing?"

The moment the question left her mouth, she wanted to request a redo. She wasn't sure if Cy caught her use of his name, but she knew Franco did, as his eyes widened. She watched as Cy and Franco exchanged a look. Then, Franco turned back toward Molly and paused, as if weighing what to say. They stared at each other for what felt like a long time.

She felt this pull, this yearning to back down while the other part of her craved his trust in her. She knew he did. He would never have shown up on her doorstep if he didn't trust her. But this seemed to be bigger than Tank.

The silence stretched between them.

He turned away from her and toward Cy. "Pull it up."

Cy got up, went back around Franco's desk, clicked a couple of times, and turned the screen toward Molly.

Molly immediately noticed the picture. As she looked at it, she briefly imagined herself and Franco in that exact pose. She felt her face get hot and quickly looked away. Her gaze collided with his, and she thought he knew what she'd been thinking. She watched his jaw clench. Then, he pulled his eyes from hers again.

"The girl in the picture is my daughter."

Molly quickly processed the statement, knowing this was the issue that had brought Franco to her, and she was relieved that Franco could now share what he had been unable to last night. She then realized, despite three years of working together, that neither knew the tapestry that made the whole of their lives. While this was a harsh reality, it was one she was glad to be reminded of.

Franco watched Molly sort out the truth. Watched her try to calculate how he could have a daughter that old. Watched her understand why he'd shown up at her house last night. Watched her glance again at the picture on the screen and saw the heat creep up her neck as she took it in. He didn't know whether she was upset that he'd shut her down last night when she sought to unfold the circumstances of his arrival or if she was feeling guilty now that she was in her role of the compliance director. He watched all of that and now recognized the error he had made in not sharing this information with her the night before. And he suddenly thought he couldn't handle Molly Magee in the right way.

The three of them sat in some kind of conversation deadlock. No one really knew how to extricate themselves from his office, so they remained where they were without saying anything.

Finally, Cy moved, breaking the uneasy silence. "So, Molly, you'll send your letter?" he asked.

"Yes, I will get it done before I leave tonight."

"Thanks, Molly," Franco said dismissively, ready for some downtime.

As they left his office, he leaned his head back and closed his eyes.

For the thousandth time, he replayed the scene with Amber in his head. For the thousandth time, he tried to figure out how this could all play out. But he came up empty. He questioned every decision he'd made about his daughter over the last two years.

He didn't know how long he sat there. But, at some point, he got up and made his way back to being a coach. As he walked out of his office toward the team planning room, he saw Tank coming back down the hall toward him. Heaving a sigh of resignation, he turned back into his office and sat down. Tank followed him in and took the seat opposite him.

Franco eyed him warily, trying to let the anger over his daughter dissipate so that he could be a coach. He should exonerate Tank. He had no idea the shit he'd just stepped into, and Franco's anger was unjustified. Tightly holding on to his temper, he waited for Tank to say what he needed to say.

"Coach, I don't want anything to mess up this season. I was a dickhead on Saturday night when I met with you and my mom." Tank stopped, waiting for an acknowledgment perhaps.

But Franco remained silent. He didn't trust himself yet.

In the absence of conversation, Tank got still. Quiet in the midst of the underlying chaos, Tank looked Franco directly in the eyes. "I'm not going to screw this up. I promise. It's over. I'm done fucking around with girls. You have my undivided attention."

Franco knew what it'd cost Tank to come apologize. After his tirade earlier, he was surprised that Tank felt the need to set the record straight. Franco had been a total ass to him, and Tank didn't even have the benefit of knowing why. If Franco had been looking for confirmation that Tank was in the right place mentally, it'd been handed to him on a silver platter.

As Franco stared up at him, he admitted to himself that if Amber hadn't been in one of those pictures, his response would have been far different. "That's good to hear, Tank."

Tank nodded his head. "Damn straight." Clapping his hands together, he said, "Let's get to work."

He started to saunter to the door but stopped right before crossing the threshold. He turned back to Franco. "Coach, just so you know, the really bad picture…it wasn't what it looked like. I mean, I'm not saying it was innocent or didn't become something, but we were doing anything but dancing when that picture was taken. I'd never do that to a girl. Ya know that, right?"

Franco nodded, because, yes, deep down, he knew that.

"But, Coach, there is absolutely something about that girl," he said as a big grin flashed across his face. Then, he was gone.

Franco leaned back in his chair and sighed. *Fuck! Of course there is. She's my daughter,* he thought. And, once again, he found himself wishing for that bottle of Jack.

FIFTEEN

Amber stashed her phone for every shift. There was a time when she'd been tied to her phone, texting with her friends and posting things on Twitter and Instagram. But, since the accident, she'd been living in a social media-free zone. At first, she could feel the addiction running through her veins, the constant need to check to see if she'd missed anything in the five minutes since she'd checked last. But, slowly, she'd weaned herself from it, and she had been very happy without knowing her friends' every thought as they broadcast it to the world. Of course, at the time, she hadn't wanted to know about anything in the world, so that had helped, too.

The Bear's Den closed late on Monday nights because of *Monday Night Football.* But, tonight, one of the other bartenders was the late person, so she finished at eleven. She grabbed her stuff from under the bar and headed out to her car when she felt her phone vibrate. She didn't want to talk to or hear from her dad. If he texted her, which would be odd, she'd feel obligated to respond.

So, she'd almost pulled up to Keira's apartment when she had to stop at a red light, and her curiosity won out. She picked up her phone. Plain numbers, unattached to any of her contacts, creeped her out. Sliding her finger across the screen, she gingerly read the text.

> *It's Tank. Don't freak out. Keira gave me your number after I threatened her life. ☺ Meet me at the football field after your shift.*

Smiling, despite the fact that she wanted to kill both Keira and Tank, Amber couldn't resist the invitation. She sat at the light through two cycles, thankful that no one seemed to be on the road tonight. She wished he'd asked her so that she could just say no, but somehow, it felt deliberate that he hadn't. She could just not show, but the temptation was too great. She wanted to go. Whether it was to see him or to go to the field, she wasn't sure.

Still sitting at the light, she glanced back at the text message. She loved that everything was all proper, like his English teacher was proofing his text. She had this thing about using punctuation and not abbreviating; it had driven her friends crazy and opened her up to all kinds of teasing.

She picked up her phone.

Coming.

It didn't take her long to get there. The field seemed to be at the center of town with all roads leading to it. To some, she supposed, it looked like a slightly overblown high school field. Definitely in the South, people just expected a stadium.

When it had been built, no one had envisioned three amazing seasons and national attention. Bleachers rose from the ground up about fifty rows on both the east and west sides of the stadium. The north and south end zones had originally been left open, but a few years before the Franco-Howard era, some wealthy alumni had built a field house in the north end zone. It housed two sets of locker rooms and office space which was used for the press on game days. Because it was far enough away from everything else that it made some people nervous, the football staff did not get the choice to reside there. They were forced to stay where they were with the rest of the department. They also threw in some cash for more seating in the south end zone.

Amber knew the stadium like the back of her hand. As a child, she'd spent the majority of her life in the stands, watching her father. Her grandmother used to load her up every afternoon and bring her here to watch practice. Even after her father had left for the pros, her grandparents had retained their season tickets. She'd grown up in this stadium, just as she'd grown up in this town. It was here she'd learned to love the game.

Mostly, she admitted sadly, because she loved her father. The thought struck her out of nowhere, and she felt a little off-balance by it.

Amber pulled in on the west side of the stadium. In high school, they used to sneak in on this side where the fence had been weak before the renovations had improved everything. It was different than she remembered it. As she made her way toward the gates, she was surprised to see most of them standing open. Walking by the player gates, she meandered out through the modified tunnel that had been constructed so that the players would have a place to run through. She noticed the big bear over the tunnel, another embellishment. It seemed like home, but it didn't—just like everything else in her life.

She quickly found herself on the field and took a minute to watch Tank.

Dressed in practice gear of green gym shorts and a gray Under Armour shirt, his concentration on the task, he looked amazing. The already tight shirt clung to his sculpted chest. He took the snap from one of the minions, rolled out of the pocket, and launched the ball through the air. She didn't feel the need to disturb him as watching him work through the drills made her appreciate what a gifted athlete he was. And maybe she had a couple of flashes of being in his arms, with him naked and her wrapped around him. So, when he turned and flashed his panty-dropping smile, she couldn't help but return it.

"When you smile like that, I think I might have gotten your nickname right after all," he yelled from the field.

Suddenly, laughter spilled from her mouth, and she almost started at the unfamiliar sound. He noticed it too because his smile got wider, exposing the dimple on one side of his mouth. Just like that, she felt her armor fall back into place. *How could this guy elicit this response from her?*

She saw Tank turn to the guy who'd been helping him out, and he quickly disappeared. Tank made his way toward her, all athletic grace and smiles, the intensity he'd displayed while he practiced gone in a blink. He startled her as he placed his hands on her hips and pulled her toward him. Their bodies came into contact with each other, and he planted a quick hard kiss on her lips. He released her as quickly as he'd grabbed her and plopped down on the ground, leaning back on his elbows near her feet.

"How was your day?"

Eyeing him while he lounged on the damp grass, she answered tentatively, "Fine. Yours?"

"Interesting."

"*Oh-kay*," she said.

He wrapped a hand around each of her ankles and tried to tug her down on the ground with him.

"Oh no," she said, trying to extricate herself. "I really have no desire to roll around on the field."

"This isn't just the field. This is sacred ground." He let her go and resumed his pose.

"This is Daily Holt Field at Tarmet Stadium. Most of the world doesn't know it exists," she pointed out quite matter-of-factly.

"I know that it exists. And, right now, the Heisman knows we exist. What more do you need?"

"Come on! You can't tell me that playing here felt anything like playing between the hedges."

He looked at her sardonically, and she wished she could take back her question.

"You're right. Playing in Athens was amazing. The roar of ninety thousand fans—but probably not ninety because, after all, we are only Kensington State. But, honestly, once I step on the field, it all fades away anyway."

She looked at him, as if he had been smoking something. "Really?"

"Really." He sat up and crossed his legs.

Briefly, she thought that he seemed awfully flexible for a guy, but then he started talking again, and she found herself only able to concentrate on what he was saying.

"I'll give you the pregame. Pregame is pretty cool and all the tradition. I always thought it would be cool to be a part of Osceola running onto the field or the eagle flying at Auburn. But it's not where I'm at, and there's no sense in crying about the difference."

His surprisingly thoughtful tone caught her in a way that made her catch her breath. Before she knew it, she was sitting on the ground next to him with her legs stretched out, leaning back on her hands.

"Do you ever regret it?" she asked. She knew she didn't have to explain it.

"Nah. Wouldn't do any good. And, to be honest, the coach I wanted to play for most was Mike Franco, and he ended up here, so it worked out pretty well for me."

She knew she was going down a dangerous road, but she couldn't help herself. "What's so special about Coach Franco?" It almost got caught in her throat, like a pill that wouldn't go down.

Tank sat for a moment, thoughtful. "He comes from the game, understands it, and has played at the highest level, but his real gift is his genuine concern for the players. He didn't bullshit me during the recruiting process. And, when he took the job here, he came to see me and tried to convince me to sign with State. Said it'd be my best bet. Who does that? I mean, that is someone who truly is looking out for his players. It's not about him." He paused. "He's a damn good coach, too. He makes me better every day. His dedication is tireless. And I guess, most of all, I respect him. He hasn't treated me any different this year, with all the hype, than he did when I was a freshman. He never lets me get away with anything. He calls me on all my shit."

Tank laughed in such a self-deprecating way that Amber glanced away. He was too much for her.

In a move she wasn't prepared for, he reached over, plucked her off the ground, and settled her between his now outstretched legs. Her hands dropped to his thighs as she leaned back into him.

Maybe not seeing him will make it easier, she thought.

"So, uh, today, he called me to his office. We'd gotten into it on Saturday after the game with my mom in the office, no less. I think he'd felt like I was acting like I was all that."

She felt him shrug against her back.

"He was probably right. I was feeling pretty good. But he'd warned me about all the girls."

She tried not to tense. She didn't want him to think she cared because she didn't.

"Anyway, we had gotten into it, and I'd left his office, pissed. Then, today, our sports info guy, Cy, pulled up this website that had pictures of me with a lot of different girls. One of the pictures was of you and me."

He stopped, and Amber tried to calm her breathing. She didn't want to have this conversation. She didn't want him to talk about her father anymore. She wanted to be far away from Tank. But she made no effort to move and no effort to stop him.

"The picture of you and me—it was intense. It was when we were dancing. Remember?"

She nodded.

"Franco was pissed. He was cussing. And I know you don't know him, but he doesn't really cuss much. Cy and Miss Magee, the compliance lady, were all a bit freaked out. Anyway, I wanted to warn you—about the website, the pictures, the other girls."

Amber took another deep breath. "You don't owe me any explanations."

If he was offended by her tone or her words, he didn't show it.

"Maybe not. But I wanted to explain just the same."

"So, do all us girls have time slots tonight?" she said sarcastically. Then, she berated herself for even asking the question.

But Tank just laughed, deep and so hard that she felt his stomach bunching up with the force of it.

"Yeah," he said when he stopped laughing. He held his arm out and made a show of looking at his watch. "I've got about thirty more seconds before the next girl shows up."

And, just like that, she started laughing, too. It still sounded rusty to her, but it felt so good that she found herself turning in Tank's arms. He lifted her again, turning her lower body so that she was straddling him. Her arms wrapped around his neck before she leaned down and captured his mouth with hers.

SIXTEEN

Franco pulled the truck into an empty spot and waited. He and Amber hadn't spoken since the week before. He wasn't even sure if she would attend Sunday dinner, but he'd bet money that she wouldn't disappoint his parents. It was fifteen minutes before he would normally pick her up, but he didn't want to miss her. So, he waited, nervously tapping his hands against the steering wheel. He heard the unfamiliar gait on the metal stairs before he saw her. It used to be that she moved with the fluidity that only dancers and athletes possessed. But now, she stuttered and paused, an uneven tendency left by the accident. Sitting up straighter in his seat, he watched as she moved toward his truck, seemingly unsurprised to see him there.

"Hey," she said as she slid into the seat across from him.

"Hi." His voice sounded hoarse, like he'd just woken up, and he realized how nervous he was to see her.

He put the truck in reverse and pulled out of the apartment complex, trying to act like this was a completely normal occurrence.

"Great game yesterday. The whole team looks really good. No real weaknesses that I can see."

He smiled. Most people wouldn't think that a twenty-three-year-old woman's opinion of football would mean that much to a college coach. But Amber knew her way around the gridiron, and if she couldn't see any weaknesses, he was in pretty good shape.

"What about Persons at center? With Marsh hurt, it's a weakness." he added.

"I know he's a freshman, but Tank's not going to drop the ball. And he blocked really well yesterday. Hardesty is not easy to contain. So, I think you are okay—at least during conference play. If you actually make it to a big bowl and have to play someone with more experience, you better hope Marsh is back in the line-up."

"Hmm. That's a more positive assessment than my offensive line coach gave me."

"Yeah, well, he's a hard-ass and a perfectionist. Persons is going to make mistakes. And, with a less experienced quarterback, you'd probably see more problems."

She relaxed back in the seat and let her head drop against it. He took that as a good sign even though they weren't actually talking about anything that needed to be said. He knew she wouldn't be able to avoid talking about how good his quarterback was, and again, he found himself waiting.

It didn't take long.

"He's really good," she said.

She didn't look toward him, and he kept his eyes on the road.

She sat up. "His numbers are phenomenal. I mean, twenty-four for twenty-eight for three hundred twenty-three yards. Are you kidding me? And he didn't panic and run as much this game. He was patient and waited for his receivers to run their routes. He's got to be at the top of everyone's Heisman list."

Franco merely nodded. Really, what could he say? She was right.

She sighed as she leaned back in her seat. "He must be so much fun to coach."

"Yes, he is."

Franco was engulfed in this sense of euphoria. This was how it used to be—when they could talk about anything. The football conversations were just a part of the give-and-take they had enjoyed. He got caught up in it, excited about the prospect of a return to normalcy.

And that was when he made the fatal error.

Reaching out, he grabbed her hand. Before he could even think about what he'd done, she snatched her hand away, as if he'd held it over a flame. Normally, at least for the last two years, he would have let it go, but he was still pissed about their confrontation the week before.

Pulling over to the side of the road, he slammed the truck into park and turned to her. He couldn't stop himself from yelling, "What? What did I do wrong this time?"

"I just figured you wouldn't want to get your hands dirty by touching a whore!" she retorted, the disdain surprising him after the momentary peace treaty.

"You're right. You can let any random guy touch you however he wants, but your father can't hold your hand. That's really reasonable."

"At least random guys don't look at me with pity in their eyes."

"That's where you're full of shit. No one in this world could look at your face and look into your eyes and not feel pity about what happened to you. Even Tank Howard. So, go ahead and continue to hold it against me that I am sorry about your accident and everything leading up to it. Keep it up. And let us continue growing apart because it's easier for you to do that than to face up to what happened. But I'm done pretending that my heart doesn't hurt every time I see that fucking scar. And that it doesn't tear me apart to know what you went through. If you want to hold that against me and put all these barriers between us, fine. But if you have any hope of ever having a normal, healthy relationship again, you are going to have to talk about what happened. You are going to have to admit that you made mistakes. And you are going to have to forgive yourself." He paused and sighed deeply.

"If I thought for one minute that letting you hate me would make you better in the end, I would let you. I'd give up the most important relationship in my life if I thought it would heal you. But it won't. So, you can keep this up. But I'm done letting you freeze me out. I'm done making this easy on you. And if it's only every Sunday that I get in your face, then so be it. But your life just got a lot harder because I am nothing if not one stubborn son of a bitch, and I am not going to let you go on like this.

"The other night, you were all about my concern for Tank and my devotion to my players. So, imagine how deep my concern is for you. Are you that obtuse, or are you feeling so sorry for yourself that you can't let me in? There are no judges here. We all fuck things up. You've just chosen to sit on the bench instead of strapping on your helmet and getting back in the game. That's on you, not me."

If he expected her to rail against him or to argue with him some more, he was mistaken. Sometime during his tirade, her face had lost all color and expression. She'd turned to the front of the car and looked out the windshield, seemingly ignoring him. But he knew she'd heard some of what he said, and he even took her tuning him out as a small victory. He'd held back for too long, and if it was too much for her, he was okay with that.

He didn't say another word as he put the car in drive and pulled back onto the road. He almost smiled as he drove on, somehow feeling lighter than he had in a while.

Four.

Four cuss words. *Shit. Fucking. Bitch. Fuck.*

Four.

She'd counted. That was what she had done during his impassioned speech. She'd listened for and counted cuss words. Because all she could think about was Tank knowing that, if her father was using foul language, he was beyond pissed, beyond control. Tank knew that. She hadn't. Sure, she had known her father didn't swear very often, but she'd never really paid attention. But, that night on the football field, Tank had described this amazing coach. She could hear so many things in his voice, like love, respect, genuine concern—traits described by Tank, an outsider, that she herself had lost sight of in her father. At that moment, she hadn't known. But now, with five days of distance, she thought Tank would be so easy to read because the emotion had rung true in his voice. She'd always know if he was bullshitting her.

As she stared out the windshield on the way to her grandmother's, it was Tank that she thought about, the words from her father floating off into some place that she hoped wouldn't haunt her. She hadn't wanted to know those things. She hadn't needed to know that her scar broke his heart. It was only a scar, just an every day, every minute reminder of her folly. Why did it bother him so much? He should let it go and get over it. She had. She barely even noticed it anymore.

Before she knew it, they were pulling into her grandmother's driveway. She almost smiled. The thing about shutting down was that the things she didn't enjoy, like being in a confined space with her father, would go by quickly. All of a sudden, they were there, and she could get away from him and the things he'd said.

She turned to open her door when the locks went down. Just like that, the anger was back, which meant that the shutters had to come down.

"What now?" she asked, infusing as much indifference as she could into her voice.

"You can't go into your grandmother's house looking like that." He reached over but paused before he touched her, waiting for her permission.

She was confused but found herself nodding.

Gently, he placed his hands on her face and wiped away the tears. She felt her eyes grow wide and saw him trying to disguise his surprise at her tear stained face. He cleaned her up, handed her a napkin, and got out of the truck. She pulled down the visor, briefly looked herself over, and followed him. Neither one of them mentioned the fact that she'd been crying. Neither one of them acknowledged that she hadn't even realized it.

The house was already full with the family, which allowed Amber to melt into the crowd. She could spend the day with twenty-five people and not talk to a single one of them. And no one would ever know. They didn't compare notes or ask if Amber seemed okay. The only person she couldn't escape was her grandmother. But, after the car ride over, the soothing presence of her Nona was like aloe on a burn. If Nona thought she looked a little rough, she wouldn't mention it. That was the one great thing about the accident; no one ever commented about how she looked. Her physical appearance had become taboo.

Today though, the house seemed claustrophobic, and her grandmother's presence made her itch to get out of there. She headed toward the bathroom with her phone to text Keira. As she turned down the hall, she was bombarded with family pictures. She always tried to avoid them, not wanting to really see who she used to be. She hurried toward the bathroom with her head down, intent on having Keira pick her up and creating an excuse to leave.

She closed the bathroom door a bit too hard. Avoiding the mirror, she found herself looking up at the pictures on the wall. It used to be her favorite picture. It was when Franco had just started working for Whitey. He was in the booth at one of his first games. She was sitting with him. Each of them had on a headset, and they were intently watching what was happening on the field. Their expressions were identical, the look in their eyes the same. Their sports information guy had snapped the picture and tagged it, *Like father, like daughter.* They'd wanted it to run on the cover of State's booster magazine, but it had hung in her room instead. Because, even back then, they'd always downplayed the fact that she was Franco's daughter.

Tearing her eyes away, she picked up her phone.

Come get me at my grandmother's.

Please.

SEVENTEEN

Tank was anxious to see Amber. When he'd walked her to her car on Monday night, he'd thought he'd see her sometime during the week. There hadn't been enough time. He'd had his first set of tests, and then they'd had an away game. But, now, it was Sunday, and they'd merely exchanged text messages. Amber wasn't about making an effort because that might indicate to him that she liked him. As long as he kept it casual, he felt like he could keep her in it.

Tilly and Iman had headed out to the bar long ago, but Tank had hung back, waiting for the elusive text from Amber to join her and Keira out. It had become hard to go out at night because, inevitably, someone would offer him something. A couple of weeks ago, he had taken. And, now, he really wasn't. Tilly and Iman could run interference for only so long. Now that Tilly was into Keira, his wingman status had dropped down from gold to silver, and Iman had his hands full with fielding his own offers.

When Tank's phone finally buzzed with an incoming text message, his relief and excitement were palpable. He unlocked his phone and found a snap from Tilly. He clicked on the picture and laughed.

Tilly had sent him a picture of Amber dancing with some guy. Her arms were draped over his shoulders, their hips aligned. She was staring at something beyond the guy's head, looking completely bored.

I'm dancing with this dweeb and wishing it was Tank.

It didn't possess the intimacy of the picture from a week ago, but Tank quickly discovered that he didn't necessarily want anyone else's hands on her. Obviously, Tilly knew how to get him to come out to play. He quickly texted him.

Where are you?

Beau's.

Coming.

Beau's was a typical college bar they frequented. When he arrived, he had a hard time wending his way through the crowd. Everyone wanted to talk to him, congratulate him, shake his hand. Without the benefit of a posse, he had no escape from his exposure to the crowd. At any other time, he would have had a lot of patience for the adoration. But, tonight, he felt rushed, like he needed to quickly get to where he was going. So, he came off a little bit short and a little bit irritated with people. But he kept moving forward, working his way to Tilly, Iman, and Marsh.

"Remind me to come out with you next time. I need my escorts," Tank remarked when he reached them.

Tilly laughed around his response, "Told you that you shouldn't have stayed at home, like some little girl waiting for the phone to ring."

Tank acknowledged the dig with a shrug and a smile. "Speaking of…"

"Bathroom," Iman said.

"You told Steele about what's been going on with this chick?" Tilly asked.

"Nah." Tank knew that Lamarcus was Tilly's gauge of seriousness.

If Tank had told Lamarcus about something, Tilly knew that it was important to Tank. Tilly loved to tease him about his bromance with Lamarcus Steele.

"Hmm. Fucking liar."

Tank refused to comment and was saved by the reappearance of Keira and Amber. He briefly looked around for Marsh's girl. He'd still pay to see a confrontation between her and Amber. Smiling at the visual, he acknowledged Keira with a nod and walked directly up to Amber.

He grabbed her hand and pulled her to the dance floor. He maneuvered them into the middle of the crowd. Satisfied with the darkness and seeming anonymity, he moved in, intertwining their fingers before his lips met hers with a too brief brush. "Hey."

"Hi," Amber said before kissing him back, harder and more thoroughly than the kiss he'd initiated.

She pushed his mouth open with her tongue, deepening the kiss. He felt one hand on the back of his neck and one slide down his ass into the pocket of his jeans. She pulled him closer and slid one leg between his, so they were one seamless being. He moaned deep in his throat, wanting her. When he felt her hand slide between them and rub the front of his jeans, he pulled back, putting distance between them. Resting his forehead against hers, he put his hands on her shoulders.

He knew she wouldn't be able to hear him, so he leaned down to her ear. "Not here, okay?" he said. Then, he kissed her near her jawline, opposite her scar.

He felt her arms drop from around him. She pulled back and looked at him with an unreadable expression on her face. Then, she turned and walked away. He watched her in confusion. Thinking she wanted him to follow, he took off after her, but she didn't go far. She merely moved over and began dancing with some random people. Unsure of what to do, he watched for a second and then left the dance floor, pissed.

Making his way to Keira and Tilly, he stood, wallowing in his anger.

Tilly looked at him curiously. "What's up, bro?"

Tank glanced at him and then at Keira. "What the fuck's up with your girl?"

"Bro!" Tilly said, surprised by the anger in Tank's voice,

"I honestly don't know. She doesn't ever say. All I know is that I got a text to come pick her up from her grandparents' house. No explanation," Keira told him.

Tank waited for more. He knew she knew more. But she didn't offer anything else.

He saw the platinum hair move closer to where they were standing. Amber looked up for a brief second, their eyes meeting. He watched her see him and then look away as she wrapped her arms around some punk-ass frat boy.

"This is bullshit!" he said. "I'm out."

As he moved through the bar, careful not to show his irritation, he acknowledged to himself that he wasn't sure what he was so irate about. He was pissed because she had blown him off., But he couldn't say if it was because he liked her or if it was because he was Tank Howard. And whoever said no to him?

Tank didn't know how long he had been asleep when his phone started going off. Picking it up, he saw that it was four thirty in the morning, way too late for a bootie call. The only things that happened at four thirty in the morning were bad things. Trying to stay as close to sleep as possible, he ignored it once. But it started again.

Coming fully awake, he reached for it, ran his finger across the screen. It wasn't a number he recognized.

"Hello?"

"Tank?"

"Tilly? What the hell, man? It's the middle of the fucking night."

"And you know I wouldn't call unless it was an emergency," Tilly said.

"What happened?" Tank said.

"We're at the jail. Got any cash?"

"What the fuck is going on? And, no, I don't have cash for bail money. Are you kidding me?"

"Nah, man. I ain't kidding."

"Fuck. I'm on my way."

Tank rolled out of bed and grabbed his team sweats. It probably wasn't the most appropriate choice as he didn't need to advertise Bears football at the police station, but he didn't think he had time to dig out clothes. Out of the house in less than five minutes, Tank made his way to the jail, the whole time questioning what he should do. *Should he call Coach? How much was bail money? How did you even post bail money?*

The jail wasn't a big building. He walked in and was surprised to find Tilly and Iman sitting in the waiting area, not languishing behind bars in a piss-permeated concrete jail cell. He caught their frantic looks and returned it with one of his own, not knowing what needed to be done. He wanted to talk to them but didn't want to be disrespectful. So, he kind of waited for someone to say something.

One of the cops seemed to notice him standing there.

"Hey, Tank," the cop said, as if knowing him. He walked over, holding his hand out to shake Tank's. "Real pleasure to meet you."

That was one of the funny things about being who he was. Everyone acted like they knew him but always acknowledged that they didn't.

"Great game the other day. Well, the whole season really. How you feeling?"

"Good, sir. Thanks."

"Can you get these guys home? They're free to go."

"Okay. Uh, thanks so much," Tank said, glancing quickly at Tilly and Iman with a what-the-fuck expression on his face.

They got up hurriedly and moved toward the door before Tank could extract himself from the cop/fan.

"We'll be cheering for you on Saturday. Glad to have a string of home games now. I mean, more work for us, but we all like to watch you play in person. You watch that Stanley kid. He's gonna be real tough for your line." At Tank's nod, the cop reached his hand out again, not wanting the chance to shake Tank's hand go by. "Good luck!"

Tank moved when the cop took a breath. "Thanks again," he said as he made his way out the door to his car, which already held Tilly and Iman.

Jumping in the driver's seat, he pulled out of the parking lot as fast as he could. He waited until he was a couple of miles away before he asked, "What the hell was that? What happened after I left?"

Tilly and Iman exchanged a look. Iman deferred to Tilly, as was his habit.

"Things got a bit crazy," Tilly said without any elaboration.

Tank waited, but his patience was at an end. "I just had to wake up in the middle of the night to come get you from jail, but you weren't even in jail. What's going on?" After another Tilly-Iman mystery look, Tank got mad. "If you motherfuckers don't tell me what happened, I'm gonna leave your asses on the side of the road."

"See, what had happened was…" Tilly looked at Iman, shrugged, and plowed forward, "Your boy Iman here, the stupid fucking freshman, felt like he needed to defend your girl's honor."

Tank felt his hands tighten on the steering wheel. "She ain't my girl."

He saw the look exchanged again but decided not to comment on it.

"Aight. The girl you've been"—Iman paused before qualifying—"wanting to bang. She was dancing with this frat boy, and when she decided she was done dancing, she tried to walk away. He didn't like that too much. Tried to hold on to her wrist." Then, Iman smiled wide, his white teeth flashing in the dark of the car. "I ain't gonna lie. She's pretty much a badass and probably didn't need my help. But I felt some sorta way about him holding on to her arm. And maybe a bit of a brawl broke out."

Tilly picked up the story. "There were some of us and some of them. It was mostly harmless. Some words—mostly. But I think the owner of the bar was afraid it was gonna blow up. So, he called the cops, and we all got paddy-wagoned."

Tank shook his head. He wanted to ask, and he knew they knew he wanted to ask, but he stayed purposely quiet.

"Don't worry about your girl. We made sure she and Keira were all right."

"She's not my girl, and I really don't give a shit."

"Mmhmm," Iman muttered at the same time as Tilly's, "Uh-huh."

Tank ran his free hand over his head. "That girl's nothing but trouble."

EIGHTEEN

It had been a week and a day. Eight days since Amber's dad had berated her. Eight days since she'd pushed Tank away. Eight days since Iman had valiantly tried to come to her defense. And she'd done nothing. She hadn't tried to fix things with her father, she hadn't called or texted Tank, she hadn't thanked Iman. That was the thing about her life in the last couple of years. She'd done a lot of nothing.

For some reason, this Monday, that mattered to her. It hadn't come upon her gradually. It hit her like a freight train. All of a sudden, she wanted to do something about the wrongs.

So, here she was, after her shift on Monday night, pulling into the stadium where she'd met Tank two weeks ago. She wasn't even sure if he'd be there, but the thought that he wouldn't, that she might have to go looking for him, left her feeling shaky. She'd been strong enough to come up with the plan to show up here, but she hadn't thought any further than that. If he happened not to be there, she'd have to try to find him. She had to talk to him.

Moving through the tunnel, she smiled as she got her first glimpse of the field and saw a sweaty Tank Howard working through his plays with one of the minions, just like he had the last time she'd come to the stadium. She watched for a long time, enjoying the view. She'd caught some of the game on Saturday, and once again, she'd been impressed with his play. His stats were amazing, and he was quickly becoming everyone's number one for the Heisman.

Ogling him for as long as she could without feeling like a creeper, she moved forward onto the field, coming up behind him. The minion immediately noticed her. She saw him glance her way and follow her progress up the sideline. Tank seemed oblivious or just so focused on what he was doing that he didn't take note.

But then the minion stopped and nodded his head in her direction. Tank turned. He didn't appear surprised, merely resigned. He turned back, and she felt her strength falter. Pausing mid step, she stumbled a little, her bum leg not enough to pull her from a stutter step. Righting herself, she continued to walk forward. She'd wanted him to be happy or shocked to see her but not indifferent.

He kept his back to her so that she had to walk right up beside him to draw his attention.

"Hey," she said as she pulled up next to him.

He looked at her sideways but didn't say anything.

Drawing a deep breath, she tried again. "Hey."

"What are you doing here?" He sounded pissed, something like impatience coming through.

"I came to apologize."

"Humph," he muttered, sounding like he'd been punched in the gut. "To what do I owe the honor?"

"Going to make this as difficult as possible, huh?" she said. "I get it. I'd definitely do the same thing."

"You did do the same thing—made everything as difficult as possible, that is."

She missed the joking, cajoling guy she'd known briefly, and she was pretty sure she wasn't going to get him back. He'd been locked away by her shitty behavior.

"Did Iman and Tilly get into a lot of trouble?"

He looked at her fleetingly before rolling his eyes. "You could have texted me to ask that question. Or asked Keira. I know Tilly's been hanging out with her a lot."

"Yeah, I haven't been at Keira's in a while."

"Shut her down, too, huh?"

Amber took a deep breath. "I'm not sure what you are so mad about. I told you from the beginning that I was not a good gamble, that I wasn't a good idea. I never lied about that. You were the one who kept pursuing me even though you could see how fucked up my life was. So, you shouldn't be acting like the injured party when you should have never gotten involved with me in the first place."

Tank turned to look at her. "This is your idea of an apology?" he asked, mystified.

Their eyes met for the first time and held. The tension between them was palpable. What she wanted to do and what she knew she had to do were at odds with each other. But, looking at him now, she admitted to herself that she wanted to reach out to him, to be surrounded by him, to melt into him. They continued to stare at each other, challenge in each other's eyes.

Take a chance on me, they both seemed to be saying.

But then he looked away, and she tried to pretend like the moment hadn't happened.

"No. My apology goes something like this." Again, with the pause and the deep breath, she tried to gather her thoughts to do, at least this, the right way. "I'm sorry for the way I walked away from you last week. And I am really sorry about Iman and Tilly. Although, in my defense, I had the situation under control, and I didn't need anyone's help. Then, all of a sudden, Iman jumped into the fray. It was kind of a mess." She stopped herself before she rambled any more. "So, that's what I came to say."

She wanted to walk away, to make it look good, like, *Hey, I came, I saw, I apologized.* But she lingered for a moment, hoping for his acceptance.

When he didn't say anything for a while, she started to turn and walk away. She made the spin successfully before his hand reached out and gently caught her wrist. They stood, looking in opposite directions, caught in the uncertainty of a feeling. She knew he didn't want to be in this with her, and she knew she couldn't be in this with him, but for some reason, they were both in it.

"Can you at least tell me what was wrong that night?" he asked softly, as if saying it at a normal pitch would somehow cause the world to tilt incorrectly on its axis.

She didn't want to tell him much, but it was difficult to always hold back from him. She struggled with telling him because, every time she mentioned her father to him, she felt like a liar. But she continued to step forward into shit with him. "I got into a fight with my dad."

He squeezed her wrist softly, as if telling her that he understood what that was like.

And, somehow, her mouth opened again. "Things with us have been rough since the accident. There were some things that happened before it that we never really talked about. And I just can't take the way his eyes cloud with pity every time he sees my scar. I mean, it's just a scar. It doesn't change who I am."

Tank's thumb rubbed the inside of her wrist, like he was settling a scared animal. She felt it and wanted to resent it, but her whole body soothed out and heated up at the same time.

"Really? You're the same girl you were before the accident?" His voice remained a degree below a normal octave.

Wounded animal, she thought.

"Not the same," she murmured. "But I'm not all that proud of the girl I was before the accident."

"That's right," he said.

"Huh?"

"You enjoy being a sarcastic, prickly-ass, stubborn female. I'd forgotten," he said, his voice returning to normal, like he was done trying to pull stuff out of her.

She pulled her wrist from his hand and pushed him in the arm. She could tell she'd taken him off guard because he stumbled a little to the side. She began walking away from him while he righted himself, but he grabbed her around the waist and pulled her back into him. His arms snaked around her middle, and then his hands landed on her hips and held on. He leaned down, around her right side, and kissed his way up her scar, making her shudder in his arms.

"I would imagine," he whispered by her ear in between kisses, "that it would be hard"—his thumbs moved up and down, lightly on her back, right above her jeans—"for any parent to see their kids hurt."

He softened the blow of his words with his kisses, so she barely knew that she was acknowledging that he was right even though she did. For the first time, she somehow knew he was right.

"What are you doing, Tank?" she managed to ask as he continued to mess with her scar, pulling the burn away.

"Somehow, I don't think I need to explain," he said.

She could hear the smile in his voice and couldn't help but smile, too.

"This is so not good for you," she reminded him.

He pulled away from her neck and rested his chin on the top of her head. His hands came around the front of her and joined, resting on her stomach. "Let me worry about what's good for me."

Neither one of them said anything for a while. They just stood together on the twenty-yard line, lost in their own separate thoughts.

"Where have you been staying if you aren't at Keira's?" he asked suddenly.

"I went back to my dad's. He works a lot, and it's easy to avoid him."

Tank pulled away from her and turned her in his arms so that she had to look at him. "Why go home if you're just avoiding him?"

That was a question Keira had asked her last Monday morning when Amber had packed up her stuff before leaving. She hadn't wanted to explain to Keira that avoiding her father at home would be easier than avoiding Tilly and potentially Tank at her apartment. And it wasn't something she would admit to now.

"You've filled your quota of questions tonight. And you even got some answers. Let's leave it at that," she said flippantly.

His eyes narrowed on her face. He studied her for a minute before he leaned in and kissed her. It was a quick, hard kiss. "Okay," he conceded. "Come home with me."

Even though she shouldn't have been, she was surprised. Being with him wasn't why she had come here. But, now, getting lost in his pretty, green eyes, she wanted to go home with him. Her conscience warred with her body. She wanted him, wanted the calm he brought her, yet there were so many complications between them already.

She continued to watch him, trying to find a way to prolong their time without getting any closer to him. She started to shake her head, knowing that walking away was the only option, when he reached down and picked her up, throwing her over his shoulder. The move forced her rusty laugh from her lungs.

"Tank, what are you doing?" she asked between giggles. She was actually giggling.

"You thought that was a question," he said as he walked toward the tunnel, shouldering her weight like it was nothing.

"It wasn't a question or even a suggestion. You're coming home with me, Sunshine," he said as she continued to laugh.

Neither one of them noticed that they were being watched.

NINETEEN

Tank opened his door and put her in the passenger seat of his car. Walking around to the other side, he quickly sent a text as he slid into the driver's seat.

"Wait! I can't leave my car here."

"Give me your keys," he said.

She looked at him, as if he were high, but she reached into her front pocket and extracted her keys. They drove around toward the player entrance and waited. The kid who'd been with Tank earlier walked out of the locker room and up to Tank's door.

"Can you drop her car off at my apartment?" Tank said.

"Yeah, no problem."

Tank handed the keys to the guy and then closed his window. He pulled out of the parking lot.

"You're going to have a minion drive my car to your place? What the hell?"

"Minion?" he asked as he pulled to a light and looked over at her.

"Yeah, minion. Those guys who hang around the football team and do whatever anyone tells them to do for a scrap of attention and a shot at a job, like cleaning helmets or coaching. Minions."

He couldn't help it. He threw back his head and laughed. "You're not right," he commented.

"No, I'm fine. Those pathetic guys will do anything you ask them to do. They are the ones who aren't right."

"Minions," he said, still chuckling. "That's fucking funny. Wait till I tell Tilly that one."

"Don't you ever wonder about them? They'll do anything for you guys."

Tank just shrugged. "He just thinks he's paying his dues."

"Whatever," she replied. "And why couldn't I drive?"

"Ha. I don't trust you. You probably would have driven straight home." He glanced at her. "Right?"

He hadn't meant to be an overbearing ass, but he didn't really want to let her out of his sight. He wanted her, and any space he gave her usually meant taking eight steps backward. He wasn't taking chances—at least tonight.

She seemed to be thinking about his question and didn't answer him right away.

"Right?" he prompted.

"Wrong," she said softly. "Right now, you would have been wrong."

"What's different about tonight?" He wanted her to be honest with him, to tell him what had brought her out tonight.

He hadn't heard anything from her since the night of the brawl. He hadn't seen her, and he'd been really careful not to ask Tilly anything about her. Then, she had shown up. He could admit that he probably would have avoided any texts or calls she'd have made to him, but the moment she'd walked onto his field, he had known he wasn't going to let her walk away.

"Ugh! All the questions. Can't you just go with it?"

"Yes. For right now."

"Then, do that. If I stop to answer your questions, I'll think about what I'm doing and how this is wrong on so many levels, and I'll run."

He took that for the confession that it was and let it go. He had gotten more of her with her nonanswer than he'd actually thought he would when he asked the question.

It didn't take long for them to reach his apartment.

"I always wondered why parents wouldn't tell their kids to run for the hills when they saw these apartments on their visits," she observed as they pulled in.

He smiled. "Yeah, they're pretty bad but cheap."

He parked and got out, meeting her at her door before she could get out. He grabbed her hand and led her upstairs to the place he shared with Tilly.

"Is he home?" she asked.

"Nah. With Keira."

"Oh. A lot?" she asked.

"Don't you know?" he said, looking at her curiously, as he unlocked his door.

"You and your damn questions."

He pushed open the door, waited for her to walk in, and then followed. "You're the one who asked the question that time," he pointed out as he put his keys on the little table that had come with the apartment.

"True," she merely said as she glanced around at the surprisingly clean room. "So, which one of you is the neat freak?"

"Believe it or not, it's a toss-up. Tilly might have a little OCD, but I have a mom who didn't let me get away with shit. So, we have a clean apartment."

"Freakishly clean," she said, wrinkling her nose. "Is one of you gay?" she teased.

He moved quickly, grabbing her arm and pulling her to him. He kissed her hard, forcing her mouth to open and invading it with his tongue. She immediately kissed him back, melting into it, her body putty in his hands. He could feel her total surrender.

He backed toward his room, his mouth never leaving hers. Turning the knob, he pulled them inside and kicked the door closed once she had come through. Then, he moved backward, sitting on the bed, before he pulled her down on top of him. They kissed for a long time until they were both impatient to move on.

Working her shirt over her head, he reluctantly let go of her mouth. He quickly got rid of her shirt and bra, and then he flipped them, so he was on top of her, between her legs. He paused to look at her. He felt her tug on his shirt, and he sat up on his knees to yank it over his head.

Then, he shifted down and caught her nipple in his mouth, making her gasp. She pulled him down, so their bodies could move against each other even though their pants were still in place.

"I didn't think I'd ever get to do this," Tank whispered as he leaned down again, placing kisses all over her breast while he played with her nipple with his left hand. "And I really wanted to…"

His hand coasted down her stomach toward the button on her jeans. Pulling it apart, he shoved her pants down with his right hand. Her underwear quickly followed. Then, his hands glided up her legs, and he buried his finger inside her.

"I really wanted to do that, too."

He watched as she arched her back, begging him for more. His gaze roamed over the plane of her torso, her olive skin contrasting the brown of his hand. He wanted to both kiss her into oblivion and scrutinize her every response. He wanted to know how she looked when he lightly grazed her nipple with his teeth and the glaze of her eyes as his fingers dipped and curled inside her. He needed to own every gasp, shudder, and spill of her body.

Mine, he thought. His finger stilled inside her as the errant word shocked him.

It took a moment.

"Tank?" Amber gazed up at him, her eyes clouded with desire.

He mentally shook off his crazy thoughts as he continued to play with her. He bent down and ran his tongue over her scar, and at the same time, he curled his finger inside her, hitting that magical spot. She cried out as her body vibrated. He groaned as her orgasm ripped through her. His mouth tugged on the ragged flesh at her neck, making her body rock against his hand as she sought to ride it out.

"Fuck," he whispered in her ear as he watched her come. "Your scar makes you crazy."

He continued to stroke her as she came. Then, he quickly took off his pants, put on a condom, and thrust up into her. He went at her hard, almost out of control, trying to make up for the weeks that he hadn't been able to be inside her. She met him thrust for thrust, her body combining with his in a frenzied slap. He pulled her legs around his waist, so his penetration was deeper.

When he knew he was close, which was so much sooner than he'd anticipated, he bit gently at the base of her jaw and ear where the spiderweb of her scar puckered up. Just like that, they shattered together.

And, if the intensity of the sex scared either one of them, they weren't saying.

Tank didn't want her to leave. He wasn't sure if her father would be waiting for her at home, but he knew that he wanted her to stay with him. He was afraid that, once she left, she'd revert back to why they should stay away from one another. She hadn't made an attempt to get up. It might have been difficult, as he made sure their bodies remained intertwined. He'd pulled her half on top of him, and he had her leg trapped between both of his.

"So, yes," he said.

"Huh?"

"You asked about Keira and Tilly. The answer is yes. They've been together a lot this week."

"He's a good guy, right?" she asked.

"Yeah."

"Good. She deserves a good guy."

"Doesn't everyone?" he asked.

"No. Some people don't deserve to be treated well."

He couldn't see her face, so he wasn't sure if she was talking about herself, but he let that one go because he wanted to ask a different question.

"Does it hurt?" he asked in his soothing voice. He knew this would be a difficult question for her. He also knew he wouldn't have to explain what he meant. He'd moved his hand up, so his fingers lightly rested against the scar on her neck.

He felt her stiffen and waited for her to pull out of his arms.

But she surprised him by drawing a deep breath and saying, "Yes. It's like it burns, but I think it's only phantom pain, like if I'd lost my arm or leg."

"You don't think it could really hurt?" he asked, a little astonished by her wanting to deny that the pain could be real.

"It's hard to explain. It feels hot a lot. When you touch it or lick it or kiss it, it feels like cool water on it. I just...I'm not explaining it right."

He shifted her, so she was beneath him, and he could see her.

"Keep going," he said. Now, he could look into her eyes when she was talking.

"What do you mean?" she said, glancing away from him, like it was too much to peer into his eyes.

"What does it feel like when I do this?" He ran his fingers along her scar, from the bottom of her neck, up around her jaw, and toward the corner of her mouth.

She closed her eyes and leaned into his hand, her breath catching in her throat. She inhaled as she opened her eyes. "It's sensitive."

"That's all you've got?" he said, smiling down at her. "What about this?" He retraced the same path—with his mouth, this time.

She took another big breath and closed her eyes. "Cool," she murmured.

"Cool?" he said, doing it again. "It seems like it gets you hot." He laughed. "I like this spot."

"I think I was right the first night I met you. You have some perv tendencies," she said, her voice sounding breathless.

He laughed. "There's no doubt about that," he said before he went about getting her all hot.

TWENTY

Franco had been leaving the building late yesterday when he ran into one of the student managers who had been coming from working out with Tank. He'd noted that they'd finished early, and he had been informed that they'd been interrupted. Tank rarely let anyone interrupt his workout.

Curious, Franco had driven to the stadium. He'd been walking through the tunnel when he heard the voices. He had known before he saw them that Amber and Tank were talking, both of their voices so familiar to him.

He didn't know what he had missed, but what he had seen shook him. Tank had held her wrist in his large hand, able to easily circle it. He had seen her push him away, and Tank had quickly moved to pull her to him. Franco had watched him kiss her down the side where her scar marred her beautiful skin. He'd observed Tank quickly kiss her and then talk to her. He had seen his daughter melt into a kid that was close to a son for him. He had seen Tank pick her up and sling her over his shoulder. And he had seen her smile.

It was the smile that was like a knife in Franco's heart. It was harder to see her actually smile than it was to see that erotic picture of her and Tank. He knew Tank was getting to her, was opening her up, was bringing her back to him.

And Franco hated Tank a little bit for it.

And he hated her a little bit for picking Tank as her white knight. She could ruin it for Tank. All her secrets and the path of destruction she'd woven through Oxford could come crashing down around Tank if he wasn't careful. If the reporters got ahold of the connections, the distractions would ruin their season. Tank needed to stay focused, not get involved with the disaster that was his daughter's past.

Franco had watched them come through the tunnel as he hid from their view. All he could think was that the longer this all stayed a secret, the more problems it would cause. He wished he could trust his daughter to trust Tank with the truth, but he knew that it would take her a long time to trust him enough to tell him confide in him.

He was torn, as he had when he first realized that their paths had crossed. He wanted them both to be okay. He wanted Amber to deal with the past. He wanted Tank to win the Heisman and be a first-round draft pick. He wanted his school to be The Little Engine That Could and somehow be in the running for the national title. And he wanted to see his daughter smile like that all the time—like she used to before her face had been so horribly scarred.

Franco got lost in his confusion, the push-and-pull of his two roles, his need to be both a good father and a good coach. *How the hell could he save the two of them?*

After Tank and Amber had left the field, Franco returned to the office. He was pretty sure that Amber wasn't coming home, but he didn't want to run the risk of seeing her, so he took shelter with his work. As he made his way back through the building, he saw the light on in Molly's office. The thought that he would need to walk by her office to get to his had never crossed his mind. He'd gotten into an unconscious habit of walking an alternate route through the building just to see her.

Leaning against the doorjamb, he watched her as she worked on her computer.

"Shouldn't you be home by now?" he asked, his voice sounding unnaturally loud in the silent building.

She didn't appear startled to see him standing there. "Pot?" she asked, smiling at him.

Her smile made him temporarily forget all his troubles. He stayed at the entrance to her office, fighting temptation.

He stared at her. Then, he suddenly got it. "Ah, kettle and black and all that."

She nodded.

"Everything okay?"

"Yeah," he said, boldly lying. "Website's down. You throwing the NCAA around seemed to work. Thanks."

"Cy told me. Said the Instagram stuff is still there though."

"Yeah. Least of my concerns right now." Franco wanted to walk in, but he figured that staying at the door was the smarter move.

"Oh?" she said, cocking her head to the side.

He just shook his head.

"You going to come in and sit down or just stand there and stare at me?"

"Standing here is safer."

She sat back in her chair, looking at him. He wasn't sure if she even knew she did it, but her eyes drifted down to his mouth and then quickly back up. Her tongue darted out to wet her lip, and she smiled wryly.

"Safer huh?" she asked, tilting her head, "Are you sure?"

Franco chuckled. "Now, I'm feeling a little reckless."

Her perusal of his mouth made him want to do things to hers.

"*Okay*?" she said, drawing the word out, like she was asking a question.

"Do you have someone to walk you out at night when you stay this late?"

"Of course. The security guard on duty always walks me out."

"Good." He took one last good look at her, enjoying the respite from all thoughts Amber and Tank. "Have a good night."

He turned to leave. He took two steps and stopped. He turned back around and looked at her. "I'm a sexual harassment case about to happen," he said, a self-deprecating smile on his face.

"How's that?" she asked, her eyes lit with mischief.

He walked toward her desk, paused, and then walked around it. He leaned down and put his hands on both arms of her chair. "Because I'm going to kiss you."

She didn't move. She just looked up into his eyes. Then, she smiled, wide. "I'll take the pressure off, Franco," she said before she lifted her mouth to meet his.

It had been a long time since Franco had lost himself in a kiss. The last two years had been about Amber. Before that, he'd been trying to build his career. And, before that, he'd avoided the entanglements because he didn't know who was genuine and who wasn't, and he'd had to think about anyone who he'd expose to his daughter. So, kissing Molly felt like a redshirt freshman's debut on the big field. His love life had been sidelined by his responsibilities for a long time.

He broke the kiss, lifted her from her chair, and placed her on her desk. She looked at him a little warily, but he just smiled.

"Told you," he said as he inched her skirt up her thighs. When it reached her hips, he smoothed his hands down her legs, from her thighs to her knees, and they lingered there for a second. He glanced down at the picture of his large hands on her. Then, he looked up at her again and leered slightly. "Reckless," he said before he yanked her knees apart and stepped between her legs. He pulled her forward to meet the thrust of his hips.

Her lids fell to half-mast as a moan escaped from her mouth.

Franco needed no further encouragement as his mouth fell upon hers. His fingers moved up between her legs, and he shifted her panties aside, seeking her warmth.

It was his turn to groan as he encountered and explored the wet depths of her. He broke the kiss and knelt down in front of her, pulling her to the edge of the desk. He was graceless in his quest to taste her. His mouth clamped around her clit as his fingers worked furiously. Molly's body bucked toward him as her hands found purchase in the thick locks of his hair. He felt her pull as he twisted his fingers and gently bit down on her. She came against his tongue, her orgasm filling his mouth and his name falling from her lips.

"Shh, baby," he muttered from between her legs. He couldn't help the laugh that escaped.

She tugged on his hair.

He stood up, and with his mouth glistening, he dropped a kiss on her lips.

"Told ya," he said as he straightened away from her. "Totally reckless." He turned and left her office.

Feeling a little smug, he made his way back through the building, happy, for the diversion of Molly, for the feel of her lips against his, for the peace she'd brought him.

TWENTY-ONE

Tank's Tuesday started at six in the morning. Although he didn't really want to leave Amber, he made himself get up. After he showered and got dressed, he sat down on the bed, gently shaking her awake. He imagined she was as tired as he was. They hadn't slept much. But he didn't want her to wake up and find him gone. He was putting an end to their hit-it-and-run tendencies.

"Hey," he said as he touched her shoulder and shook her again. "I gotta go."

Her eyes opened slowly. He liked how she looked in the morning.

"What time is it?"

"Six," he said.

"Ugh! Why are you so bright-eyed?"

"Ha. I got some action last night. I'm feeling pretty good."

"Trust me when I say I've seen the pictures, and I know getting action is not something you have a problem with."

The smile left his face. "Wow. Sunshine's back."

"Just stating a fact."

He wanted to tell her that he hadn't been with anyone since they kissed against the barn, but somehow, he thought that would do more damage than her thinking he was with a different girl every night. So, he went with changing the subject.

"Can I see you tonight?" he asked with as little interest as possible.

"I have to work."

"Is that a no?"

"It's not a no. I just have to work. And you have to sleep this week. You do have a game on Saturday."

For some reason, that pissed him off. "Let me manage my football."

"Okay. I'll text you when I'm done," she responded hesitantly.

"Good." He leaned down and kissed her on the forehead. "I'll see you later." He stood and walked backward toward the door. "Right?"

"Right," she said.

And he thought she actually meant it.

Franco felt good as he exited the field. He'd felt good since he'd been between Molly's thighs the night before. It provided this artificial bubble of hope and light that he knew would pop soon after he met with Tank today. He tried not to think about what he was about to do. He'd made up his mind, and he was going to see it through.

Franco knew Tank wouldn't think anything of the request to come to his office following practice. They often talked, dissecting his play. Most of the time was voluntary, but tonight, Franco had summoned him.

"What's up, Coach?" Tank entered the office and lowered himself into the chair in front of Franco's desk. Comfortable. Relaxed.

"Great work today," Franco remarked. Now that the time was here, he felt strangely calm, as if making a decision and taking action were what he'd been meant to do.

"We look good. We all believe."

Franco studied him. How this young man had fallen into his lap was still a bit of a mystery. He was grateful every day for the opportunity to coach him even though Franco often questioned his good fortune. Looking at Tank now, he could still see the hints of the fifteen-year-old kid he'd first watched on the field. But there was also a maturity and a determination in his face that hadn't always been there, and Franco knew that had come from his time at Kensington. He would have gotten it anywhere he had gone.

That was the thing about Tank. It wouldn't have mattered where he was or who coached him; he was just destined to be great. It was in that moment, during that recognition, that Franco knew he was doing the right thing.

"I'm not going to keep you long. I just have something I need you to do."

"Whatcha got?"

"When you have some time, I want you to do some research."

Tank looked at him questioningly. "I've been at film this week, Coach. I watched the defense. I know what's coming for me."

Franco took a deep breath. "Not that kind of research. I want you to Google *Rowdy Daniels.*"

Tank looked at him skeptically and shrugged.

Franco knew that Tank would eventually get around to doing what he'd asked; he didn't ask Tank to do much. He also knew that he had just set in motion a series of events that he was unable to predict. The lack of control over what would happen next scared him a bit, but he also knew that he'd made the best decision he could for everyone involved. He had to hope that they would all see that one day.

When Tank left Franco's office, he was slightly confused. Their meeting had been strange. But it didn't seem like that big of a deal. He pulled out his phone and texted Steele.

What do you know about Rowdy Daniels?

Lamarcus didn't immediately answer, so Tank headed out to his car and started the trek home. It'd been a long day, but he was pumped from practice and eager about the prospect of seeing Amber. He got home and headed upstairs. As he was unlocking his door, his phone buzzed. Then, it buzzed again.

He went inside and pulled it out. Two texts—Amber and Steele.

Defying the partner-in-crime protocol, he clicked on Amber's first.

Be done around 10. Good?

Yep. Come here.

Then, he scrolled to Steele's text.

WTF? All I know about the dude is that he's dead.

Amber's shift seemed to drag. It had been a long time since she'd been thrilled about having plans. Why it had to be this guy, right now, she didn't know. She wished that she could have somehow avoided all of this…him. She thought back to Keira's red-flag analogy and wondered if perhaps her friend had a point. Would she have ever gotten involved with him if she hadn't known how wrong it was?

"You seem awfully dreamy tonight," Keira remarked, pulling Amber from her thoughts.

"Maybe," she admitted ruefully. "I'm supposed to go to Tank's after work, and I'm really excited about it." Shaking her head, she met Keira's stare. "I was just thinking about what you said."

Keira cocked her head to the side, attempting to figure her out. "The red flag and all?"

"Yeah."

Shrugging, Keira said, "Sorry about that."

"Why are you sorry?"

"I don't know. I was being all judgy."

"Judgy? What kind of word is that?"

"A mixture of judgmental and bitchy. Look, I had no right to tell you what to do. And Tank's a big boy. He can take care of himself."

Amber leaned against the bar, looking at her friend. "Yeah, I don't think you need to worry about Tank."

"What about you? Do I need to worry about you?"

Amber blew right by that question and moved to one of her own. "How are things with Tilly?" She watched as her friend blushed and smiled wide.

"Good," she said briefly.

Amber waited, but Keira didn't offer anything else. "That's all I get? Seriously?"

"That's all you get for now because he just walked in, and it's time for you to go."

Amber turned and saw Tilly ambling toward the bar, looking directly at Keira. Smiling, she glanced at her watch, saw it was ten, and cashed out. Keira didn't need to tell her twice.

Amber hurried to her car. She wanted to shower and change, the smell of the bar heavy in her hair and on her clothes, so she detoured to her house, and seeing the driveway empty, pulled in. She ran inside, trying to move quickly in case her dad came home and because she didn't want Tank to think she wasn't coming.

Even though she didn't have time to dry her hair, she felt better with the smell of fried food and stale beer washed from her body. Donning her standard-issue outfit—jeans and a T-shirt—she left the house, thankful that her luck had held and she'd avoided her father.

As she drove, she tried to fight her enthusiasm. She really didn't want to be giddy to see Tank. It meant all sorts of things that she wasn't ready to deal with. How could she be with him without sharing her past? Or telling him who her father was?

God, she thought, *what the fuck am I going to do about that little secret?*

For the first time, she thought about Tank and Franco's relationship. What would Tank think of his coach when he found out that Franco had seen Tank with his daughter in a compromising situation, and he hadn't admitted to Tank his relationship to the mystery girl? That he'd virtually lied to his star to protect the identity of his daughter?

As she pulled into the parking lot of Tank's apartment, she was overwhelmed by the impossibility of the situation. *What the fuck am I doing?*

She almost kept driving, as if she'd pulled into the parking lot in error. But then her phone buzzed. She put her foot on the brake and picked up her phone.

You close?

Another moment of truth. She could ignore it, keep driving, and go home. But her fingers seemed to have a mind of their own as she typed a message back.

Just pulled in. Be up in a second.

She parked the car and rested her head on the steering wheel. Taking a few deep breaths, she got out of the car and walked toward Tank Howard.

Tank finally sat down on the couch. Noticing the time, he texted Amber and then pulled out his iPad. He had gotten caught up with other stuff and hadn't taken the time to do his research. Curious about Franco's directive, he typed *Rowdy Daniels* into the search engine and waited. When the results came up, he clicked on the first one.

TRAGIC CAR ACCIDENT CLAIMS LIFE OF OLE MISS FOOTBALL PLAYER

Friday, April 15, 2011. By Shannon Marshall, Staff Reporter, Oxford Eagle

Ole Miss football player, Rowdy Daniels, was killed Thursday morning in a one-car accident at the intersection of State Road 7 and US 278. The cause of the accident is not known at this time.

The driver, whose name is being withheld, pending notification of her family, is in critical condition at Baptist Memorial Hospital.

The article went on to list his stats and his high school bio.

Tank didn't understand the significance. There was nothing in the article to tie him to Rowdy Daniels. He scanned the other links until one caught his eye. Clicking on it, he began to read.

FATAL CRASH RULED AN ACCIDENT

Tuesday, May 3, 2011. By Jack Sargeant Staff Reporter, Oxford Eagle

He'd only read the headline when Amber knocked on the door. Quickly putting his iPad away, he stood up. Seeing her was much more interesting than trying to look up stuff on some guy. As he opened the door, he took her in. Predictably, her platinum-blonde hair was pulled to her right side, covering the ghastly scar. She wore a pair of well broken-in faded jeans and a white V-neck T-shirt.

"Hey," she said, not necessarily with enthusiasm.

He pulled her inside and directly into his arms, hugging her. "I'm not gonna lie. I didn't think you'd show up."

She leaned into him, her arms wrapping around his waist. "I almost kept driving."

"Nice," he said, laughing.

She pulled away from him. "What have you been doing?" she asked.

"Some schoolwork. How was work?"

"Uneventful. Tilly just got there. I guess he's going to keep Keira company tonight."

Tank sat on the couch. He wanted to pull her down next to him, but he hesitated to force her into anything and opted to let her pick out her own seat. She sat across from him, the table between them.

"Keira's family down with the swirl?" Tank asked.

"Huh?" she said, looking at him like he'd spoken a foreign language. "The swirl?"

"The black-white thing," Tank explained.

Amber looked at him before she laughed. He loved the sound of it, but he could tell that it always startled her when she did it. She would look around for the source, surprised that it was coming from her.

"I mean, I'm pretty hip, but I've never heard that. The swirl." She laughed again.

"So, are they?"

She stopped laughing and took some time to think before she answered, "I wish I could say with complete certainty that they would be good with it, but I don't really know. Keira's their only daughter and the youngest. And they are old-school Southern people. But they've always been so open that I can't imagine it would bother them. I've definitely been wrong before though."

"What about your family?"

"My family's cool with it," she said quickly with conviction.

"My dad's family wasn't cool with it. They didn't want anything to do with my mom and me. But I think they thought she was a groupie and a gold digger." He stopped himself from saying more. His dad wasn't someone he usually talked about and definitely not someone he offered up without being prompted. A little thrown by his willingness to open up to this girl who held so much back, he stopped himself before he went any further.

"Do you have an Xbox?" she asked.

He eyed her skeptically. "Is that a trick question?"

Again, with the laugh. She was all lit up. "No. Call of Duty?"

"For real? You're not just fucking with me?"

She smiled, and it hit him directly in the gut. "I am not fucking with you. I grew up with a lot of boys. Keira says I need to trade in my girl card."

"Trust me when I say, you do not need to worry about your girl card." And just like that, everything was all hot and intense.

"No?" she asked, the smile gone from her mouth but not her eyes.

Tank got up and walked toward her. He held out his hand for her. She took it, and he pulled her to her feet and into a open-mouth kiss. He felt her arms wrap around his neck as he grabbed her hips and pulled her toward him. They continued to kiss as he maneuvered her into his room.

He broke the kiss. "I can't believe I'm saying this, but can we have a rain check on Call of Duty?"

She laughed. "Sure."

He moved to kiss her scar, eliciting a gasp.

"You know, Sunshine," he said as he continued to kiss her, "I could get used to that laugh."

He thought he heard her murmur, "Me, too," but he wasn't sure.

And then he didn't hear anything else.

They didn't come up for air for a while. When they did, it was late, probably too late to be having a conversation about anything. But, somehow, Tank found himself talking about football and the guys. He even told her about Steele, laughing as he admitted that Tilly had referred to his friendship with Steele as a bromance.

"Do you regret your decision?" Amber asked.

"Being here?"

"Yeah."

"Are you asking me about signing day? If we are going there, I've got a shit-ton of questions for you."

"I recant then."

"You gonna ask me if I need a dictionary?"

Amber winced. "I was a bitch for saying that," she said with what sounded like a little bit of regret.

"Yeah, you were. But it's okay. I asked Iman the day after I met you if he knew what necrophilia meant, and he said no, so I'm letting you slide on that."

She gifted him with a laugh again. "Poor Iman."

"Poor Iman, nothing. He's doing just fine."

"Don't you need to get some sleep?" she asked.

He glanced at the clock. "Shit. I didn't realize it was so late. I have to finish something for Coach." He turned back to look at her. "Fuck it. I can finish tomorrow."

"What do you have to do for your coach?"

"He wanted me to look up some dude. But I have no idea why, so it can wait."

"Who did he want you to look up?"

"You know anything about Rowdy Daniels?" he asked.

TWENTY-TWO

Amber heard a whooshing in her ears. Everything fell away, including Tank's body, which had so recently been inside her. She felt far away, like she was Dorothy and she'd just landed in Oz.

The moment Rowdy's name had fallen from Tank's lips, she'd known that her time was up. Her laughter faded away, her scar burned, and her heart broke. Her father had given Tank Rowdy's name. He'd betrayed her to save Tank. To say that her heart was breaking would be an understatement.

For the better part of the last year and a half, Amber had blocked all of her memories of the crash. But the mere mention of Rowdy's name catapulted her back to that night when she had been in Rowdy's car, trying to get away from him and the party. She had known she'd made a mistake in not driving herself, but it was too late to repair it. She'd begged him to stay away from her, but he kept coming. When she started to leave, the passenger door opened, and Rowdy threw himself into the car.

She had thought he said, "I'm coming with you, so we can figure this out."

But, later, when she'd tried to explain that to the police, the words had flitted away, like water slipping through her fingers.

She'd pulled up to the Stop sign and had turned to Rowdy. "It's over. I told you that the moment you did that. You knew I'd walk, and you did it anyway. I don't care…"

That had been the last thing she had said. The last thing she had remembered.

From somewhere far away, she heard Tank trying to talk to her, but she needed to get away from him. As she tried to unravel herself from him and the sheets, her uncoordinated movements brought her closer into Tank's body, pulled her deeper into the tangle of the remnants of the sex they'd shared. She could smell him, feel his hands on her, but she couldn't concentrate on anything, except for attempting to get away from him. She finally found her feet. She stood unsteadily, and she noted that she needed clothes. As she leaned down to pick up her jeans, her heart began to beat faster, her upper lip beaded with sweat and her hands dampened. Dizziness overtook her, and then there was nothing.

Tank scooped her up and gently placed her on the bed, his mind screaming at the fucking insanity of the last couple of minutes. Yes, he'd checked the time quickly; the whole thing had lasted about sixty seconds. It had felt like an eternity, but it had only been a minute. He'd never seen anything like the full-blown panic attack that Amber had just experienced.

He ran to his bathroom and got a washcloth. Dousing it in cold water, he placed it on her forehead. When she still didn't move, he got worried and ran to get his phone. He needed help and although it was late, he quickly, he texted Glenna.

> *Amber just had some kind of panic attack and passed out. She's not waking up. What do I do?*

When Glenna didn't immediately answer, he parked himself on the side of the bed and continued to drag the wet, cold towel over her head and neck. His phone rang, and with relief, he saw Glenna was calling him.

"What happened?" she said without preamble.

"I don't know. She freaked out and tried to get up. When she stood, she passed out. I've got a cold towel on her forehead, but she's still out."

"She's breathing?"

"Yes."

"She's fine. Just keep doing what you're doing. I'll call back in a bit and check on her."

Somewhat relieved by Glenna's assessment, Tank watched Amber carefully as he continued to smooth the washcloth over her face. He thought back over the last couple of hours, trying to figure out what had prompted her freak-out.

For the second time since he'd met her, he wondered if he should have listened to her when she told him to stay away from her. He didn't know what secrets her past held, but whatever it was, he knew for certain that she hadn't dealt with it. His feelings for her were starting to scare the shit out of him. He liked her, liked the feel of her, liked the thought of her. But he didn't think he could handle the weight of her issues without knowing where the pressure came from.

Much like the first night in the bar, when she'd come awake, it was with a jolt and a sense of hyperawareness. She didn't flutter back to consciousness; she sprang back. Her eyes were suddenly staring into the depths of his, challenging him to look at her with pity. But he didn't feel any pity. All he felt was a deep and utter resolve to figure out what the fuck had just happened.

"You okay?" he asked.

She pushed up with her hands and bent her legs to give herself the momentum to sit up. She leaned back against the wall, where a headboard should have been. Running her hands over her face, she wiped at the dampness left behind by the towel, and then she folded her arms across her chest, belligerence shooting from her deep brown eyes.

"Yeah." She looked at him.

He saw her note their positions. With his arm over her, he had her caged in. He decided to stay exactly where he was.

"You want to tell me what that was about?" His tone was patient, but the soothing tone he'd infused to get her to talk to him at other times was noticeably absent.

Her face continued to radiate mad, but he held his ground, his pale eyes boring into her dark ones.

"No."

He shot a quick glance to the clock. "Thirty minutes ago, I was inside you. Five minutes ago, you had an all-out panic attack. What just happened?" He could hear the frustration in his voice, and he was fairly certain she heard it, too.

Her arms came unwound from her chest and pushed against his arm. "I need to go," she said as she tried to slither out from under him.

Part of him wanted to let her go, to be done with this whole mess. But another part of him, the part of him that was more than a little bit entranced by her, needed to get beneath all the craziness, all the scar tissue, and get her to open up to him.

A quick thought came at him—the memory of her telling him that it was a one-for-one—and before he could even second-guess what he was about to do, his mouth opened.

"I was going to go to State. There was no doubt in my mind. There hadn't been since I met Franco and Whitey. There was just something about the combination of the two of them. They fed off of each other, and I knew that they were going to be number one at some point. The only time I questioned my decision was the day that Franco called me and told me he would be branching out, taking a shot at a head job at Kensington. And it was really only a second of indecision. Then, Franco told me that I needed to be at State with Whitey because he would take me to the next level, and I'd leave his program as a first-round draft pick.

"I didn't even want to do that damn press conference on signing day. But there I was, the number one recruit, a true five fucking stars. With the fanfare surrounding signing day, my dad couldn't let it pass. The shit of it was that my dad had never been involved, at any point. But, for some reason, maybe because my mom felt like she needed guidance—who the fuck knows? Anyway, all of a sudden, at the beginning of my senior year, he was there, involved, at my games. It was bizarre. And I guess some part of me couldn't resist having him care." He rolled his eyes at his own stupidity.

Amber had settled down, resuming her defensive position but watching him with both trepidation and blatant curiosity swimming in her big brown eyes.

"He insisted I take my five official visits even though I knew I was going to State. He wouldn't let me post anything on Twitter that might let people know where I was going. It was like he scripted the whole thing so that everyone would be drooling over my choice.

"When I think about it now, it's almost funny. You have these coaches wooing you, trying to get you. You feel like you could ask for almost anything, and they would find a way to promise that you can have it. The power…it's a shitload of power for a seventeen-year-old kid. And, ya know, by default, their parents. Now, I know that. I know that, for Richard, it was all about the power and the attention."

He stopped, thoughtful for a moment, and then continued, "They set it up for me to be the last signee"—he rolled his eyes again—"milking me for all I was worth. Anyway, we'd spent five months in the dark, not saying anything to anyone. The guys who were supposed to be my recruiting class, they knew. We'd planned it all—Steele and I. We met during a 7v7 tournament and then we'd taken our official visit together. The number one quarterback and the number one receiver, we'd be together at State. It was perfect. I just had to get through the day. So I'm up on the stage, and all my high school teammates are in there with me. And no one in the room truly knows where I'm going, except me and my mom. Then, that motherfucker shows up right before I'm about to pick up the hat. He comes in all State gear, letting everyone know that's my choice and broadcasting it to the world that he already knew. It hit me right then that the five months leading up to that moment hadn't had a thing to do with me. He was the same piece of shit he'd always been, except he wanted to steal my thunder now.

"It was a split-second decision really. I looked down at the hats in front of me. They were all the big ones and would challenge State every year as all of them fought for the title. I didn't want to play against the guys I considered my recruiting class. And, in the back of my head, I knew Franco was here. It made all the difference. It was the best *fuck you* I could come up with.

"Maybe I cut off my nose, despite my face—as my mother liked to point out. But it doesn't feel like that. I'm getting everything I thought I'd get there. And I'm not gonna lie; I couldn't have embarrassed my father more. And it felt really fucking good."

He'd purposely looked beyond Amber's eyes for the last half of his story, not wanting to know what lurked in the depths. But, now, he swung his gaze to hers, and what he saw there made his throat tighten and his heart slip—a burning compassion mixed with understanding and desire.

He cocked his head to the side and said, "I go; you go, right?"

She unlocked her arms again, but this time, her hands came up to slide smoothly across his face, cradling his head. She leaned forward and kissed him deeply, pushing all her fears and uncertainty at him. He returned the kiss until she pulled away.

As she leaned back against the wall again, her hands dropped to her lap. "Yeah. You go; I go."

And she began to talk.

TWENTY-THREE

Amber would probably never be sure what had prompted her to talk. Maybe it was Tank's willingness to open up to her or the way he'd recalled her one-for-one philosophy. As he'd relayed his tale about signing day, she was struck by the significance of that one decision he'd made. It didn't leave him permanently scarred, like her, but that one reaction had changed the course of his life. And, in the end, wasn't that the same thing that had happened to her? One split-second decision had changed everything, brought her here into his realm, directly in his path.

When he'd finished, she could sense how raw his story had left him, his feelings gutted and on display for her to pick through. It didn't seem fair to her for him to put himself out there and for her not to reciprocate.

But she'd never spoken about the events leading up to the accident—not to the police, not to her father or Keira, not to the therapist they'd all insisted that she see. She wanted to lay it all out there for him. The look in his eyes said he was ready for her, ready for her to bare it all. She could see that.

As she studied him, he reached for her hands that were still clasped in her lap, sensing that she needed some physical tether. It seemed so innate that she briefly wondered about their more than physical connection.

Looking down at her limp hands in his strong ones, she laced her fingers through his, seizing the opportunity to hold on to something.

"I know pretty much everything there is to know about Rowdy Daniels. Most importantly, I guess I should tell you that I killed him." She paused to take a deep, stuttering breath. As she exhaled, she felt Tank gently squeeze her hand. She continued to look down at their intertwined hands. His long caramel-colored fingers were wrapped around her feminine hand. She wasn't willing to look at him yet, but she could feel herself tying their lives together.

"I wish I could give you details about the crash. I tried for months to remember exactly what had happened, but the therapist thinks the memory is too painful, so my brain has been blocking it. I guess that could be true. Could also be the coma I was in for those first few weeks.

"What the skid marks told the police was that I was trying to avoid something and that the car careened for a while before wrapping itself around a tree. I'm alive because of my seat belt. Rowdy is dead because he wasn't wearing one. But that kind of has its own questions because I rode in cars with Rowdy a lot, and he always wore one, so why he wasn't on that night is a complete mystery. His body flew through the windshield, and he collided headfirst with a tree. He was dead on impact."

Still looking down, Amber stopped for a moment, lost in the memories of her first meeting with Rowdy. She'd been fooled from the beginning, thinking he was someone so different than who he truly was. But the year that it had taken her to figure it out left her an integral part of his life and his family. It'd made it difficult to extract herself.

With hindsight, she could admit that had she moved quicker, made a cleaner break, Rowdy might still be alive. Instead, it had been six months of angst with her gradually pulling away from her father and even Keira because she just didn't know how to admit to them that she was in a situation that she couldn't quite figure out how to get out of. For the strong, independent girl they thought her to be, she wouldn't admit to them that she needed help.

Her pause had turned to a long silence. She wanted to continue but didn't know how to restart the conversation. But she could tell that Tank was going to push her when he extracted one of his hands and moved it to her chin, lifting tenderly so that she was forced to meet his eyes.

"It sounds like it was a horrible accident." That was all he said—no accusation, no questions, no demanding that she keep talking.

But it was enough to get her move her forward.

"It was a horrific accident."

Tank still held her chin in his hand. He moved it to the back of her neck and gently pulled her forward into a brief kiss.

It surprised her more than once that Tank seemed to sense her needs and would react to them before she could even understand that she wanted something. It felt good to have someone respond to her so intuitively. It had been a long time since anyone had looked out for her. She could admit now though—and only to herself—that she hadn't allowed anyone to get close enough to know what she needed.

"It took me a while to figure Rowdy out. Ronald Wendell Daniels IV was a Southern gentleman from a really old Southern family. Aside from coming from Southern royalty in Mississippi, he was a better-than-average football player. All that combined made him a bit of a celebrity on campus. He was hot and charming and really fucking mean. But you didn't see the mean. No one did. It got overlooked because of the charm. Without all that charisma, everyone would have seen it a lot quicker.

"As it was, I was with him all the time, and it took me almost a year to understand that his behavior was suspect. When I got it though, I was in too deep to get out easily. So, I stayed and became one of those really pathetic women you see in Lifetime movies who stay with the bad guy. He never hit me or anything like that. He just had this desire to verbally hurt people. And he was controlling. I found myself doing shit and thinking, *What the fuck am I doing? This is so not me.* But it was just confusing and hard and crazy." Sighing, she said, "I think I was crazy for a little while."

"Then, one day, my dad just showed up at school. And I couldn't deal with him seeing me like that. I didn't realize at the time that he probably wouldn't have noticed. Who really notices when you feel crazy on the inside? But I needed him to go away. When he left, I knew I couldn't go on like I was. I couldn't be that person. So, I began to pull myself out, pull away. But Rowdy was smart and determined and possessive. He didn't want me to go anywhere. He didn't ever hit me. If I had to pinpoint abuse, I'm not sure I'd be able to. Like, if I had to prove it to someone, I couldn't. There wasn't anything concrete, except when there was."

"We'd gone out one night, and he could tell things were different and that something was going on with me. He could probably see the crazy. I think all crazy can recognize crazy. But whatever. He knew something was up. We got home, and he wanted to have sex. It was nothing we hadn't done hundreds of times before. But I didn't want to. I needed distance. It's hard to have distance when someone's inside you." For some reason, she chose that moment to look at Tank. She saw him glance away from her at that stark statement, but she couldn't do anything to lessen the frankness of it. She squeezed his hand, using her touch to soften the blow.

Thinking about what she was about to tell him made her stay stopped. She'd said it before in a detached, clinical retelling. But, admitting this now to him would forever change her and her relationship with him.

"When I told him that I didn't want to have sex, he tried to convince me. At first, it wasn't anything that concerned me. It was kissing and gentle persuasion. But, when he started to realize that I wasn't going to change my mind, he morphed. He became this version of himself that he normally kept under wraps. I could look in his eyes and see that he wasn't the person he showed to the small world of Oxford. He was someone who wasn't going to take no for an answer.

"I started to get scared and tried to get away from him. He tackled me in a full-body hold. I think my body probably felt how you must feel when you get blindsided by a defensive end who has fifty pounds on you. For a minute, I lost all sense of what was happening. That one minute of disorientation cost me everything. When I shook myself out of it, he was inside me, taking what he thought he deserved, I guess."

She felt Tank stiffen, but he continued to hold on to her and wait. She remembered the fight, her complete shock when she'd realized what was happening to her and then her realization that she wasn't really shocked. This was the Rowdy she'd seen more and more often. The cruel guy who she had known she needed to get away from. She'd tried to buck him off of her, but he had her hands and her body pinned. Rowdy had known her body, what it would take to get her to respond. In the ultimate horror and degradation of everything that had happened to her, she had responded to him, and he'd managed to wring out an orgasm. The humiliation of that moment would haunt her forever. It wasn't anything she would ever admit to a single soul.

But when Rowdy had laughed and whispered in her ear, "Yeah, baby. I knew you'd like it rough," her resolve to do something about Rowdy Daniels had become resolute.

"When Rowdy left, I got my purse and drove to the sheriff's department. I told them that I'd been sexually assaulted and that I wanted a rape kit completed. One of the female officers took me to the hospital where they did the rape kit, and I filed my report with them. When they learned the extent of my relationship with Rowdy, they tried to discourage me from reporting it. We already had a preexisting sexual relationship, they said. No one seemed to mention that I had bruises all up and down my arms from where he'd held me or the bruising on my thighs. I had known reporting it would be a long shot. It's why I went to the sheriff rather than the campus police. I mean, we are talking about Rowdy Daniels. But I wasn't going to let it go. They told me they'd hold onto it so I could think about what I wanted to do.

"A week later, Rowdy was killed in a car accident with me driving. And the whole incident went away.

"I was in a coma. And, when I woke up, I couldn't remember much of what had happened. I guess there was enough physical evidence to prove that it was truly an accident, but when I couldn't answer questions, things were pretty rough for my family."

Taking a deep breath, Amber looked up at Tank. "That's what I know about Rowdy Daniels."

Tank's eyes reflected all the emotions she was sure she'd experienced while she spoke. Anger and disbelief. She could see all of that lurking in his green eyes.

"I'm not really sure what to do right now," Tank admitted.

Amber smiled sadly. "I don't know either." Shrugging, she said, "I haven't ever told anyone any of this. You know how people say that you'll feel better if you talk about it? You'll feel lighter?" At his nod, she continued, "I don't feel any of that."

For some reason, that made him smile. "That's a lot of shit you've been carrying around with you."

He moved closer to her, studying her. She watched him watch her. Then, he picked her up and slid behind her, settling her in between his legs, wrapping her up in him. She felt him lean over and kiss her neck, right on her scar.

"I'm sorry," he said.

She leaned into him, enjoying his sooth. She had more that she needed to say, but she hated what she was about to do. She vaguely wondered if her father had thought this through. Now that she'd shared everything with Tank, she didn't feel like she could or should hold anything back.

"Tank," she murmured as she laid her head back on his shoulder, "do you know why Franco wanted you to look into Rowdy Daniels?"

He stiffened a bit. "To be honest, since you started talking, I forgot that I'd brought it up."

"He wanted you to figure out what had happened to Rowdy so that you would stay away from me," she said matter-of-factly.

"Why would Franco care about who I'm with? And why would he want me to stay away from you?"

"Because he's my father."

TWENTY-FOUR

"Mike Franco is your father?" he asked, knowing he hadn't misheard her but hoping he had.

"Yes."

"But your last name isn't Franco."

"No. My mother gave up custody to him when I was born but not before she gave me her last name. By the time anyone thought about changing it, they were more concerned about protecting me. So, it just made sense to keep my name."

"I didn't even know Franco had a daughter."

"It's a complicated and involved story. One for maybe another night when you don't want to get any sleep."

At her gentle reminder about the time, Tank looked over and groaned at the lateness of the hour. "Fuck, it's late."

"I'm sorry," Amber said, meaning it. "I shouldn't keep you up so late."

He hugged her closer to him and rubbed his chin on the top of her head. "I'll give up sleep anytime you need to talk."

She shook her head. "I didn't need to talk, Tank."

He lifted her and set her on his right thigh so that he could look at her. "You had a full-blown panic attack at the mention of that motherfucker's name. You might not think you needed it, but you definitely did."

She merely nodded at him, and he knew she was just appeasing him, not really agreeing with him, but he was so tired that he let it go.

"Franco's your father," he said as he studied her. "Same eyes," he observed.

Nodding her agreement, she continued to stare at him.

"He saw that picture of us. He must have wanted to kick my ass." He smiled but managed to hold back a laugh. "I'm surprised he didn't lay me out."

For some reason, that made Amber burst out laughing. "Oh, yeah, I'm pretty sure he wanted to."

"I know I should be feeling some sorta way about this, but I think there's way too much to think about for me to work up any kind of emotion." He flashed her a weary smile. "I think, tomorrow, I'm going to be mad at him for manipulating me, but it's going to have to wait until then."

"I get that," she said.

He shifted her between his legs and pulled her back into his chest.

"Will you stay?" he asked. He put it out there like a question, wanting her to feel like she had a choice. If she insisted she wanted to leave, he'd deal with that when it happened.

"Yeah."

He knew he shouldn't push her, but he wanted it all, all she was willing to give. So, he pressed forward. "Tell me the rest of it. Tell me about this," he said as he gently ran his hand down her scar.

He felt her inhale and thought she was going to shut him down. "Uh, let's see…ruptured spleen, punctured lung, the ribs on my left side were all broken. All the bones and my ankle on my right side were crushed. And, my face, the windshield shattered, some spattered battery acid from the impact. My jaw and cheekbone were shattered. You think this looks scary now; you should have seen me right after the accident."

"It doesn't look scary," Tank said. "It looks pretty badass."

He got the reaction he had been searching for when she laughed.

"Again, you're a perv."

"Yeah, maybe a little," he said, laughing lightly.

"You need to get some sleep."

Glancing at the clock again, Tank figured he'd forfeited his night of sleep, but he imagined she was spent. Turning off the light, he pulled her down next to him and wrapped her in his arms.

"Sleep," he murmured in her ear.

Tank felt all the tension release from her body as she gave in to her exhaustion. He seemed to absorb it. Watching the clock as it ticked closer and closer to morning, he thought of all they'd shared over the last couple of hours. He looked down at her, cocooned in his arms, and wondered what it'd cost her to talk to him tonight. The memory of her panic attack played across his mind. How did she carry the weight of her story around with her all the time?

What is it about this girl?

Tank had never been in love; he'd probably have a hard time figuring it all out. Since he was fifteen, everything had been about him. His mom had definitely kept his ego in check when he was in high school, but when he thought about what he'd done, who he'd been with over the last few years, he admitted to himself that it was a bit shocking.

He'd always kind of wondered why girls were so impressed by someone who could throw a football—not just girls, but everyone. What the fuck did he know about life? He hadn't come up with a cure for cancer, saved a buddy on the battlefields of Afghanistan or Iraq, or contributed to alleviating water and food shortages in Africa. He was a twenty-one-year-old kid who lived in a bubble, was catered to, and played football. And, for some reason, it meant he had an unlimited supply of women who wanted to sleep with him, people who wanted to talk to him, and kids who wanted to grow up to be like him.

And what was Franco's game?

Tank had held back much of his surprise when she dropped that on him. From their conversation, he already knew Amber and her dad had a contentious relationship. He'd seen her twice after she'd had a fight with him, and her reactions had been extreme.

Was Franco trying to get him to stay away from her, or did he have some other motivation for sending him down the Rowdy path? And why now?

They were six games into the season—halfway—and undefeated. Tank was leading in the Heisman race. He didn't think being with Amber was affecting his play, and he was pretty sure Franco would have a hard time saying that he wasn't focused.

So, did this have to do with him or with Amber?

It was a conversation he needed to have with Franco.

Glancing again at the clock, he was relieved to see it was six and that he needed to get up. He untangled himself from Amber, dropped a kiss on her head and headed to the shower. He got ready, grabbed his stuff, and sent her a quick text, so she'd see it when she got up.

He wanted to see her tonight, but he knew his body was going to be shot. He needed sleep. But he didn't want her to think he'd freaked out and that he didn't want to see her. He knew he couldn't make a worse move than not being around for her tonight. And when it hit him that he didn't want to make a wrong move with her, he almost groaned. He didn't want to think about the fact that the one girl he actually wanted was his coach's daughter, that the one girl he found himself caring about had more shit in her past than he did.

Fuck, he thought as turned back to looked down at her sleeping, *what is it about this girl?*

Tank had to be in the training room by seven. His first class was at nine thirty, and then his next class was at eleven. He wasn't hurt, but the constant pounding had taken a toll, and he liked to stay on top of the aches and pains. He'd briefly forgotten that he'd texted Glenna in the midst of Amber's panic attack but she hadn't. Glenna enjoyed distance from her student-athletes personal woes, which was one of the reasons he'd chosen to text her.

While she hooked him up to the electrical stimulation machine, she merely asked, "Everything work out okay last night? You didn't answer my text."

"Shit, sorry. Things got a little intense."

At Glenna's raised hand waving him off, he stopped his explanation, thankful once again for her need-to-know attitude.

When he finished rehab, texted Steele.

The girl—she's Franco's daughter. ☹

LMFAO. How did he not kick your ass?

Lamarcus was always good for some perspective.

Tank had a twelve-thirty appointment with his academic adviser because registration for next spring was the following week.

He grabbed a quick lunch and had position meetings at two fifteen. They had to be on the field at three thirty.

As he made his way out there, he felt the weight of the night pressing down on him. He was nervous about looking Franco in the eyes, knowing how he'd had his daughter. He was anxious and weary. For the first time all season, he felt unfocused. He kept thinking about the night before—Amber's tale, his story. He kept seeing her in the midst of her panic attack, her eyes focused only on the past. It hit him right then as they were about to run through their first series of plays. He completely got Franco's motivation.

He heard the call, ran the play, and hit Iman with a perfect pass. As they were about to start the next series, he stepped away, breaking the rhythm.

He walked toward Franco, not really knowing what he was going to say or even why he needed to say it right now. But he was having a hard time continuing without flashes of Amber interrupting his concentration.

"What's going on?" Franco asked as Tank approached him.

This wasn't a normal occurrence. Any conferences on the practice field were called by Franco.

Tank removed his helmet, another oddity. His quarterback coach walked toward them, but he was waved off by Franco, as if he knew what Tank needed to say.

Franco eyed him, and Tank knew he knew.

"I did your research."

"Okay," Franco said quietly, maybe trying to calm the confusion.

"I didn't know she was your daughter. But it wouldn't have made any difference. I'm all in."

"I counted on that," Franco answered matter-of-factly.

Tank nodded his head, telling Franco that he'd known that already. "Why that way?"

Franco signaled for the backup quarterback and for his coaches to move forward with practice. Tank could feel the flurry of activity start. He and Franco moved away from practice, toward the other end of the field.

"Somehow, I didn't imagine this conversation taking place in the middle of my practice," he said, rebuking Tank for the timing. Tank shrugged – Franco had started this. "I saw you two together.

And, for the first time in I can't remember how long, I heard her laugh. She used to have a laugh that made you want to join her."

Franco looked away, maybe trying to collect his thoughts. Tank wasn't sure, but he waited patiently.

"I'm not sure if I did the right thing. That's the shit thing about being a parent. You're kind of flying blind. But she was opening up to you, and I thought you could help her. I wanted you to help her because I'm not the right messenger for her, and I want my daughter back."

Franco placed his hand on Tank's shoulder pads, looking him directly in his eyes. Tank was struck by how similar Amber's eyes were to Franco's.

"But it didn't have everything to do with her. What she'll think is that I did it to save you. She'll know that I wouldn't want you to get blindsided by her past, and I wouldn't want you to be tangled up in the emotional mess that is in her head right now. I want both of you to come out of this better and stronger. That wouldn't have happened if you didn't know what had made her who she is right now. So, I threw you the Rowdy bone, hoping that you would run with it."

"I did. I didn't mean to, but I ran with it." Tank paused, thinking about Amber and who he knew she was. "She might not forgive you for it."

"Oh, don't think that I don't know that. But when it came down to what was more important to me, I was a bit shocked by the realization that there's no contest. She's my life. If she can get better, whole, with you, then I don't care if she hates me for the rest of her life. Sometimes, it's just the price we have to pay as parents, and I'm willing to pay any price for her..." There was a notable pause. "Are you good, Tank?"

"Yeah, I'm good, Coach."

TWENTY-FIVE

Sometimes, Amber hated the empty spaces of time in her day that weren't occupied by work or rehab. Boredom could be difficult to handle when your mind had all sorts of events and emotions to pick through. Knowing that today of all days, there was a litany of things that could preoccupy her, she headed into the Bear's Den, hoping to pick up the lunch shift and stay through dinner. As she walked through the doors, she realized her intent had been much more focused than she was willing to admit to herself because the only one behind the bar today, on a very slow day, was Keira.

Sliding onto one of the barstools by the service bar, where most patrons knew not to sit because of the constant stream of servers retrieving drinks, Amber grabbed a menu and waited for Keira to make her way over to her.

"Hey," Keira said with a smile. "Are you actually thinking about eating?"

"Hi," Amber returned, looking up from the menu. "Yeah, I'm kinda hungry."

Keira looked her over. "Well, that's different. What do you want?"

"Still looking."

"Do you really need to look? The menu hasn't changed in fifteen years."

"I know. But I'm not sure what I want. I figure, something will jump out at me."

Shrugging, Keira turned away to check on her other customers. Circuit complete, she returned and leaned forward, resting her elbows on the bar. "So, what's happening with you? I've heard some rumors, but I'm not sure I believe them." When Amber lowered the menu to look at her, she continued, "Is it true that you actually tracked Tank down and maybe apologized to him? Because that's what I heard, but it doesn't sound like my best friend, so I've chosen to be skeptical."

Amber smiled. "Maybe. There might actually be some truth to that."

Keira raised both hands to her cheeks and widened her eyes, feigning surprise. "Oh, my. Whatever has gotten into you?"

"Tank Howard," Amber answered with a mischievous grin spreading across her face, actually lighting her eyes.

Keira drew back, in true shock this time. "Are you smiling?"

"Maybe?" she said with a question in her voice.

"I don't mean to go all dramatic on you, but it's been a long time since I've actually seen you truly smile. I missed it."

At Keira's seriousness, the smile disappeared from Amber's face. "I know. And I'm sorry."

"You don't have anything to be sorry about. I'm really happy to see you smiling. Please don't apologize."

Amber took her statement for what it was worth and shrugged, not fighting the smile that somehow couldn't stay away. Knowing she needed to talk to someone other than Tank, she leaned back in her chair and braced herself for what was about to come out of her mouth. "My father asked Tank to do some research on Rowdy." She tested his name on her lips. When no residual panic ensued, she continued, "Tank asked me about it in passing, not having any idea what it all meant. And I had a massive panic attack. Like batshit crazy panic attack." She shook her head and rolled her eyes at Keira. "I'm talking beyond batshit."

"Do you get that phrase yet? 'Cause I really don't. Batshit crazy. Very strange."

Amber laughed. "Well, it's a good way to describe the way I acted. Anyway, after I came out of it, he made me tell him what had triggered it. And I did. I told him everything, Keira. All the stuff I haven't been able to say, things I haven't told you or Franco…I put it all out there."

There was no faking the astonishment on Keira's face. "I know I should be a little jealous that you can talk to him and not me, but I can't tell you how relieved I am that you are finally talking to someone. How do you feel? You look really good."

"I don't think I feel any different. Maybe. I don't know. Everyone says you're supposed to feel lighter after sharing, but I didn't feel that way. I felt a bit exposed, really vulnerable, and a little cray-cray."

Keira rolled her eyes. "You are not cray-cray," she said, laughing lightly.

She reached over and took one of Keira's hands in hers. "I was a little crazy for a while. I am really sorry I kept you out. I just didn't want you to think I needed anyone. I didn't want to disappoint you."

Keira looked around the bar, still holding on to Amber's hand but making a production out of looking for something.

"What?" Amber asked.

"Am I being punked? Or did you just offer me a crumb of an explanation?"

Amber smiled, despite the ribbing. "Yeah, Gretel, I just offered you some crumbs."

Quickly, the laughter drained from Keira's face, and she got completely serious. "I can't stand to see you blame yourself for everything that happened. I just want you to be okay."

"Thanks," Amber said, feeling the threat of tears well in her eyes. "The only shit thing about what happened last night is that Franco gave Tank Rowdy's name. I just can't believe he'd betray me like that, ya know? I mean, don't get me wrong; I am sure it's been killing my father to know that Tank's been with me. And I wasn't playing nice in our fight the night Franco saw that picture. I flat-out told him that I was having sex with Tank. But I just thought he'd pick me."

"You don't know that he didn't."

"I absolutely do know. He asked Tank to research Rowdy. Seems pretty clear to me."

"But you don't know why he did that. Give him the benefit of the doubt."

Amber shrugged her shoulders, not giving on the issue but not engaging in a battle about it. "So, I need a favor."

"Okay."

"Well, two favors. First, can I work for you the rest of the day?"

Keira eyed her curiously.

"Look, last night was pretty emotionally draining. And I don't want to have any time to wallow in it all."

"I get that. What's the second favor?"

"Tank's going to be spent tonight. He probably got, like, two hours of sleep last night. I'm definitely not going to see him. And there's something I want to do, but I need your help to do it. Would you be okay with not seeing Tilly tonight, so you can help me?"

"Of course," Keira answered without a second thought.

"Thanks!"

"Are you going to tell me what we are doing?"

"I don't think I can keep it from you because I need your connections." At Keira's raised eyebrows, Amber continued, "Can you call your cousin Kelly? I need her."

Keira smiled as it all clicked. "Absolutely!"

"You going to see Keira tonight?" Tank asked as he and Tilly made their way home after practice.

"Nah, she has plans with Amber, so looks like it's just me and you and Call of Duty," Tilly said, flashing a big smile.

"I don't know how much Call of Duty I have in me tonight. I didn't really sleep last night, and I definitely need to get some tonight."

"What was that conference between you and Franco about? You've never walked away from practice like that. It was fucked up."

Tank took a deep breath, pretending like he was in the midst of looking for something, so he could bide his time. He hadn't thought much about what he would or wouldn't tell Tilly. Tank wouldn't be sharing Amber's secrets. It all seemed so surreal to him today, like it couldn't have gone down like it had.

Part of him longed to see her today, to make sure she was okay, to assure himself that pushing her last night had been the right thing to do. Part of him didn't want to see her yet. He felt raw and gritty, like his body had been dragged across asphalt and the remnants remained, pieces caught in his skin. He wanted this girl;

he just didn't know if he was ready for everything that would come with her, and that made him feel shitty.

"I'm just saying, leaving us with Coach Higgs was wrong. You know the way he yells. You want to laugh, but you can't. '*Watching you run that play was like getting bent over and dry-humped. Can't you give me some finesse?*'" Tilly imitated in his best Southern accent.

Tank laughed, despite his mood. "Sorry, man. Franco and I had some things to discuss."

Tilly's eyes got wide. "Did some new pictures show up? Did you do something I don't know about?"

"Nah. At least not that I know of, and I haven't seen Cy hovering lately, so I should be good."

"So, what's up?"

"Franco is Amber's dad."

Tilly looked like he'd just been sacked. "What the fuck?"

"Yeah, that's kinda what I thought."

Then, Tilly laughed. He laughed till he couldn't stand up anymore and had to rest on the sofa. He grabbed his sides and rolled onto the couch, hysterical. "He must wanna kick your ass."

Tank was good-natured enough to get the humor of the situation. He'd shown Tilly the picture of him and Amber, and he had relayed his conversation with Franco. So much of that conversation made sense now when it hadn't before. The tidbit he'd thrown Tilly was enough. He didn't ask any more questions or want to know any of the other details, to which Tank was eternally grateful.

"So, what's up with Keira?" Tank asked, happy to turn the tables.

Tilly shrugged his big shoulders, trying unsuccessfully to fight the inadvertent smile that spread across his face. "She's cool."

Tank laughed. "That's all I'm getting, huh?"

"Yep."

"That says it all," Tank acknowledged.

"I knew it would." Tilly laughed.

At that, Tank retreated to his room, thankful that the day was over and he could go to bed. It had been that kind of day where he was looking forward to the end of it. He lay down on his bed and stared at the ceiling, trying to ignore the smell of Amber that lingered all over his room. If he were more ambitious tonight, he would have changed his sheets, needing some distance. But being tired from the past twenty-four hours overwhelmed him.

Reaching for his phone, he tapped out a text.

You okay?

He hadn't communicated with Amber all day. His phone beeped almost immediately with her response.

I'm good. Hope you get to catch up on your sleep.

That was it. No lamenting over not hearing from him all day, no subtle hints that she wanted to see him, no guilt for not checking up on her today. Suddenly, the lingering scent of her in his room felt welcome, like a kind of balm from the grittiness of his emotions. Her response assuaged his feelings, and the burden of her sort of faded away to be replaced by a longing for her to be there with him. Rubbing his hands over his eyes, he turned out his light, thinking that he was in way deeper than he ought to be.

TWENTY-SIX

A week after the first Bowl Championship Series poll was released, Kensington State University won their seventh game in a row, one of eight teams who remained undefeated. Even with their impressive numbers, they debuted in the poll in the seventeenth spot. They'd all secretly hoped that the voters would think they were better than seventeen, but for a team that had been flirting with the top twenty for two years, breaking through felt good. They watched the games of the teams in front of them with vested interest—never wanting anyone hurt, but definitely hoping for less than stellar performances, so their games would resonate with the pollsters.

As Tank, Tilly, and Iman left the field, with the late afternoon sun rippling across the parking lot, they looked like the perfect picture for a victory poster. Three football players, a lineman, a quarterback and a receiver were leaving their field in triumph. With the adrenaline of the game still pumping through them, there didn't seem to be any question about where they were headed. Two of the three of them had girls working at the Bear's Den, and Iman kind of enjoyed being able to roam around while his two partners in crime were otherwise engaged. His dance card had been completely full since Tank had pulled himself out of circulation. Tank didn't think there wasn't anything wrong with Iman reaping the rewards.

Tank's excitement built as they pulled into the Bear's Den parking lot. He hadn't seen Amber since they'd traded war stories. There was something about being with a girl who understood his schedule that appealed to him in a way that he hadn't anticipated. He'd always assumed that having a girlfriend meant having to explain everything. Amber didn't seem to want or expect that. He knew part of that had come from her time with Rowdy. She wasn't going to become anyone's other half. It was just another thing that he decided he liked about her. There were still all sorts of things that he was on the fence about, but the lack of curiosity over his whereabouts wasn't one of them.

He did a quick but thorough sweep of the place, looking for that platinum-blonde hair. When he didn't see it, part of the edge from the game wore off. He felt a major letdown, and again, he found himself questioning the depths of his feelings for this girl. He followed Tilly to the bar and sat down between him and Iman.

Keira immediately came over and greeted them. "Amazing game!" she gushed without really meaning to. "Tank, they were talking about you after the game on *SportsCenter*, saying how you were putting up numbers that people couldn't argue with. It was awesome."

Keira leaned over the bar and gently swiped her lips across Tilly's. Tank watched with amusement and a little bit of envy.

Iman just laughed. "PDA!" he chanted a couple of times.

Tank and Tilly rolled their eyes and murmured, "Freshman."

Tilly picked up the mantle for Tank. "Where's your PIC?"

Keira nodded her head to the side. "She's over there, waiting on a couple of customers," she delivered matter-of-factly. "She'll be over in a sec. What can I get for you?"

They placed their orders and were watching the multitude of TVs when Amber bounced around the side of the bar with a smile on her face, excitement evident. Her fist was out, heading for a down-the-line fist bump. "Now, that was some amazing fucking football," she said.

Three pairs of eyes widened, three mouths dropped open, three fists bumped with hers, but no one said a thing. They could only stare.

Keira laughed. "She didn't tell you about the hair, huh?"

Amber stood before them, but her platinum hair had disappeared. Gone was the long hair that she constantly pulled to her right to cover the scar that would always be with her. Instead, her natural black hair, hung in a silky curtain to her shoulders. She'd cut bangs to draw the attention away from her chin, and the effect was startling. As the stunned silence continued on, Amber started to fidget, and the perma-grin left over from the thrill of the game started to fade.

Tank saw Keira's eyes widen as she attempted to communicate something to him. He fought his shock and tried to come up with an appropriate response. Amber looked amazing, but he felt like whatever he said at this point, after the prolonged silence, was going to come out wrong.

"No," he finally said to Keira, "as you can tell from my shock, she didn't tell me." He looked directly at Amber and said, "You look amazing."

No one could doubt the sincerity of his words, and Tilly and Iman sat on their stools, nodding their agreement. She smiled tentatively at the three of them, but Tank could tell that his reaction wasn't what she had been hoping for. Trying to find a way to put them on equal footing, he cocked his head slightly and asked, "What's the critique for the night? I know you have something to say about our play."

Again, Tilly and Iman followed his lead, waiting to hear her opinion on how they played. Tank could see her try to regain her momentum.

"You guys played amazing." She said the word *amazing* exactly as Tank had, a perfect parody of him. "I've got to check on the other side of the bar," she offered as an explanation before her abrupt departure.

Tank's eyes found Keira's. "Seriously? Not even a clue? Shit!" he exclaimed, shaking his head.

Tilly and Iman were mute, leaving Keira to try to help him with the situation.

"Look, she wanted to surprise you. I forgot that you guys didn't know her before…ya know, before everything went down. That's how she used to look, so it didn't shock me. Sorry!" she shrugged.

"Two steps forward, ten steps back," Tank muttered as he glared at her.

She glared back, saying, "What the hell do you expect? That's just Amber!" Then, she left them, too.

The elation the three of them had felt when they entered the bar had gone flat.

"You gotta get my girl mad, too?" Tilly lamented.

Tank threw his arms up in the air. "Fucking women!"

Amber bounded to the other side of the bar—this time, with anger and embarrassment rather than excitement and hype. Wow, she'd misplayed that. She'd thought Tank would fall all over himself when he saw her—mostly because it'd been five days. But, instead, he'd gone all speechless and stupid. She'd been anticipating this moment since she'd made the decision to put her hair back to right. She'd imagined it a number of different ways but not like it'd just happened. *Maybe he only liked blondes?* Somewhere in the recesses of her mind, she remembered the website and all the women. The only thing they'd all had in common was that they had a vagina. So, she didn't think she could blame hair color.

This was the problem with expectations. She'd always been a glass half-empty kind of girl, so it had been a bit odd for her to be so excited about seeing Tank. He was just a guy in a bar who hadn't given her the reaction she wanted. Big flippin' deal—except that he was also the guy whom she had bared her soul to five nights ago and hadn't seen since.

She went back to being a bartender and handling her customers. It was game day, which meant that they'd remain busy through the night. She never got busy enough that she forgot that Tank was on the other side, but at least she was busy enough that her mind wasn't replaying that awkward scene over and over on repeat. When she got a break, she carefully made her way to the back. Thankfully, she was on the side of the bar that allowed her to slip away without any notice. She headed back through the kitchen into Mark's office, knowing that he wouldn't care if she took a couple of minutes to regain her inner bitch.

She closed the door behind her and sat heavily in the chair in front of the desk with her back to the door. When she heard the door open, she almost sighed in relief, knowing that Tank had followed. She stood up quickly but awkwardly and found herself face-to-face with Tilly.

"You were thinking he'd follow you back, huh?" Tilly said knowingly.

She turned her back on him and fell back into the chair again. "Shit shouldn't be this hard," she said more to herself than to him.

Tilly walked around the chair and leaned on the desk behind him. "He feels like an asshole."

"He should," she said quickly.

Tilly just laughed. "Look, I feel like a dickhead, too. I didn't expect you to come out, looking all not blonde and shit."

She smiled reluctantly. "It's not really that big of a deal. I'm making more of it than it should be. I wanted to look different, and now, I'm crying in my beer because I do."

"Just cut him some slack. I mean, you set him up with Franco. You kind of owe him a free pass."

"Ouch!"

"I'm just saying. A man's gotta feel some sort of way when he knows the kid who's banging his daughter. You kinda put them both in a shit spot."

Amber was taken aback by Tilly's stance. She was so used to garnering sympathy that having someone call her on some shit felt a little new. "Tilly, just so I'm clear on this, you've got Tank's back, right?" She'd said it like a joke, but it wasn't received like one.

"Never doubt that," he said like a warning.

"You don't like me?" she stated but with enough emphasis on the end that it sounded like a question.

"I haven't decided yet," he said as he pushed up from the desk before leaving the office.

Amber's head rolled back on the chair. She was tired. *Were twenty-three-year-olds supposed to be this tired?* she thought.

When the door opened again, she braced herself for another confrontation. But, once the door closed, her body knew that Tank had come looking for her. He didn't say a word. He just leaned down and dropped a kiss on her head before he came around to the front of the chair. Taking up residence in the spot recently vacated by Tilly, Tank looked down at her with apprehension starkly reflected in his eyes.

"Hi," she said as she smiled tentatively at him.

"Sunshine," he said. He smiled back, obviously appreciating the opening.

"I know it's not supposed to be this hard. And I would love to be able to claim that I'm worth it, but I can't even guarantee that."

He laughed. "There ain't no guarantees."

"I'm not even a good bet."

"We'll see."

"I missed you the last couple of days." It was not something she would have considered saying even five minutes ago, but Tilly had shaken her, and on some level, she knew he was right.

Tank dropped to his knees and filled the space between her legs, resting his forearms on her thighs. She sat up and scooted forward, so their upper bodies were flush, and his hands had no option but to wrap around her waist and hold her tight.

"All you had to do was ask, and I would have made time to come see you."

She hated being this close to him and trying to have a conversation. She couldn't think straight. Being so close to him made her forget any of her reservations.

"That's never gonna be me," she said.

"I know. But I want you to know what kind of response you'd get if you asked."

He leaned forward and lightly kissed her lips. It was a teaser, meant to merely connect them briefly. But, somehow, it always seemed like more. Before she could think or stop herself or form another thought, her mouth opened on his, pulling him in. She explored and tasted, as if she hadn't been there before, learning his mouth all over again. She didn't know how long they kissed, but when her body screamed for more, she gently bit on his lower lip and then pulled away. Resting her forehead on his, she worked to catch her breath.

"I have to get back to work," she said, forcing her breathing to slow and her body to unravel itself from his.

"I know." He scooted away and held her from him.

She saw him scan her, starting at her new/old hair and moving down to meet her gaze, before looking hungrily at her lips. Then, he softly kissed her.

Pulling her to her feet, he hugged her. "See you after work?"

"Of course," she said, as if it was the most natural response in the world.

He turned her around and gently pushed her to the door. Before she opened it, he leaned in and said, "Your hair is badass!" Then, he kissed her on the spiderweb on her jaw.

And she went back to work with a smile.

TWENTY-SEVEN

When Tank asked Amber sometime during the night, he'd been somewhat apprehensive. Taking her with him to breakfast with his mother, Chantel, was a gamble. But he found himself thinking about Amber virtually anytime his mind was not otherwise engaged. Somehow, it just didn't seem right that his mother hadn't met her. He knew Sunday breakfast was sacred mother-son time, but there wasn't another opportunity for them to meet.

The question, while rather innocuous last night, seemed to throw Amber out of whack on Sunday morning as they were getting ready. She was jumpy and short, and he almost immediately regretted his decision to bring her along.

"Look, you don't have to come if you don't want to," he conceded to her, hoping just a little that she'd take the out he was offering.

She been sitting on the bed, lacing up her boots, when he tossed it out there. "Ugh!" she said as she fell backward on the bed and dramatically threw her arms over her head. "I'm just not ready. I'm sorry. Just meeting your mom seems like…so…formal. That's not the right word."

"Dictionary?" he said, like a complete smart-ass. He wasn't sure what he'd been hoping for with that remark—a laugh or a fight.

He got neither. She merely rolled her eyes at him.

"Now, I'm definitely not going," she said matter-of-factly.

"Whatever," Tank said. "I've got to go." He saw her watch him with her big brown eyes, trepidation pooling there.

"Okay. I've got dinner at Nona's tonight, but I don't have to work. Catch up later?"

Knowing he was being an ass but not really caring, he shrugged his shoulders. "I'll text you, see if we can work something out." Then, he grabbed his jacket and left—no kiss, no backward glance, just a whole lot of pissed, which was never good when seeing his mother.

Marie's, the diner where they always met, was a couple of streets over from the Bear's Den, tucked into a strip mall, next to the Kroger. They'd stumbled upon it one morning when stocking his apartment with food, and they had been coming ever since. Not because he was Tank Howard, just because they were regulars, they had a booth in the back that was theirs on the Sunday mornings after home games and once a month in the off-season.

As the season had played out, he would walk into Marie's to applause and, "Great game," and, "That was some pass."

Today, someone had taken it upon himself to start chanting, "Heisman, Heisman," as he made his way to the back.

He high-fived and fist-bumped whoever held out a hand, so it took him a couple of minutes to join his mother in the back. He couldn't disguise his pleasure at the big deal everyone was making of him this morning. He almost wished Amber had been watching, so he could smirk and stick his tongue out at her. He didn't need her apprehension. He was Tank Howard.

As he sat down, the adulation of the diners warred with his anger with Amber, so his mother got a pissed off, arrogant Tank.

"Morning," he said.

She glanced at her watch. Without knowing what time it was, Tank knew that glance meant he was late. She wasn't a tyrant by any means, but Chantel knew her way around respect.

"Sorry," he grumbled, silently cursing the women in his life.

"Good morning." She eyed him like only a mother could—scrutinizing his face, his eyes, looking for signs that she could recognize and those that she couldn't.

She could always guess his mood in the first few minutes of seeing him without any words being exchanged. He knew that, at some point in his life, someone would know the ins and outs of him better, but right now, his mother owned that ability. He waited for it, and she didn't disappoint.

"What's going on, honey?" she stated with a soothing tone, pulling a smile from him.

"Nothing. Just the morning didn't play out the way I'd expected, I guess."

She shrugged and harrumphed, telling him that life didn't always play out the way you wanted and you needed to strap it on and get over it. He'd seen it enough to know exactly what she was saying.

He smiled. "So?" he asked, knowing she'd want to talk about his game. He also knew exactly how she'd start.

"I love watching you play," she said, to which Tank smiled again.

Since he had been small, she'd start every conversation about his game with that phrase. Today, he waited, but nothing followed.

"That's it?" he asked, about to sit back and relax into the booth. He saw her eyes dart away from his, and the first little frizzle of uneasiness buzzed through him.

"It was a good game."

"Yeah," Tank answered, his brow furrowed.

She took a deep breath. "You know, I knew that the time would come, and when it did, I thought I'd be ready. It's going to be complicated because, of course, that man wants a piece of you."

At her pause, she looked down again, and Tank's stomach knotted.

Fucking Richard, he thought.

"Agents have been calling for a while. You know that already." She looked up for his confirmation. At his nod, she continued, "It's gotten pretty crazy. Franco and I discussed it the last time I was here. He gave me the names of the agents that are registered with the state and school, for reference. Anyway, I think we are getting to the point when you are going to have to make a decision about next year."

Tank leaned back into the booth, studying his mother. At the beginning of the season, they'd decided that he would wait until after the season before he even started thinking about next year. First, Chantel and him had met, and then they'd met with Franco. He'd agreed. There was no reason he needed to be thinking about this right now.

"I can't make a decision at this point. We've got a month left with four games to run the table and then the bowl game. Why would I decide that now?"

She inhaled deeply. "Tank, I have a bad feeling. He's been circling, saying some crazy things. He wants me to agree to get you to sign with an agent. Of course, it's not with anyone on Franco's list."

Tank hated his mother's bad feelings. They always meant something. But she really wasn't telling him anything that they hadn't already anticipated.

"What's changed?" he asked, exhausted by the conversation.

"It just felt different this week. Almost like he was baiting me."

Tank kept himself from rolling his eyes. "Okay?"

"I don't know how else to explain it. I feel like he's going to pressure you, us to do something rash." She didn't need to mention signing day; it was always there.

"What does that mean?"

"I think it means that he's got something up his sleeve, and we're not going to like it."

Amber had made her way out of Tank's bed and apartment as quickly as possible. She knew her reaction to his invitation to meet his mother had not gone over well. She got it. It wasn't something he had done lightly, almost like a royal summons to a commoner. She understood Tank had an ego. You weren't the number one prospect in the country and then the leading candidate for the Heisman without some sense that you were just a little bit better than everyone else. She'd been around her father enough to get the ego of an athlete. Even knowing all that and understanding that Tank would do something to remind her that he was who he was, she didn't think she could meet his mother today. Today, she had to deal with her father and with the little devil Tilly sitting on her shoulder, reminding her that she'd gotten them all into this twisty knot of intermingled relationships.

Since coming home from Oxford, Sunday evenings at her grandparents' had stirred up a myriad of emotions in Amber. Part of her longed for the comfort of the house she'd grown up in, surrounded by all the people who loved her. But, mostly, it turned her stomach because it put her into such close proximity with her father. Their relationship had disintegrated into a series of battles where the victor's spoils were not ever something to celebrate. The battleground known as Tank Howard had become particularly bloody, and Franco's giving up of the state secret of Rowdy Daniels had her brain screaming, *Traitor.*

But then Tilly's reprimand had snuck in and made her feel like she wasn't the wronged party. She'd known who Tank was, she'd known his relationship with her father, and she'd hooked up with him anyway without any forewarning to him about who she was. When she spun it around, looking at it from another angle, maybe she couldn't claim to be the victim in this case.

Why did she need Tilly to point that out to her? *Oh*, she thought, *because it has to do with Franco, and I've lost all objectivity where he's concerned.*

With the bitter sting of Tilly's jab fresh in her mind, she attempted to get ready for her confrontation with her father because, today, there would be a confrontation. She just wasn't sure who would win. What she could be certain of was, they'd both come out a little bit bloodier than when they'd started. Some part of her—the part that Tank had reawakened, the one that was getting used to the startled laughter and rusty smiles—had some hope that maybe, just maybe, this would be the final battle.

So, she showered, did her new/old hair, and got dressed. She donned her armor but in a much more subdued manner than she had done in the past.

It was funny; even though they hadn't spoken a civil word in weeks, Amber knew her father would pull up to the house at three forty-five. So, she sat on the front steps, waiting. When he drove in, she made her way around to the passenger side of the truck.

In a scene that she had played over and over, like repeat on an iPod, Amber took her seat and mumbled, "Hey."

Franco looked over at her. "Hey. I like your natural color. It looks great," he said. He left the car in park and turned toward her.

Going on the offensive, she thought.

"Remember two weeks ago, when I said I was going to make this a lot harder for you? That I was going to push and stop letting you push me away?"

Amber cautiously watched her father. Even though she thought she'd prepared herself for their time together, she found that she wasn't quite ready for his direct confrontation. She reluctantly admitted to herself that she liked him better when he treated her like she was fragile even though she hated that, too. She guessed she wouldn't let him win, no matter what he did.

"Yes," she said, nodding.

"Telling Tank wasn't about that."

She continued to stare at him. He waited her out, not saying anything.

"I don't get it. What do you mean?" she finally asked.

His left arm draped over the steering wheel, as he pinned her with his steely brown eyes. "I saw you with him."

At that statement, Amber shuffled uncomfortably in her seat. *What exactly did that mean?* "Okay?" she said in a manner that sounded more like a question than a statement.

Franco smiled, like he was caught in a pleasant memory. Amber noted the smile with a small amount of amazement. It had been a while since she'd seen him smile like that. She knew he could say the same about her, and that made her heart hurt a bit.

"You were at the field, and you smiled and laughed." He paused, like he was gathering his thoughts, but he never looked away. "It's been so long since I've seen a genuine smile on your face and even longer since I've heard your laughter. I've probably never told you, but as a parent, at least for me, genuine laughter is like a miracle when you hear it in your child. It makes you think you can fly."

He shrugged but held her gaze, allowing the sentimentality of the moment to wash over both of them. Franco had always had remarkable timing.

"After I saw you two together, it made me think that you could be happy again—not the same as you were, but that you could find some happiness." He watched her, and she felt herself nod, unknowingly acknowledging what he was saying without even checking her actions. "But none of that would be possible if Tank didn't know what had happened to you. And I knew that you'd never voluntarily give it up. So, I pushed him in the Rowdy direction."

"You expect me to believe you did that for me?" she heard herself saying, but the bite that normally accompanied her interactions with him was missing.

Franco laughed humorlessly. "No. Unfortunately, I don't expect you to believe me. But I wanted you to know just the same. I know you won't believe this either, and that's probably my fault. I guess, in my own way, I've shown you that my career is more important than you are. But you will always win. There's no contest. Between you and Tank, I pick you." He made sure she saw the sincerity in his eyes before he turned and put the truck in reverse.

They didn't say anything else on the way to her grandmother's, nor did they talk on the way home. But when he dropped her off before heading back into the office, Amber had to admit that the battle lines had been redrawn. She could fight her father's pity, even his anger, but she had no defense against his declaration of utter devotion. Because she absolutely believed him.

TWENTY-EIGHT

It took Amber about two seconds to text Tank once she entered the front door.

I'm done. You busy?

She thought his response would be instantaneous.

But, in the interim, she washed her face, changed her clothes, and brushed her hair. When she finished, she checked her phone and found that there was no response from Tank. Disappointed but not alarmed, she waited. The thing with waiting for a text was that your head would get all caught up in the possibilities behind the delay. For Amber, the possibilities were endless. He'd definitely not appreciated her hesitation to meet his mother. And he seemed not to like the way she moved around his sarcasm. But, back in those moments of uncertainty, she faltered in the meaning. Why did he want her to meet his mother? What if, like Tilly, she wasn't an immediate fan? Amber wasn't sure she could handle being persona non grata with both his mother and one of his closest friends. So, she had balked. Now, she wondered if he was making her pay for it.

She debated for a while—text him back or just go see him. *Which would be more humiliating?* she weighed. *Another text ignored or a door in her face?*

Throwing herself on her bed, she picked up her phone, willing a ding. But watching it didn't do any good, and she was too amped up to sit at home. So, she decided on the more radical approach. Grabbing her stuff, she headed out the door to see what was up.

Tank's apartment complex was jumping when she got there. Bass was thumping through the parking lot, and many of the apartment doors were ajar, allowing people to roam freely from one spot to another. Yesterday had been an active day for the BCS teams, and everyone was fairly certain that the Bears would break the top ten. She imagined that was the reason for the party atmosphere.

And, she thought thankfully, *the reason I haven't heard back from Tank*.

After circling the parking lot once, she pulled down the road and parked in the first open spot she could find.

She saw Iman first, sitting on the trunk of a car with some hoochie-looking girl taking up space between his legs. He flashed a smile when he saw her and nodded toward Tank's apartment. She checked herself as she started to move quickly up the steps, her excitement getting the best of her. She tried not to think too much about it—this shiny new feeling inside her—because she didn't want to admit to herself that it was wrapped up in a big Tank Howard bow.

The door to their apartment was open, and the first thing she saw was a wide-eyed Tilly Lace, leaning back in the kitchen table chair, his hand filled with cards. She took the look to mean he either had a good hand or a bad one, and she had a momentary feeling of pity for his lack of a poker face. But, as she entered the apartment, she knew the face had nothing to do with his cards but instead with the girl straddling Tank on his sofa.

She pushed herself to walk all the way through the door and even managed a very casual, "Hey," to the apartment at large.

She had a vision of walking over to the blonde, grabbing her by the hair, and yanking her off of the guy whose bed she'd woken up in this morning. Instead, in an unconscious gesture, she reached around for her recently sheared hair, attempting to pull it over the right side of her face and neck. Tilly saved her by standing up and walking over to her, all Southern hospitality-like.

"Hey," he said, obviously used to playing this role with the women in Tank's life. He moved her toward the kitchenette and grabbed a beer from the fridge. "Drink?" he asked.

She took it even though the only thing she wanted to do with the beer was break it over Tank's head. Tilly seemed to recognize the look in her eyes because he smiled wide, his gold teeth gleaming in the fluorescent kitchen light.

"Not worth it," he mumbled, nodding his head in Tank's direction and turning her around.

Tank's light-green eyes were trained on her but he made no move to disengage himself from the other girl.

"What happened this morning?" Tilly asked, leaning against the counter.

"Huh?" Amber said, too shocked by the blatant fuck-you happening right in front of her.

Tilly just looked at her, like she was being stupid.

"You think I did something to deserve that?" she whispered furiously.

"Nah. I didn't say that. I'm just wondering why he's watching you but all up on another girl."

She shuddered at the direct, accurate description of the last few minutes. "I don't know, but I'm too old to play these little games."

She set the beer down and almost took a step when Tilly said, "Wasn't that you a few weeks ago when you walked away from him and started grinding on some frat boy?"

Amber looked up at him, kind of surprised by his observation. "I thought you didn't like me."

"Never said that."

"Didn't trust me?"

"Good reasons."

"So, what does it matter if I just walk out of here?"

"Nothing. I'm just saying, didn't you have some reason you were all over some other dude not two weeks ago?"

"Fucking Dr. Phil," she said sarcastically.

Tilly threw his head back and laughed loudly. His laughter drew everyone's attention, and Amber reluctantly smiled at him.

"Look, Tilly, I appreciate the subtle intervention, but I'm fucked up enough as it is. I can't get into this pissing match with him." She shrugged her shoulders. "That's what it would be because what I really want to do right now is go find one of your teammates and screw him. So, do you really think this is worth interfering?"

Tilly looked at her with a little bit of pity in his eyes. "That's pretty sad," he said.

"Yep. Sad but true. But, because you've been such a good guy, I'm going to just walk out of here and go home. No harm done. Okay?" she said as she reached out and patted his huge arm. "Have a good night." She made her way to the front door.

She wished it were closed, so she could take out some of her frustration with a good pulling open and slamming shut. But, because there was little choice, she merely walked through the open passageway without a second glance toward the couch. Down the steps and across the parking lot, she nodded at Iman whose wide eyes reflected his surprise at her quick departure. When she reached her car, she was more than ready to go—do not pass go; do not collect two hundred. She was almost away when two hands wrapped around her biceps, and she was pulled to a halt.

She wasn't scared. She didn't freak out. She knew it was him by the gentle hold on her arms and the familiar smell.

She wanted to step on his instep and elbow him in the balls, but she merely stopped walking, took a deep breath, and said on a sigh, "What do you want, Tank?"

"Don't leave," Tank said, keeping enough distance between them to both frustrate and excite him.

Again, with the sigh. "Why? Did you want me to watch you fuck that girl, too?"

He almost laughed at her assessment of the situation. "Nah, I wasn't planning on fucking her," he said as he gently turned her around. Then, he dropped his hands.

"What do you want?" she said, her frustration and anger radiating off of her.

"I don't want you to leave," he said, understanding the complete discord between his words and his actions inside his apartment.

She rolled her eyes. "Could have fooled me."

He knew that he should insert the word *sorry* right there, but he wasn't sure if he was, so he didn't. After her *no* to his invitation this morning, he was feeling a bit spiteful and pissed. He definitely didn't mind that she was mad; he kind of felt like she deserved it.

"Look, I asked you to stay. You gonna turn me down twice in one day?" He sorta spit the words out at her, his little bit of mad mixed in with the invitation.

"Ah," she said, nodding her head, as if she'd just solved a complicated equation.

"What?" He bristled.

"So, that's what this is about. Breakfast?"

"What do you mean?" he asked with feigned innocence.

"The ignored text, the girl all up on you. This is all because I didn't go to breakfast with you and your mom?"

He bowed up, spoiling for a fight, so he could let loose some of his frustration with the day and the way it'd turned out. "Am I not supposed to be with other girls? Had we gone there?"

She glared at him. "Nope. I don't think we have gone there. But, next time, you might want to space us out better."

"Last I checked, I didn't ask you to come here tonight," he fired back, his sense of self-righteousness growing by the second.

"Funny, I swear you followed me out here to beg me to stay."

Maybe it was the word choice or her mocking glare, but whatever it was, Tank felt he'd been pushed too far, the day unbelievably heavy on his back. He almost scoffed at her. But, instead, he pushed in close, moving her back against her car, his body flush against hers. He could sense the change in her breathing, feel the curves of her body giving against the solid metal beneath her. He ran his hands up from her thighs to her arms, from the tip of her fingers to her shoulders, across her collarbone and her neck, until her face was cradled by his hands. He rubbed his thumb across her bottom lip and then followed it with his tongue and his teeth as he gently caught it and tugged. Amber's breath hitched, and she seemed to melt into him. He felt it, too—this incredible desire to sink into her and forget all the shit of the day.

His body was taut with desire, so when his mouth captured hers, the kiss took on a life of its own with his tongue moving in, exploring her mouth, his hands moving down her body, beneath her shirt. He pulled her closer and then leaned them both back against the car. He almost got lost in her, but then he heard the moan escape her throat and as she hauled him closer, and he remembered that he was mad. He drew away from her mouth but kept their bodies pressed together.

"I never beg," he stated simply as he put space between them, breaking all contact.

Her eyes snapped open, but they were still glazed with the desire that had immediately ignited when they kissed. Her languid look told him that what he'd said hadn't hit her yet. So, he waited impatiently for his statement to take hold. He watched her eyes as the comprehension sank in, and they filled with the same kind of mad he was feeling.

She pushed away from the car, backing him up. Then, like a fury, she lit into him.

"I get it, you know. I really do. I understand you put yourself out there with that invitation, and I hate that I disappointed you and left you hanging like that. I just…I couldn't do it. I still had Tilly's little pep talk in my head, and I just…I wanted to go but—ugh! I know I'm hard, but so are you. You go all, 'I'm Tank Howard. Bow down before me,' on me," she said as she threw her hands up for the air quotes. "And I get it. I so fucking get it. You are Tank Howard. Mr. Five Star. Mr. Heisman. But, shit, cut me some fucking slack. Can't your ego just cut me some fucking slack?"

He hated to admit, even secretly to himself, that he was pissed off at her for not coming with him this morning. Yes, he'd asked her to go with him to meet his mom in the afterglow of some really hot sex, but even he could admit that he wouldn't have asked her if he hadn't wanted her to come with him. And she'd essentially turned him down, bruised his ego. She seemed to forget a lot who he was. He could be with any girl that he wanted. But he wasn't, didn't want to be. He just needed her to respect that he could. That she knew all that and called him out on it scared the shit out of him.

So, instead of being mature and admitting that everything she'd said was true, he slid right into being Tank Howard. "Nah," he said. Then, he turned his back on her and walked away.

TWENTY-NINE

Cy came barreling into the coaches' meeting room with a piece of paper in his hand and a smile on his face. "With South Carolina, Nebraska, and Michigan's losses, we just broke the top ten. We're number nine!"

If he'd come a couple of minutes earlier, he'd have gotten a reaction worthy of his excitement. Unfortunately, Franco had gotten a congratulatory text from Whitey, and he'd shared it with the rest of his staff.

"Thanks, Cy," Franco said, a hint of a smile lurking around his mouth. "We just heard."

"Oh," Cy responded, masking his disappointment. "Well, congratulations."

Cy turned to leave as Franco and his staff got back to the business of discussing practice for the following day. They worked a couple of hours longer and then broke for the night.

Franco made his way to his office and was surprised to find Molly standing there. He hadn't seen much of her since the night in her office. He wasn't sure if she had been avoiding him or if he had been avoiding her or if their jobs had just inserted responsibility in their way. Seeing her now though made him wish that he'd seen her in the interim.

"Hey," he murmured as he made his way to her, caught up in some overwhelming desire to put them where they'd been last week.

He had almost reached her when she sidestepped him and purposefully put the chairs in front of his desk between them. He tried to recover from his surprise by acting as if walking directly to her hadn't been his intent.

"What's going on?" he asked as he ran his hand through his hair and walked behind his desk, trying to overcome the awkwardness of the last few seconds.

"We have a problem, Franco," she said, taking a seat in the cockblocking chair.

He sat and leaned back in his chair, throwing his legs up on the desk. He looked at her like, *Whatcha got?*

"Tomorrow, President Holdiman is going to receive a letter of inquiry from the NCAA," she said matter-of-factly, like she'd just told him that his shirt was green.

Franco shed his air of nonchalance, quickly dropping his feet and leaning forward in his chair. "What exactly does that mean?"

"It means that they have reason to believe that we've committed a violation, which needs to be investigated."

"What the fuck? What violation? We haven't committed any violations."

He saw her take a deep breath and knew he wasn't going to like what was about to come out of her mouth.

"The violation in question has to do with Tank receiving benefits from an agent."

Franco snapped back, as if he'd been slapped. "An agent? Tank hasn't had any contact with any agent."

"I'm just telling you the little I know. Unfortunately, I don't know anything else right now."

"Why the hell not?" he barked, anger and confusion taking over.

"I'm probably not even supposed to know about the letter of inquiry since it hasn't reached campus yet. It was a courtesy call because I happen to know some people."

Franco got up and started pacing, running his hand through his hair, as he tried to figure out what was going on. "Explain it to me," he said. "What's a letter of inquiry mean?"

"The letter of inquiry will explain the alleged violation and give us a list of people that we have to talk to. It will essentially detail the charges and tell us how they want us to go about investigating it. We'll have to interview everyone on the list. Then, we have to send a response in writing to the NCAA. If they don't agree with what we send, they could send an investigator to come and interview everyone again. After that would come a notice of allegations, which would specifically spell out the violations and potential infractions."

"Who does the interviewing?"

"Initially?"

"Yes."

"I do."

Franco nodded. "Worst case?"

"I don't know and won't know until we know what we are dealing with."

"Guess," he ordered as he stopped pacing and looked at her.

"Worst case is that it would affect Tank's eligibility to play and, of course, the season."

"What? We can't pull him. It would ruin his chance at the Heisman. Plus, everyone would think he's guilty of whatever trumped up allegations are out there. That's bullshit!" His voice rose as he got angrier at whatever this was.

He couldn't get over the timing. They'd broken the top ten, Tank was leading the Heisman race, and suddenly, there were some crazy allegations about him talking to an agent.

"You asked for the worst case," she calmly stated. "Worst case is that whatever is in the letter of inquiry is true, and we have to declare him ineligible. If he played and we found out that the allegations were true, then you'd have forfeit any game that he'd played in. That's the worst case."

"Tank and I have been over this a number of times. He hasn't been talking to an agent, much less getting anything from one."

"Coach, let's be honest. You don't know if he's been talking to an agent or if his parents have been talking to an agent."

"Wait, what?" Everything around Franco slowed down as the reality of her words reverberated in his office. "What do you mean, his parents?"

"I mean, his parents. It's a violation for him or any of his family to receive anything from an agent. Marco Smith ring a bell?"

Marco Smith definitely rang a bell. He was an all-American receiver whose parents had moved into a house provided to them by an agent. It had cost him and his university greatly. Franco had conveniently chosen not to think about Marco Smith.

Franco's world shifted a little at the seams. He could feel Molly watching him, gauging his knowledge, judging his reactions. He tried not to let the horror of the situation seep into his facial expression.

"When will you get the letter?"

"The letter will go directly to the President, but the faculty athletic rep, the athletic director, and I will all be copied on it. We'll probably all meet tomorrow to figure out how to go about this. I imagine Cy and the university's press person will be there to come up with a strategy for the media. I'll probably have to set up interviews this week. We need to be able to have a good idea of if we can refute the letter before we take the field on Saturday."

"Why's that?" Franco asked.

"Because, Coach, it's going to be up to me to determine if his playing will force us to forfeit wins later and bring bad press to the university. Whether or not Tank plays on Saturday isn't going to be left up to you. It's probably going to be my call."

Ah, this is why you don't kiss your director of compliance, he thought.

But he could only guess what she was thinking because she wasn't giving anything away.

This is why you don't get involved with a man you work with, Molly thought as she watched Franco process her statement.

Yes, it would be her call about whether or not Tank stepped on the field on Saturday. And, right now, she wished it could be anyone but her.

She watched Franco pace his office, his hands running through his hair, frustration and helplessness swirling around him. She wanted to move toward him and offer him any comfort he would be willing to take. But she knew what she wanted was impossible.

When she'd first seen him and he'd walked toward her earlier, she'd almost met him halfway, almost thrown herself into his arms, almost begged him to shove the papers off his desk and take her. But then her career had flashed before her eyes, and she'd cockblocked him with a chair. Not very graceful or subtle, but certainly effective.

Molly was already all mixed up about what she'd shared with Franco. She'd done a good job of staying out of his way over the last couple of days, content to just think dreamily about how good it had felt when their lips met and his tongue tangled with hers, when he spread her open on her desk and taken what he wanted from her. She wanted him. Badly.

Then, she'd gotten a call from her former boss. A school had filed a report of a violation with their compliance director, who had forwarded it to their conference office. From there, it had escalated, and here they were, on the eve of receiving a letter from the NCAA that would put a cloud over their dream season and on the career of Tank Howard. No matter the outcome of the investigation, people would now associate them with cheating and Tank with doing something below board. There were no winners in this. In the court of public opinion, an NCAA investigation meant guilty. Everyone would always wonder.

She didn't know what this whole thing was about, but she was intrigued by the timing also. If they weren't a BCS buster this year, would they even be dealing with this? She wasn't a conspiracy theorist kind of person, but she could appreciate where Franco was coming from.

Ha, she thought. She could appreciate Franco.

"So, what happens tomorrow?" Franco asked, interrupting her thoughts.

She managed to bite back a sarcastic retort. "Uh, tomorrow, we'll get the letter and probably meet. Then, we'll determine the course of action."

"Tomorrow's Tuesday. It's a big day for practice. Then, we leave on Friday. So, break it down for me. Think it forward. The violation is about Tank. You interview him. You interview me—"

"I don't interview you, Coach," she said, interrupting him.

"What do you mean?"

"I'm bringing in general counsel to help me conduct the interviews."

Franco's brow furrowed, and he stopped pacing to study her from a couple of feet away.

"General counsel will conduct the interviews. I'll recuse myself from asking questions and making any contribution, other than coming up with questions and directing the general counsel on what he needs to do."

Their eyes met, and they stared at one another from the expanse of a couple of feet, but the memory of Molly splayed open on her desk and Franco's head between her legs seemed to shimmer between the two of them. Molly felt her cheeks heat.

Franco sighed audibly before looking away from her. "That makes sense," he commented.

She shifted back, trying to put distance between them. "I just think that, after last week, I shouldn't be the one asking questions."

"No reason to explain, and I agree."

"It's just the right thing to do, Franco. And I don't regret it," she said. She knew she was merely reiterating her point, but she couldn't seem to stop herself from saying it again.

"Molly, I'm not arguing with you. I agree," he said.

The impatience in his voice seemed to snap her out of her bumbling explanations.

They stared at each other again, the tension palpable between them.

"General counsel will interview Tank and me. Who else do you think will have to be interviewed?" Franco asked.

Molly took a steadying breath. His proximity had made her body want to be closer, but now, she could think better. "Without knowing the specifics, I would say his mother and his father. We might need to ask for phone records, text messages. I just don't know yet."

"You have to interview Richard?" Franco asked, incredulous.

She looked at him warily. "We're going to have to interview whoever we feel we need to, so when Tank steps on the field, we are confident that he is clear."

Almost like she'd drawn a line in the sand, Franco removed himself from her proximity completely. Running his hands through his hair again, obviously frustrated, he faced her, in complete coach mode. "It's Monday. We leave on Friday. And, when we leave, Tank is coming with us. So, we have three days to figure this out." He raked her with his gaze. "Let's get started."

You can pull the coach card. Watch this, you motherfucker.

"I'll have a schedule of interview times on your desk first thing tomorrow. But make no mistake; if I feel like Tank shouldn't play this weekend, he won't play. And there's nothing you can do about it."

THIRTY

Tank slung the towel around his neck and sat on the bench, staring through the mirror in front of him, as he relived the events of the last few days.

When Franco had called him into his office, the atmosphere had swirled with some unnamed tension.

"Tank," Franco had begun, "we have a problem."

Tank, like the shithead he could be, immediately thought of Amber and grimaced internally. *Really, my coach is gonna give me shit 'cause I got into it with his daughter?* But he waited, trying not to shift uncomfortably in his chair.

"The NCAA has launched an investigation into some activities between an agent and you and your family."

Tank had leaned back in his chair, shocked by the subject. *Fucking Richard,* he thought. In the back of his mind, his mother's feelings and warnings from over the weekend had bounced around, pelting him with doubt and fear like a barrage of hail.

Tank realized that he hadn't responded to Franco, and for a brief moment, he wondered if his actions were already being judged and weighed.

"That's messed up, Coach. I haven't spoken to an agent. I swear to you." Tank questioned if there was some blood oath he could take to prove his innocence.

"I know, Tank. Your actions are not what I am concerned with." Franco made sure that Tank looked him in the eyes when he said, "I know that you haven't done anything wrong."

Somehow, Franco's statement made most of the anxiety shift, so it was still there but not lodged in his heart, thinking he might have let down someone he cared about.

"But," Franco said, one of his ironic smiles playing around his mouth, "I'm not so sure I trust that Richard might not have done something stupid."

Tank merely nodded his head. He really wanted to argue, to stand up for this person he was associated with, if only to say that he wasn't connected just because he had the blood of a crazy person running through him. But how could he argue? Hadn't his mother warned him that something was going to go down?

Tank looked up at Franco and knew he could trust him with what he knew.

"Look, Coach, remember signing day?" At their shared memory, they both smiled a little. "I told you that my mom had this bad feeling, and even though she never said anything to me directly then, I knew she thought something weird was going to happen. Well, when we had breakfast the other morning, she said that the agents have been blowing her up. And Richard's been circling, talking about me signing with some dude who's not on anyone's good list. I guess he threatened her—nothing specific—but she's been worried. I don't know what that all means, but now, I'm nervous. And I wasn't on Sunday."

Franco sat back and had taken in what Tank had said. "Tank, this is going to get worse before it gets better. Miss Magee wants to interview you today with the general counsel for the university."

Tank eyes widened.

"They are also interviewing Chantel. I think they are talking to her this afternoon. Let Chantel tell them. She's the one who's been dealing with Richard. What she's said to you is not your story to tell. You need to just answer their questions."

So, he had. He'd answered every question they threw at him. The thing was though it was a short interview because he answered most of the questions with, "No." He hadn't spoken to any agents and hadn't received anything from any agent. His car was in his mother's name, he hadn't had access to more money recently, he hadn't met or associated with anyone whom he didn't know before, he hadn't even determined if he was staying for his senior year or not. Yes, he'd gotten text messages and Facebook messages by the thousands, but he'd only responded to those people he knew.

When he got up to leave the conference room where the interview was being held, he felt pretty good. But then Miss Magee stopped him before he reached the door.

"Tank, I know you are worried about playing this weekend. We are going to try to get as much information as possible so that we can get an answer for you and Franco about whether or not you can play. I'll do everything I can to get you on the field this weekend."

Tank's shock must have shown on his face because Miss Magee's eyes narrowed.

"Franco didn't mention that, I guess?"

"No, ma'am." Tank tried to be as respectful as possible, but what he really wanted to do was break something.

She took a deep breath. "We have to make sure that we are protecting the university and the program. If we don't…" She paused, as if she wasn't really sure she wanted to put whatever it was she was thinking out in the open. "If we don't have enough information, then we will have to withhold you from the game on Saturday."

Then, that respect his mother had beaten into him rose up in his throat like bile. "Yes, ma'am," he returned.

He calmly walked out of the room and headed straight for Franco. As he relayed his conversation with Miss Magee to Franco, he watched his coach get angry.

"Look," Franco explained, "you are going to have enough to think about and deal with over the next couple of days. Let me worry about the politics of all of this. Okay?"

Tank nodded, as a good portion of his confidence drained away. If Franco was worried about getting him on the field this weekend, things were starting to look a whole lot worse.

When he had left Franco's office, part of him had wanted to check out for the day, to just not show up anywhere—not classes, not meetings, not practice. He had wanted to wallow a little bit and take a hiatus from the shitstorm brewing around him. But the thought of leaving his teammates to fend for themselves for the day didn't work for him. Plus, this time, if he dropped off the radar for forty-eight hours, everyone would think he was guilty.

So, he went about his day. He attended classes and went to team meetings and practice, as if his world wasn't somehow crashing in around him. And practice helped. Every one of his teammates and coaches had done something to show him that they believed in him—tapping him on the helmet, looking him in the eyes, throwing him a fist bump. It was all the little ways men in pads could show their team captain that they didn't doubt him.

His departure from the field after practice sustained him for a while. But then TV, Twitter, and the Internet intruded and reminded him that, while those people around him believed in him, the rest of the country had started to doubt. When that reality kicked in, he found himself making his way to the weight room to pound out some of the mad that was starting to settle in around him.

Tank tapped his phone, looking for the time and quickly surveying the waiting text messages. Here, in the solace of the weight room, with its weak light and thumping music, Tank could admit to himself that he was looking for a message from Amber, was waiting for some indication that she was worried about him, some lifeline to hold on to, while the storm raged around him.

But there was nothing.

THIRTY-ONE

Amber had been silently livid for the last couple of days. After her cathartic discussion with Franco on Sunday, she'd been looking forward to seeing Tank, because Franco has sewn some healing stitches in the holes in her heart. She was ready to move forward. Then, Tank had dressed himself up in his ego, and she hadn't known how to rip it off of him. She didn't really want to care that he had been a complete asshole, but she so completely did. Shaking it off, she entered the Bear's Dean for her shift, happy to have something to occupy her mind and hands.

"What's going on?" Keira said to Amber as soon as she entered the bar.

Amber shook her head, not knowing what she was talking about. "Huh?"

"Tank?" Keira said, dropping her voice.

Amber shook her head, frowning. "I don't know. I pissed him off on Sunday morning. Then, we got into a fight Sunday night, and he hasn't been in touch since."

Keira scrutinized her. "What? Well, that sucks. What happened?"

"I got freaked out when he asked me to have breakfast with his mom. Then, he went all, *I am Tank Howard; hear me roar*, on me. I haven't talked to him to know exactly what's going on." She shrugged her shoulders, disguising her hurt.

"Have you not watched the news today?"

"No. Why?"

"It's all over ESPN."

"What?"

"Something about the NCAA and a letter of inquiry and Tank being investigated."

Amber's heart dropped. "Investigated for what?"

"Something about an agent. I thought you'd know." Keira looked a little bit sorry that she'd made the assumption that Amber would know what was going on.

"I don't know shit," Amber replied.

She watched the television, looking for the telltale lead. It didn't take long to scroll, just following the NCAA BCS rankings, NHL scores, and NBA scores. Seeing it live, in print, she felt all the horror that her father and Tank must be experiencing. The fact that neither one of them had reached out to her left her feeling adrift, useless, and shut out.

THE NCAA IS INVESTIGATING ALLEGATIONS OF THE RECEIPT OF EXTRA BENEFITS INVOLVING HEISMAN CANDIDATE TANK HOWARD. SOURCES TELL ESPN THE NCAA SENT A LETTER OF INQUIRY TO KENSINGTON STATE UNIVERSITY PRESIDENT MICHAEL HOLDIMAN LATE TODAY.

When it ran across the ticker, everything inside her flickered with indecision. He'd been a complete asshole to her on Sunday night. She'd meant what she said. She totally got it. She'd gotten why he was hurt and mad and all the stuff in between. She probably would have even forgiven the ho who had been astride him when she walked into his apartment.

Part of Amber, the hardened cynical girl who was all beat up and scarred, wanted to wait him out. Because she should wait him out. But the girl who'd bared her soul to him a week ago wanted to jump out from behind the bar and run as fast as she could to his side. She wanted to be there for him, to wrap him up in her, the way he'd engulfed her the other night.

"Fuck, Keira, I have no idea what to do. He was such an asshole the other night that I want to let him stew in whatever is happening. I mean, the whole Karma-is-a-bitch theory," Amber told Keira when she'd returned from bussing some empty tables. "But, holy shit, this is beyond big, and his head has to be spinning."

Keira just kind of shrugged her shoulders. "I don't know what happened the other night."

Amber quickly related the story. She saw Keira cringe at the image of Tank with the girl on top of him. As she watched Keira's reactions, she remembered why she'd kept so much of her relationship with Rowdy to herself. Sometimes, you just went through things in relationships, and you didn't always want the people who cared about you to remember the bad stuff. So, you'd end up holding it close to your chest, protecting all the people you loved.

"So, what do I do?"

"Can I opt out?" Keira said, laughing uncomfortably.

"I really wish I were more Zen or enlightened or whatever. Instead, I'm a grudge-holding bitch."

Keira laughed, more like herself this time. "If it were me, I'd have a hard time getting over what happened Sunday night. Does that help?"

Amber nodded. "It absolutely does. Thanks."

"Good. I haven't heard from Tilly tonight, but when I do, I can ask him about Tank."

Amber nodded. "So, did Tilly tell you that we had a little discussion on Saturday night?"

Keira looked away sheepishly. "Maybe," she said, drawing it out. "Yes, he did. I'm sorry."

Amber shrugged. "You don't have anything to be sorry about. I get it. And, actually, I don't blame him. I kind of appreciate that he has Tank's back."

"That's different."

Amber laughed. "I guess. When I thought about what he'd said, it made a lot of sense. Kind of made my chat with Franco go a little differently."

"You talked to Franco?" Keira asked, surprise evident in her voice.

"Yeah. It was…good." She shrugged, as if the action could infuse the topic with the proper amount of uncertainty.

"So, are you and Franco on speaking terms now?"

"I'm not sure. You know he's like a ghost during the season. So, even though Sunday afternoon went well, I haven't seen him since."

"Maybe you can ask Franco," Keira suggested.

Amber weighed the option, deciding if she could actually talk to Franco about this. *What would that be like?* At least she would be able to find out what was happening without having to break down and actually check on Tank.

Keira continued to eye her.

"Maybe," she conceded.

But, as the night wore on, Amber felt the idea taking root in her head. And, when she completed her shift, she found herself driving to the athletic department in search of her father.

When Franco had coached at State, even though Amber hadn't lived with him, she spent enough time there to know all the staff and basically walk wherever she wanted in the building. During Franco's tenure at Kensington State, Amber had been gone. And, when she'd returned, she'd been all dinged up and damaged. So, while she knew her way around, the staff, security guard included, didn't know her. Of course, she didn't think about that until she pulled into the parking lot and tried to enter the locked doors.

Leaning heavily against the wall next to the door, she tried to come up with a plan. She really didn't want Franco to know she was here until she was right in front of him. For whatever reason, she thought he'd send her away or ask her to wait until they got home. She wasn't in the mood to wait. So, she banged on the door.

As the security guard approached, she slid the right side of her hair behind her ear. She wasn't against invoking the sympathy card when needed.

"Hi," she said shyly when the door was opened. She saw the guard's gaze lock on her neck, and she attempted not to smile. "I know we haven't met, but I'm Amber Franco. My dad is Coach Franco, and I'm supposed to meet him here."

He studied her, and then his face broke into a big smile. "Of course. You probably don't remember me, but I go to church with your grandparents. Ed Wells," he said, holding out his hand for her to shake. "Come on in. I bet Coach will be excited to have a visitor, especially after today."

Amber chatted with him while she walked toward the elevator. Once the doors closed, she felt her nerves jump. She couldn't really remember the last time she'd initiated a conversation with her father. It seemed monumental that she was about to do it now, but she was nervous about how she'd be received. Oftentimes, she'd forget how easy their relationship had been in the past, how close they had been. And even though she wanted to blame Rowdy for coming between them, she knew that she was the one who'd wreaked havoc on what was probably the most important relationship in her life. *Wasn't it just two days ago when she'd been wondering what they would say to hurt each other at her grandmother's?*

She left the elevator and made her way down the hall to the football offices. Entering the reception area, she paused, not knowing which way to go. She heard voices coming from one of the offices and headed in that direction. She didn't need the sign to know which was his office. His voice carried down the hall, directing her where to go. The door was slightly ajar, but she heard him speaking in deliberate tones, as if he were controlling some emotion. It was such a familiar tone, the only one she'd heard over the last couple of years. Not wanting to appear as if she were eavesdropping, she gently knocked on the door.

She heard the deliberate pause, as if everyone in the office were trying to ascertain who was outside, before a woman with blonde hair opened the door.

They both seemed to study each other before the woman spoke, "It's Amber, right?" She extended her hand.

"Yes," she responded as they shook hands.

"I'm Molly. Come on in."

"Uh, I don't mean to interrupt—"

"Amber?" her father said as the door opened more.

Franco came from around his desk. She took in his appearance and noticed the tired lines around his eyes, his rumbled shirt, and finger-tousled hair. He genuinely smiled at her before the worry claimed his expression.

"Everything okay?" he asked as he gestured for her to enter.

Amber noted that the blonde woman stayed.

"Yeah. I'm sorry to just show up, but I needed to talk to you." She left it at that.

She wasn't going to throw Tank's name out there with a stranger in the room, but she tried to communicate silently to Franco. Unfortunately, it seemed as though their telepathy had died under the weight of their neglect.

"Franco, we can finish this tomorrow. It's late anyway."

Amber watched as the indecision played across his face. Then, he looked at the woman with something different than Amber was used to seeing. Her eyes narrowed as Franco reached out and patted her on the shoulder before he walked around her to the woman.

"All right, Molly. I cleared my calendar, so I have all morning. When will general counsel be here?"

"Eight thirty. Nice to finally meet you, Amber."

She nodded in acknowledgement, and Molly left them alone.

Franco turned from the door and walked back to Amber. "You here about Tank?" he asked.

"Yes."

He scratched his head and then ran his fingers through his already disheveled hair. He must have been doing that all day, based on the way his hair stood up. He gently pushed her into the chair in front of his desk and sat in the one next to it, turning it slightly so that they were almost facing each other.

"There's not a whole lot I can tell you," he said apologetically, like he really wanted to talk to her about it but couldn't.

"I mean, I figured that. Confidentiality and all that."

He nodded.

"I just…is it going to be okay?" She felt like a child all of a sudden, needing her daddy's assurances that everything would be all right.

"I honestly don't know. What I know is, it all has something to do with Tank's father. The good thing about that is, Tank hasn't had any contact with his father since he signed his NLI almost two and a half years ago. So, we definitely have that going for us. I'm sure if you asked Tank about it, he'd tell you. He probably needs someone to talk to who has a little distance."

"Yeah, about that…" She almost spilled her guts. "I just don't want to bring it up and make it worse, so I thought I'd check with you first." It hit her just then that Tank hadn't been the only reason she was there. She'd wanted to make sure her father was okay, too. "What about you?"

"Me?" He raised his eyebrows in surprise and then smiled tiredly. "I'm okay. Just trying to hurry this along, so we can have Tank on the field this weekend. Keep your fingers crossed."

"I can do that." She looked around the office, listening for sounds of life. "You done for the night?"

Again, he scrubbed his hands over his face and ran them through his hair. "Yeah, I'm done."

Her tongue burned with the desire to move them forward, to bend a little and offer up some small caveat of a peace treaty. She opened her mouth to chip away at the wall between them, but she came with a lame, "Okay, well, I'll see you at home."

Then, she stood up and turned toward the door, escaping as quickly as she could, wondering how she could get over the two years of withholding information and emotions from her father. She imagined it'd just take an opening, one that would gradually grow bigger with each sentence she might be willing to share. Theoretically, she got it; she just wasn't sure what it would take to actually apply it.

THIRTY-TWO

"Is he going to play on Saturday?" Higgs asked, worry creasing his brow.

Franco leaned back in his chair, attempting to infuse confidence into his answer. "I'm not leaving campus on Friday without him."

His coaching staff was finishing up their post-practice meeting, and Franco had desperately tried to keep the agenda focused solely on practice prep and game-planning, but he could tell his coaches' minds were elsewhere, wrapped up in the turmoil of Tank's situation.

"But will they clear him to play?" Higgs said, asking the same thing in a different way. "Shouldn't we start running Jackson through more?"

At that moment, with their questioning gazes focused on him, Franco wished that he ran a dictatorship. *Don't fucking question me,* he wanted to say. But that wasn't his style. His was a cooperative leadership.

So, he kicked himself forward and placed his elbows on the table. "We are not doing anything different at practice than what we always do. I'm not going to give anyone the impression that we don't think he'll be playing on Saturday. No one's told me he can't play, and until the moment the party line changes, we are proceeding as usual." His tone, his demeanor, didn't invite questions or doubts.

As they finished up and made their way out of the room, they didn't necessarily look relieved, but he could tell that they knew he wasn't holding anything back from them.

But the glimmer of doubt that reflected in the eyes of his coaches burned the remainder of his good humor away and pushed him toward the compliance office without him even remembering that he'd made a decision to go. When he rounded the corner, he heard the din of a conversation being softly spoken, coming from Molly's office. He recognized both her voice and that of the general counsel. He took a seat in the chair outside her office and leaned forward, forearms on his thighs, so he could try to make out what they were saying. Perhaps he should feel guilty for eavesdropping, but his protective instincts were too churned up to allow him to give much thought to the sliminess of trying to listen in without making himself known.

"But you believe him, right?" Molly asked.

"Yes. I don't think that Antony knew anything about what'd been happening. But how would we prove that if there were something unsavory happening with his father? Chantel Jones's assessment of things has me worried."

"Me, too. But not enough for me to want to hold Tank out of the game this weekend. The moment we do that, people are going to think he's guilty."

Franco found himself smiling at her words, words that he'd spoken to her not twenty-four hours ago. Feeling better than when he'd ventured down there, he was contemplating leaving when the door opened, and they both filed out of her office. Molly's eyes widened when she noticed Franco sitting close to the door, and he knew that his face reflected his guilt.

He stood quickly and held out his hand to Joe Grant.

"Coach Franco," Dr. Grant gushed, "it's a pleasure to finally meet you."

"Dr. Grant," Franco said charmingly as he extracted his hand from the slightly overzealous pumping. "Nice to meet you. I wish it were under better circumstances."

"Yes. Terrible business," he said. "But I think we will get it worked out quickly," he said, reassuringly.

Franco smiled and looked toward Molly just in time to see her roll her eyes. "Well, that's good news," Franco said before he held out his hand to Dr. Grant again. "I really appreciate all of your help with this." Franco grabbed Dr. Grant's shoulder. "We'd love to have you down on the field sometime, if I can get my compliance director to agree to that." Franco glanced at Molly. He made sure

Dr. Grant's attention was focused away from him and then Franco winked at her.

Dr. Grant puffed up like he'd just been handed the winning lottery ticket. "My wife would really love that."

"Great. We'll send some passes over next week," Franco promised him.

"Thanks so much," Dr. Grant said before he left.

The moment he was gone, Molly turned her back and trudged into her office. Franco followed, a huge grin on his face. When she threw herself into her chair and glared at him, Franco laughed.

"That was the most ridiculous case of groupie worship I've seen in a long time. It's such bullshit. He hasn't had a pleasant thing to say all day. All day, I've been defending Tank, and he's only worried about the image of the university. Then, you walk in, and it's like he wants to kiss your ass."

Her frustration radiated off of her, and Franco would have felt a little bit sorry for her, but he was so used to his role that he just accepted it. Knowing that, he didn't attempt to appease her.

"I don't mind a bit of worship every once in a while," Franco teased.

Molly rolled her eyes. "No shit."

"Wanna try?"

"Don't you wish?" she retorted, regaining some of her humor.

Suddenly, all sense of playfulness evaporated as heat flamed in Franco's eyes. "Actually, yes," he answered, the volume of his voice dropping.

He saw Molly's eyes shift away from him, and the pulse point in her neck fluttered faster. He willed her to look at him, unable to gauge her thoughts when she refused to meet his eyes. Tired of circling his attraction to her, he got up from his chair and walked around her desk. When she still refused to look him in the eyes, he moved between her chair and the desk. Leaning back on the edge, he crossed his arms over his chest, his presence forcing her to look up at him.

When he finally had her attention, he asked, "Aren't you tired of fighting this?"

Molly was pretty much in the throes of her worst nightmare—sitting in her office, the door partially ajar, with her head football coach waving their attraction in her face as she attempted to investigate his number one player.

Okay, so maybe having Mike Franco want her was an amazing fantasy, but why did it have to be now when she could end up embroiled in a major NCAA investigation? Why, after three years of working together, was he interested in starting something? The timing made her nervous. Not that she really thought he'd seduce her in an attempt to impede the investigation, but she wanted some sort of guarantee that one didn't have anything to do with the other.

Looking into his chocolate eyes, she lost her way out of the maze of denial. She did want him, and she was tired of fighting it. "Yes."

Franco cocked his head to the side. "Yes what?"

"Yes, I'm tired of fighting this."

He looked slightly surprised by her honest answer.

"You weren't expecting me to say that?" She'd meant it as a statement, but it managed to come out as a question, like she couldn't believe he didn't believe that she'd gone there.

He smiled.

Oh, the things Mike Franco's smile did to her—and probably any woman in his vicinity.

"As a matter of fact, I didn't expect you to say that."

She shrugged a little and looked away. Did she admit that she hadn't really intended to say that either, but she'd gotten lost in his gaze and lost her smarts? She tried to focus on a spot on the wall, so she could avoid his stare, but after her admission, she knew it was a losing battle. She felt rather than saw him push himself off the desk and lean forward. His hands circling her upper arms, he pulled her out of the chair and into his body. She found herself between his legs. He held her hips in his hands as he pulled her in close.

She fidgeted because she wasn't sure what to do with her hands. She knew she wanted to wind them around his neck and plunge her fingers into his thick black hair, but she continued to hold back. Almost like he knew the problem, he pulled his hands from her waist and grabbed ahold of hers. He placed them on his shoulders, leaving the rest up to her. But, still, she hesitated. He didn't.

His mouth captured hers. It was just like the last time, except she was now resigned to her fate, not cursing it. In fact, as her lips parted for his, all her thoughts just faded away. She forgot about Tank Howard, she forgot about her open door, she forgot that she was the director of compliance and she was kissing her head football coach. She wanted him, and as wrong as she knew it was for her career, it was every kind of right for her body and soul.

Her fingers tangled in his hair, his hands roamed away from her waist, and her breath mingled ever so intimately with his. Every thought and fantasy that she'd had about Mike Franco played out in her kiss. She left it all out there for him.

Franco pulled away from her mouth to kiss his way down her throat. "We shouldn't be doing this here," he murmured as he bit gently on her earlobe. "We should go."

"I know," she managed to say, breathless as he'd stolen it with a nip at her throat.

"If I let you out of my sight, are you going to disappear?" he asked.

She pulled away from him. Her dazed eyes met his, and he looked at her, the question hanging in the space between them.

She shook her head before her mouth could form any words. "No, I'm not going to disappear."

"Okay. Can I meet you at your house in thirty minutes?"

He hadn't released her, but she could feel the weight of her job pressing down on them. She thought she'd covered it up, but he seemed to sense her hesitancy. He met her lips with a hard kiss.

"Don't." He rested his forehead against hers. "Thirty minutes?"

Checkmate.

"Molly?"

"Thirty minutes," she responded.

THIRTY-THREE

Amber had successfully avoided Tank in the training room since her first day of rehab. She had no reason to think that today would be any different. As she made her way back to the pool though, she saw him sitting on the edge, almost like he was expecting her. Shaking off the droplets of happiness at the sight of him, she kept walking toward Glenna, who was waiting for her at the treadmill.

As she got closer though, she realized he was talking to Glenna, seemingly oblivious to her approach. She almost turned back, but she'd become so good at pulling down the shutters that she moved forward, cloaked in nonchalance.

"Hey," she said to the room at large.

Glenna smiled at her, and Tank noted her appearance but merely nodded.

"Same as Monday?"

"Yes," Glenna said, getting the machine ready to hook her up.

As she attached Amber to the machine, Tank got up, leaving them alone and moving to the front of the training room. An exasperated sigh escaped from her lips, and she flinched inwardly as she saw Glenna take note of it. Averting her eyes, she began her workout, dreading the thirty minutes of a blank mind and nothing to keep her thoughts at bay. She tried to keep from looking toward the front of the room and the beacon that was Tank's presence. But he was a magnet for her, even as she fought against his pull.

It wasn't like her to let someone else determine her actions. She was worried about Tank even though he'd been a complete dickhead to her. He had deliberately hurt her, but she still felt the compulsion to reach out to him. And trying to deny it was starting to wear her out.

As she finished up, she realized that she was done trying to stay away from him.

Glenna appeared as her time expired. "How are you feeling?"

"Tired. Shouldn't this be getting easier?"

Glenna just smiled. "It will eventually."

Amber rolled her eyes. "It's been eventually."

"Are you doing anything aside from this three days a week?"

"No."

"So then, it will get easier. Eventually."

Amber snorted. "Gee, thanks."

As she was untangled from the treadmill, she tried to track Tank's movements through the training room, hoping he wouldn't disappear before she could catch up with him. Even though she could feel Glenna's gaze on her, she chose to ignore it. Finally released from the tether of the machine, Amber grabbed her towel and dried off quickly, watching to make sure she had Tank in her sights.

"Got somewhere to be?" Glenna inquired innocently.

Amber stopped what she was doing and looked at Glenna. "Yeah, sort of."

"Oh. Well, you have about fifteen minutes before you need to move, so you can take your time."

Grateful for the information, Amber sat down on the bench and proceeded to get dressed. "Thanks."

Since she didn't have access to the locker room here, she always brought sweats and just pulled them over her wet clothes, the drive not too far. She slid on her sneakers and bided her time, trying to look like she had a reason to continue to sit there. When she saw Tank grab his backpack and head toward the door, she made her move. Following him out into the hall, her hope for subtlety failed her. Because his pace was so much quicker than her own, she found him to be too far away to touch.

Swallowing her remaining doubts, she grabbed the last option. "Tank!"

The sound of Amber's voice stopped Tank mid step. Turning to face her, he stood impatiently, waiting for her to catch up to him. He probably should have met her halfway, but he stood there, holding his ground, feeling belligerent and hopeful all at the same time.

"Hey," she started, a little breathless from her struggle to catch him.

He acknowledged it with a nod.

He watched her bristle a little, her eyes narrowing with a what-the-fuck look.

Oh, Sunshine, he thought as he fought a smile.

Standing directly in front of him now, she looked around, noting the increased activity, as the building started its day.

"Is there somewhere we can talk?"

Did he want to talk? was more the question. He knew where talking to her would lead. The moment he'd felt her presence this morning, he had known that he'd missed her, wanted to talk to her about all the shit that had been going on. It'd hit him hard, like a sack from his blindside, this thought that he wanted her around all the time. And that scared the shit out of him, just like his reaction to her on Sunday night. He wasn't normally that much of an asshole, but something about this girl made him stupid.

He hesitated because he couldn't figure out if he was man enough to navigate this with her.

She got antsy with his prolonged silence, and he could almost see her force herself to look him directly in the eyes. That was where he lost his pseudo resolve—when he got caught up in the emotions dancing in the brown depths.

He glanced at his watch and nodded. "I've got some time before I have to be in class. Let's go to my place." He grabbed her hand and gently pulled her to his car, not allowing her the opportunity to escape.

The silent short drive had them pulling up to his apartment in no time. But the confined space had amped up his desire to both touch her and talk to her. Following her up the stairs, he had the absurd notion to just pick her up and run, so they could get to where they were going faster. In the last couple of days, he'd felt her absence, but he hadn't realized how much he wanted her until he had seen her. Not quite out of sight, out of mind. More like, out of sight, easy to deny.

When he opened the door, he fought not to tackle her and get inside her as quickly as possible. So, he moved to a place where there could only be distance between them. She sat awkwardly on the couch, the exertion from rehab and following him through the corridors catching up with her.

"What's up?" he asked, donning the asshole again for reasons he tried not to think about.

She leaned forward, her forearms on her knees, and stared up at him. There was some unfathomable look in her eyes that pulled at him, causing his stomach to knot up.

"Are you okay?" she asked.

"Yep."

"Okay, well, I know that's bullshit, but if that's how you want to play this, that's fine." She took a deep breath, almost like she was still trying to catch it. "I've been really worried about you, and if I were a better person, I would have tried to find you as soon as I found out, but I'm not very forgiving, so I didn't."

The shared memory of Sunday night compelled them both to look away to preserve their own self-righteous role in the mini drama.

After a brief moment of silence, Amber continued, "I can only imagine what must be going through your head with all of this chaos. I just wanted you to know that I'm here…if you need me."

"Why?"

She looked away and then back. "I guess because I have this innate attraction to the wrong kind of *boys*."

He heard an emphasis on the word *boys* and tried hard not to smile. Then, it hit him that she'd somehow lumped him in with Rowdy, and that pissed him off.

"I'm not anything like that asshole," he said, his anger at being generalized along with that other guy apparent in his tone.

"No"—she nodded, agreeing—"you're not. But, let's be honest, Tank. Your little stunt on Sunday was immature and definitely uncalled for. So, I think *boy* applies." Her pissed got thrown at him.

Rubbing his hand over the back of his head and down his neck, Tank felt the tension of the last couple of days bunch up and coil. He didn't want to be in limbo with her. Somehow, he knew that, if he'd had her around since Tuesday, when it all came down, he'd have felt lighter. But it was a trade-off. He could opt to have her in his life, but he knew that he'd have to be able to think about her, too.

Amber leaned forward again, suddenly very intent. "Tank, I've been around college football my whole life, so there are some things I just get that a lot of other people don't. Honestly, part of me feels sorry for you guys because, for so long, everyone around you has let you think you can do no wrong and that the world will cater to you because of your ability. What happens when that stops? No one seems to want to prepare you for that." Stopping, she looked at him. "Sorry, soapbox."

She paused and smiled at him—to soften the blow, he figured.

"I chalk Sunday night up to you flexing your ego at me. But you can't do that again. I mean…"

"You mean?"

"I mean, if you want…you know, if you want to be with me," she said, meeting his eyes. Then, she quickly looked away.

He sat back in his chair and watched her squirm. She'd totally taken him by surprise, and he was a little stunned that she'd put herself out there like that. It was so sunshiny and hopeful, somehow different than the girl who had fallen at his feet not so long ago.

Was he any different though? If his football career weren't on the line and he wasn't feeling all sorry for himself, would he try to work this out with her?

He thought about their last kiss. Then, he tried to picture himself kissing someone else. When he thought about her kissing someone else, he felt uncomfortably angry. Thinking that was as close as he was going to get to an answer, he reached over the table and grabbed her hand.

"Come here," he said, hauling her toward him.

Amber stood, not even trying to resist his pull, and walked around the table to him. The hand not holding hers landed on her upper thigh, and he tugged her down until she was straddling him. His hands moved up, so he had one on the small of her back and the other on her neck, his thumb caressing the scar on the side of her mouth. An image of Tank in this exact position with a different girl on Sunday flashed through her mind. It must have been on his mind, too, because he grimaced when he felt her tense.

"So different," he said as he met her eyes.

"What's that?" she asked, wanting clarification.

"Sunday, that girl. I wasn't with her. I didn't kiss her, and I definitely didn't fuck her."

"I thought we hadn't gone there," she countered, apparently not able to let it go. *So much for being mature*, she thought.

He moved her forward, gently pushing with the hand on her back and pulling slightly with the hand on her neck, placing her exactly where he wanted her on his lap. "We're there," he murmured.

He drew her in, leaning up slightly to place his mouth directly on hers. He kissed her hard, like he needed to have her, their teeth grazing each other as he forced his tongue into her mouth. But it was quick, and then he moved back. Continuing to move his hand up and down her neck, he traced her scar with his thumb.

"You just have really shitty timing," he explained. Smiling up at her, he kissed her again. "I'd just sat on the couch, and she jumped on top of my lap. Then, you walked in. I wasn't expecting you to show up. I was mad at you, and it was the perfect opportunity to show you."

"As opposed to just talking to me about it?" she asked as she leaned a bit away from him.

Part of her appreciated that it was a spur-of-the-moment decision, not completely calculated. But the other part of her remembered the hurt, the surprise, and their interaction after.

He shrugged and flashed a smile. "No one said I knew how to do this."

But she couldn't let it go yet. "Do you know what I wanted to do?" she asked, putting distance between them by placing her hands on his chest and pushing away from him slightly.

He cocked his head to the side, taking her in with his green eyes, and shook his head.

"My first instinct was to walk out your door and find one of your teammates to mess around with."

His grip on her waist tightened, and a steely glint flashed in his eyes. "That would have been bad."

"I know. That is why I refrained. But that's who you're dealing with. Eye for an eye and all that."

He surprised her with a laugh. "Oh, I know it, Sunshine."

Something warm, like pleasure, flowed through her, lighting her up. She wasn't sure if it was his acceptance of who she was or his complete confidence that he could handle it, but she felt something slip through her. An elusive confidence that she hadn't had for a long time settled in around her heart, and she knew it had everything to do with him.

She gifted him with a bright smile. He returned it right before he settled his mouth against her neck, opposite her scar.

"Let's just take this slow," he murmured as he continued to kiss her neck and grind against her.

"Slow, I can do." She wanted to get lost in him and let him get lost in her, but she also wanted him to talk to her and tell her what had been going on. But his body was wreaking havoc on her, and she couldn't quite string any cohesive thoughts together.

He pulled away from her, glancing at his wrist. "I gotta go. I have class in fifteen minutes."

But then he kissed her, sliding his tongue along the seam of her lips, begging for entrance. She acquiesced easily, and he pushed in, invading her mouth, exploring, coaxing her to do the same, until the kiss turned so that neither one of them could control the outcome. His hands settled on her hips, maneuvering her so that she stroked him exactly how he wanted her to, moving them toward the point of no return. She felt her body open up to him, her heart following, the joy from being back in her arms spreading through her.

"I thought you had to go," she murmured as he kissed his way down her throat.

He looked at his watch again. "Shit!" he said as he leaned his head against her chest, regret radiating from him as he started to disengage himself from her. "Can you meet me at twelve? I have a break before position meetings. We can grab lunch."

She pushed up onto her knees and placed her left leg on the ground before her right followed. It was numb from the position she'd been in and already sore from rehab. He leaned forward and rubbed his hand down her leg, from her knee to her ankle, pushing the blood back through.

"I didn't even think about what the position would do to your leg," he acknowledged with a mischievous grin. He continued to help with her circulation.

"It's okay," she responded. Then, she quickly added, "But that helps a lot," so that he wouldn't stop. "So, you want to meet for lunch. Like a date?" she teased.

He grinned up at her, still bent over with his hands on her calf. Continuing to massage her with his left hand, he ran his right hand up the inside of her leg, from her ankle and up to her thigh, and then he moved it along the seam between her legs and placed it on her ass, pulling her forward. He kissed her stomach and looked up at her. "Yeah, like a date. But kind of a short one because I have film at two fifteen and need to be dressed."

She looked down at him as he gazed up at her and felt herself fall a little bit deeper. "Sounds good. Where should we meet?"

"Marie's. You know it?"

"Of course."

"Your leg better?" he asked as he went to stand up. He held on to her waist as he gently pushed her backward.

"Yeah. Feeling has been restored."

Kissing her, he grabbed her hand to head out of his apartment.

THIRTY-FOUR

Franco was a master at compartmentalization. Work was work; play was play. When he'd rolled out of Molly's bed at five in the morning, after the best sex of his life, he had no qualms about the day ahead, even knowing that Molly would hand down her verdict on Tank. He'd gently kissed her on the spot right between her ear and her jawline, promising her that he'd see her later, making sure she knew he wasn't talking about at work. He knew, after last night, that he needed to see her again. And again.

When he entered his office following his morning workout, Miss Beverly informed him that a nine thirty meeting had been scheduled with Molly, the general counsel, and his athletic director. His first instinct was to call Molly and ask her what was going on, but he hesitated, suddenly not knowing the protocol for dealing with his compliance director whose thighs had been wrapped around him not so long ago. Although hesitant, he picked up the phone and called Molly's office line, but when she didn't answer, he put it out of his mind and started his day.

At the appointed time, he stepped into the administrative conference room, slightly apprehensive about the meeting.

"Coach, how are you?" his athletic director, Carl Wheeler, greeted, extending his hand toward Franco.

Franco returned the greeting. He generally liked Carl, who managed to stay out of his way on a daily basis. He didn't micromanage or question Franco's coaching decisions. Aside from that, Franco didn't really have much of an impression. They'd never had a crisis that required Carl to take the lead, so Franco didn't have a reason to look to Carl for any kind of direction. The fact that Carl didn't push him to do so either meant he was confident in his ability to do so when warranted, or, in Franco's experience, he didn't have the ego to do it. He'd always treated Franco as a good ole boy rather than someone who he employed. Franco had been around college athletics long enough to know that he had his own power, and on the grid of Kensington State, Franco managed it just fine.

Franco greeted Dr. Grant and then turned to Molly. The moment he met her gaze, he felt like he'd been trucked. His whole body felt her presence, and he almost groaned at the impact. Smiling tightly at her, he sat in the chair at the head of the table, which somehow said something about the dynamics in the room, but he dismissed it as he directed his attention to Carl.

"We just came from the President's office," Carl began.

Franco tried not to, but he looked at Molly with a hint of betrayal sliding into his eyes. "I didn't know that was happening this morning," he commented.

Here, Molly interjected, "President Holdiman called the meeting this morning."

He wasn't sure if she was defending herself or just filling in the gaps, but he suddenly realized that he needed a better poker face.

Franco nodded.

"We also spoke with the enforcement staff at the NCAA. They have requested phone records from Richard Howard, Chantel Jones, and Antony Howard."

Fighting to maintain his horror at that bit of information, Franco moved forward and rested his arms on the table. "Why? I thought we were charged with investigating," he asked, directing his question to Molly.

Franco had questioned Molly at length about the ins and outs of NCAA investigations. He'd also called Whitey.

"There's enough evidence at this point to move forward with the investigation. Apparently, this inquiry has been going on for quite some time. They're looking into things." She delivered this last sentence with a shrug.

Franco felt his patience and composure start to slip. "How in the hell are we just finding out about this? I thought you were up-to-date on everything that was going on with the investigation," he said, his tone accusing.

One of the things he had always appreciated about Molly was her composure.

She met his gaze calmly and answered, "I am."

Franco's ire doubled. Frustrated, he got up from the table and moved to lean against the wall. He looked away from her and turned to Carl, suddenly sick of the meeting and feeling the need to get out of the room. "So, where are we?"

Carl took a deep breath, which Franco didn't take as a good sign. "On the advice of counsel, we are going to allow Tank to play this week, but as we continue to move forward with the investigation, we will reevaluate."

Franco cocked his head. "Reevaluate?"

"Yes. Week by week. If we find something in the next few days that makes us think that Tank will be implicated, we will pull him from play."

"This is bullshit!" Franco said.

From his peripheral vision, he saw Molly flinch at his vehemence, but he didn't care. He didn't care that he'd just cursed in front of his boss and the president's right-hand man.

Pushing away from the wall, he moved back toward the table and put both hands down, leaning toward the three of them. "You don't know anything about this young man. If you did, if you took any time to know Tank Howard, you'd know that he wouldn't jeopardize his career or the reputation of this university for something as stupid as talking to an agent at this point. He's the best player in the country right now. Everyone knows it. He's going to win the Heisman. He's probably going to lead this team to an undefeated season and potentially a BCS bowl. His stock is only going up. He'd never gamble that. He's too damn smart.

"He grew up with the legacy of his father's gambling scandal even though he barely had any contact with him. Since he signed with us two and a half years ago, he hasn't talked to Richard Howard. If Richard has made some deal or been promising Tank's signature with an agent, it's a bogus promise. Now, I realize your job is to protect this university. But my job is more than protection. It's about developing young men and about fighting for them. You both have an obligation to fight for our student athletes, too." He looked at Carl and Molly. "Do your damn job!"

With that, Franco left the room, his anger coursing through him. He was mad at himself for losing his temper. He was pissed at his athletic director for not taking a stand for Tank. He was furious at Molly for ambushing him like that. In his mind, he saw her as she'd been when he left the conference room, disappointment clearly stamped on her face, her eyes reflecting that sentiment but spiking with anger at his parting statement. Then, he saw her as she had been the night before—in her naked glory, beneath him, on top of him, moving with him, wrapping him with her in an envelope of passion like he'd never known. His body immediately responded to the images of her. Groaning in frustration, he made his way to his office, delineating everything he needed to do so that he could dispel the memories of the night before and shut out the crazy feelings he didn't want to feel for this woman who had suddenly become his adversary.

Molly sat in a stunned kind of silence, impatient for the mood to be broken so that she could steal away to her office, close the door, and wallow in the mess she'd just made of her life.

Carl was the first to move. "Well, that didn't go so well, now did it?" he said with a shaky laugh.

She didn't know if he was embarrassed about the confrontation because of Grant's presence or if he felt the charge that Franco had forced on them to protect his student-athlete. Whatever it was, he looked a little ashen and definitely out of his league.

Dr. Grant cleared his throat, maybe a little nervous. Molly wondered if he feared losing his opportunity to go onto the field the following week. She knew it was petty, but she couldn't quite get the image of him kowtowing to Franco out of her mind. She was also pretty sure that Dr. Grant didn't have to deal with that kind of dressing down from the members of the faculty senate.

Oh, Dr. Grant, she thought, *welcome to college athletics.*

Since no one seemed to want to pick up the mantle of the conversation, Molly took it upon herself to bring this little soiree to an end. "You had to know that Franco wasn't going to like this decision." She wanted to tell Carl that she'd warned him on the way back from the President's office when they had a moment alone. But she wasn't one to question her boss in front of someone else, so she just added that gentle reminder without the *I told you so* that she wanted to include. "But we all decided that this was the right way to handle this. I know Dr. Grant agrees with me that Tank is innocent in all of this. Unfortunately, based on NCAA rules, his family is responsible for doing anything in his name. That's going to be the biggest issue. In the end, we are probably going to have to declare Tank ineligible and have him reinstated. I wish Coach Franco had given us the opportunity to dump that into his lap today. Then, he could have gotten all of his temper tantrums out at once."

She could hear the bitterness and hurt in her voice, but thankfully, neither one of the men in the room knew her well enough to recognize it.

Dr. Grant smiled weakly at what he read as an attempt at humor, but Carl didn't even attempt a smile.

"Cy is meeting with the university's press people. I want to make sure we all know that this subject is off-limits with the press." Carl said.

Molly nodded because she felt like Carl wanted to know she understood his directive.

Then, he dropped a bomb. "Molly, I want you to travel with them this weekend. I think it's important to have compliance present with our team right now."

Molly felt the bottom drop out, and her heart went with it. There couldn't have been a worse sentence for her. It was as if she'd committed some crime and this was her punishment. If things hadn't gone down like they had last night, she would have completely agreed with him. It was the right decision. But she knew that Franco would resent it. And her. She also knew she couldn't argue the point or not follow through on the directive.

Nodding her head, she answered, "Yes, sir."

"I'll make sure Franco knows and that arrangements are made for you."

Dr. Grant and Carl stood, signaling the end of the meeting. Molly took a moment to gather her planner and pen but mostly her composure. Part of her wanted to be a fly on the wall for that conversation between Carl and Franco. She could only imagine Franco's anger. Part of her wanted to run away.

Where was the damn motorcycle when she needed it?

She vaguely recalled Franco's parting actions this morning—his kiss on possibly the most sensitive spot on her body, which had taken him only moments to discover—and his words. He'd promised to see her later. She knew that he hadn't been referring to work. And the part of her that had capitulated last night would be waiting for him to be inside her again. But the woman here, now, still attempting to stand up after their confrontation, knew that she wouldn't see that Franco tonight, maybe not again. And she wanted to cry for her loss.

THIRTY-FIVE

Molly was wrong.

She pulled into her driveway to find Franco's truck sitting there, and he was waiting on her front stoop with his arms draped over his legs so that his hands lay motionless over his knees. The pose struck her. He looked like a lazy sort of predator biding its time.

Taking a deep breath, Molly checked her emotions, mostly because she couldn't focus on one in particular, and got out of her car. Stopping in front of him, she looked down. "Hey."

Franco lifted his head slightly and merely nodded.

His lack of greeting set her on edge, more so than when she'd pulled up. Fighting the desire to scream at him for his rudeness and boldness and arrogance, she strode around him and unlocked her door. Stepping over the threshold and dropping her bag, she opened the door wider to admit him. But he remained where he was, still facing the street.

Neither one of them moved for a minute, striking a weird display with her standing in the doorway and him sitting on the step, both looking in the same direction but seeing different things—a twisted tableau for where they were. She might have laughed at the disjointed picture, but she couldn't find anything funny.

Impatience finally winning, Molly struck out at him. "Are you coming in or not?"

"I can't decide." He paused.

His stillness disturbed her.

"*Oh-kay*," she said, sounding like a petulant child waiting for her parents to give her what she wanted. "Why? Or why not?"

"Part of me wants to throttle you, and part of me wants to be inside you. I can't decide which part of me is going to win out. And, even if I don't throttle you, I don't know if any part of me is feeling gentle right now. Even as pissed off as I am with you, I don't want to hurt you."

And how am I supposed to respond to that? she thought.

Her body got all hot and needy, but her head wanted to tell him to fuck off. Feeling sullen, pissy, and horny all at once, Molly made a *humph* noise that she knew he would hear and backed away from the door with every intention to shut it and him out. But for no reason she could come up with, she lost her composure.

"What has you so pissed off? You're acting like what happened today was personal. The events of today had nothing to do with the events of last night." She sounded whiny instead of forceful, and she hated herself for it.

Mad that Franco was right in front of her and refused to talk to her or look at her, she lost it and yelled, "Grow the hell up!"

She stepped back and started to slam the door, hoping for an exclamation point to her directive, so when the door stopped before the resounding slam, she was surprised. Then, Franco was in front of her, easing her back into her house, gently shutting the door before moving into her space and pinning her to the wall. He didn't say anything. He just looked down at her, his eyes searching hers. He looked tired and mad and sexy all at the same time, and Molly knew she was in trouble because, against all of her best judgment, she wanted him badly.

He still didn't say anything, and everything in her ratcheted up—her want, her mad, her confusion. She could feel it all show on her face, and she watched him ingest it. His desire to throttle her and be with her played out in his eyes, and she felt every emotion flowing between them. When his hand reached out to cup her nape and his thumb slid across her bottom lip, she thought she was going to implode. As he leaned forward, his forehead met hers, and a ragged breath escaped from him. No longer able to meet his eyes, she closed hers.

When he started to speak slowly and carefully, she tensed. "My mother is famous for saying that there is a time for everything. This isn't the time for us, but I can't seem to grasp that."

She knew this. It plagued her. Knowing that, she couldn't seem to stop herself. That he was feeling the same thing, the same pressure, should have reassured her—maybe. But it didn't. It made the space between them seem like an hour and a millisecond. He hadn't moved, except to slowly lead his thumb back and forth over her mouth, like he was trying to get his fill with this subtle yet completely sexual motion. She waited for it to break the plane, to give her a reason to draw him into her mouth, but he continued to fight it, much like she knew she should.

"Franco," she sighed.

Her body tight with tension, she pulled her hands away from the wall, brought them to his chest, and gently pushed him, trying to give herself space. She hadn't made any decisions or come to any profound conclusions, but being so close to him sort of robbed her of any ability to reason. But that motion seemed to propel Franco out of his stupor. Suddenly, his mouth was on hers, and his body pressed her into the wall, stealing her space. The kiss wasn't gentle; it wasn't full of regret. It was carnal and rough and electrifying. She felt their teeth knock as the grace of their sex the night before gave way to the knowledge of the forbidden, their desire for each other winning out. Last night, she had felt satisfied, a little bit guilty, and relieved. Now, with their bodies coming together in all the right places and their confusing attraction taking over, with the practiced lovemaking giving way to their base desires, she felt scared as hell by her sense of complete fulfillment.

Somehow, Molly and Franco found their way to her bed. It was the first conscious thought Franco could hold on to since the moment he'd entered her house.

We made it to the bed.

Then, he rolled out from between her thighs, pulled her into the crook of his neck and shoulder, and gently rubbed his hands up and down her back, calming their breathing and racing hearts. Their clothes were strewn around the room, the sheets tangled around them. Franco rubbed his jaw against her hair, letting the silence descend and take up space. It wasn't his normal MO, but he'd pretty much broken all his rules, and out of his normal comfort zone, he didn't know how to move forward. Knowing all of that, he was surprised to find that he wasn't uncomfortable in the quiet of the room. When he considered it though, he wasn't surprised. It was Molly after all.

"Grow the hell up, huh?" he said, his voice laced with humor.

He felt her head duck into his body and vaguely wondered if she was embarrassed.

"Yeah," she finally replied with none of the supposed embarrassment in her tone.

"You think I'm taking this personally?"

She groaned against him.

"Seriously, Franco? We are going to do this right now?"

He managed to grab her by her biceps and pull her up so that she was looking at him in the face. "Do what?"

"Have this conversation about what happened today, right now?"

"When else would we have it?"

"I don't want to do this when I am still lying on top of you, and I can smell you all around me."

He saw the faint blush creep up her neck. He flashed her a smile before teasing her, "You were surrounding me not ten minutes ago, and yes, we are still naked. It doesn't matter. We need to have this conversation, Molly."

"Fine!" she said indignantly before jumping off of the bed and flinging herself into the bathroom, seemingly to wash up. She returned minutes later, her body wrapped up in a robe, most of the sexy parts of her covered.

He couldn't hide his smile as she sat as far away from him as the bed would allow her. He almost reached for her, but because she was glaring at him, he figured it was best if they had some physical separation.

"What was discovered that suddenly has everyone on edge?"

The surprised look on her face soothed him in ways words wouldn't have been able to. "There isn't any bloody glove at this point, Franco."

"Why do you have to travel with us? And let me go back and say that I've never had a problem with having you on the road with us, not that you have ever asked. But I don't really like being told that you have to come."

"Yeah, I figured that would go over really well," she replied sarcastically.

"Do you blame me?"

"No, of course not," she said, waving away his question. "It's a good plan for right now though. If I'm on the road and monitoring the player-guest gate, it looks like we are taking this seriously. It's a concession to the NCAA—a preemptive strike, if you will."

He nodded, understanding and appreciating the strategy. It made him feel better that they didn't think that his program was doing anything illegal. "What other concessions am I going to have to make?" he asked, dreading her answer. He saw her take a deep breath and garner her strength. *Shit,* he thought, *I am not going to like this answer.*

"Look, Franco," she began, pulling her legs underneath her, getting comfortable with the space in between them, "I can predict how some of this will play out, and you are going to hate it."

She didn't say anything else.

"Okay," he said, hoping to prod her to continue.

She looked away from him, and in that moment, he knew that she was wishing there were a conference table and business clothes between them. A very small part of him felt like an asshole for putting both of them in this position. But most of him just couldn't be sorry that he was still in her bed.

"At some point—and I'm not sure when that is—we will have to declare Tank ineligible."

"What the hell are you talking about?" he raged. Forgetting that he was naked, he jumped up from the bed and walked toward her, his bellow reverberating in the room.

She merely raised both eyebrows and looked at him like a teacher patiently waiting for her student to realize he'd just stepped over the line. As her glower festered between them, Franco sat back where he'd been sitting.

"Franco, don't act like you don't know the rules. Any arrangement with an agent and a member of the family is a violation. Even if Tank hasn't talked to Richard in however many years, he still has to suffer the consequences. But since he hasn't talked to Richard, he should be reinstated fairly quickly."

"Let me see if I understand this. We are going to declare him ineligible. Then, he'll be reinstated. Just like that?" At her nod, he got all pissed off again. "Doesn't that seem pointless? If he's just going to be reinstated, why do we have to go through this anyway? Why do we have to say he's guilty of something merely to have the guilty plea waved aside? That doesn't make any sense."

She sighed heavily. And he wished he could go back to the moments before this conversation had started, when he'd been wrapped up in her, and wringing better sighs from her.

"Come on, Franco. Don't be an ass. This is just the way it has to be. You need to get on board with it because Tank will take it a lot better coming from you than from anyone else."

Franco leaned back against the headboard, overcome by the futility of the situation—Tank's and his being with Molly. He shouldn't be here with Molly right now—or ever—while they worked together. They'd both been stupid and irresponsible.

He slowly got up and retrieved his clothes without looking at Molly, afraid of what she'd see in his face. When he was dressed, he walked over to her. He reached down and rubbed his thumb against her bottom lip.

"I'm sorry," he said.

They both knew he meant good-bye.

THIRTY-SIX

Since their fight two weeks ago, Amber and Tank had managed to spend all of their free time together. Granted, it wasn't much, but they'd made it count. Tank had surprised her with his desire to experience all of the traditional dating rituals—like taking her to dinner and a movie, strolling through town square while holding hands, having her meet him at the stadium when her shifts had ended. Watching him put himself through extra workouts topped her list of favorite dates. And even though she loved her time at the stadium with him, she still hadn't gone to a game. She should have been prepared for his question, but she wasn't.

"Come to my game this weekend?"

Amber's startled gaze met his. "Huh?"

Tank seemed to take a deep breath, almost like he was girding his strength. "Come to the game. It's not that far of a drive. I can sneak you into my hotel room," he suggested, a look of obvious mischief sliding into place.

Laughing, Amber said, "That's definitely not happening. Do you know what Franco would do to both of us if he caught me in your hotel room the night before a game?" She shivered, as if in fear.

Tank answered with a laugh, "Yeah, that'd be bad. I'd like to survive to play in the game."

Suddenly, Amber's smile disappeared. "Did you ever talk to him?"

Tank nodded, but when he didn't say anything, Amber felt the need to fill the silence, perhaps letting him know that whatever transpired between the boy and his coach would be okay with her.

"Me, too," she said.

"What?"

"Huh?"

"You and Franco talked? And you didn't go all self-destructive after?" he said in a teasing way.

But she knew he was serious. It made her want to tell him, to share the conversation she'd had with Franco with him. The realization made her shudder with hesitation. She so didn't want to go where they were going—or where she was going. She didn't want to feel so much for him. But there was something compelling in his face, and again, she found herself telling him about her conversation with Franco when he'd explained his motivation for telling Tank about Rowdy. He didn't say much during her retelling, but he listened.

She finished with, "Look, I don't want my relationship with Franco to come between you and him. I know…I know that you are pretty tight."

"It wouldn't," he answered a little too quickly. "When I met you, you weren't Franco's daughter, and most times, I'm not even thinking about it." He laughed again as he maneuvered her so that she was lying on top of him. "Except when you're pissed. Then, you kinda really look like him, and it's sorta freaky."

"Just don't piss me off."

At her playful glare, he flipped her over, so she was on her back, and he was lying on top of her, between her legs, his mouth on her scar.

"Come to my game," he said this time instead of asking a question.

He kissed up her neck, along the spiderweb, clearly trying to entice her. She giggled and immediately started at the unfamiliar, ludicrous sounds bubbling from her mouth. She tensed, and because of where he was, so intimately connected to her, he felt it.

"What?"

"Nothing," she said. She hoped to redirect him with her own question. "So, your game?"

Seeming to know her strategy, he shrugged and got back to attempting to tempt her. "Yes, my game. Saturday"—kiss, suck—"three thirty"—kiss, tongue in mouth—"quarterback"—kiss back down her neck—"undefeated."

Then, he stopped talking, so he could concentrate all of his effort on kissing her mouth, delving into the warm depths, stealing her breath while he surrendered his. Amber lost all thoughts of the conversation, everything instead focused on him, his mouth, his tongue, his body. She always seemed to want him, even when he was attempting to push her into something she wasn't sure she was prepared for. She pretty much wanted him all the time.

"Okay," she breathed as his mouth left hers to blaze a path down her neck.

Tank stopped, looking up at her. "Okay what?"

"Okay, I'll come to the game."

He smiled then, and she felt like she'd been punched in the gut. It lit him up from the inside.

"I'll drive up on Saturday for the day."

"Yeah, yeah," he murmured, "Saturday."

He continued to stare at her, catching her in some sort of happiness haze. She could feel his delight from her decision to go to the game. For the first time in a very long time, Amber took some pleasure in making someone else happy.

He ducked his head, kissing her stomach, turning his attention to commandeering her body, reading and penetrating her defenses, delivering the perfect play. As her mind relinquished all of its worries and hesitations about Tank, her body took him in, sheltering him in her depths, providing both the escape he needed and the home he craved.

When he was buried deep, he paused, focusing on her with his gaze. Bracing himself with one arm, he placed his left hand on her jaw, spanning almost the length of her scar. "Thank you," he said before he resumed movement.

She wasn't sure what the thank-you was for—the sex, agreeing to go to the game. But something in the way he looked at her told her all of the things she needed to know.

It was that moment, that exact moment, she gave up the fight and fell in love with him.

"I'm worried," Tank admitted, looking down at Amber, as she raised her eyes to meet his.

"That they'll find something to implicate you?" she asked, her face a mask of confusion.

He could tell she wasn't questioning him, but his worry somehow gave her a reason to doubt.

"I don't know," he answered truthfully. He really didn't know. He knew that he hadn't done anything wrong, but he felt disoriented, like there was something that he couldn't quite see, and it made him nervous.

Amber shifted away from him and sat up, dragging the sheet with her so that it covered her breasts. She noted his wandering eyes with a smile and said, "No way a serious discussion is happening if you keep looking at me like that." Adjusting the sheet, she leaned against the cinder-block wall, not even grimacing as her back hit the unforgiving cold stone.

He could tell she was waiting for him to continue, but her movement had both distracted and discouraged him from continuing. Looking into those brown fathomless pools of her eyes seemed to make it real and scarier. She studied him. Then, she reached out and grabbed his hand off the bed, pulling it toward her and cradling it in her hands, drawing lazy circles on the center of his palm with her thumb.

"I wish I could say that there's nothing to worry about. And it makes me sad for you. Because, I'm sure, somewhere in the back of your mind, you have to be thinking that this taints everything."

Startled, Tank looked away from her. She'd somehow plucked all of the worry from his scattered ideas and arranged them in an ugly picture that he'd been afraid to look at too closely. His eyes widened, and he was thankful that she couldn't really see what he was thinking. In that moment, it seemed to him that she would have no trouble piecing together his thoughts. He wasn't able to control the involuntary clenching of his fist though, and she caught it with her hands, smoothing it out, smoothing him out.

"Pure," he murmured.

"What?"

"I wanted it to be pure. Not like the spectacle that was signing day. Not like Richard's fall from grace, ya know? I wanted one thing to be completely clean. And, now, no matter what happens, it won't be. I have to share this with the NCAA and people picking it apart, questioning if I deserve the Heisman, the hype. I don't want that. They'll pick apart my character. I'll become another Heisman candidate who has some shit going on. I wanted it to be so different. And it won't be."

There, he thought, *I said it.*

Relief skittered through him after laying his worries out there for her to sort through.

Amber didn't say anything. She just continued holding his hand in hers. He still faced away from her, and suddenly, he wanted to see her—to look for censure or acceptance, he wasn't really sure. Sitting up abruptly, he pulled the sheet out of the holding place under her arms and scooped her up so that she was sitting across his lap, her right arm draped across his shoulders, her black hair hanging down in front of her neck, the smell permeating his nostrils. He loved having her close, her badass attitude disarmed but present, her nimble mind dissecting the maze of his words.

She looked directly at him.

"The shit thing about it is, I'm sure they're right. I am sure that he did something to jeopardize what I've worked so hard for." Tank shrugged, as if to indicate that he'd expected nothing less from Richard Howard. "It would be fitting, ya know?"

"Fitting?" Amber questioned, horror lacing her words.

"Fitting. I fucked him on signing day and haven't spoken to him since. And then I went about my business, acting like he wouldn't try to get me back for that."

"Tank," she said. He could hear the pity in that single word. "No one should go through life, expecting their father to get them back for something they did when they were eighteen."

"You don't know him," he snapped.

He expected her to pull some Amber attitude shit on him, but she merely said, "You're right."

"I let my guard down. And my mom tried to warn me; she knew something was happening, but I just…I didn't believe her. I didn't think I could be touched."

"Untouchable. Ego can make you feel that way," she said so softly.

If he hadn't been looking directly at her face and thus her mouth, he might have missed it.

He wanted to be mad at her statement, but it was so true that he bit back his sarcastic retort. She reached up to stroke his jaw, rubbing her thumb over his lip, when he paused to collect his thoughts. He wasn't sure if she was trying to coax him to speak or to rub out any incriminating thoughts.

"Yeah," he finally admitted, "ego."

Maybe she sensed his disappointment in her assessment, or perhaps she knew that he wanted to pull away, not wanting to be stripped bare. So, when she leaned forward and kissed him, he met her lips in a frantic search, pushing his tongue insistently into her mouth, wanting to take the words from her, to somehow draw them back in so that he could forget that he'd started them down this path. His hands gripped her hips and lifted her so that she could straddle his lap. Then, his hands moved up so that they cradled her face, as his kiss turned urgent, all of his confusion, anger, aggression wrapped up in the mating of their mouths. He felt sure the intensity of the kiss would scare her, but she met him thrust for thrust, barrage for barrage, giving him all the acceptance and understanding he was searching for, forgiving all of his shortcomings. He broke from the kiss and rested his forehead against hers, trying to gather his thoughts and control his desire.

"Tank," she breathed, the loss of breath still apparent in her speaking of his name.

He pulled back, so he could see her. Leaning forward, he dropped a quick, gentle kiss on her abraded mouth. "Yeah?"

"You know I believe in you, right? For me, it's pure. And it should be for you, too."

He continued to stare at her as her words washed over him, soothing him in a way that surprised him. He didn't say anything, and his hesitation allowed her to go on.

"And Franco and your mom, your coaches and teammates, they all believe in you. Sometimes, that has to be all that matters. Because there won't be a whole lot you can do to sway public opinion. It's already been dismantled and put back together in a way we can't control. But you? You deserve to enjoy this ride. Try to take comfort in the purity of our belief in you."

He wanted to respond. He meant to. Rather than speaking, he captured her mouth with his, smothering the need to put feelings he was just starting to understand into words.

THIRTY-SEVEN

Amber entered the stadium, both trepidation and excitement coursing through her. She hadn't fought Tank on this, like she had his invitation to breakfast with his mother, and she tried not to think about the reasons. She knew his mother would be here, and it was essentially the same thing that she'd tried to avoid a few weeks ago. But so much had seemed to change over the last forty-eight hours, and it stole her breath every time she let herself think about it.

She hadn't been to a live football game since before her accident. The reasons for her reticence abounded, but somehow, now, standing in the bowels of the stadium, they all faded away, making her giddy. When she'd first made her decision to come, she'd decided she'd go about it like a normal spectator, sitting in the stands among the masses. But, as the day had drawn near, she had shaken off her hesitation and called Franco. She'd counted on a fight, but after a brief pause, he'd agreed.

One of the minions met her at the gate with a pass and led her up to the box. When she walked in, Higgs greeted her with a huge smile, a hug, and a headset. She couldn't keep the smile off her face. Taking a seat next to her father's offensive coordinator and longtime friend, the excitement came back to Amber, and she silently thanked Tank for inviting her to the game.

As the team left the field, following their pregame warm-up, Amber caught Higgs's eye.

"Thanks, Higgs. I know you are usually in the locker room right now, and I just wanted you to know that I appreciate you staying in the box with me."

Higgs didn't say anything for a minute. He just took her in, looking her over, as if making sure she was really there. "Don't you ever scare us like that again," he said gruffly.

If it had been anyone else at any other time, she probably would have told him to fuck off or walked out or done something mean or stupid. But all of her darkness seemed to be giving way to the light of Tank. So, she smiled gently at the big bear of a man next to her and nodded. The moment held as they both seemed to assess each other.

"Let's see what your boy can do today," he said with a wink.

She noticed his reference and actually blushed—not something Tank's Sunshine would do. Then, she laughed. *Oh, Tank,* she thought, *what the fuck have you done to me?*

As the Bears took the field, Amber left all thoughts of introspection behind. Poised on the edge of the chair, the headset in place, she became someone who looked a lot like her old self. But, in the midst of the atmosphere, she didn't recognize it, nor would she have acknowledged it if she did. In the booth, denial wasn't an option.

Amber had watched Tank put himself through workouts; she'd watched him on television. But, now, here, in person, she was able to take in and appreciate his greatness. His physical presence alone would be attractive to the NFL. He looked right at home among the beasts named Marsh and Tilly. He demanded their attention and their respect. She saw Iman, whose confidence and swagger was a phenomenon in and of itself, look to Tank for reassurance and direction. He took to the field like a general commanding his troops, and he led every attack.

In the first quarter, his line faltered under a blitz from the defense. Everyone in the stadium watched with bated breath for the bone-crunching sack, but somehow, Tank evaded the defenders and hit Iman on a crossing route for a touchdown. In the second quarter, he ran for a fifty-yard touchdown off the option.

At halftime, he'd played a near perfect game, and Amber sat back in her chair, awe coursing through her. Pulling off her headset, she looked over at Higgs with a radiant smile affixed to her face.

"He's amazing," she murmured.

"He is," Higgs confirmed, laughing softly at her expression.

"I knew he was good, and I've watched him play, but holy shit, Higgs! How could he not win the Heisman?"

"I don't think there's any doubt that he'll win. No one is putting up numbers like him. And our record doesn't hurt either. We just need to keep playing like we're playing and keep our eye on the ball."

"Where's the stat sheet?" Amber asked, all business.

"It'll be here soon. I'm going to run down to the locker room. I'll be back shortly."

Higgs handed her the stats before he left her alone to wait for the second half to start. It was then, sitting there, perusing the stat sheet, that her conversation with Tank really sank in. All he wanted was for what he could do on the field to be his, to get the recognition he deserved for being the best at what he did.

It's not so much to ask, she thought.

He didn't take his gift for granted. He worked at it, honed it, made himself better every day. She understood his desire for the taint to be absent, but until this moment, with the nearly perfect stat sheet in front of her, did she understand the travesty of the controversy swirling around him. She meant what she'd said to him about it being clean for everyone around him, but it was no longer that way for him. It wasn't pity for him that took up the spaces in her heart; it was anger for the craziness of it all. He didn't just want to win the Heisman; he wanted everyone to think that he deserved it and that he had done it the right way.

Her ever-present worry about her reasons for wanting Tank Howard dissipated like a shimmery mirage on a hot summer day. He was so much more than a football player to her. The irony was not lost on her. She'd needed to be immersed in the game to realize that his appeal stretched far beyond the hundred yards of green. It wasn't the cleat-chaser in her that had fallen in love with the star quarterback; it was the broken, scarred woman who loved the optimistic, intelligent man-child who happened to play football. Every stroke of his fingers across the marred skin of her face had stripped away the anger and fear that she hoarded like one of those people who stacked and collected stuff until their lives were overrun.

When the Bears took the field in the second half, Amber watched Tank with a new perspective. While she marveled at his grace and skill, she saw him through the hopeful eyes of a woman in love.

Following the game, Tank left the field hyped up on the adrenaline of their victory. He could feel it coursing through his body—that natural high that so many tried to mimic by other means. He'd only faltered once when a reporter had touched on the taboo subject of the investigation, but Cy had been there, waiting in the wings, to swoop down and rescue him. Even that brief reminder of the shitstorm brewing around him couldn't take the edge off. He didn't need to see the stats or even see Franco's face to know that they'd played their asses off.

As he came through the tunnel on his way to the locker room, he saw Amber. In the space of a heartbeat, he took her in. Dressed in her ever-present jeans and a green T-shirt, a set of credentials hanging around her neck, she looked to him like every single dream he had about who he wanted to sink into. He didn't notice anyone or anything else once he'd spotted her.

Walking directly to her, he scooped her up with his free hand, wrapped it around her waist, and slammed his mouth down on hers with little finesse. The pads impeded him from feeling her body against his, but her hands came up to cradle his face as he plundered her mouth, immune to the people around them. Retreating from her mouth, he kept his forehead banked against hers.

"Hey, Sunshine," he murmured.

"Hey yourself."

He nipped at her lips again but held himself in check, suddenly aware that they weren't alone. "Glad you're here."

"Me, too," she said.

He could hear the smile in her voice, and that made him want her right then.

Instead, he cocked his eyebrow at her, gauging her sincerity. "Really?"

Then, because he couldn't help himself, he kissed her again. The murmurs around them started to penetrate his haze, and he reluctantly set her down, belatedly realizing that she hadn't answered him. Looking around at the people surrounding them, Tank tried not to sheepishly duck his head. He held on to her hand though, not ready to release her.

Franco was leaning back against the wall, waiting by the door to the locker room, not willing to enter without his team captain. His mom stood unmoving in the middle of the corridor, an incredulous statue frozen by Medusa's icy glare. Cy and Miss Magee hovered around, looking lost in the mini drama about to play out around them.

Tank felt Amber squeeze his hand before she broke away and walked toward her father.

"Good game, Coach," she said.

Here, he watched her hesitate. He could tell that the momentum had been carrying her forward and that she'd been about to embrace her father, but she'd caught herself. For some reason, a bit of the edge fell off of his excitement.

Still holding back, huh, Sunshine? he thought.

He watched in a sort of frustrated fascination as Franco struggled to keep in check. He could see his coach visibly still as Amber came back toward Tank. Knowing he had his own family issues to tackle, he grabbed Amber's hand and pulled her toward his mother. He knew he'd already breached family etiquette, and he prayed that his mother would make him pay and not her.

"Hey, Mama," he said, letting go of Amber's hand to lean down and place a kiss on her cheek. Looking to make his intentions excessively clear though, he stepped back to pull Amber into their small circle. "This is Amber."

"Son, great game," she said.

Tank had never forced his mother on anything. He'd never tried to get her to see an opposing point of view or to get her to allow him to do something that she'd already told him he couldn't. You just didn't defy Chantel. That was not how things worked. As he stood, waiting for her to acknowledge Amber, he thought of that—with some anxiety. He hadn't intended to introduce them here with the sweat of his game still clinging to his body, his stench taking over their small circle, in front of Amber's father and the staff. He'd meant to do it over breakfast with some clear warning.

As the silence lengthened, a different kind of sweat started to trickle in between his shoulder blades. He felt rather than saw someone move, and suddenly, Franco stepped into the fray.

"Hello, Chantel," he said, kissing her in the exact same spot that Tank had only seconds before.

This seemed to snap her out of her trance. "Franco, great game," she said, some life coming back into her face.

"I don't think you've met my daughter, Amber," he said, pulling her forward, letting Chantel know that whatever was going through her mind about the girl in front of her, she needed to rethink it.

Tank knew, at that moment, that Amber hadn't helped herself with her hesitant congratulations to her father. Had she embraced him, had Chantel seen her as something other than some groupie with her son, this meeting would have been much smoother.

Chantel finally looked at Amber and extended her hand.

Tank found himself mentally trying to prod Amber to get this right. He knew that, even if she didn't, he'd figure it out, but right now, he didn't need Sunshine breaking through.

Amber stepped forward to shake Chantel's hand. "Hi, Miss Jones."

Tank noticed she kept her left side prominent and her hair forward, hiding as much of her scar as she could.

"It's nice to meet you. I've heard a lot about you."

Chantel smiled—a real one, Tank noted. "I'd actually forgotten Franco had a daughter. I've heard quite a bit about you, too."

They made some small talk for a short time until Franco reminded them that he and Tank needed to get into the locker room. Tank said good-bye to his mother and then pulled Amber to the side, completely cognizant of the watchful stares around him.

"Meet you at the Bear's Den? Around eight?" He held both of her hands in his, trying like hell to make sure she was good.

She nodded, and he couldn't get a read.

When she didn't answer him, he leaned forward, bringing his mouth to hers. Kissing her chastely, he asked, "Are you good?"

Again with the nod, her big brown eyes locked on his.

"Can you speak, Sunshine?"

"Yeah, I'm good. Yeah, eight o'clock."

He let loose a visible sigh of relief, believing her. "Good." He moved around toward her ear. "But I don't want to stay out long.

I have other plans for you." Then, he kissed her on the spiderweb of her jaw, his spot. He started to walk away.

"Tank," she said.

He turned toward her, walking backward toward the open locker room door, waiting for what she had to say.

"Really."

And, just like that, the adrenaline rush was back.

Tank took longer than everyone else. During his family introductions, they'd all showered. So, when he left the locker room, he entered a deserted tunnel, twenty yards from where the bus waited outside the stadium. As he hurried out, his tie undone around his neck, his sport coat half-on and half-off, a man stepped into his path. Looking around, unsure of what was happening, Tank stopped.

"Tank Howard?" the man asked.

"Depends on who's asking." He didn't mean to be a dick per se, but he knew the bus containing his team was close by if he needed them.

"I'm John Barnett. Richard sent me."

THIRTY-EIGHT

N*ew. Shiny. Happy.*

Amber sat in her spot at the insanely busy Bear's Den, drifting in a haze of unfamiliar emotions. The day played over and over in her head, a montage of pleasant images that seemed to do battle with those suddenly rusty memories of the past couple of years. The only blight on the past twenty-four hours was her fumble with Franco and those tense minutes before meeting Chantel. Where, even yesterday, she would have found a way to blame anyone but herself, she could at least acknowledge that she'd blundered. She didn't think that she would soon forget the look on Franco's face when she'd aborted her hug. It wasn't horror or anger but rather a knowing resignation in his eyes that seemed to momentarily strangle her happiness.

Here, a number of hours later, she held her hands on the reins of two very different desires—to tell Tank how she felt about him and to fix things with Franco. Both scared the shit out of her.

The atmosphere at the bar didn't invite solitude or even thought. Players had been arriving in waves with groupies in their wake, a sea of green and silver. When Keira and Mark started to drown in orders, Amber jumped behind the bar to help them out. It was probably why she didn't notice the time. It wasn't until she saw the huge smile breaking across Keira's face that she even started to think about it. When Tilly and Iman arrived at nine, Amber could no longer contain the excitement. Her stomach rolled with the anticipation of seeing Tank.

But when Tilly's questioning glance met hers, she scurried out from behind the bar and pushed her way to him and Iman.

"Where is he?" she asked.

Tilly leaned down, so she could hear him. "I thought he was here with you."

They both pulled back to look at each other, concerned.

Amber couldn't help it when doubts settled in her gut. She leaned forward into Tilly's mass, and he lowered his head, so he could hear her. "Should I be worried?"

Tilly moved back, away from her, so she could see his face before he dived back down toward her ear. "Nah," he said, shaking his head, which she could feel in the confines of the space they were allotted. "You don't need to worry about that. I promise."

Her relief felt like a presence of its own in the bar. "Where is he?"

But Tilly merely shrugged, not with indifference but with uncertainty.

"I'm going to go look for him. Will you tell Keira?"

"I got you. Text me when you find him."

Then, Tilly scooped her up, hugging her tight. "We're good," he said before he released her.

She wasn't sure what she'd done to change his mind or win his approval, but all of a sudden, all that happiness flooded her system again, a wave that carried her out the door in search of its source.

Amber started in the direction of his apartment, but halfway there, she changed directions and headed toward the stadium instead. When she found the stadium empty and dark, she doubled back to his apartment. She wasn't sure what had happened between the magic in the tunnel outside of the locker room and the designated meeting time. The pessimist who lived in her head started planting uncertainty, like a bomb specialist might lay land mines—strategically placed so that one misstep could blow you away. It made Amber take each step toward Tank's apartment with careful consideration. Tilly's words and Tank's greeting earlier in the day seemed to fade in and out. She remembered the other time she'd shown up here, unannounced.

Reaching the front door, Amber paused, laying her forehead on it, her hand on the doorknob. Without knowing why, her heart stuttered and dropped. She almost walked away, but she moved forward, sensing that she must know what was happening behind that door. Without knocking, Amber turned the handle and stepped over the threshold.

Tank's beautiful half-naked form was sitting on the couch, his head lolled back, his knees spread, as some unknown girl's mouth was wrapped around him. She must have made some noise because Tank's translucent eyes found hers. But they didn't widen in surprise, nor did they cower in fear with his discovery. They simply took her in, raked her from head to toe. Maybe they filled with regret or even resignation, but she was so far gone that she couldn't process it.

Backing out of the door, Amber turned and flew down the steps. Her left foot missed the bottom rung, and she sprawled on the concrete, her hands bitten by the asphalt, her chin bearing the brunt, jarring her teeth with a resounding thud. Jumping up, as if she hadn't just face-planted, she moved as quickly as she could to her car. Before she opened the door though, the horrible scene flashed through her brain, ripped through her stomach, and pulled her to a halt as she vomited, almost projectile-like. When it passed, her shaking hand wiped across her mouth, attempting to put herself to right.

As she climbed into her car, the last couple of moments hit her again—her throbbing hand, her sore jaw, her rolling stomach. She'd been here before where her body seemed to operate on its own without heeding her head. And she waited for it because she knew it was coming, if she could just be patient.

Leaning her head back on the driver's seat headrest, closing her eyes, she willed her natural response. It was a pleasant sensation, allowing her to float through the bad without really feeling it. She'd mastered it in the hospital. It was an old friend who gave her comfort and peace, allowed her to move on, swimming instead of treading water. When it hit, it was almost orgasmic.

She was numb.

Sneaking in through the kitchen door of the Bear's Den, Amber grabbed the first aid kit and headed to the bathroom, keeping her head down and avoiding as many people as possible. She waited in line but when the biggest stall, with a sink and a mirror, presented itself, she barged in front and sequestered herself inside. Examining her face in the mirror, she almost groaned aloud. Her abraded chin swelled with ribbons of black and blue, making her resemble Humpty Dumpty.

Giving up on her face, she ran her hands under the water and washed off the dried blood, careful not to disturb the deeper cuts. Lubing them up with Neosporin, she slapped some Band-Aids on her hands. Rinsing out her mouth, which was bothering her more than anything else, she almost felt put back together. She glanced in the mirror, admiring the cursory overhaul, until she saw her eyes. Then, she realized she didn't look put together at all. Her haunted, lifeless eyes resembled the girl she'd been just a few weeks ago.

Dousing her face with cold water, she messed with her hair and headed out to the bar.

Thankful for the dimness of the Bear's Den, Amber picked her way through the celebrating football players, their groupies, and their fans, heading directly to Keira and the bar.

"I need Patrón," she demanded when Keira greeted her from behind the bar.

She recognized the questioning look in Keira's eyes but ignored it as Keira placed the glass in front of her. Throwing down the first shot, she immediately placed the empty shot glass in front of Keira for a refill. Amber smiled at her when she refilled the glass.

"Are you okay?" Keira asked as Amber threw back the second shot.

Slamming the shot glass on the bar, silently demanding a third, Amber merely nodded, looking Keira directly in the eyes. Keira shook her head but again filled the glass.

With the tequila burning through her system, Amber turned from the bar and moved directly toward the dance floor, looking for someone, anyone, to fill the quiet within her. Unfortunately, the bar was filled with most of the team, and they knew about her and Tank. Even though they respected him and most of them liked him, she knew there was always one, someone who hid their jealousy and spite under a veneer of general indifference. That was what she looked for as she stepped out onto the dance floor. It wouldn't be hard to find; she'd be able to see it because it was easy to pick out when it was leveled right at you.

And, just like that, one song in, someone took the bait. The junior cornerback, Tony Smith, put his hands on her hips and pulled her into him, her siren song working. Turning, she looped her arms around his neck and kissed him. It was nothing like having her mouth attached to Tank's, and she was so thankful for the numbness as Tony moved it through her, spreading it around, instead of desire. She kept her eyes closed, blocking out any lurkers, not wanting to actually meet anyone's glare.

She knew the moment it'd gotten out of hand. She could feel him pull her closer, could feel the length of him against her stomach. Part of her wanted to puke again, and part of her wanted to hold on, to keep pushing so that the detachment would stay. Then, suddenly, she was yanked backward, and she opened her eyes to see Tony being pulled back, too, in a direction opposite of her, rage masking his features.

"What the fuck, Iman?" Tony yelled, trying to extricate himself from Iman's grasp.

She watched in fascination until she realized that she was not touching the ground, and the arms around her weren't very gentle.

"Put me down," she insisted, the numb fading away. She wasn't completely sure who had her, only that he was big and strong, which made her resist the temptation to fight against him.

"What are you doing, Amber? You're gonna ruin this team."

Sagging with relief when she realized Tilly had her, she let him pull her through the bar and out the back door. Setting her down, he spun her around, so they were facing each other, both of them trying to contain their anger.

"What the hell is wrong with you?" he yelled at her, his voice booming in the darkness.

"Me? What's wrong with me?" she sputtered. "Are you fucking kidding me?"

"No! How in the hell could you hook up with Tony? What's the matter with you? Tank's gonna lose his shit."

"Ha! Don't you worry about Tank giving a shit about me. He doesn't fucking care about me."

"Are you kidding? He loves you." Tilly's rage was evident, but he seemed to heave a deep breath after the words had left his mouth. He visibly calmed, the rage from moments before seeping out of him. He took a step forward, imploring her. "Look, Amber, my boy is head over heels in love with you. He's gonna lose it when he finds out that you were hooking up with Tony. He's gonna fucking kill Tony. Do you know what that's gonna do to our team right now? Do you even care about that?"

"No!" she screamed at him. "I don't fucking care."

Tilly didn't respond to her hysterics. He merely watched her, and suddenly, silence stretched between them.

"What happened?" Tilly asked. His tone had changed completely from accusatory to conciliatory. Eyeing her warily, he reached out to squeeze her shoulder. "Tell me what happened."

She averted her gaze, no longer able to look him in the face, ashamed of what had happened, humiliated in a way that she couldn't share. Tilly's finger touched her chin gingerly, lifting it. He peered at it in the feeble light, inspecting the damage. Batting his hand away, Amber stepped back, needing the distance. But that drew attention to her hands, and suddenly, Tilly reached out to grab her wrists and flipped her hands over to inspect them.

"Amber, I know Tank. I know he wouldn't hurt you, but can you please tell me what happened? I'm starting to freak out here."

Afraid to meet his gaze, she looked down at her palms, still held in Tilly's hands. Now that his anger had dissipated, he was like a gentle giant, holding on to her, coaxing her to spill her secrets.

"I went to find him. I thought he was maybe at the stadium, but when he wasn't there, I went to your apartment. And…it's funny. I hesitated at the door because of what I'd walked into the last time I showed up unexpectedly, but this time, Tilly, it was so much worse."

Tilly shook his head, like he was preparing himself for denial.

"He was mostly naked, on your couch, with some girl giving him head."

"No fucking way. He wouldn't do that to you."

"Oh, he did, Tilly. And the shit part of it, what hurt the most—well, I guess there are two things. She had platinum-blonde hair, which speaks a lot for his preferences. And he looked right at me, Tilly, looked me dead in the eyes, and didn't say a word. Just let me take it in to do with whatever I wanted."

"I believe you, but I just don't believe it. He's in love with you. I know he is."

"Well then, he doesn't love right," she said simply.

"Then, what happened? Did you get into a fight?"

"No. I ran, missed the last step, and face-planted. My leg just doesn't allow me to be graceful."

"And then you came here to have your revenge?"

"Ah, Tilly, you know me so well," she responded, sarcasm lacing her words.

Tilly didn't say anything for a bit. He just moved to lean against the brick of the building, silent in the quiet night. "Something's wrong."

Amber turned to look at him. "What do you mean? I mean, I know shit's messed up, but that's not what you mean, is it?"

"No." He met her gaze fully. "I know that you can't believe me right now, but Tank loves you. I don't mean kinda sorta likes you. I mean, soul-deep, love-of-his-life kind of love. Something happened tonight that pushed him away. It's the only explanation."

"Tilly, Tank might love sex, and he might love women—apparently, women with platinum-colored hair—but he doesn't love me. There's no way he slid his dick into someone else's mouth just because 'something' happened," she said, throwing up the air quotes.

"Why not? You slid your tongue into his teammate's mouth!" he said. His tone blazed through her, all sense of sympathy absent. He took a deep breath. "Think about it. Think about when you left the bar earlier tonight. You felt it. You know I'm right."

She felt the denial all the way to her soul, but she had to admit to herself that she was sort of captivated by Tilly's faith in his friend's feelings for her.

"Come on," Amber said.

"Where are we going?" Tilly asked.

"If you really think something's wrong, then we need to talk to Coach."

THIRTY-NINE

Tank was in his bed when he heard the front door open. His eyes popped open at the sound of the footsteps walking through his apartment. Surveying his room, relieved to find it empty, all evidence of his earlier encounter was absent, except for the ugly images emblazoned on his brain.

When the knock sounded on his door, he rolled toward the side of his bed, letting his feet hit the floor while he pulled the sheet over his lap. He couldn't contain his surprise when the door opened to admit Franco and Tilly. He watched Franco survey the room.

"Get dressed," he snapped before the door closed, leaving Tank alone, apprehension filling him.

He couldn't stop the replay of his night. It ran continually. His conversation after the game, his realization on the bus, his deliberate hook-up, Amber's face when she had seen him, his future fractured, his dream shattered—it was all right there in front of him. Slowly, he stood up, his soreness from the game setting in, leaving him achy and lethargic. Or maybe it was the mess of his life that made him feel like that. Whatever it was, he moved as if through water, grabbing a pair of sweatpants and a T-shirt. As his hand reached for the doorknob, he paused, leaning his head against the doorjamb, praying for something that he couldn't quite name.

Walking into the living room, he was surprised by the people waiting for him—Tilly and Franco, Miss Magee, Coach Higgs and Amber. Franco was in the recliner, and Miss Magee was on the couch. Amber, Tilly, and Higgs were leaning against the counter in the kitchen. He couldn't look in Amber's direction, but that she was there, at the scene of his crime, fucked with his sanity. His stomach seized up, leaving him nauseous. He didn't look anyone in the eyes but Franco.

"Take a seat," his coach barked.

Tank sprawled on the couch, next to Miss Magee, his only option. It didn't escape his notice that, a few hours ago, he'd sat, naked, in this same spot, trying to escape his reality in the mouth of someone who now left him feeling greasy and worthless.

Franco leaned forward in his chair, making sure he had Tank's every attention, before he said, "Explain to me why your roommate and your girlfriend showed up at my house at one o'clock in the morning, worried about you."

Without any control of his actions, Tank shot a withering glance in the direction of Tilly. "I have no idea," he managed to say with an innocence and nonchalance he didn't feel. "Too much to drink?" he quipped.

In his peripheral, he noticed Tilly shake his head, obviously disgusted with him. He knew right then that Amber had told Tilly what she had seen. His shame multiplied. He just barely managed to keep his eyes from going wide as he contemplated the idea that Franco also knew. Trying to focus, he noticed that some time had elapsed since he'd answered Franco. Shifting his gaze back to his coach, he found Franco looking at him with a puzzled expression on his face.

"Lift up your shirt," Franco said.

"What?" he asked, indignation blatant in his tone.

"Just do it."

Tank, not sure of where Franco was going, pulled his shirt over his head and cast it away in anger.

Franco studied him. "Where'd you get those bruises?"

Tank was taken aback. He looked down and noticed the bruises riddling his left side. This explanation was easy. "I just got done playing a game," he scoffed, confident in his answer.

Franco looked disappointed. Shaking his head, he said, "Funny, Higgs and I just watched the film. No one even came close to touching you during the game. No way you got those on the field."

Tank remained silent.

"All the people in this room have got your back. They left their houses in the middle of the night because they were worried about you. Are you going to blow that? You going to shut us all out?"

Tank couldn't help himself. He looked around the room, meeting their worried faces—Franco, Higgs, Miss Magee, Tilly, Amber. He stopped at Amber. She wouldn't look at him, which was appropriate. But he noticed the bruise on her chin, and this time, he couldn't control the widening of his eyes, the questions in his face when he looked back at Tilly. Tilly merely shrugged while he narrowed his eyes and crossed his arms over his chest, here supporting Tank but obviously pissed off at him.

Part of him wanted to answer. He knew he was in over his head, drowning really in the morass of lies, money, and deception caused by the man who was somehow his father. But admitting everything to a roomful of people who, with the exception of Miss Magee, made him who he was seemed much harder than trying to navigate it on his own. Leaning forward, he rested his elbows on his knees, clasping his fingers together, looking back to Franco.

"There's nothing going on. I don't know what Tilly's thinking." He deliberately didn't mention Amber, a purposeful omission.

He saw her move, and he hated himself for what he knew was necessary. He'd preferred to put the hate in her eyes in his own way. He couldn't give his father that, too. He watched her grab Tilly's hand, and then she made her way out of the kitchen, through the apartment, and out the door. He watched Franco's eyes follow her. Then, Franco looked at Tilly, and Tilly followed Amber out too.

"All right," Franco said as he leaned back in the chair, "stop fucking around, and tell me what happened with John Barnett."

This time, Tank couldn't contain his surprise. All pretenses were stripped away. He wanted to pretend like he didn't know what Franco was talking about, but he suddenly realized that Franco wouldn't buy it.

Before he could contemplate it, he said, "How do you know about John Barnett?"

"Miss Magee saw him when he came into the stadium. He's one of those people who has been flagged. When he's around, people know it."

Tank merely shrugged, pretending like he actually already knew this.

Franco leaned forward again. "Do you want to know why people know who John Barnett is?"

Tank could sense a trap, but he couldn't help but step into it. "Nah."

Franco nodded his head, like adults did when they knew you were full of shit. "John Barnett is often credited as the man who destroyed Richard Howard's NFL career."

Franco watched Tank with a combination of pity and anger. The pity was easy. No matter what Tank had done, he couldn't escape the stain of Richard's crimes. And, for that, Franco couldn't help but feel sorry for him, even though Tank had been blessed as one of the most gifted athletes he'd ever seen. The anger was harder to deal with. Tank had always had the cockiness that came with his ability, his looks, his attitude. But his nonchalance tonight coupled with his blatant refusal to acknowledge Amber ate away at Franco's inherent respect and liking of the kid.

Facing Tank now, Franco merely wanted to wipe the smug off of his face. His statement about Barnett had done that. There was no ego when Tank raised his eyes to Franco. Again, with the pity because he knew that Richard had always been the best way to manage Tank's ego.

"Look, Tank, I don't know for certain that you had any interaction with Barnett tonight. But I am guessing from the look on your face that you did. All this agent stuff is starting to make sense to me. We want to be able to help you. I'm not sure what that will look like, but until you talk to me, my hands are tied."

Franco had always been one of the athletes who had the itch to move around, his kinesthetic energy moving through him and putting him constantly in motion. Tank was never like that. Even now, even knowing that his mind must be racing with this latest disaster, Tank was immobile. If you didn't know him, you might have thought he was indifferent. Franco knew better, but he could almost feel Molly's frustration.

When Tank started to talk, Franco breathed a sigh of relief.

"I came out of the locker room after everyone. And I was thinking of other things"—he looked up at Franco, telling him with a hopeful mind that he had been thinking about Amber—"so I wasn't paying attention. But when he came up on me, I looked to the bus—mapping the distance, ya know. It wasn't that far. I thought if there was any trouble, I could yell or take off, and I'd be fine. He told me his name and said that Richard had sent him."

Tank's head dropped down, hanging loosely between his shoulders, his arms resting on his knees. When he looked up, his misery was etched starkly on his face. Franco was really the only one who could see it, and he knew that it was Tank's intention to keep it that way.

"I should have taken off running for the bus right then. I should have known better." Tank paused to collect his thoughts.

"But I didn't move, Franco. I just stood there. Out of nowhere, two guys came up behind me, each grabbing an arm. One of them put his hand over my mouth. In my head, I was thinking someone was going to notice that I was taking a long time, that they were going to walk out and see these motherfuckers, and this would all be over. But no one came. That dude, Barnett, he started reciting figures. I had no idea what he was talking about. All I could think was, *I'm being held by Rain Man.*"

He paused to laugh and shook his head at the visual. Franco felt his stomach tighten at the fear that Tank must have been feeling.

"He went into this explanation about how all the alimony my mom had received over the years had come directly from him, an agent, how it'd been funneled through Richard, and how he owned me. And he said it was time for me to pay him back, that he was ready to take his cut. You know, right?"

Franco nodded his head, hating that he knew, hating the position Tank was now in.

"The bruises?" Franco asked even though he knew this answer, too.

"Exclamation points?" Tank quipped.

Franco looked to Molly, hoping she could offer some salvation.

"Is it as bad as I think it is, Miss Magee?" Tank asked, turning away from Franco for the first time.

"I'm not sure, Tank. I need to do some research, search precedent."

When Tank looked away from her, she met Franco's questioning eyes, shrugging her shoulders, effectively telling Franco that she wasn't holding anything back, which he appreciated.

"Tank, regardless of where this goes from here, we are going to have to declare you ineligible and request reinstatement. Obviously, you haven't done anything wrong, and your mother hasn't done anything wrong. But it's not so very cut and dry anymore."

Tank's head dropped again. When he looked up, Franco almost flinched at the bleakness he saw in Tank's eyes.

"I can't play next weekend, can I?"

Molly shook her head. "I'm not sure. I wouldn't count on it."

"Fuck!"

"Tank, how do you want this to end?" Franco asked.

"What do you mean?"

"I mean, where do you see yourself next year?"

"Here, Coach. I want to be here."

"Humor me for a minute. You are a first-round draft pick right now, potentially the number one pick because Detroit, Miami, Cleveland, and Denver all need a quarterback. Have you thought about declaring for the draft? You can have your pick of agents. No one has to know that's what you are planning. We can interview them on the low. Then, you can pick one and declare for the draft. It takes this guy's power if he doesn't have that hanging over you. The NCAA, college, the rules are restrictive. There are no recruiting rules in the NFL. He wouldn't be able to mess with your eligibility." Franco took a deep breath. "I know you don't want to do that, and God knows I don't want to lose you, but it might be the best thing for you in the long run."

Tank merely shook his head.

"Look, it's really late. Let's take some time to think this over. We'll regroup tomorrow." He looked at Molly and Higgs, who both nodded.

Higgs pushed himself away from the counter, and Molly stood up. Together, they headed toward the door.

"I'll catch up with you," Franco said.

Sitting for a moment, collecting his thoughts, Franco felt the weight of Tank's fears. He'd done all he could as Tank's mentor and coach tonight. But he hadn't quite fulfilled all of his responsibilities. He stood slowly, drawing Tank's attention to him. He didn't move any closer for fear of the retribution for the hurt Tank caused Amber; it thumped through his tired body.

"I don't know what happened with my daughter. And I swore to myself that I wouldn't go down this road with the two of you. But I trusted you with her."

Tank looked away from him, not meeting his eyes. Franco's anger notched up, and he had to hold the dad in him in check.

"Something you did hurt her, and you'd better fucking fix it."

FORTY

He wasn't ready to fix anything with Amber. That was Tank's first thought when he woke up on Sunday morning, the burden of his decisions pressing heavily on his chest, choking him with their implications. Having to think about the mess he'd orchestrated threatened to pull him under. Although it proved more difficult than he thought, Tank forced any thoughts of her from his mind, so he could focus on his impending career. This was the resolution he came to before he rolled out of bed, heading to the shower. It lasted about fifteen minutes.

When Tank walked out of his room, on his way to the stadium, Tilly sat in his chair, shoveling cereal into his mouth.

"What up?" Tank said, walking toward the fridge.

When Tilly remained silent, Tank pulled open the door of the refrigerator with more force than necessary, rattling the bottles inside. Grabbing some juice, he slammed it shut and leaned heavily against the countertop. "You're not talking to me now?"

Nothing.

"What the fuck, Til? Two weeks ago, you didn't even like this girl."

At that, Tilly cut his eyes at Tank, casting out a glare that made Tank's eyes widen. Tank waited, but Tilly just went back to eating his cereal. He stayed trancelike, watching Tilly finish his breakfast, stuck in a weird limbo. Tilly stood up when he finished, making his way to the kitchen, and Tank felt the need to pull back from his relaxed lean, like he needed to be ready. Tilly noticed his movement and smiled, telling Tank that he knew he'd intimidated him.

Dropping his bowl in the sink, he turned toward Tank and crossed his arms over his massive chest. It looked like he was going to say something. Then, he smiled wide and shook his head, his gold teeth catching the sun, casting little streams of light.

Laughing, Tilly said, "I hope you're ready for the shit you just stirred up."

Just like that, he walked right past Tank, grabbed his bag from the floor, and left the apartment. Tank merely shook his head. He wasn't ready to think about what had led him down the skank path the night before. But Tilly's words shattered his earlier resolve. He'd done a good job of blocking out the look on Amber's face when she'd walked in on him. Even when she'd stood in his apartment, having called in the cavalry, he'd shut her out. Right now, he wished he'd blocked her out the night she'd fallen at his feet. She didn't need to be involved in this mess. He'd already been warned, and as much as it killed him, he needed distance.

As he walked out the door though, with Tilly's words ringing in his ears, Amber's governing mantra beat a tattoo in his head and heart. *One-for-one, one-for-one, one-for-one.* With a sense of complete horror, Tank braced himself. If he'd been with someone else, she'd responded in kind.

Impossibly, his day got worse when Iman met him outside the doors to the training room.

"You don't need to go in the training room, man," Iman said.

When Tank looked at him, Iman shuffled his feet and looked away.

"You don't know, do you?" he asked.

Maybe, Tank thought, *I haven't given Iman enough credit.*

Dropping his bag, Tank leaned back on the brick wall, waiting for Iman to divulge the secret that he just couldn't keep to himself. Tank didn't even have to nudge him.

Looking up and away from Tank, Iman mumbled to himself, "Why didn't Tilly spill this shit?"

Reluctantly, Tank smiled. Out of nowhere, he thought he would miss Iman next year and felt the loss of not being here to help him be a better player. The errant thought caught him unaware. It was with a kind of bilious resignation that Tank knew how this was all going to play out, and he felt sick to his stomach.

"Tilly didn't tell me."

Iman was trying to puzzle that out. Tank could see his brain racing behind the almost black eyes. Tank knew, without Iman saying a word, exactly what was running through the freshman's mind. *Why wouldn't Tilly tell him? Maybe I'm not supposed to tell him. But I can't let Tank just walk into this without knowing, so I have to tell him.*

Again, Tank smiled.

"Smitty was all up on your girl last night," he said quickly, as if the quicker he said it, the less hurtful it would be.

And even though Tank thought he'd prepared himself for this, thought he knew what she had done, the truth felt like a dagger to his heart. He knew he was a hypocrite, knew he was the one who had started this volley, knew he could only blame himself, but the thought of anyone's mouth on her, their hands moving over her curves, someone else wanting to taste her, it made him want to puke. He couldn't even play it off in front of Iman because he saw the freshman move toward him, about to grab him, as if he'd staggered.

"I ain't gonna lie, man. She didn't seem too bothered by it. After Tilly and I broke it up, she and Tilly had it out."

Tank's eyes narrowed. "You broke it up?"

"Yeah, man. Tilly grabbed Sunny, and I grabbed Smitty. Then, she went batshit crazy, and Tilly had to take her outside."

Tank almost smiled at Iman's nickname for her, but then the reality of the scene played out in his mind, and he forgot all about being amused at the nickname.

"Ya a'ight, man?"

Tank thought he might have nodded because Iman kept talking.

"Where were ya, bro? You never showed up. Sunny went to go find you but came back alone. Then…ya know."

"Yeah, man."

"A'ight. Oh, and Coach is looking for you."

Tank glanced at his watch. "Yeah, I'm coming."

With an image of Amber wrapped around Smitty, Tank made his way upstairs for the strategy meeting. He wasn't sure what Franco could have come up with in the nine hours since Tank had last seen him, but he hoped that it was something brilliant, something that could make all of this seem like a distant nightmare that he would be unable to remember in the morning.

Three forty-five. Clockwork. Precision. Routine.

Franco's truck pulled up. Amber got in. They exchanged polite greetings, and then they each got lost in their own thoughts. She welcomed the silence.

Twenty-four hours ago, Amber had been awash in feelings of love and happiness and hope. Now, her thoughts lingered in a borderless desert, deprived of water and escape, just the reality of the relentless sun beating down on her with harsh images of a naked man and an unknown woman. No matter what she'd tried today, the image remained the focal point of her brain, much like a fluorescent light lingering long after you'd stopped looking at it.

She didn't know what had gone down with Tank after she and Tilly had vacated the apartment. They'd gone back to the Bear's Den and then spent the night at Keira's. She wanted so badly to know what had happened, but Franco was a vault when it came down to it. She probably wouldn't be able to get anything out of him even if she could bring herself to ask, which she couldn't because of her major bobble yesterday after the game. When that memory crept in, she felt her cheeks flush with the heat of embarrassment over her behavior. Sometimes, she could really be a horrible person, like when she'd lured that boy last night—another not-so-shining moment.

Maybe I'm meant only for destruction, she thought.

"You did the right thing last night," Franco said suddenly, startling her.

She turned toward him, meeting his eyes as he looked away from the road toward her. She shrugged because she wasn't really sure what to say.

"Was it your call? You knew something had gone down?"

She wanted to pretend to know what he was talking about so that he would share his information with her. Maybe if he thought Tank had told her, then he'd let her in.

But, when she responded, there was only raw truth in her voice, "No. It was Tilly actually. He knew something was off."

"Did he tell you what had made him think that?"

She wanted to answer. She wanted to rage and spill the truth about his golden boy, to tell him that he'd hooked up with someone else and that Tilly had found that odd. *But how did you say that to your father?*

"I think…I think it was something to do with me."

Franco nodded his head, and his grip on the steering wheel tightened so that she saw the color in his knuckles fade to white.

"He's in some bad shit, Amber. I don't know if that makes you feel better, but knowing what I know…"

He paused, and she could tell that he wanted to say something but was afraid of the way she would take it.

"Knowing what you know, you're not surprised?" she asked, bailing him out.

"Knowing what I know, I'm not surprised that he did something stupid."

She made some scoffing noise in the back of her throat, and she thought she could see Franco struggle with a grin.

"Are you defending him?"

"Absolutely not." His answer was quick, and she believed him. "Look, things are going to get bad here. Really unreal."

At his description, Amber's confusion played across her face.

"His hand is being forced; his plans are being ruined. This next week is going to be really hard for all of us with things we have to do that none of us want to do." He looked over at her, gauging her reaction, looking for her understanding. "Do you understand what I'm trying to tell you?"

"That I shouldn't take everything at face value."

He nodded his head, looking back to the road so that she couldn't really see his face.

"Where does that leave you, Franco?" she asked.

"Nowhere different. Right where I've always been. Trying to be a good mentor and a good father. I failed at one. I want to try and get the other right."

"You never failed me. I failed myself, and I just couldn't face you knowing that you couldn't be proud of me." It flew from her mouth without any thought or censor. And it felt like a magnificent weight had been lifted from her.

He didn't respond. But, when he came to a red light, he turned in his seat toward her. "I can't recall a day since I was sixteen and I held you that I haven't been proud of you."

He turned away from her as the light changed, and silence descended again. As they pulled up to Nona's house, Amber reached out for Franco, catching his forearm.

"Thank you for yesterday, for coming to my rescue. I didn't really deserve it, but…I just really appreciate it."

He shrugged a bit. She saw him hesitate, like he was stuck between two decisions. Then, he reached over with his left hand, placing it on her cheek. He moved forward and kissed her on the forehead. He quickly pulled back, looking like he feared a strike from a snake. Then, he turned from her and stepped out of the truck.

It took her a couple of seconds before she followed. Once again, she was reminded of the damage she'd done over the course of the last few years. If Franco had given her a chance, she would have leaned into him.

FORTY-ONE

It was as if someone had pressed the pause button. For a week after that fateful Saturday night, nothing had changed, nothing new had happened, everything had seemed to remain status quo. Amber never spoke to Tank, and since they didn't run in the same circles unless they wanted to, she didn't see him, hear him, or even speak his name.

She was back to numb, and she reveled in it.

Except with Franco. If she could chalk it up to one thing, she would have said that Franco smoothing her way with Chantel Jones had opened her up in a way that allowed him to get closer to her. In seemingly small increments, Amber worked on her relationship with her father. The embrace in the car was step one in that it'd punctuated how closed off she'd made herself to him over the last few years. His immediate withdrawal from her after his embrace had felt like a knife cutting through her hard exterior. Her father was afraid to touch her, and that realization hurt her in a surprising way.

If life was all about timing, her time to forgive her father was now upon her. So, she allowed herself to follow her impulses on the small things with him. When she came home from work and knew her father wouldn't be far behind, she would find herself waiting up to talk to him. They'd discuss Xs and Os, they'd gossip about her aunts and uncles, and they'd laugh. It was sweet and poignant, and it started to heal her in ways that she hadn't realized she needed.

They never talked about Tank, and she rarely allowed herself to think about him. When the images of him flashed across her mind, she would block them out. She felt she'd dodged a bullet. Things wouldn't have ever worked out for them, and now, with some distance, she could appreciate that. The unwelcome memory of how she'd felt that day of the game was locked away.

When she walked into the Bear's Den that Monday night for work, she felt pretty good, considering where she'd been a week ago. *Monday Night Football* helped keep the Bear's Den hopping, and Amber looked forward to being busy. The Monday regulars were KSU Bears fans first, so it wasn't surprising to find them talking about their football team, even with the thirty-two flat screens ablaze with professional football. It was in the din of the game that Amber heard the news.

"Shame, isn't it? Think this will hurt his chances of winning the Heisman?"

She couldn't help but hear the discussions. Finally, after catching snippets of the conversations, she leaned on her forearms and asked the question, "What is everyone all freaked out about?"

"You haven't heard? And you call yourself a Bears fan." That was Al Stevenson, a faithful Bear.

"Yeah, yeah," she said, playfully swatting his arm. "So, what's going on?"

Al shook his head, dropping his eyes. "Tank Howard got hurt at practice today. Concussion. Can't play on Saturday in the championship game."

Amber felt her jaw slacken and hang open. She couldn't even muster up a response.

Al took pity on her and reached out to pat her hand. "Shame, isn't it?"

Pulling herself together, Amber managed to ask, "Does anyone know what happened?"

"Well, you know Lauren Hayworth works as an ER nurse. She was there when the ambulance arrived with the trainer and Tank. Said he was conscious but that they didn't want to take any chances with him. Coach Franco was there, too. He's out. Tank is, I mean." Al took a sip of his beer, drowning his sorrows. "I know Franco is a good coach, but I don't know if we can win without Tank."

Amber stopped listening. Grabbing a towel, she started wiping down the bar, so she looked too busy to talk to anyone. *Why hadn't anyone told her?* Keira hadn't said anything. Reaching in her back pocket, she pulled out the old-school flip phone. There weren't any text messages.

She'd been Tank-free for one week and one day. And, with just the mention of him and the thought of him hurt, there she was again. But she wanted to fight it, and she did. Jumping back into interacting with her customers, the constant work kept her desires at bay.

Until she got home.

Sitting in Franco's favorite chair, with her feet curled up under her, Amber waited for her father to walk through the door. She figured it would be late because they were probably working through their plan B for the game, getting their backup quarterback up to speed. She must have dozed because she didn't hear Franco pull up, open the door, or walk into the house. When he nudged her leg, she came awake instantly.

"Is he okay?" she asked without any preamble.

She noticed Franco look her over, study her, try to pry into her heart and mind with that look he'd leveled at many a player over the years.

He cocked his head a little and then nodded. "He's okay."

"Out for the championship?"

"Yeah."

"Can you still win?"

Franco flashed that cocky smile of his that, back in the day, she'd shared. "Yeah."

"Heisman?" she asked, not really sure why she cared.

Franco shrugged. He must have realized that this wouldn't be a quick conversation because he dropped his bag by his feet and found his way into the chair across from her. "I don't know. He's got to be so far ahead in voting that it shouldn't matter, but no one knows for sure."

She merely nodded. She felt the relief flood her body, like her worries had been held at bay by a dam of uncertainty. She saw Franco's eyes get wide, and he was suddenly out of his chair. It dawned on her that he was worried, scared even. It wasn't until he pulled her out of her chair and into his arms that she realized she was crying. And when she was protectively wrapped up in her father's arms, the dam shattered, and she sobbed. She cried for Tank, she cried for the splintered pieces of their relationship, she cried for the hell she'd put her father through. She cried for the ruined burning skin on her neck and face and the girl she'd been.

Franco held her the whole time, saying nothing. When the hiccupping sobs stopped and her tired body sagged against him, he picked her up and took her to her room. He literally tucked her in bed. When he smoothed the hair back from her forehead and placed a kiss there, she reached for his hand and squeezed. He ran his hand across her hair again and walked toward the door.

I owe him, she thought as he flicked the switch to turn off the light.

"Franco?" she said just loud enough for him to hear and turn back.

"Yeah?"

"I love him."

"I know, baby."

It had been a shitty day, a shitty eight days. There was no end in sight. As Tank left Miss Magee's office on his way to Franco's, he found himself wondering if there would be a day soon when he would wake up and the ever-present pit in his stomach would be absent. It was all about to come to a head, so he hoped it would be soon. He had to go see Franco, but it was becoming harder and harder to be around his coach. He wasn't sure what had happened. He'd gotten to know Amber better and could suddenly see all the similar mannerisms between her and Franco and he missed her so much that being around her father made him aware that he couldn't be around her.

Franco hadn't said another word to him after the warning he'd leveled at Tank's apartment that fateful night. Perhaps now, with some distance, Franco could see what Tank had seen, what had driven Tank to make the decisions he'd made. Whatever it was, the thread of Amber had snapped.

He'd just gotten his draft prediction back. No surprise it was first round. Just like Franco had promised, they were keeping it all on the down-low. With him out for the championship game, they were trying to clean up some things, like his ineligibility and reinstatement.

He'd reviewed his letter for the Student Athlete Reinstatement Committee with Miss Magee. He'd signed his Buckley Amendment. Tonight, once again, he'd be the lead story on ESPN. But, this time, he'd resigned himself to what was about to happen. It was for the best. He would declare for the draft. The die had been cast.

There would be no championship game, no bowl game. They couldn't run the risk that Richard Howard and John Barnett wouldn't try to bring everyone down. It had been Tank's suggestion really. He needed to stop playing to protect his team, his university, his coach. It was the honest thing to do. In exchange, he'd pick a good agent, he'd enter the draft, and he'd move on.

He would run the scenarios every night before he fell asleep. And the verdict was always the same. It got easier every night. So far, with the news of his concussion over twenty-four hours old, it still appeared that he was on the Heisman ballots, the body of his work speaking for him.

"Tank," Franco said, when Tank arrived at his office, "everything handled?"

Tank found his way to the chair in front of Franco's desk.

"Signed, sealed, emailed," he responded as he sat.

"How ya feeling?"

Tank seemed paralyzed in that moment. He knew what he'd talked himself into feeling, much like how he'd talked himself into the haphazard blow job. But, now, with Franco's gaze leveled at him, he couldn't put his pat answer into words. He shrugged.

Franco sat down next to him. "I can tell you how I feel," he said. At Tank's nod, Franco began, "I feel like I've lost my way."

Tank's inward reflection stopped, and he looked, really looked, at his coach.

"I have no doubt that we did the right thing," he said reassuringly. "Getting you off the field, declaring for the draft. Barnett has no hold over you in the NFL. If this situation were put in front of me one thousand times, I'd do it the same way. I just hate that I have to do it. Football should be pure."

Tank smiled at his choice of words.

"Pure. I get that, Coach."

"I just want to coach players, win a few games." He winked at Tank. "I don't want to have to be creative and sneaky to do what's best for a player who just wants to play the game. So, anything you're feeling, it's all good. You might not be able to see it right now, but this will all work out in the end. It's not going to be the way we envisioned it, but it will be okay."

"I wanted one more. One more with you and Iman. I wanted one more year to be here. And I'm not going to have that."

"No. But life has a funny way of working out. You never know. You might be throwing the ball to Iman in two years, making a hell of a lot of money to do it."

"True," Tank said with the first genuine smile he'd felt in days.

"Get some sleep tonight. You're going to need it over the next couple of weeks."

Tank got up to leave. He almost made it to the door, but something stopped him. He wasn't sure if he'd regret bringing Amber up, but he couldn't help himself.

"Coach?"

Franco looked up. "Yeah?"

"Will you…" He paused, not knowing how to go forward. "Can you tell her that I'm sorry?"

Tank held Franco's gaze, noting the quick flare of anger. They both stood stock-still, Franco judging and Tank allowing him to.

Franco slowly shook his head. "No, Tank."

"I understand," he said. And he did. Truly. He just hated it. He turned and started out the door.

"She loves you," Franco said quietly.

Tank didn't turn around. He stood, his hand on the doorknob, his body rigid. It dawned on him that he did know, just like he knew that he loved her. That was why he had to walk away.

FORTY-TWO

Tank was here. In New York City. In December. Getting ready to make his way to the New York Athletic Club. It seemed surreal.

He'd always wondered what people felt like when they achieved something they'd dreamed about forever. Like an actor who won an Oscar or an Olympian who won a gold medal. *Was it a sort of self-righteousness? I've worked hard for this my whole life, and I deserve to have this honor.* Was it a complete shock? *Oh my goodness! I have worked so hard for this, but I never, ever thought I would be able to achieve this.* Was it thankfulness? *I am so thankful that I have been able to achieve this great honor.* Was it a combination?

He imagined that it took some ego for anyone to be recognized at the top of their game. You had to believe wholeheartedly to propel yourself to those heights. It was hard work and luck and probably a whole lot of arrogance. He smiled a little and gave a silent shout-out to Sunshine because he imagined she would vote for ego above all.

As he pulled on his suit jacket and made his way to the lobby, he acknowledged to himself that he had thought he'd share this night with Amber. Even over the last couple of weeks, he had some silly vision that she'd show up with Franco, and they'd all walk in together. But he knew that wasn't possible. He'd made sure of it. He was surrounded by good people though, people who'd supported him for a long time. Franco, his mother, Coach Hayes from his high school, Higgs. Steele, Tilly, Iman, and Marsh had all FaceTimed him earlier. They were all together to watch him on television.

He wasn't nervous at all. His concussion and subsequent absence from the conference championship game had given other hopefuls a leg up, just like Franco thought. He had no expectations of winning, and he thanked God for that. He didn't deserve it. It wasn't pure. He and Franco had discussed it at length. Tank had wanted to withdrawal his name. But, in the end, they'd felt like he'd had enough controversy attached to his name, so they'd just left it alone.

Even though Richard had played in the NFL, Tank hadn't been a part of his life, so he'd never been around the football scene. Again, he found himself thinking that Amber would love this and would know exactly how to handle herself. But he found himself a little star struck as he met the past Heisman winners and the past and present NFL greats. It was funny though. The commonality of football, talent, and recognition acted as an equalizer. They assumed he belonged there with them because of who he was and what he'd done so far. It was a good ole boys' network at its core, and it was impossible to feel like he didn't belong. After the awe wore off though, he found himself mingling just fine.

It went by quickly, and soon, they were finding their seats, the ceremony about to begin. As Tank sat down and they began to go through each player, he found himself thinking about everything that had gone down in the last month. The memory that played out in front of him over and over wasn't John Barnett or all the meetings or any of the bad. It was that moment after his game when he'd grabbed Amber in the tunnel, and he'd realized that he was in love with her.

He was almost home free. Just a couple of weeks, he'd be free of all the complications around him. Then, maybe, just maybe, he could convince her to take a chance on him again. He looked up to find his mother watching him. When she reached over and grabbed his hand, he knew that she somehow understood what was going through his head. He didn't know how he knew that, but he did.

Then, she squeezed his hand, and he shifted his focus back to what was happening around him. It was the moment, that moment, when they would announce the winner. Right now, the moment before the announcement, he could admit to himself that he wanted it. He'd wanted to win it for as long as he'd been playing football. Maybe it was to put the Howard name back to right. Or maybe it was because he wanted to know that everyone thought he was the best player in the country. There were thousands of reasons. For the last couple of weeks, he'd convinced himself that he didn't want it, but now, with the lights and the cameras and the atmosphere, he could admit that he did. He wanted them to call his name.

Dreamlike, Tank made his way to the stage with the rest of the nominees. He returned to his seat and watched as the past winners came up and were introduced. Finally, it was time for the announcement.

"The Heisman Memorial Trophy winner is…Tank Howard, Kensington State University."

It rushed him. Beat at him. He wasn't supposed to win. They'd fixed this. Done everything that they could do to keep this from happening. He let his mother take him in her arms and hug him.

"You deserved to win this," she whispered, confirming for him that she knew what he was thinking.

Coach Hayes was next, then Higgs, and then Franco. The two men merely stared at each other. Franco extended his hand, and when Tank accepted it, Franco pulled him in for the one-arm, one-hand man hug.

"I know you said you didn't want this, but there's no one even in your league. You had to sacrifice something special this season. Let this be your reward."

They both pulled back, meeting each other's eyes. Franco's bore into Tank's, trying to impose his will. Tank had to smile. He turned, making his way to the stage, trying not to think about the piece of paper that Franco had placed in his hand when they shook.

Glutton for punishment, Amber thought as she parked herself in front of the television, flipping through until she found the channel.

Making herself as comfortable as possible, she sat back to watch the Heisman. That she was doing it from the comfort of the Waldorf Astoria certainly helped.

"I have an idea," Franco said to her.

"Okay," she said, waiting for the punch line.

"Why don't you come with me to New York for the Heisman?"

"Absolutely not!"

"I'll put you up at the Waldorf, and you can walk through the city. You won't be anywhere near the proceedings. I've got some stuff that I need to do in the city on Monday. We'll head home Monday night."

"I don't know, Franco."

"I do. Come."

So, she had. She'd flown up by herself and had dinner with Franco. Then, she'd been left alone. It felt good to be away from everything. She'd walked the city, and she'd been able to forget for a bit about the hurt. She was tired, her leg aching from her explorations.

But she couldn't fight the pull tonight. *Glutton for fucking punishment.*

When the camera stayed fixed on Tank, she thought she was going to combust. She hadn't seen him in weeks, but just the sight of those freakishly beautiful green eyes juxtaposed with his caramel-colored skin was enough to make her body respond. She smiled ruefully as she thought of all the women watching this right now and adding Tank Howard to their Top Five list.

When they called his name, she felt like she'd won something. Her happiness for him and pride in him overwhelmed her. And then, because she was Sunshine, she remembered him with the other girl, and she let the anger slide right back into place, next to the disappointment and hurt. She watched him step to the podium, knowing that she wouldn't be able to listen to his speech.

She took him in for a second as she heard his opening line, "One of these days, you'll have a winner who can stand before you without a hint of controversy. I wish it could have been me."

Then, she turned it off, pounding the Off button on the remote so hard that her finger hurt. Even though it was early, she showered, made an ice pack for her leg, and got into bed. Exhaustion overtook her quickly, and she fell asleep.

When she came awake, she wasn't sure what had woken her. Then, she felt the throbbing in her leg and knew. Groaning, she rolled out of bed and headed back to the ice bucket to make another pack. As she refilled the bag with ice, she heard a knock at the door, and it dawned on her that it was the sound that had woken her up. She headed to the door, imagining it was Franco.

"Congratulations!" she said as she pulled open the door.

But she found Tank standing on the other side.

"Thank you," he said, a wide smile on his face, obviously leftover from the euphoria of the night.

But when Amber's smile slid away, his followed, and they both stood, staring at each other in the doorway.

"Can I come in?" Tank asked.

Amber stood, motionless, unable to move or really speak. It all rushed at her—a barrage of images, a relationship flashing before her eyes. She saw herself in increments—a little battered when she'd met him, a little hopeless when she had gotten involved with him, a little happy when she had fallen in love with him, a little sad when he'd broken her heart.

Without any thought of what she was going to do, the door slammed forward, blocking him out. But it didn't catch because Tank's hand shot out, hampering its trajectory, forcing it back toward her, leaving it open and swinging, with both of them on either side of the threshold.

"Just give me a minute to explain."

"Explain what? What are you explaining? The girl?"

"I don't know. Are you explaining Smitty's tongue in your mouth?"

"No," she said, slowly shaking her head. "That doesn't need any explanation."

"Do you know what I wanted to do to him? What I almost did to him?"

She pursed her lips and widened her eyes, feigning innocence. "So, it upset you that I kissed someone?"

She watched his hands clench into fists.

"You fucking kidding me?" he asked.

Shaking her head, the wide eyes still in place, she said, "So, it was upsetting to you to hear that I kissed your boy? Imagine me naked, lying on a couch, with his head between my thighs. You have that image in your mind?" She knew he did because he blanched, the color leaching from his face. "Now, you know how I felt, you fucking asshole!" Her voice stayed quiet, monotone, like a professor delivering a dry lecture. "So, Mr. Heisman, you can turn around and walk away. Please. Before I lose my shit and cause a scene that will keep Twitter ablaze for weeks, providing your precious Heisman even more controversy."

She turned away from him and waited to hear the door close. When she did, she turned around, breathing a big sigh of relief. But he stood there, inside the room, leaning against the wall, right next to the door. She opened her mouth to scream, to scream the walls down, anything to get him away from her, but he was on her before she could make a noise, his mouth settled against hers, her hands held loosely in his grip behind her back.

"Please," he murmured, "let me explain, apologize, make it up to you. Don't send me away."

He was right up on her, so she could feel his lips moving against hers, the vibrations jolting through her. She wasn't sure if it was his words, his tone, or his proximity, but she found herself capitulating, nodding to him so that he understood she wouldn't be screaming. He released her in sections—his mouth pulling away from hers, his body moving backward, his hands dropping her wrists so that they were apart from each other.

She looked up at him, studying him, falling for the sincerity she saw on his face. Taking a deep breath, she moved away and sat on the corner of the bed. "Win me over, Tank."

FORTY-THREE

Tank almost smiled at Amber. It was just like her to put the burden on him to make her like him. He was so thankful for the opportunity to talk to her that he was tongue-tied. So, he simply stared, taking her in. Her eyes looked hyperalert but red-rimmed, like she'd been up for way too long. Her hair was in a short little ponytail with her bangs in disarray, her scar on display. He took a little joy in the fact that she didn't seem at all self-conscious about it in his presence. He was having a hard time with her attire. She'd definitely been asleep or in bed, so her tiny little shorts didn't hide any part of her legs or ass, and her shirt clung to her like a second skin. After a quick perusal, he did his best to keep his eyes averted.

Sensing her impatience with his muteness, he tried to think of the best way to start.

"When I left you outside the locker room, I was…I'm not even sure I can describe it. I've never felt like that. Almost like everything was right in the world."

He stopped and looked at her, trying to see if she got what he was trying to say. But she continued to glare at some point behind his head.

"Anyway, when I came out of the locker room, a guy was there, waiting for me. He introduced himself and told me Richard had sent him."

That made her react. Her eyes got wide, and she glanced at him but then quickly looked away, focusing elsewhere.

"At first, I didn't think it was any big deal. But, then two other guys came out of nowhere and grabbed me, basically restraining me."

This time, she pulled her eyes away from the wall and focused on him.

"He went into this elaborate explanation about Richard's finances and how he's been footing alimony to my mom with Richard's promise that he could represent me when I came out. This dude…I guess he's smart enough to do his homework, and he thought it unlikely that I would follow Richard's advice. So, he came up with a different way for me to make good on his investment. He wanted me to shave points, basically fix the games."

He waited for some reaction from her but got nothing.

Sighing deeply, he continued, "Not sure if you realize it, but my collegiate football career is over. Aside from the obvious, that Richard took money from an agent, as did my mother…well, you get the point. Plus, when Franco and I sat down and really talked through it, we realized this dude would always have something on me as long as I was trying to play college football. That's what the concussion was about. We had to get me out of the games. If we didn't meet the point spread or if we did, there would always be questions."

"Don't you think you should have gone to the police or something?"

"We did. We talked to the police and the NCAA. I've had so many interviews and meetings in the last three weeks that, if I never have to sit in a conference room again, I'll be happy. I also interviewed agents, declared for the draft."

"You've been busy."

"Got declared ineligible and requested reinstatement from the NCAA. I got it, but still, after everything, it just makes sense to go."

"What about graduating?"

"Yeah, that's my final hurdle. I also met with my academic adviser and dean. I have fifteen hours left. But because of the combine and then football season, I'm not going to be able to do anything this spring or in the fall, so I'm going to have to play that one by ear."

"It sounds like you've got it all figured out."

He nodded. She continued to sit stock-still, focused back on the spot on the wall.

She turned toward him then, meeting his eyes for only the second time since he'd started talking. "Sounds like it's been a rough couple of weeks. I'm glad you worked it out, Tank."

It was a dismissal, and he knew it.

"I'm not done."

She shrugged, and he got angry.

"Look, he threatened you and my mom. He saw us in the tunnel. I needed to get you away from me. I didn't want you to get messed up in this."

"Ah, the infamous blow-job reference."

Her sarcasm grated on him, and he felt his frustration growing. "It was a stupid decision. I know that. I just wanted you to have a reason to stay away from me."

"Actually, Tank, it was a brilliant move. I'm away from you, and I intend to stay that way."

She slowly got up then, keeping her weight off her right foot, which he noticed. He noticed those things about her now, her subtle hints that her body hurt or that she was self-conscious. He knew her, and unfortunately for him, he understood now that he'd made an irrevocable choice.

"Amber, I fucked up. I know that now. I knew it then. But, at the time, before you all showed up at my apartment, I was scared. Scared shitless. I'd just realized an hour before everything went down, when you were waiting for me in the tunnel, that I was in love with you. I…I wanted to protect you. And I know that I could have gone about it in another way, but I needed for you to hate me enough to stay away from me because there was no way I'd be able to stay away from you."

She didn't say anything, but she'd stopped moving, balancing precariously on her left foot.

"What happened? Why does your foot hurt?"

She rolled her eyes at him but answered, "I walked around a lot today."

He tentatively moved toward her, afraid she'd bolt. He grabbed the desk chair on the way, pulling it toward her and gently pushing her into it. When she was sitting, he sat in front of her with his knees bent and extended her leg so that it rested on his knee. He massaged her foot and her leg, hoping to ease some of the ache.

"You have no reason to have any faith in me. I know that. But I love you. I wanted that Saturday night so bad. I wanted to tell you. I wanted to question you about what had happened with Franco and laugh with you about my mom's reaction. I wanted to share my high with you." He took a deep breath before he continued, "Even if you have to walk away from me, I need you to know that I love you."

Not one of Tank's words penetrated Amber's mind. It seemed to be protected by this super unbreakable force field where words just bounced off. But when he got down on the floor and touched her foot, her leg, she felt vulnerable. She had seen when he'd noticed her hurt leg right away, like he had some line on her aches and pains. She resented that about him, that he could tune into her and figure her out without any effort. It made it all so much easier for him. She had to guess when it came to him, and things felt unbalanced between them.

"How did you know to go get your father?" he asked.

She was lulled by his ministrations, and the answer came out easily, "I didn't. Tilly guessed something was wrong because of the girl with her mouth wrapped around your dick." She saw him flinch and didn't really care.

"You really have a way with words, Sunshine," he mumbled.

"He kept claiming that the only way you would do something like that was if you were in trouble. So, we went to Franco."

"He was right."

"So it would seem." The languid feeling in her legs was starting to spread through her body, and her earlier exhaustion caught up with her.

Tank stood, picked her up, and moved her to the bed. He laid her down and pulled the fluffy comforter up to her chin. Then, he sat on the side of the bed. She watched all this through half-lidded eyes.

He smoothed the hair back from her forehead as her eyes closed.

"I just don't think I can forgive you, Tank, even if I wanted to."

"You don't want to?" he asked, his surprise evident in his voice.

"I can't handle that kind of hurt again. Even though I can understand your reasons, I just can't get that image out of my head. And if that's how you're going to solve any problems that come our way, I'll spend a whole lot of time feeling that shitty."

He laid his hand on her scar, dragging his thumb across the rippled skin. Her body immediately responded, a moan escaping the confines of her throat. She'd told him one night about the burning, and whenever they spent the night together, he would help her sleep by keeping his hand on you scar.

Her eyes snapped open, and she saw his face, his eyes, and this indescribable look, the look she knew would reflect on her face when she let herself go and allowed her feelings to show. She knew that look, recognized it, reveled in it really. She pulled her hands from under the covers, seeking his skin, the slightly bristly strip where the fade of his hair tapered down and disappeared. She threaded her hands together and yanked him down to her, opening her mouth on impact with his lips, her tongue searching. He capitulated under her assault, desperately trying to get closer to her.

The comforter melted away with his clothes and her pajamas until their bare skin pressed together, and she felt every carved, ridged muscle warm beneath her wandering hands. Their frantic hands traversed hills and valleys—his praying for forgiveness, hers for forgetfulness. When the clamoring of their desire was too much to bear, Amber wrapped her legs around his back, her fingers around his length, and she pushed up toward him, taking over. Tank reached down, grabbed her hands, and brought them up, pinning them on the sides of her head. Her eyes snapped open, and she found herself staring into the confused depths of his.

"What does this mean?" he asked, his voice a scratchy, low version of his real one. "You forgive me?"

She couldn't look away but needed the distance, something to give her the strength to answer him truthfully. "Why are you so fucking stupid?" she whispered instead.

The bewilderedness disappeared as her question penetrated. He shook his head. "I don't know."

"How do I know you won't be stupid again?"

"You don't," he said on a sigh.

She'd needed a different answer even though she could appreciate his honesty. "Let me up," she demanded as she wiggled her wrists from the shackles of his hands.

He immediately released her, and she shoved against his shoulders. He rolled over onto his back as she jumped up from the bed. She turned her back on him as she tried to reason through his answer. If he'd answered in any other way, she probably would have hit him, but still, his candor made her sad.

"Fuck, Tank," she said, still facing away, her naked ass directly in his line of sight. Her comfort with him was not lost on her.

"I know, Sunshine. I know."

Later, she would think back on his response and remember it as the exact moment of her decision.

She turned around and made her way back to the bed. She didn't let him move, but rather, she climbed up onto his spectacular body. Her eyes raked over every smooth inch of his cocoa-colored skin. Her fingers and hands followed the same path—eyes, mouth, the dip of sinew on his shoulders, the ridges of his abdomen, and his powerful hard quads. She kissed every inch of him until she couldn't contain her need to have him inside her. She left him to retrieve a condom and rolled it on before taking every inch of him in one glorious rush.

"Jesus," he groaned, his hands clenched in fists.

When he tried to move them to her hips to take over, she batted them away. She rode him hard until she was dripping with sweat and every horrible image of him with another girl was expunged from her mind. When he came, she followed him. She stayed atop of him with her eyes closed, letting her heart rate settle back to normal, gathering her thoughts and emotions. He tried to pull her down to him, to wrap her in his arms, but she merely rolled off of him before gathering her clothes and heading to the bathroom.

She ran the water and took a quick shower. Standing in the heat of the steamy bathroom, the reality of their situation lodged itself in her throat. She leaned over the sink, trying to catch her breath. She wanted to be able to forgive him; she wanted to build something with him. Even the folly of his disastrous decision seemed to pale in comparison to the love she had for him.

But she couldn't be that girl—the one who let it go, only to go through it again.

Resolved, she returned to the room. Tank sat, shirtless, on the edge of the bed, his elbows on his suit pants-clad knees. He jerked his head up at the sight of her, and it took every ounce of willpower she had to stay on the other side of the room.

"How did you know I was here?" she asked as she sat back in the desk chair.

"Really?" He kind of snickered. "When Franco was giving me a mini pep talk to go get the Heisman, he slid a piece of paper in my hand."

"Traitor."

"Mmm, maybe. I asked him a couple of weeks ago to tell you that I was sorry. He said no. But then, as I was leaving his office, he told me that you loved me."

"Total traitor," she said again without any heat.

"Is that true, Sunshine?"

Amber let his question linger in the air, unanswered. She didn't say anything for some time. She merely gazed at him, memorizing his face, basking in the beautiful translucency of his eyes, remembering him. "Sorry, bud. You don't get any feel-good statements tonight."

He chuckled at that, and she couldn't help but laugh with him.

Then, growing serious again, she said, "I don't think I'll ever be able to trust you again."

"You have to give me a chance to earn it back. That's really all I'm asking for here—a chance."

"You'll be going to camps and the combine. We won't even be in the same town. How are you going to do that?"

"KSU is going to be my home base. I'll be around. I'll earn it back."

The earnest look on his face and the words he was speaking wreaked havoc on her intentions. She thought back to the day she'd figured out that she would always be able to tell if Tank was bullshitting her. Amber believed what he was saying. She knew he loved her; she felt it. She also knew he would do anything in his power to win back her trust.

She closed her eyes for a moment, imagining a different ending. When she opened them, they were damp with unshed tears. Their eyes met, and she knew he could see the decision reflected in her eyes. She watched the disbelief harden into disappointment and then shatter into disillusionment. The look on his face was eerily reminiscent of the haunted eyes that had looked back at her from the mirror in the Bear's Den.

"I'm sorry," she whispered. "I wish I could be the girl who could forgive and forget. But I just don't have it in me." The collected tears overflowed, coursing down her cheeks.

"What was that about?" he said as he swept his hand behind him to the bed, his anger apparent.

"It was about good-bye," she said quietly. And although her voice was soft, her tone relayed finality.

He blinked, and the fall of his eyelids banished all of his feelings. Like an eraser wiping a chalkboard clean, the smattering of dust was all that was left of what they'd shared. She watched it from her side of the room—a clean slate.

He gathered his things—his shirt, his tie, his coat. He bent down and snatched up the used condom and the wrapper from the floor. He walked to the garbage can and flung it in. Now that it was over, she wanted him to go, needed him to get the hell out of her room, so she could wallow with her unforgiving heart.

Shrugging into his shirt, he walked to the door. He flung it open, and then he stopped and turned toward her. "I wish all that I felt for you were enough," he said, his anger seemingly gone.

It was a simple statement with a truth she couldn't quite face because, even though she knew what was between them, she couldn't let it go. The wordlessness reverberated in the room around them, damning in its silence. Tank shook his head, turned, and left, the door closing peacefully, an insufficient punctuation point on the end of whatever had been between them.

EPILOGUE

Franco placed the box on the floor beside Amber's bed. Then, he reached up and wiped the sweat from his brow. "You had to move in July right?" he joked, smiling over at her, as she glanced his way.

She grinned. "Of course. You know I never take the easy way." She turned, taking inventory of the space around them. "The good news is, that's definitely the last box. And there were no stairs involved."

"True," Franco replied.

Amber slowly spun around. "This is going to be good," she said convincingly.

The little bungalow she rented sat on a quiet street, a family neighborhood with a basketball hoop at the foot of the cul-de-sac, well-kept yards, and according to Franco, a low crime rate. They'd toyed with her living closer to campus, but in the end, they'd decided that when she actually had downtime, she'd probably want to be far away from the action. She wasn't counting on a lot of idleness in the coming months. She preferred busy with little time to dwell.

"You excited?" Franco asked.

She glanced back toward him. When he moved to the family room, she followed, knowing the time had come. They both sat on the love seat she'd inherited when he moved to Atlanta and decided to downsize.

"Are you?" she countered as she snuggled back into the depths of the couch corner.

"I asked you first."

She managed a smirk before she took a moment to think about her answer. Things with Franco were getting easier, but it was still difficult for her to share.

She took a deep breath. "I'm excited. But nervous, too. I mean, I know I went through the whole interview process, and I feel like I earned the position, but I can't help but think that other people will scream preferential treatment." It had been on her mind for a while—the fear of other people's opinion—but she hadn't realized it until she told Franco.

He nodded his head, and she knew he understood what she was saying, validating her feelings. "I get it. But there is no way in hell that Whitey would have let you around his program if he didn't believe you could do the job. He and I are tight, but he wouldn't sacrifice his team just to help me out."

Franco moved closer to her and tentatively reached out, looking for her hand. The touching thing had gotten better between them, but he'd still wait for her to offer some gesture of approval. When she reached out for him, his hand swallowed hers.

"I haven't told you this because I wanted to wait until you needed it."

She couldn't help but roll her eyes. "Just tell me."

"Whitey didn't weigh in. He said he didn't need to. You impressed the hell out of everyone on his staff. He said he was glad he liked you because, if he would have tried to hire someone else, he would have had a mutiny on his hands."

Delight spread through her. "Really?"

"Have I ever lied to you?"

"You have not, even when I've really wanted you to," she answered.

"I think this is a great opportunity for you, and I think you are going to be an amazing director of operations. I wish I could hire you."

"I don't think I'm quite ready for the NFL."

"Not yet," he said.

He squeezed her hand, and she suddenly knew that the next thing out of his mouth was going to be something she didn't want to hear. He watched her, judging her openness.

"Just say it, Franco. I know you want to say something."

"I'm really proud of you. You've been on a mission the last six months. You graduated and worked with Higgs to get some experience. You found something you wanted, and you pursued it."

He was bragging on her, and she was proud of what she'd accomplished. Yet she waited for the *but* she knew was coming. When Franco didn't say any more, she grew impatient.

"But?" she prompted.

"But nothing. There's no *but*."

"You aren't going to say anything about running away from my problems?"

"What problems?" he ventured.

Rolling her eyes again, she released his hand and sagged back into the couch. Sighing, she turned her head toward him. "I'm not running away from Tank. That's not why I moved."

He leaned toward her. "I know that."

"You do?"

"I do."

He ran his hands through his hair, and Amber acknowledged his nervousness. He'd still get antsy about talking to her about some things. She hoped it wouldn't always be like that, but maybe fathers and daughters everywhere were leery about these kinds of conversations.

"Look, I don't know what went on between the two of you in New York. But what I can tell you is that you both have been resolved on your positions. I see you're trying to move on and put it behind you."

Although it was exactly what she was trying to do, it still hurt to hear that Tank was doing the same thing. Because, as hard as she tried, she wasn't over her feelings for Tank. She'd been glued to the TV on draft day, watching, hoping, praying for him to get what he wanted. When he'd gone to Atlanta, where Franco had been named the head coach, in the first round as the sixth overall pick, she'd cried happy tears. So, even though Tank and Franco didn't get to finish what they'd started at Kensington State, she was fairly certain they'd get their chance together in the NFL.

"I am trying to put it behind me. Got to admit, it's a little more daunting than I thought it would be." She hadn't meant to say that, didn't want to share her monumental task with anyone, but Franco had that effect on her these days. Things just slipped out.

"It'll happen," he assured her.

"Promise?"

He laughed. "Yes, I promise. You will get over Tank Howard."

She laughed, too. "When?" She'd meant it as a joke, a way to continue the lightheartedness she was surprisingly feeling. But, when she'd opened her mouth and the word had escaped, it sounded jagged and rough, like the edges of her heart.

Franco didn't hesitate this time. He didn't wait for permission. He merely pulled her into his arms and held her.

"Eventually," was all he could offer.

THE END

Thank you for reading the beginning of Tank and Amber's story.

The next book in the duet is *Superstar*. Find out if Tank and Amber can find their way back to each other.

Love *Five-Star* (even if you hated the ending)?

Please consider leaving a review on your favorite book site.

Connect with J. Santiago

Sign up for J. Santiago's newsletter:

https://mailchi.mp/bf94c1c685b4/jsantiagosubscibe

Read on for an excerpt from SUPERSTAR.

Then, Tank came around the side of the table and took a seat. "So, are we scouting?" he asked as he looked at the monitors. He did a double take when he noticed the uniforms, the game, the play frozen in front of him. He rubbed his hand over his head. Turning to her, he asked, "Why are you watching this?" A trace of accusation and embarrassment colored his tone.

"I was curious." She almost reached out to touch him, reassurance for both of them maybe, but she stayed her hand.

"You were curious about the worst game of my career?" The question flew out of his mouth, the accusation heavier this time.

Easy.

She wasn't sure how to play this.

Tank had always taken her analysis well. He'd never gotten defensive if she lobbed some constructive criticism his way. But he

also hadn't gotten stomped and humiliated in a game that millions of people were watching. Even worse, she knew he was going to hate what she had to say because the loss of the game had nothing to do with the Xs and Os; it had everything to do with his leadership.

His eyes flickered back and forth between the screens and her. Frozen in front of him was one hell of an ugly sack, a picture of his body pinned under the left tackle. Something in his eyes flashed when he studied the scene, like he remembered the crunch of the helmet on his shoulder pad. Maybe his body remembered the impact of the hit that had driven his right shoulder into the unforgiving ground. Possibly, he could recall the smell of the field as his facemask sprayed a healthy dose of grass and dirt up into his nose. It could have been anything, but she guessed he remembered it all.

"You could at least acknowledge it was the worst game." He was pissed.

Part of her wanted to laugh at the return of man-child Tank, who basically wept when his precious ego was bruised.

"Well," Amber began, "based on the score, I would guess it was. But, because I haven't seen you play since college, I don't know."

His jaw dropped, incredulity a mask on his face. "You haven't seen any of my professional games?"

"No."

His eyes literally bugged out of his head. She had this image of him having to force his eyes back into his sockets, and she worked hard to smother her smile and laughter.

"Why not?"

She waved him off, not deigning to answer his question.

He shifted in the chair, obviously uncomfortable. Then, he nodded. "So, what'd you think?"

She bit her top lip, fighting another smile. She couldn't help it; she found him so cute when he was in a huff. It inserted some humanity into the perfect specimen of Tank Howard, and it made her like him even more. His arrogance was insidious, but his vulnerability was endearing.

"I think it's hard to throw and run an offense when you're clenching," she said her piece, putting it out there in the film-room universe. Then, she waited for the explosion.

Tank's eyes blinked, like residue was in the way of him seeing clearly. "Did you…" he sputtered. He looked around and then back at her. "Did you just say it's hard to throw when I'm clenching?"

Amber smirked. "Yep."

Tank leaned back in the chair and cackled. His laughter filled the space, permeating the air, and he looked at her with a big, dopey smile on his face. She returned it.

"That's your expert analysis?" he said, the smile lingering. "Yeah, dude. You lost that game because of nerves." "Clenching?"

"Right, clenching."

He reached up and rubbed his index finger and thumb across his chin. He pinned her with his gaze, which had somehow darkened with lust. "What can *you* do when you're clenching?"

ABOUT THE AUTHOR

J. Santiago is a graduate of Villanova University and the University of Pennsylvania. She gets her love of sports from her fifteen-year career in the field and a houseful of boys who love to play. A former English and history teacher, she understands and embraces the power of stories in our lives.

Connect with J. Santiago

Sign up for J. Santiago's newsletter:
https://mailchi.mp/bf94c1c685b4/jsantiagosubscibe

Like J. Santiago on Facebook:
@j.santiagonovels

Join J. Santiago's Reader Group:
http://www.facebook.com/groups/184363652197039/

Follow J. Santiago on Twitter:
@skywalkerxnl

Connect with J. Santiago on Instagram
@santiagonovels

Made in the USA
Las Vegas, NV
16 December 2020